Spark Out

Spark Out

Nick Rippington

Cabrilon Books

Published by Cabrilon Books

ISBN: 978-0-9933323-1-9

Typesetting services by BOOKOW.COM

For my Dad Trevor Rippington, who has supported me forever and told me my first novel was 'just like a real book'

ACKNOWLEDGMENTS

First I must thank my wife Liz, who has not only been patient when bins needed emptying or food needed cooking but also proof-read Spark Out meticulously, even though she prefers chick-lit and squirmed at some of the more graphic scenes.

My new American Editor Vanessa Gonzales came in like a breath of fresh air and got the gig because she made me laugh. She pointed out a few minor tweaks but mostly encouraged me and had nice things to say about my characters while giving me ideas on how they might be strengthened. Her belief and encouragement gave me a new lease of life when I was flagging. Writer pals Ian Sutherland, Stephen Bentley, FD Lee, Maxine Ridge and Laurence O'Brien have always been supportive, while reading Dick Kirby's books about life in the Special Branch gave me a few ideas that he may notice I've pinched! This book has also been a great learning experience and some of the reading material on the Falklands was an eye opener, particularly Nicholas van Der Bijl and David Aldea's book '5th Infantry Brigade in the Falklands' and John and Robert Lawrence's hard-hitting 'Tumbledown' about Robert's experience in the Scots Guards. Jane Dixon-Smith's amazing cover work speaks for itself.

'A mighty flame followeth a tiny spark'
– Dante Alighieri

PROLOGUE

EVERYONE was scared of Reg. Dad's special friend lodged in the back room, keeping his own counsel – until trouble flared. Then he would spring to life, dishing out his unique brand of punishment.

Reg wasn't that big, but he was squat, unyielding, terrifying. He and Dad had an unbreakable bond. Maurice 'Big Mo' Dolan kept Reg around because life was all about respect and discipline and sometimes people needed reminding of that. You couldn't take the piss, swing the lead or tell porkies without Dad nodding at Reg to remind you The Enforcer was on hand to ensure you bucked up your ideas.

When Reg was in full swing, little could stop him. A squad-car full of Filth tried once and crawled away nursing their wounds. A postman was on the receiving end another time, ending up in the hospital with two cracked ribs and a concussion. His only crime was to deliver a parcel to the wrong address. Children, women, ordinary folk going about their daily lives – no one was immune. Named after the legendary Reggie Kray, the enforcer's reputation was as fearsome on the estate as the one nurtured by those gangster twins across the East End.

For those incarcerated within the mould-dappled walls of No 625 White Tower, Reg sat dormant, like a life-threatening illness preying on the mind of a patient in remission. Little Chuck cowered in his presence, though he had never personally experienced The Enforcer's wrath. The boy had seen plenty of his old man's companions come and go – a procession of rock-like creatures – but they were quickly forgotten. Reg was a constant, grafted onto the family unit since that day Dad had brought him home from a tour of duty around the spit-and-sawdust boozers of Ilford, Barking and Dagenham.

"Just minding his own business, he was, sitting in the corner," Maurice Dolan confided in his first-born son. "I thought: He'll do for me. Hasn't let me down since, 'ave ya, Reggie old son?" The words were accompanied by an affectionate pat while Reg remained mute, his life one of action, not words.

Early memories for Chuck were cloaked in casual violence. Small for his age, the boy was often told by Dad that the remedy for his lack of stature was to "toughen up", a long-term project Big Mo insisted on supervising personally. The mean-spirited nature of this indoctrination manifested itself in one incident destined to remain burned on Chuck's memory forever, even though he had been a toddler at the time. It involved a pink pushchair.

Chuck was happily pushing it around in the playground at the back of the flats when the old man returned from tour. Keen to show it off to the person he idolised, the boy ran across the asphalt on bowed, unsteady legs, the pushchair out in front. Big Mo stopped in his tracks.

"Da... da...look," Chuck said, pride shining on his cherubic face as he nodded in the direction of the toy, a female doll nestling inside. Big Mo sank to his haunches. He directed his gaze firstly at the object of Chuck's affection then straight into the little boy's eyes. He grasped his child firmly by the forearms.

"Chuck, son, pushchairs are for girls," he said. "Are you a little fackin' girl?" Chuck shook his head vigorously, tears flowing due to the thick, gnarled fingers boring into his delicate skin. Despite his discomfort, he maintained his focus on the craggy, fault-lined face in front of him, nestling beneath a roof of short, black bristles. The smell of hops and smoke filled the air, a blend of odours he associated with his father's unique brand of love.

As he struggled for a reply, Big Mo answered his own question. "Of course not! You're a boy, ain't you? So let's get rid of this nasty, girly thing." Relief flooded through Chuck as his dad released his arms and hoisted the pushchair in one meaty hand. The fingers, misshapen chunks covered in black, matted hair, reminded Chuck of a nest of spiders he had found in grandad's garden once.

Standing there in tearful confusion, he watched Big Mo march to a nearby roundabout. It was winding down from a spin cycle started by four teenagers who had moved onto the swings in the dilapidated playground. "Clank!" the noise reverberated around the park as pushchair met roundabout, the metal-on-metal sound bouncing back off the surrounding high-rise walls, the doll flying off and landing under the see-saw. "Clink!" Chuck stared open-mouthed as bits of metal and plastic went flying, wheels from the pushchair detaching and spinning off, one of them performing ever-decreasing circles beneath the climbing frame, mesmeric in its progress.

Chuck was shaken from his trance-like state by a raised female voice. A woman in tight white jeans, flowery purple smock-top and cork-platform sandals was running towards the playground. "Hey! Stop!" she was shouting, looking back over her shoulder at the bench where Chuck's mum was sitting. "Bloody 'ell Beryl, your old man's gone mental! Look what 'e's doing to our Jill's pushchair. Shit! Mo, stop that you nutter! It ain't yours, it's Jill's."

Big Mo's facial expression never changed as he looked at the tangle of cheap plastic, flimsy metal and ripped nylon that lay in his hands. He switched his attention to the woman arriving in the playground, and for half a moment onlookers might have expected him to admit his mistake, apologise and offer to replace the damaged item. Chuck knew better. His dad never had reason to say "Sorry".

"You stupid cunt!" shouted Big Mo, stopping the woman in her tracks with the brutality of his words. "You think it's a good fackin' idea letting my boy play with a spazzy girly pushchair? Here..." He flung the remnants of the toy in her direction, forcing her to jump back hastily to avoid being hit. "Next time you do that, it'll be you I'm smashing into the roundabout, you hear me, you slag! No one turns my boy into a faggot."

Chuck noticed the woman was visibly quivering from the verbal battering. There were tears running down her cheeks as she span on her heels and ran back to the bench, losing a shoe in the process and having to stop briefly to fit it back on. When she reached her destination she took her daughter from Chuck's mum, clutching the little girl tightly to her chest. Chuck saw his mother mumble a few words to the woman who, without reply, marched off in the opposite direction from the playground.

When Chuck looked back to where his dad had been standing, the old man was gone. Detritus was scattered around, by-products of the human whirlwind that had passed through. The kids on the swings talked excitedly now and though Chuck couldn't understand exactly what was being said, he got the gist. "God, that was Big Mo!" said one. "You wouldn't wanna mess with him, he's mental!"

"They say he carries this big club, and belts people when he feels like it."

"Yeah," said a third. "Brilliant!"

"Come here Chucky boy." His mum arrived, arms wide open. He waddled over and she engulfed him in such a suffocating embrace he thought his ribs might snap. "Never mind, baby, never mind." He inhaled the rose scent he associated with his mother, as comforting and safe as a warm blanket, and started to feel better again. "Your daddy only wants what is best for you," she whispered. "We don't need silly pushchairs anyway, do we? You've got your own toys at home and they're much more fun. Let's go and play with your cars, shall we?"

Later, lying in his bed, he heard raised voices along the corridor. "He's only a little boy!" his mother was protesting.

"He has to learn sometime," said his dad. "You can't mollycoddle him forever, it's a tough world!"

"Forever? It's hardly forever. He's barely two, for God's sake. I know you had it tough with your dad but..."

"Don't bring him up... Hell! I turned out all right, didn't I? At least I can look after myself and my own... That's what he taught me. Look after family. Blood's thicker 'n water and all that. Your lot were hardly a good example, were they? That fackin' woman..."

"Oh don't start on my mother again, please..."

"It makes me sick though. Snooty cow. All them airs and graces and she facks off and leaves... Discipline is important and there was none of it in your family. Your old man was far too soft, letting her get away with that. She needed a good slap. To my mind you ain't never too young to learn... or too old. Fack! Maybe you could do with learning some lessons yourself, girl."

"No... no. Don't even joke about it. Why don't you settle down, have a beer and stop getting yourself all wound up. You know it's not good for your blood pressure and them headaches. Here let me..."

"Fack, no. You don't get 'round me that easy. Maybe I'll get Reg in to adjudicate..."

CHUCK first witnessed the destructive qualities of Reg just after his fourth birthday. One afternoon Dad bundled him into a van despite his mother's protests. He waved goodbye to her as she stood caressing her bump with one hand and wiping something from her eye with the other. Chuck shared the passenger seat with his dad, looking around to see who else was coming along on the mystery trip.

The driver was a bloke called Cozza, who looked like someone had scribbled over him with crayons. In the back was Handsome Frank, an ironically nicknamed ex-boxer, and a scrawny bloke in dungarees called Shooter. Reg sat comfortably between them, resting against the back door.

"He's a nice looking lad. He's got your eyes, Big Mo," said Frank, nodding in Chuck's direction as the boy carried out his reconnaissance.

"You think?" replied Big Mo. "Hell, it makes me laugh, you know? Them bints get together and say 'Ooh don't 'e look like 'is Dad'? I can never tell. Them babies all look like Winston bleedin' Churchill to me. Still, I think I see the resemblance more now 'e's getting older. Bit on the small side, though. He needs to beef up a bit."

"Don't sweat it," said Cozza. "I got a picture of our Shaun on the piano at our mum's. Tiny little thing. He's 13 now and won't stop growing. We'll have to make a hole for him in the bloody car roof soon... you know, like they did for that dinosaur in the Flintstones?"

"Bloody Flintstones!" said Shooter, letting loose a honking laugh at the reference to the cartoon series about Neanderthal cave dwellers. In a few seconds the van was rocking with mirth, the happy banter continuing until it juddered to a halt outside an imposing, red-brick building somewhere near the river. The streetlamps were on, the cold, misty air drifting up from the River Thames to cloak London's docklands in fog as intimate as a lover's embrace. It was late for Chuck to be up and, though he adored being with his dad, he was feeling tired. "Come on Chucky, time you started to learn what life is all about," Big Mo said, lifting him out through the passenger door and onto the cobbled street.

"Wapping Tobacco; This the one?" Shooter was pointing to a sign on the side of the building.

"Yeah, hang on." Big Mo removed a key from his pocket, fiddled with the padlock and swung open a small door. "Right boys, in you go."

Chuck's immediate reaction was to screw up his nose in response to the dank, musty smell that reminded him of the small cupboard in the hallway at home. At the same time his ears detected the constant drip-drip-drip of water not far away. The darkness was impenetrable and he felt scared, letting a whimper escape.

"Don't be frightened, boy," growled Big Mo. "Time to be a brave little soldier. Nothing to worry about. Wait here..."

Strip lights flickered on, buzzing like angry wasps. "There... feel better?"

Chuck nodded, looking around. Packing crates were stacked in corners, old newspapers covering the floor.

"Is this the stuff you got me out on quiz night to lug around for you?" asked Shooter, pointing to a collection of crates stacked in the centre of the room. "Dot isn't happy, I can tell you."

"Aaah, ain't she? Shame. See, here's the thing..." Big Mo curled a finger, indicating for Shooter to approach him with the unspoken promise that he could learn something to his advantage.

"What's up, Big Mo?"

"I need your help with something, son."

Chuck noticed the light was reflecting off a damp patch on the man Shooter's top lip, as if his nose had been leaking water. A tall, gangly figure, he moved hesitantly forward to where Maurice Dolan was fiddling with something in his pocket.

"What is it, Big Mo?"

"Do up me buttons, would ya?" Turning his back on the other man, Big Mo pointed to a spot at the back of his head.

Shooter sniggered nervously. "Eh?"

Big Mo swivelled, a metal contraption now fitted snugly around the knuckles. Without warning, it clattered into the side of Shooter's face. The man staggered back, Cozza and Handsome each grabbing an arm.

"What the..?" he mumbled through a mouth frothing red.

"You heard me, you mug. I asked you to do up the buttons."

"Buttons?"

Smash. A cut opened on Shooter's temple. He bucked and pulled in a wild attempt to escape the vicious assault, but was unable to shake off his two bodyguards.

"Fackin' 'ell, am I speaking Swahili here, boys?" demanded Big Mo of his two accomplices. They shook their heads, neither wanting to be the next victim of the knuckleduster. "My fackin' buttons. Do 'em up!"

"Jeez, Mo. OK, OK! Give me a chance to understand... I can't see no buttons. You ain't got any, Mo."

Big Mo nodded his head slowly, his eyes rolling. "That's right, Shooter, me old mucka," he said. "You've finally got it... have a gold star." He gave a mirthless chuckle, pausing before delivering the punch line with perfect comic timing. "Strange, though, because the way you've been acting I can only assume you believe my head buttons up the back."

Everything was still, silent for a moment, the only sound that of laboured snorts coming from the prisoner, who was trying to clear the blood from his airwaves.

"Wh... what sh'you mean?" Shooter stuttered eventually.

"Ripping me off," said Mo. "I know what you took away from that Holland Park raid. You owe me a lot more – a couple of grand, I reckon – and it's a bloody cheek you've held out on me after I tipped you off to the opportunity. Don't you know there's a recession on? I got a wife and kid to feed, with another on the way. I'm sorry Shooter, truly. You always seemed a loyal soldier and a good mate, but now I've got to make an example of you. I can't afford people thinking I'm a soft touch. Seems no one can be trusted these days. Handsome? Keep hold of him. Cozza, get Reg, would you?"

"Oh shit. No!" pleaded Shooter. "Not Reg. Look, I'll make it up to you. Pay you extra, if that's what you want. Do another job especially for you. It wasn't on purpose, honest, I'd never do that to you, Mo, you know that. I must have miscalculated is all I can think. I've always been useless at maths..."

Chuck let out a whimper. He didn't know what it was all about but he didn't like seeing his daddy so cross. Big Mo looked at him and winked as if to say, "It's all right son, none of this is real". Chuck told himself what he was seeing was a magic trick, the red stuff on Shooter's face not blood but tomato sauce, like he had at home on his chips.

HOURS later Chuck was in bed, crying himself to sleep. Big Mo told his wife the youngster was overtired. They had popped into the pub after their 'bit of business', just to take the edge off things, and Chuck had fallen asleep. Beryl Dolan looked at her husband.

"You've made him a part of it, haven't you?" she said. "I asked you, even begged you, but you couldn't help it. You had to 'toughen him up'. I can only guess what you've been up to. You took that... thing ... with you. I can see the blood. There's a stain on my carpet and a trail on the tiles in the hall."

Big Mo looked out from beneath his thick, black, caterpillar eyebrows, pushing his hand wearily through the bristles on his head. He didn't feel like justifying his actions. It had been a long day. He had done what he had done, and in his mind he had made the right call. A row with the missus was the last thing he needed.

Lifting himself from his favourite armchair, Mo reached over and switched on the television, turning up the volume to dissuade his wife from carrying on with the conversation. A well-dressed man was standing in front of a weather map pointing at various areas of the country, but Mo wasn't interested.

Bending down slowly, he picked up the three-foot length of wood he had propped beside him on the sofa. Noting the dark stains for the first time, he vowed to rub it down with a hot, damp cloth in the morning to get rid of any 'evidence'. Shame. To his way of thinking it just added to the character, like when you had a champion conker as a kid and the more messed up it looked, the more scars it had, the more you knew it had done its job. Walking out through the sliding glass-partition doors, he swung the sawn-off curtain pole at his side, the spherical ball on the end reflecting the light. Resting it gently against the wall in the corner of the small parlour room, he patted it affectionately.

"Night, Reg," he said.

Part One

ONE

October, 1981

BIG MO parked on double yellow lines outside a rank of scruffy shops in the East London area of Forest Gate, stuck a badge in the windscreen and strolled to the pedestrian crossing. The sticker had been given to him by an acquaintance at the council who owed him a favour and wanted to stay in his good books.

"Hey, you... excuse me, old chap!"

Big Mo ignored the posh-sounding voice, convinced the words couldn't be directed at him. After all, there were few with the barefaced cheek to speak in such disrespectful tones to a bloke who stood 6ft 5in in his stockinged feet and tipped the scales at close on 16stone. If that wasn't enough, the skinhead haircut discouraged interaction.

"You in the sheepskin coat... You do realise you aren't supposed to park there, don't you?"

Mo stopped in his tracks halfway across the street, his actions met by a screeching of brakes as a taxi pulled to a shuddering halt, other traffic squealing to a standstill behind it. A cacophony of car horns filled the early-afternoon air. Winding down his window the taxi driver, a young Asian, leaned out, took one look at the imposing human roadblock in front of him and quickly wound it back up again. Big Mo turned with the considered slowness of a heavily laden oil tanker.

"You talking to me?" he asked, fixing his inquisitor with an icy glare. The line was from his favourite film, *Taxi Driver*, Mo intent on delivering it with the same menace as Robert De Niro.

"Yes, man... you." The scrawny character seemed oblivious to the danger in which he had placed himself. Mo noted the bloke's rimless spectacles and pinstripe suit; bank manager, accounts clerk or office know-it-all, he guessed. "Look, I don't know how you came to be in possession of that, um, badge in your window," his accuser continued regardless. "It seems perfectly obvious from where I'm standing that you have no disability of any sort and are quite capable of parking somewhere else and walking to your destination. There are people who need that space far more than you. It's right outside a doctor's surgery, for goodness sake. Be a good chap and move it to the car park around the corner, would you? You're a fit young man. It will take just five minutes of your time." As others gathered to watch, Mo saw smug, self-satisfaction etched on Mr Pinstripe's face, as if he was the spokesman for every decent, law-abiding citizen.

Shame I don't give tuppence for the law, thought Mo, heading back towards the car at a steady pace, the metal segments attached to the bottom of his black brogues performing a relentless tattoo on the tarmac. Behind him, the traffic started up again, the horns more infrequent. Believing he had succeeded in his quest, Mr Pinstripe began walking off.

"Oi, geezer!" Big Mo's grating cockney accent was so menacing it stopped passers-by in their tracks. "Would you like one of these disabled discs for yourself?"

When the man in pinstripes looked over his shoulder, Maurice Dolan was rummaging around in the boot of his Daimler. "Eh? Well, no... I don't have a disabili..." The word stuck in his throat as Big Mo jacked himself up to his full height and turned, the thick wooden curtain pole in his hand. Colour drained from the responsible citizen's face.

"No disability?" said Mo. "That can be arranged."

"Now... steady on old chap... wait... you can't..."

Mo cut down the distance between them, swinging Reg over his shoulder like a baseball player. "Can't what, eh? Can't what?" Anger lines jagged across Mo's exposed forehead. As it suddenly dawned on him that reasoned argument wouldn't be his saviour, the retreating target broke into a run, feet sliding in an effort to gain purchase on the grubby pavement. His comfortable, expensive slip-ons weren't suited to a foot race. "Help! Someone call the police!" he shouted.

Mo ate up the ground between them, never breaking into a run. People who had earlier impeded his quarry, moved aside in respect of Mo's bulk. When he had narrowed the gap to less than 100 feet, Mr Pinstripe reached out in desperation, pulling over a table of ripe grapes, plums, tomatoes and bananas. The burly female shopkeeper emerged to remonstrate with the culprit, presenting Mo with a formidable obstacle. As he sought to avoid a collision, the beloved segs in the soles of his shoes became his downfall, combining with crushed grapes and tomatoes to send him flying. He landed flat on his back on the pavement, but was too psyched up at that moment to feel any pain. He lost vital seconds racheting himself into an upright position.

The irate shopkeeper now provided another barrier. "Look what you've..." Mo poked the woman's flabby stomach, Reg pushing her backwards across another of her displays. "Get lost, you fat slag," he said, finally refocusing his attention in time to see Mr Pinstripe disappear through a train station entrance.

Brushing crushed fruit from his beloved sheepskin, he bellowed, "Fack!" and bought Reg crashing down on an escaped melon. Juicy lumps of its flesh flew everywhere, sending passers-by scurrying for cover.

"IF you will permit me, you seem a bit tense today." Mo tried to relax as Sunil Prabhakar dug his fingers into his knotted shoulders, working the flesh as if kneading dough.

"Not fackin' surprised, Suni," said Mo. "Everyone seems to think they have the divine right to make a Muppet out of Mo these days.

What's that about, eh? On the way here some string bean insulted me about my parking... made a complete mess of my clothes. The jacket's fackin' ruined, I tell you."

"Sorry to hear that, Mr Mo, sir," said the confused Indian, failing to make the connection between parking and ruined clothes. His own uniform was pristine, white shirt, trousers and trainers, a knee-length apron draped over the top. "Did you hear about that IRA business?"

"Case in point," said Mo, though the attack on Chelsea barracks had nothing to do with him personally. "How they managed to smuggle a nail bomb into the heart of bloody Westminster is a mystery to me. Those bloody left footers killed a bunch of civilians, even though their target was the military. Disgraceful." The Irish Republican Army were firmly at the top of his rapidly expanding hate list.

"At least it was Chelsea Barracks," said the guru. Though it was no laughing matter, Mo smiled. The guru was making a sporting joke, knowing that if his client hated anyone nearly as much as Irish Republicans it was the Chelsea football team. Sport was one of a vast array of topics they discussed during Mo's monthly visits, which had started two years earlier after he had completed a short stint inside for a nightclub ruck that left a rival in hospital.

While incarcerated, Mo suffered blinding headaches which the doctor put down to high blood pressure. Refusing to spend a lifetime taking pills, he agreed to try alternative forms of treatment. "Try this bloke," the prison medic had said. "Name's Sunil, nice chap, Indian, bit of a guru. To be honest, I see him myself..."

Mo had been sceptical at first, doubtful about putting his trust in a bloody foreigner, but had quickly changed his tune once the guru got to work. The pressure the Indian applied to Mo's temples as part of his massage technique almost earned Sunil a broken nose on the first visit. Mo somehow restrained himself, though, and was amazed at how well he felt after the session. He was even happier a few days later when he realised he hadn't been plagued by migraines at all since his initial treatment.

Not only was Sunil a wizard with his hands, he was also a damn good listener. Mo found their conversations liberating, convinced that everything he told the guru was bound by the same rules of confidentiality that applied to a priest in the confessional or a GP in his surgery.

"How's your brother?" asked Suni.

"Ain't seen him in ages," said Mo. "I've been too busy really. Last time he was around I brought him here."

"Nice bloke," said Suni. "And the missus? Any problems like we talked about?"

"Well… you know how it is. It's all about the young 'uns for her at the moment. I guess I shouldn't expect the same treatment as I got before they were born. I miss it, though… the attention."

"Then why not go and get some?" said the guru.

"You mean prostitutes?" asked Mo, shocked. "Out of order, mate. I couldn't do that to Beryl."

"Oh I know, Mo, sir," said the guru, backtracking. "I wasn't thinking ladies of the night, though some of the greatest men who ever lived had concubines to ease their tensions. Look at Kennedy… a great president, but a man with a wandering eye. He was having the nookie with Marilyn Monroe, you know. Everyone needs a distraction – it doesn't have to mean anything. What about all those army generals, far from home, protecting us? You can't tell me they don't find another way to relieve stress when their wives aren't around. If it isn't up your street I'm sorry I mentioned it, though I reckon some families have even benefited because the breadwinner returns home not so 'strung out'."

Mo allowed the calm voice and soothing effects of the treatment to spread through his aching body. "I hadn't thought of it in those terms," he said. "If my missus found out, though, I'd end up a fackin' eunuch."

The two men laughed. "What about that Mr Tebbit eh?" said Suni, changing the subject seamlessly. "He wants us to all ride bikes to work. You wouldn't catch me doing that in this horrendous traffic."

"He don't mean it that way, Suni old son. It ain't aimed at you. You've got a job. He's on about these scroungers, says they should travel to find work. Get on their bikes."

"You agree?"

"I can carry out my business from most places," said Mo. "I don't have to stick around here. Some lazy bastards expect to fall out of bed into a decently paid job. I tend to agree with Tebbit, and with this Maggie Thatcher in charge I reckon some things will get well and truly sorted."

"Like the invasion of all these bloody foreigners," interjected Suni.

Mo had to use all his willpower to stifle a laugh, the irony striking a chord. Fortunate he was lying face down, so the guru didn't notice.

MO left the guru's apartment feeling much more relaxed and was soon driving through the traffic-clogged streets of Ilford. As he approached the town centre he noticed something which made his eyes light up. A thin figure in pinstripes was just departing a local newsagents, a briefcase under one arm and a copy of the Evening Standard under the other. "Well I never," muttered Mo.

Reg being stowed away in the boot, Mo knew he wouldn't have time to park up without the risk of losing his quarry. He had to act now. Pulling down the flap to the glove compartment he reached inside and found exactly the kind of thing he'd been looking for. He hefted it in his hand. Just right. If only he could get a bit closer...

Spotting a break in the traffic, brakes screeched as he shifted into the left hand lane, drawing level with the target. Winding down the window, he took a deep breath.

"Oi, disability boy!" he shouted.

A few heads turned but Mr Pinstripe continued walking. "You! The arsehole in the pinstripes!" This time the man looked up. Locking eyes with Big Mo Dolan, for the second time that day the colour drained from his face. "Catch, you cunt!"

The large, square battery caught him smack in the middle of the forehead and Mo watched in wonderment as his victim sank to his knees, a crowd of onlookers gathering to see what had happened. That will teach him respect, Mo thought, putting his foot to the floor and heading in the direction of home.

TWO

BIG MO cursed under his breath between large gulps of pissy lager. He was sitting at a scarred bench near the door of the 3 Wishes pub in Dagenham, his ire directed at the flamboyantly dressed teens gathered in the corner, pooling their pocket money to put a procession of tuneless dirges on the jukebox. His ears were being battered by the 'pop sensation' of the moment, a weirdo called Adam Ant who obviously spent too much time as a kid plastering on his mum's make up. The yodelling nancy boy thought his bizarre game of "dress up" entitled him to the name Prince Charming. "Prince Arse-Bandit, more like," mumbled Mo. It was as if the singer heard the insult, assuring him "Ri-di-cule is nothing to be scared of".

It had taken barely seven hours for Maurice Dolan's buzz from the guru session to wear off. The feelgood factor that once lasted all week, became less effective the more treatment he had. He supposed it was like developing immunity to a particular brand of painkiller or being addicted to an illegal substance. The original high could only be replicated by feeding your habit with increased amounts of the poison.

The word poison made him recall a visit to his dad's earlier that day, arranged so that Billy 'The Kid' Dolan and his wife Viola could fawn over their eldest grandson. The love-in was mutual. Chuck believed every word his grandad said was an incontrovertible fact, feeding Big Mo's in-built paranoia. In irrational moments he feared he came a distant third behind Beryl and Billy in his son's affections. Billy reinforced those feelings of insecurity with regular barbs disguised as jokes and designed to lower his esteem in the eyes of the boy. On this occasion, Billy had opened the door to them pleasantly enough and led them into his study. It didn't take long for him to start, though. Walking to the ornate drinks' cabinet in one corner of the room, Billy had pressed a button which sent electric gadgetry whirring within. After seconds, a door slid open and bottles and glasses magically appeared on a circular tray from within the contraption. Billy honestly believed the fancy piece of tat was a status symbol owned by such dignitaries as the Lord Mayor himself.

"What's your poison, son?" he had asked, holding a bottle of whisky up to the light for inspection. "This is a good one, a wonderful oaky single malt. It was a present from one of my Jock pals. Not to everyone's taste, only the discerning palate. I expect you would prefer a beer."

Mo had felt the tension creep across his shoulders but refused to take the bait. "No, no... whisky's fine."

It was at that moment Chuck chose to show off the garish painting he had produced in school. It reminded Mo of one of those weird psychedelic cartoons from the 60s, like the one on the cover of The Beatles' Yellow Submarine album.

Billy had taken the rolled scroll and unfurled it as if it was a priceless piece of art that had been on display at the Tate Gallery. "Fantastic, Chucky boy," he'd said, nodding approvingly and patting the kid on the head like an obedient dog. "The only things your dad brought home were letters from the teacher telling me how naughty he'd been."

Dig No.2 had been right on cue. Chucky had glanced in Mo's direction, unsure whether he had permission to laugh. For the boy's sake, he had manufactured the briefest of smiles while inside the knotted ball of angst grew and mutated. Later, Grandad Billy would use the picture again as a weapon with which to batter Mo's sense of worth.

"What's this Chuck?" Billy had asked, pointing at a splurge of bright colours.

"That's the garden, with lots of pretty flowers in it," Chuck had explained excitedly. "There is a swing for the children and a round-about over here."

"You don't have a garden, do you, Chuck?"

"Naaah!" the boy had exclaimed.

"Shame. You boys could really do with somewhere to play safely." Billy had looked over his thick-rimmed specs, something he did when he had a serious point to make. "Maybe one day Daddy will buy you a bigger house and you will be able to run around to your heart's content."

The words had stung. Studying the spotless interior of the dining room in this relative palace in Chigwell, Mo had felt inadequate. Yet it wasn't as if his dad had lived in such splendour when Mo and Clive had been growing up. It was only after a particularly lucrative bank job and some life insurance facilitated by their mum's passing that he had invested in property. By then Mo and Beryl, desperate to free themselves from parental restrictions, had moved in together and Chuck was on his way.

When Chuck had gone to watch his grandma ice a cake for Billy's birthday, Mo felt able to vent his frustration. "What was the point in that, Dad? Eh?"

"What's that, son? Don't remember saying anything to upset you."

"About the garden... "

"Just thinking out loud, that's all. That playground at the flats is a shithole. On the rare occasion I've taken the boys over there I've seen needles, empty cans, dog mess... It's not suitable for your boys. They can come here any time they like, but it's not always convenient for you to drop them, I know."

"How do you propose I conjure up this house with its nice garden then?" Mo had challenged his father. "Are you going to let me in on one of the 'big jobs' you're planning?"

"Big jobs? There aren't any. Who told you that?"

"People talk. Rumours get around."

"Can no one keep a soddin' secret around here?" Billy's show of temper had at least allowed Mo the opportunity to chalk up an imaginary point on his side of the board. "Don't you dare go blabbin' your mouth off, you hear? You always were a..."

"A what, Dad? Eh? A what? You can't label me a blabbermouth. None of us could get a word in edgeways at home, in the court of 'King Billy'." Spitting out the last two words venomously, Mo had gone in for the kill. "Come to think of it, there you are pouring shit over my school work to my son, when I don't recall you taking any interest at the time. In fact, you and Mum were quite happy to pull me out of school at a moment's notice so I could look after our Clive and Cilla while you went gallivanting off down the West End. Talk about double standards..."

"Calm down, son, you'll give yourself a bleedin' heart attack," Billy Dolan had said. "Me and Vi ain't getting any younger and we're the ones who would have to tidy up the mess if you dropped down brown bread. How heavy are you? Eighteen stone or something? Tsk tsk. You should trim down, boy. You look a likely candidate for a failed ticker if you ask me. Take a leaf out of your brother's book. Fit as a flea, he is."

"Yeah, maybe if I cut out eating I could save enough money for a fackin' house," Mo had responded. "In London. That what you're saying? You're kidding, right? You do KNOW how much they cost these days? Still, let me in on the action and I'll soon be able to afford it... Deal?"

The question was greeted with silence, Mo breathing heavily having got the rant out of his system. After what seemed like minutes, Billy had replied: "You know I can't do that son. We've got our team and we don't need any substitutes."

Finally, Mo had run out of energy to fight his corner. Instead, he made a vow to himself that he would be entirely supportive of his own children. He was still fuming long after he left the house, dropped Chucky home and wandered into Dagenham to drown his sorrows.

"HEY good looking, what can I get you?"

The girl's blonde hair wound itself around her head and stretched upward to a point, reminding Big Mo of a Mr Whippy ice cream. The look was enhanced by a hint of pink running through it like raspberry sauce. Retro.

"Same again... lager," he leant against the bar, his attention again drawn to the youngsters, who were mock-fighting in the corner. Handbags. He wondered whether they would be so full of their own bullshit if Reg got involved.

"Wow, you're the talkative one." The barmaid was leaning towards him, heavy breasts fighting for space inside her low-cut red dress. She had a finger dangling from the corner of her mouth as she chewed on a cuticle.

"Sorry?" He had been so wrapped up in his own thoughts it was as if he was seeing her for the first time. *Pleasant, green eyes with an air of wickedness about them.*

"It's a joke, lover," she said. "I can see you're the strong silent type. Will Stella do you?"

"Eh?"

"You know, the drink... Stella?"

"Oh yeah. Course." He watched her wiggle off to the far end of the bar, dress stretching tight across a shapely ass and finishing mid thigh, fishnet stockings encased in impossibly high stilettos. He figured she wouldn't be dressed in such a provocative manner if she didn't want to attract male admiration. The click-clacking of her heels announced her return, interrupting his internal debate.

"Here you go." She put the pint down in front of him and he handed over a fistful of coins. "You're a regular?"

"Yeah. I drink here, The Hope in Barking and sometimes over in Ilford," said Mo. "I haven't seen you here before, though."

"Tommy, the landlord, agreed to give me a stint behind the bar." She returned his change. "He thought I might be able to attract a classier brand of customer." Posing in profile, hands on hips and nose in the air, she only realised her mistake too late. "Oh shit, sorry, that came out wrong, didn't it? I'm not having a go at you. You're about the classiest bloke in here." Blushing, she carried on talking in an effort to hide her embarrassment. "Better than those little scrotes over there; spent about a fiver between them all night. One drink each and they think it gives them the right to batter our ears with this tuneless crap."

"Not a fan, then?"

"Hell, no..."

"Audrey! The longer you spend chatting up the clientele, the less they drink," shouted Tommy from the far end of the bar. "Sorry, Big Mo, but there are customers waiting."

She leaned across, winking. "Better go... don't want to get the tin-tack on my first day."

"I can't see him sacking you," said Mo. "You seem to have quite an audience." He nodded his head in the direction of a sea of leering faces, the dodgy punters clambering up the side of the bar to get a better look. They waved their paper money around to signal they were men of means though Mo suspected broods of kids were at home fighting over fatty cuts of belly pork.

She smiled, resting her hand on his a moment longer than necessary. "Thanks. I'll see you later. Oh, and if you wanted to change the music... I like Ghost Town. The Specials?"

THREE

"HEY, watch it!" A youth with long, greasy brown hair swung around – the beer stain creeping across the front of his ruffled, white cotton shirt. Dark brown eyes peered out from below lids painted in glowing pink. Mo wrinkled his nose as a stench of body odour hit him, mingling with the sour aroma of spilt beer. Somewhere in the bouquet he detected the pungent scent of joss sticks, the incense burners widely used to disguise the equally revealing smell of dope. He pushed the boy again.

"Get out of my fackin' way then!" The kid was about five years younger than him and a world apart when it came to fashion. He was dressed like a modern Dick Turpin, the legendary highwayman famous for conducting a reign of terror throughout rural Essex. Mo knew a few boozers named after the criminal up Epping way. Out East they appreciated their bad guys.

It was highly unlikely anyone would name a boozer after this skinny runt, he thought. The freak was in no position to put the fear of God into anyone. Still, there was no point in causing a scene.

"Look, I only want to put something on the jukebox," said Mo. "So sorry if some of that nasty beer splashed on your pretty clothes but just because you dress all fancy don't give you the right to dictate what music is played in here." The boy raised his arms in surrender and stepped aside. Mo bent forward, pressing buttons on either side of the jukebox, watching the cards flick around until he saw what he wanted. "Specials: *Ghost Town*". He put in two 10p coins, which entitled him to five songs.

"Come on, mate, get a move on," someone shouted behind him. Ignoring them, his eyes lit up when he saw a song that reminded him of Youth Club back in the day. The artist was Prince Buster, the song *Al Capone*. Pushing the appropriate buttons, he was poised to choose again when he felt a jolt in the kidney region. What the..? Some cheeky bastard had poked him!

He span around, a mixture of surprise and anger bubbling inside him. A youth with short, blond hair stood there. He was roughly the same height as Mo but weedy. A large hoop dangled down the left side of his face and he was kitted out in some kind of vintage army uniform, blue coat rimmed with red-piping, white collar and cuffs, red lapels, cuff flaps and shoulder straps, augmented with brass buttons. Hardly worth bothering about, thought Mo dismissively. He didn't want to get into a ruck and ruin all the hard work the guru had done to get him to relax earlier that day. What was it Suni always said? Focus on something else. His mind drifted over which song he should pick next. He was about to turn back when the New Romantic recklessly chose to continue the dispute. "Mr Big Man, are you?" he shouted in Mo's face. "Think you can just barge in among us and push Pete here cos he's dressed different? That's out of order." Raising his fists in response, Mo felt another shove from behind, followed by a couple more as a chorus of heckling started up.

"Fuck off, bully boy!"

"Pick on someone your own size, skinhead!"

"Fascist pig!"

Feeling claustrophobic, Mo thrust his arms backwards to give himself breathing space. There was a squeal, then a crashing sound. Glancing over his shoulder, he saw a teenage girl with bright purple plaits lying prone across a collapsed table, blood streaming from a cut across her eyebrow. "Oh, hit girls, do we? Such a big man," shouted the blond bloke.

"Shit! That was an accident," Mo responded, unsure of himself. "You lot were attacking me... what did you expect?"

The bloke in the blue army jacket aimed a haymaker in Big Mo's direction, but it lacked accuracy and grazed his shoulder. He thought about cutting his losses, making a break for it and rounding up some of the troops or, at least, grabbing Reg from under the table by the door where he had left him. Only, now he was trapped, his brightly dressed accusers blocking the escape routes. Regaining his composure Mo lunged forward, grabbed and pulled, hearing the scream. The younger man doubled over, holding a hand to his ear. Blood poured from it, the hoop stained red and lying forlornly under the jukebox. "You've ripped my fuckin' ear open!" he shouted.

The words were drowned out by a familiar sound. "Al Capone's Guns Don't Argue!" barked a heavy, echoing voice, followed by the chick, chick, chickity, chick, chick rhythm of the Prince Buster Ska classic. As the horns broke in it was as if Mo had switched to auto pilot. Like a dancer, he twisted and turned, firing out punches in time to the beat.

"Don't call me Scarface..." Bang! Blood flew from a split lip as he connected with a stunned face on his right. "... I'm Alias Capone." Crash! Another New Romantic rocked backwards, knocking over a wooden stand, coats and umbrellas scattering across the floor. "C... A... P... O... N... E. Capone!" Blam. Shit! That was the landlord. He'd cuffed him in the ear.

"Sorry, Tom, I didn't..."

"Think you'd better go, Mo," shouted the landlord above the din. "Not your fault! Hell, I'll have to ban these fuckers. No good for business. Trying to turn a proper boozer into a bloody youth club." As if to demonstrate his disdain he pulled the guy called Pete towards him and sent him reeling with a head butt. "Give me a chance to get things straightened out here," he continued, breathing heavily. "Cops are on their way. Come back in a couple of days and I'll have a pint waiting."

Mo turned to leave, only to be confronted by the girl with purple hair, a screaming banshee lunging towards him waving a small, broken Babycham bottle. She was just about to strike when a hand appeared from nowhere, grabbing one of her purple plaits and clouting her around the ear with a closed fist. She dropped the bottle.

"Thanks for the tune, mate!" said the barmaid, shaking her hand to relieve the jarring pain caused by the impact her fist had made with the girl's face. "Like Tommy said, it might be time to go!"

Mo didn't hesitate, retrieving Reg and making a strategic withdrawal from the war zone. "Fackin' 'ell Reg," he said. "A proper bar brawl... You missed all the fun."

THE more Maurice Dolan thought about it, the more riled he was by the cheeky fuckers who had accused him of starting trouble. They were way out of order. He'd only wanted to use the jukebox but these little brats didn't seem to respect anyone. Fucking hell, what a day it had been: first being lampooned by some dipstick in pinstripes, then being made to feel an inadequate parent by his own father and finally being targeted by a bunch of clowns in panto costume.

He stood in one of the alleyways that criss-crossed the Dagenham housing estate, watching the entrance to the 3 Wishes. He was pretty much unscathed apart from a small cut below his left eye and the beginnings of a bruise on his shoulder. He also had a cut on the back of his head where one of those delicate creatures had broken a glass on his skull. Very romantic, he thought.

Plotting his revenge, he considered picking off the fuckers one by one as they left the boozer, but didn't want to attract the attention of the law. While tangling with the police hadn't bothered him in the past, he had a family to worry about now. It felt like a defeat, though, and Big Mo couldn't afford to have his reputation smeared. He banged the back of his head softly against the wall to the tune now escaping through the open door of the pub.

"This town..." Yeah, he thought, it's like a ghost town. He took a long drag of his cigarette and closed his eyes, relaxing to the latest hit by ska revival band The Specials.

"My hero!" The voice came from his left. Turning, he saw the barmaid wrapped in an imitation fur jacket.

"Oh, hi," he said. "Where did you spring from?"

"Tommy let me go out back, just in case. I need to head in the other direction but was gonna hang out here 'til those troublemakers left. I'm Audrey." She held out a hand and he accepted the greeting. "You, I hear, are Big Mo. You got a spare one of them?" She indicated the cigarette and he pulled the packet from his sheepskin coat, removed one, put it in his mouth and lit it from the one he was smoking. He passed it to her.

"Name's Maurice actually but, yeah, you can call me Big Mo."

She smiled, dimples showing on her cheeks. Her face was on the chubby side but he liked a girl with a bit of meat on her, better than one of those skinny models he had glimpsed in Beryl's magazines. Since having the kids Beryl's own natural curves had disappeared after the crash diet she had undergone to regain her pre-baby weight. Not that he had been given much chance to investigate further. They lived in different time zones these days – she up early with the kids and he staying out late.

"Why the nickname, if you don't mind me asking?" she said, watching him casually swing something wrapped in brown paper at his side. Mo always carried Reg that way so that if questioned he could say he had recently bought it from a hardware store. "Is it because of that? What's the line? Is that a table leg in your pocket or are you just pleased to see me?"

He smiled, lifting it so the light reflected off the brown paper. "It's a curtain pole, actually," he said. "Umm..."

"There he is, get him! He's with that slag who punched our Rita, too." Turning swiftly, Mo watched the end of the lane fill with New Romantics. They had tooled up. Mo pushed Audrey behind him as a bottle hurtled through the air in their direction, smashing against the wall next to their heads. Mo smiled coldly. Though he hadn't wanted it particularly, trouble had found him. The blond boy in the army uniform stood facing him, a metal bar in his hand. The crusted blood around his damaged ear was visible in the misty glow of a streetlamp.

"Get out of here, and I'll catch you up," Mo told Audrey.

"Sod that!" she said. "You can't tackle them on your own."

"Watch me!" As the iron bar came hurtling towards his head he ducked and struck with the speed of a cobra, his fist uncoiling into the attacker's throat. The boy's mouth gaped open and he dropped the pipe. Quickly, Mo lifted Reg and swung the gift-wrapped weapon from over his right shoulder, catching his attacker with a direct hit on the knee, sending him reeling back into the rest of the gang. Out of the corner of his eye Mo saw Audrey scrambling on her knees, reaching for the metal pipe.

"You want it, you bloody ponces?" she demanded, standing upright again. "Come on then!" One boy waving a broken bottle stepped forward out of the crowd, but Audrey was quick, bringing the pipe up between his legs. He gagged and fell backwards in agony.

Swinging like a latter-day Babe Ruth, Mo demanded: "Who's next, eh? Who's next?" Their leader out cold on the floor, the others backed away. Mo jogged after them, Audrey close behind, hanging on to the tail of his sheepskin coat. He was about to break into a full run and lay into the stragglers when a blue, flashing light appeared at the end of the lane. "Shit, filth!" he shouted to Audrey. "Run!"

"We ain't..."

"Don't argue, just do it! I can't afford any trouble." Turning, he grabbed her hand and they set off at a sprint, the sound of pounding feet and raised voices close behind.

"Hey, you up there... stop! Police!"

Mo hurdled the prone bodies of two of his victims then raised the pace, his brogues slipping around on discarded rubbish. There was an overwhelming stench of dog shit but it was too dark to see where he was treading. Audrey was doing a good job keeping up with him as he changed direction, entering an adjoining lane. Hearing more raised voices and a pounding of feet he feared he had entered a dead end.

"Here!" said Audrey. Grabbing his foot she launched him into the air. Clambering like a squaddie on an assault course, he found himself on top of a yellow gate and toppled over into an adjoining garden, hearing a rip and sensing he'd damaged his favourite sheepskin. Landing with a "whump" on his back he looked up to see Audrey hurtling through the sky above, treating him to a full view of fishnets, suspenders and knickers, the red dress billowing like a parachute. He rolled quickly away and she landed on her haunches beside him, her expression that of a wild animal, senses honed by the adrenaline of the hunt.

"Shit!" he whispered. "Where did you learn to fight like that?"

"My dad, mainly. He wanted me to know self-defence to fight off the boys. Didn't factor in my mum, though. She..."

He pressed his finger to her lips. They lay like that for ages, listening to the sound of voices going to and fro, sticks rhythmically beating at the overgrown weeds on the other side of the gate. Slowly the night regained the upper hand. There was a roar of powerful car engines then silence.

Mo studied her face in the half light. She looked younger, more vulnerable. He pushed his finger gently into her mouth and felt her suck it, other parts of his body responding to the stimulus. Then he sent his lips crashing into hers and felt her tongue shoot inside his mouth, her hands massaging the bristles of his cropped hair, sending tingles shooting through his body to offset the aches and pains.

She guided his hand up her dress to where the stockings finished and the cold, dimpled flesh of her thighs began. He massaged the skin, pushing his calloused fingers inside her knickers, finding her wet. She gasped and he did, too, a cold hand slipping inside his flies and discovering his hardness. He couldn't remember the last time he had felt so alive and so aroused.

"Fuck me, Big Mo," she whispered, breath hot on his ear.

"I... I'm married."

"Fuck marriage," she said.

He did as he was told.

FOUR

STARING at the three hulking grey monstrosities in front of him, Big Mo listened to the sounds of a city coming to life. There was no melodic bird song or excited cockerel crow to welcome the new day, just a repetitive grinding noise provided courtesy of the council's refuse collection team. As the bin lorry ravenously chewed up whatever delights had been discarded by the citizens of the estate, seagulls circled above, hovering on the fresh morning air as they studied the ground for scraps. Sitting on a bench in the playground amid an array of cigarette butts, beer cans and discarded chewing gum, Mo's nostrils were invaded by a cloying mish-mash of smells. Rotten veg and decomposed meats competed for supremacy with the eye-watering ammonia from hundreds of disposable nappies.

Mixed with his hangover, this battering of the senses told Mo that however badly intentioned his comments had been, essentially his dad was right. His sole focus had to be about looking after family, bringing up his kids in an environment where fun outside didn't involve having to slalom through a landscape of discarded needles and used condoms. He loved his city, but deprived areas like this spread through the outer boroughs like a cancer. Trying to survive in London, even at this low level, was a full-time job. Blokes like him spent every waking moment dreaming up schemes which might improve their lives a fraction.

It was a Catch-22, though. The higher up the rung you climbed, the more of the good bits you left behind. Billy 'The Kid' provided testimony to that. Mo's father waxed lyrical about the East End and the good old days while isolating himself in the country, a world away from the places he claimed to love and the people he idolised. If Mo was reluctant to follow suit it was because he didn't want to give up his mates, the boozers, the clubs, the betting shops and the banter. This was his manor. It was who he was. A unique brand of camaraderie existed here and to leave would be akin to surgically removing a piece of his soul.

His dad wittered on about the blitz spirit shown by his grandparents when Hitler's bombs were dropping on the capital. To a certain extent that still existed, though rather than bonding in the face of a war-mongering tyrant, these days the enemy had set up camp just down the road in Westminster. Mo vividly remembered the winter of discontent, piles of rubbish forming on street corners as the binmen went on strike, Green Goddess fire engines racing around the neighbourhood as the Army stepped into the breach left by protesting firemen. Still, this latest Prime Minister seemed a different proposition, prepared to stick up for her citizens and determined to make Britain Great again. He liked her conviction, believing Margaret Thatcher did things because she thought they were right rather than because they would win votes at the next election. Putting out his cigarette he got to his feet, gagging involuntarily as another pungent whiff attacked his senses. Then he made his way reluctantly towards the entrance to the flats.

Stepping into the decrepit lift, the whole saga of the previous night flashed through his mind. It had been like a *Play for Today* drama on the telly; the fight with a bunch of kids in bizarre fancy dress, the escape from the police and the act of infidelity with the barmaid. It was as if they had happened to someone else and he had been an innocent bystander powerless to intervene. Even now, thoughts of Audrey brought a stirring to his groin and, though he was completely alone, he reflexively moved his hand to cover his embarrassment. He could hear her voice begging him to push "harder, harder" as he recalled pounding into her without even having bothered removing the lacy black knickers she was wearing. His skin tingled at the thought of her legs wrapped around his back, her heels pushing him deeper until he came in a flood of guilt, embarrassment and ecstasy. He had laughed out loud, only for an angry voice to interrupt. "Hey, you, what do you think you're doing down there? Bleedin' Ada, love, there's a couple 'aving it off in our back yard!"

He smiled to himself at the recollection of them leaping to their feet, adjusting their clothes and sneaking out of the gate just as a grumpy dog arrived to protest their trespass. Having been dragged back to her flat, he was on her again the moment they were through the front door, pinning her to the passage wall with his hardness, trousers gathered at his ankles, her fists gripping the collar of the sheepskin. When it was over they drifted into her tidy little bedroom and fell asleep on top of the sheets until the chill of early morning alerted him to the fact he was supposed to be somewhere else. "Shit!" he had exclaimed, pulling on trousers and racing from the flat.

"You know where I am!" she had shouted at his retreating back as he stumbled outside to get his bearings, lost in the maze of Dagenham streets which looked like carbon copies of each other. He had found the main road eventually, flagged down a cab and headed back to Barking. Once on home territory he had delayed his return, smoking a couple of cigarettes in the playground because he feared Beryl would detect the scent of illicit sex on him if he climbed into bed next to her. He reasoned it was better to get in at a time when her mind was preoccupied with preparing breakfast and getting Chuck ready for school.

Nearing the sixth floor, the reek of urine and cheap disinfectant intensified. His eyes scanned some new, unfamiliar graffiti in the lift and it made him chuckle. Next to a sticker which said "Jesus saves" a wit had scrawled "But Brooking scores the rebound".

Jarring to a halt, a few clanking noises suggested the rusted internal contraption was struggling to cope. The bloody things broke down all the time. It was a couple of seconds before the doors slid open and he stepped out. Letting his eyes adjust to the natural light, the first thing he noticed was a yellow and red splodge like a piece of nouveau art decorating the uniformly grey balcony walls. It was a neighbour's puke and his stomach lurched in empathy. Old Alfie at No 641 was prime suspect, having never been able to handle his ale. Swallowing hard, Mo looked out over the tired view from the balcony and drew in a deep breath before putting his key in the lock, twisting it and entering the flat.

Chuck was already up, playing with a toy aeroplane in the hallway. "Dad! Dad!" the kid said, eyes sparkling, "Look at this Spitfire! Grandad gave it to me yesterday. He said the men who flew these were heroes, shooting down German planes in the war."

Mo squatted and took the plane from Chuck's hand, noticing the boy flinch as he did so. "It's all right, son," he said. "I ain't going to break it. My, but this is a beauty, ain't it? Hope you thanked your grandad. I made one similar when I was a boy. In fact, yeah, come to think of it this is probably mine. They came in packs and you had to use special glue to stick them together. This was my first, I reckon." He handed it back and threw open his arms, Chuck running into the warm embrace.

"I thought I heard voices," said Beryl from the kitchen doorway. "You're back. Late one with the boys, was it? Hey, what happened?" She moved forward and put a cold hand to his cheek, turning his face to the light. "You've got a cut over your eye and that lovely coat of yours looks like it's been dragged through a hedge backwards."

"Bit of a misunderstanding with a bunch of young punks," he explained. "No big deal... well, I say punks, but they were dressed up to the hilt with strange hairstyles, make up, the works."

"I've read about them in one of my magazines, love," she said. "They call themselves New Romantics."

"Yeah, well I call them Nancy Boys."

"You want breakfast? I bet you could do with a cuppa. I know Cozza's bint ain't the most hospitable. In fact, I don't suppose neither she nor that lazy bloke of hers was up when you climbed off their sofa, were they?"

He grunted, non-committal, reluctant to tell a lie that might catch him out later. He made a mental note to ask Cozza to be his alibi.

Beryl could go on thinking he stayed there until someone told her different. "Tea would be nice," he said. "What you up to?"

"I was thinking that after the school run me and Sly could pop into the supermarket, get something for tea and a few supplies. We're low on a few essentials: milk, eggs, cheese, cereals, you know..?"

"Sure. Go steady though, eh?"

She looked at him. "To be honest, love, I was hoping you might be able to sub us a few quid. Family allowance isn't due 'til Friday."

"I know," he said. "Hard times. I'm hoping to get a bit of business come my way over the next few months and then we won't have to scrimp and save so much, but at the moment... well, I ain't got a penny on me. Sorry. Maybe one of the twins might lend you some dosh, you know, just until I can sort out this temporary cash flow situation."

"Oh, come on, Mo," she said, raising her voice out of frustration. "I can't keep begging my family. They aren't made of money like... Look, we have to do something. I've been saving those supermarket stamps for food, but Christmas is around the corner and you know he's set his heart on that b...i...k...e." She spelled it out to prevent Chuck overhearing, but for a moment it was Maurice who struggled to grasp the meaning – English wasn't his strongest suit. Silence.

"Sure," he said, the penny dropping. "Don't worry about that. I'll sort it."

"If you say so." She grasped the bull by the horns. "Would it really be too much to ask your dad for a sub? I mean, they're living out there in that big house, just having to look after the two of them, and he dotes on his grandkids, I'm sure..."

"No!" Mo spat, becoming animated, the colour flooding back into his cheeks. "I told you, I ain't putting out no beggin' bowl to that facker. It's what he wants, can't you see? He wants me to grovel to him, admit I can't look after my own family. I ain't playing into his hands like that." He closed the distance between them, his grip tightening around Reg. "I told you... I'll sort it."

Beryl stood her ground courageously as he moved towards her, maintaining eye contact in the presence of the weapon. "As long as you've got it all taken care of," she said, her tone full of irony and doubt. "You might be needing a new coat, too, by the looks of things. The pocket looks ripped and, jeez, there's a tear in the collar, too. I can patch it up on the sewing machine, but you've had that one so long it must be time for a replacement."

Distracted, he looked at where she was pointing, remembering long fingernails decorated in bright red varnish pulling at his lapels, hearing a rip as he sank deeply into... shit, he was getting aroused again. "You're right, sure," he said, breaking eye contact. "Damn, I'm busting for the loo. Cup of tea would be lovely, babe. Don't worry," he shoved passed her. "...Leave it on the table there if you have to go straight out and I'll have it in a minute."

"It ain't even 8 o'clock yet, hun," she said, confused. "My, you did have a right bang, didn't you?"

"Eh?" his heart skipped a beat.

"You know, on your head, from those bloody kids. Maybe you're concussed." He grunted and marched on, slamming the toilet door shut and pulling down his trousers. Grasping his erection he let his mind drift back to the previous night, oblivious to his wife muttering under her breath: "Perhaps it's a warning to cut down on your drinking a bit. Maybe then you might be able to feed your damn kids."

FIVE

"I'M telling you, it can't lose!"

"Yeah, cos you Irishmen aren't in the business of backing three-legged nags, are you?" Big Mo held the phone in one hand, using a towel to wipe his head with the other. A second towel was around his waist. He had sluiced half the contents of a Dagenham back garden down the plughole and was feeling human again. Now, the money issue pressing, he was determined to show Beryl he could manage without his dad's intervention. "With all these 'unbeatable' horses you Paddies must be millionaires. I can see you sitting on your yacht off the Costa Del Crime now. How is Marbella these days?"

"Hang on a wee second," said the Irishman, rising to the bait. "There I was thinking it was you who rang me for a tip and I was doing yous a favour. Sweet Jesus! Take it or leave it... Rockin' Rupert in the 2.30 at Market Rasen. It's well weighted with the handicapper, loves the track and gets the distance. Still, if you want another tip, don't play with your balls when you've been chopping chillies!"

Mo waited for the other man to stop guffawing. "Ha ha, funny man," he said. "Thanks for that, Pat Molloy, if it wins I'll get you a drink."

"Might as well shout 'em in now, fella. Mine's a Guinness." Mo replaced the handset without another word.

An hour later he strode along Barking's North Street, his brogues tapping out a purposeful rhythm. School kids loitered in doorways followed his movement with their eyes, cigarettes concealed within closed hands. Break-time, he guessed. They had invested their dinner money in a packet of 10 menthol and would make do with crisps and a cake for lunch. He knew this to be the case because he had done exactly the same when he was a teen.

He'd left the sheepskin at home in favour of a brown leather bomber jacket like those RAF pilots favoured in movies, the tenner burning a hole in his pocket. He had retrieved it from the emergency tin on the top shelf of his closet, the special rainy day fund now so depleted it would barely shield him from a mild shower.

Stopping off at the newsagents he invested in 10 ciggies and a copy of *Sporting Life* so he could study the form, spending a brief moment discussing football with Ron, the chatty shop owner. "Reckon they can qualify for the World Cup next year, Mo? Switzerland did us a favour, winning in Romania the other day. With a few results going our way it should mean all we have to do is beat Hungary at Wembley next month and we're in. It will be our first appearance at the World Cup finals since 1970 if that happens. The country will go mad for it."

"Sure," said Mo, smiling. "Well, we've got a Hammer in charge, Ron Greenwood, so where can it go wrong?"

Waving his paper in farewell, he moved next door to Albert Kemp's, the independent bookie who had set up on his own thanks to the proceeds of a windfall on the Pools. Inside, he was greeted by the usual suspects bunched up at counters ringing the interior as they scribbled down their doubles, trebles and Lucky 15s – their plan for long-term financial security still a work in progress as was evidenced by their clothes. While Mo always tried to look presentable in his neatly ironed white shirts, this lot could have emptied out from the local Salvation Army hostel.

Benny the Bounce, named for the way he walked from stool to counter on the balls of his feet, sat just inside the door sucking on a small complimentary pen, studying the boards above. Next to him, Twitching Trev leaned in as if to impart some valuable information, only to jerk his head away at the last moment as the other man moved closer to hear what he had to say. Mo had fallen into the same trap in the past. Though the twitch was outside the man's control, Mo found it difficult to suppress a snigger, particularly when the poor unfortunate had an embarrassing comb-over that flopped to the side each time his affliction kicked in.

"Well, if it isn't Barking royalty paying us a visit!" Albert Kemp peered out from behind the counter.

"It's tough being a royal these days, Kempy," said Mo, walking up to him. "Too many Republicans around wanting to chop off our heads. I really don't know how we are supposed to survive on the measly millions the taxpayer gives us. Maybe you could find it in your heart to contribute a few pennies to our beloved monarchy."

He held out his hand, but Albert shook his head. "Sorry, Big Mo, but you got to earn it like the rest of us. Anyway, when did you last pay tax?"

Mo ignored the jibe. "I've had a pretty good tip that this nag at Market Rasen might do the business... Rockin' Rupert. What's your thoughts, Albie?" Albert Kemp's face screwed into a sneer. "You've made that face because you want me to stay well away from him, haven't you?"

"It's a fine horse and it's entirely up to you," said Albie. "If you ask me, though, she prefers softer ground. It's pretty firm today and there's one or two in the field that have the beating of her... mind you, what do I know? I'm just a poor, impoverished bookie."

"No such thing," said Mo. "How's the new Roller anyway, Albie? Silver Ghost I was told, special edition."

"Don't believe everything you hear around these parts," said Albert Kemp, "especially off this lot."

"So..?"

"Yeah, OK, it is a Silver Ghost." He laughed. "Nice little runner, too. Look, I haven't got time to shoot the breeze with you, I got a shop to run... you betting or what?"

"Maybe in a minute." Albie's comment about the state of the ground had raised doubts in his mind. He retreated to find a seat and study his paper. It was happening more often recently. Mo would enter the bookies sure of what he wanted to do, only to change his mind at the last moment. His confidence had taken a knock with a few tips going against him lately.

He let his eyes skim the cards. It was such a minefield. Whose advice should he follow? Two people who knew their horses were giving him conflicting opinions. He looked at the screen to see the latest odds. Rockin' Rupert was 3-1, not even an each-way chance. He let his eyes drift down. Coming to the Huntingdon card, the 'Eureka!' moment hit him. If it wasn't an omen, he didn't know what was. In the 2.15 there was a horse called Magic Mo. He returned to his paper and studied the form guide. The horse had appeared only once this season, finishing back in 12th, but the *Sporting Life* expert said it would come on leaps and bounds for the run. In the previous season it had been out injured but was now coming back to its best. Two seasons ago it had raced three times over course and distance, winning twice and coming second once. It liked good-to-firm ground and its owner was confident it had completely recovered from its past problems. It had a top jockey on board and when Mo checked on the price he discovered it was going off at 16-1. It meant he could take it each way and scoop a decent pay out if it won, while also being up on the deal if it finished in the top four. He scrawled down his bet and returned to the window with a smile on his face. The girl who had replaced Albert Kemp behind the counter printed off the bet and gave him the slip, reflecting his optimism back at him. "Hope it's a winner!" she said cheerily.

Commentary crackled out of the speakers in the four corners of the elongated room. For a while he heard no mention of the horse that carried his cash. Then, after a couple of fallers, he felt a tingle of excitement as the commentator drawled: "... and keeping up a strong pace on the stand side is Magic Mo. Jockey Peter Scudamore has him well tucked in behind the leaders and he is looking veeerry smooth at this moment."

Magic Mo hit the front with three furlongs to go and it was now a two-horse race between his pick and John Francome's mount

Crosstown Boy. The commentator's voice rose an octave. "... And it's Magic Mo, leaps the second last brilliantly, showing a clean pair of hooves to Crosstown Boy. The grey looks like it's tiring but, master that he is, Francome is getting every last ounce out of him. There seems a lot more running in Magic Mo, though, and remember he's won a couple of times here over this distance. They are approaching the last, a two-length gap developing. It's Magic Mo, Crosstown Boy and.... ohhhhhhhh!"

What? Thought Mo. Tell me you twat! What's happened? His face went pale, his breath caught in his throat, his heart pounded. "He's gone! He's gone!" shouted the commentator. Who's gone?

"Magic Mo was looking so good, Scudamore doing everything right but maybe this race came too soon. He clipped the top of the last, overbalanced and fell, leaving the way clear for Crosstown Boy to complete a 12-length win over Mr Chimp with Opening Times in third and Magic Mo, the tragic Magic Mo, still down and, I regret to say, looking badly injured. I hate to be the bearer of bad news but it could be they will have to put the poor gelding out of its misery."

"Its misery?" stormed Mo, heads turning to face him. "What about my fackin' misery, eh? Ten quid down the Swanee and all because a horse couldn't make one decent fackin' jump. It must have been rigged. They knew..."

"What? That you had £4 each way on the nag?" said Albert Kemp, standing behind him. "I think you're clutching at straws there, old friend."

"Yeah?" said Mo, turning, a look that could freeze lava pasted on his face. "Well why don't you fack off and collect your millions, Albie, another fackin' punter stitched up, you..."

The bookie made a hasty retreat.

"Calm down, will you?" A hand touched Mo's shoulder and he swivelled, fists raised, though if he had thought for a second he would have recognised the voice. Clive, his younger sibling, stood there, a big grin stretched across his face.

"What the fack..?"

"Know my brother pretty well, don't I?" said Clive, who was the same height as Mo but on the thinner side, his hair now modelled in an unfamiliar buzz cut. A light-brown moustache crawled across his top lip. They hadn't seen each other for more than six months, but that didn't mean they weren't close. "I thought I'd better show my face, let everyone know I'm all right," he continued. "I suppose it was telepathy which brought me here... after all it's not as if you are in the same place most afternoons." He winked, indicating the opposite was true.

"Damn Scudamore!" Mo's mind was on the lost bet. "Supposed to be in the running for the jockey's title and can't clear the final hurdle when the race is in the bag. Must be some sort of fix."

"Doesn't a fix normally involve the favourites? Magic Mo went off at 16-1."

"Yeah, well..." Mo nodded his head in the direction of the bookmaker. "Dare say he's got a buzzer through to Huntingdon, some sort of alarm that says he is about to lose so make something happen to change the course of the race."

"Jeez, talk about conspiracy theories. How much did you lose, Maurice?"

"Eight pound in all, but it's the thought that counts. Magic Mo was leading right up to that final hurdle only to run through it as if its feet were stuck in treacle. It's a travesty I tell you."

"Shame," said Clive.

Suddenly the light went on in Mo's eyes again as a TV screen flickered into life above him. "Hey, you want a good tip? Sub me and we can both come out of this up on the deal. There's a crackin' horse running in this one."

"Really? Like the last one?" He still had a grin on his face.

Mo swatted at him with his hand, but Clive was expecting a reaction and dodged out of the way.

"Come on little brother!" pleaded Mo. "When do I ask you for anything? This is a Molloy tip... it's good."

"Paddy Molloy? Doesn't he just bet on rigged boxing bouts?"

"No. Yes. Well... Look, he's an Irishman. They know their horses."

Clive dipped into his pocket and pulled out a fiver. "You'd better hurry," he said. "They're at the starting gate."

Mo grasped the lifeline and joined the queue behind Twitching Trev, who was taking his time to explain exactly what he wanted. "Hey!" he said, poking Trev in the back. The man turned slowly, leaned forward as if to speak in Mo's ear, then jerked away at the last moment, catching Mo on the chin with the top of his head. "Christ!" said Mo, rubbing the affected area. Collecting his change, Trev got out of the way.

"And... they're off!" shouted the commentator. Mo leaned across the counter, throwing the fiver at the friendly female assistant. "On the nose. Rockin' Rupert," he shouted.

"Sorry, sir, the race has started. We can't take any bets now."

"Fack off! Nothing's happened yet," he said. "It wasn't my fault I couldn't get to the window, that bleedin' twitcher was in the way."

The girl stood her ground. "I'm sorry, sir, those are the rules."

"Fack your rules! Get Albie out here."

"I'm afraid the manager can't do anything either."

"Sure he can," said Mo. "Albie!"

Instead of seeing the bookmaker poke his head around the corner, he felt his arms grabbed by a hulking, shaven-headed man in a cap-sleeved tee-shirt. "Time you left, mate," he said with the trace of an Eastern European accent.

"Fack you!" protested Mo. "You know who I am?"

"Another mug punter who wants to take issue when he's lost his money fair and square? If you can't afford to lose it then don't come here in the first place."

Shuffling his prisoner away from the counter and towards the exit the bouncer was confronted by another unhappy customer. "I suggest you leave him alone," said Clive. "Otherwise, you might regret it."

"Yeah? Who's going to make me?" asked the bouncer.

"Wrong question." Clive brought his head crashing down against the tough guy's nose. There was a crack like a whip and he released his grip on Mo immediately to examine his damaged nose. A moment later he was on the floor, put there by Mo's elbow.

"Albie you cunt, come out here!" he shouted at the top of his voice.

"No time," said Clive, "Come on, he's probably in the back room calling the Old Bill. I can't afford to get in trouble and neither, I imagine, can you."

"True," said Mo, picking up Reg from where he had left the weapon, lying against a stool. Turning, he brought it crashing down on the shoulder of the bouncer. "Who's the mug now, eh?" he asked as his victim emitted the kind of scream only dislocation can cause.

SIX

CLIVE DOLAN handed over the mug of coffee with the West Ham football club logo on the side and took a seat opposite his brother. The cosy one-bedroom flat nestled above a bakery in a rank of shops, the smell of sausage rolls and other tasty pastries wafting in through the small window. "Are you making it your mission to get banned from everywhere?" he asked as Mo put the mug to his lips, the hot liquid dispersing much-needed caffeine throughout his body.

"Don't worry about Albie, he'll come around," said Mo. "Don't know why he appointed that fackin' blown-up muscleman anyway. Damn lot of use he was."

Clive laughed. "You're supposed to be the older brother, keeping an eye on me, and there I am wading in for you. I ain't had a fight in ages, then one minute in your company and it's like World War II all over again. Seriously, Maurice, you're a grown man now, with a family and responsibilities. When are you going to calm down? Look at all the cuts and bruises on you."

"Oh those! Just a disagreement with some young idiots last night," explained Mo. "I didn't go looking for it. Anyway, life ain't easy, mouths to feed and the rest of it. That's why..." He stopped suddenly.

"... You're doing your nut over a missed betting opportunity? Come on, bruv, it's me you're talking to now. If you've got worries you can tell me. It's always been me and you. Maybe that's not been the case lately, but..."

"Nothing to tell," said Mo. "Haven't had a lot of work, I guess. We got Christmas coming up and Beryl's nagging on about cash, but it's not as if every other family around here is rolling in it. Something will turn up."

"Like more trips to the bookies?" said Clive. "Followed by more screaming and shouting at some poor girl because you can't get a bet on a certain race?"

Mo lapsed into thought. Then his eyes lit up. "Speaking of which, put Ceefax on, see how it did."

"Yeah? And what good will that do? If it won you'll throw your toys out of the pram again, probably tear my gaff apart."

"Maybe." There was a smile on Mo's face as he pushed thoughts of the race from his mind. "Probably not. Got to keep an eye on the blood pressure, you know? Anyway, it's great to see you. Where have you been? One minute you're around our house every minute, begging to take Chucky out and stuff, the next you've disappeared. I can't remember when we didn't see each other for so long."

"You know where I am," said Clive.

"I know. I called around a couple of times but got no answer. Then things got busy with the kids and Beryl and... well, I started to think you just weren't answering the door because of somethin' I said. There was that row at Christmas..."

"Christ, it was a disagreement about bloody football. We've always been like that. You know I don't hold grudges."

"I know, but even when I first moved in with Bee you were around our place regularly, kipping on the sofa," said Mo. "Then when our Chuck arrived you couldn't get enough of 'im, taking him over the park to play footie and the like. It was strange not to hear anything."

Clive nodded. "There are reasons," he said. "Truth is I haven't been here. I've been getting into shape, training and stuff."

"Yeah? What's the occasion? Ain't getting spliced are you? Who's the lucky girl?" Mo sat forward, taking another drink of coffee, the fumes filtering up his nostrils and making him feel awake for the first time since he had stumbled out of Audrey's flat that morning. "Have you put some poor unfortunate bird up the duff?"

"Nothing like that," said Clive coyly.

"Oh, hang on, I know: you've gone all Village People on me," said Mo mischievously. "You're batting for the other team. Had my doubts mind, seeing that moustache and that hair cut. You look a bit like Freddie Mercury's younger, uglier brother. Hell, a year ago you looked like a German porn star or a blond version of Kevin Keegan. What happened?"

"Stop taking the piss," said Clive. "You know I'm not gay. You're just jealous because I've got decent looks and my hair doesn't resemble one of them cheap loo brushes with which our mum used to clean the bog."

Mo leapt forward, dragging Clive over the back of the chair. The younger man issued a swift elbow to the ribs and Mo responded with a rabbit punch to the kidneys.

"Shit, bruv, no need for that, you could have broken something!" Clive protested. "I've a medical in a couple of weeks, I can't afford to get damaged."

Mo got to his feet, sucking in oxygen to replace the air driven from his lungs. "What the fuck are you talking about?"

"I've signed up," said Clive.

"On the dole? I thought you were doing OK in that supermarket... you said they were training you for management. Bastards! They've sacked you?"

"No, Maurice, the job was fine," said Clive. "What I mean is I've enlisted in the Army. I'm going to do my bit for Queen and Country. I've been in Hampshire for the best part of the year doing my basic training. I've joined the Scots Guards."

Mo stared at him, silent for seconds, trying to digest the stunning revelation. "You're joking, right?"

"Deadly serious," said Clive. "I wanted something for myself... didn't want to be a shelf-stacker all my life. You remember all those stories grandad used to tell? He fought in the war, you know, he was a guardsman, too. The regiment are quite big on family tradition. They were delighted to have me when I told them about him."

"Yeah, but you ain't a Sweatie!" said Mo, disbelief painted across his face. It took a while for the younger man to work out the rhyming slang. Sweatie sock meant Jock which was slang for Scotsman.

"I don't have to be," said Clive. "Grandad wasn't either. Provided you ain't all lairy and you give as good as you get, they accept you well enough. A lot of the boys are from places like Preston and Carlisle, good lads, though they all speak a bit funny. Strange really, because they take the piss out of my accent! It's all in good humour, though. The camaraderie is one of the reasons I joined up... and the chance to see new places and experience new things."

"Like getting something vital blown off," said Mo.

"Oh come on, don't be so dramatic! It ain't like that," said Clive.

"Oh yeah, Monkey?" Mo used the nickname he had given Clive back during their childhood. "Tell that to the poor bastards maimed or killed at Chelsea barracks."

"Funnily enough, I'm going to be based there," said Clive. "After that business I reckon it's probably the safest place in the whole of the UK with all the new security measures. Most of the stuff I'll do is ceremonial, you know, changing of the guard and the like. It ain't any more dangerous than going for a night out around here... in fact, by the look of you it's a darn site safer." He laughed, letting the words sink in. Then his expression turned serious again. "The modern Army is a place you can learn a trade, feel part of something. I quite fancy being an electrician or an engineer. There's a better chance learning those types of skills in the Army than around here. Notice all the apprenticeships the companies here are handing out?"

Mo shook his head.

"Exactly! There ain't any. I'm fed up with seeing the same faces all the time, struggling to make ends meet. I'm fed up with living in this crummy flat with no chance I'll ever get a decent holiday. Weekends in Southend-on-Sea and Clacton lose their appeal after a while. The only mates I have are the same ones I had at school, and they've all gone off and got themselves hitched. Shit! Even you've got other priorities. I'm taking the plunge while I'm young and not tied down. I want to see the world."

He fell silent, the sound of an ambulance siren splitting the air en route to one of the nearby hospitals. It shook Mo into a response. "You want to see the world, Monkey?" he said. "Is that the world as in Belfast? Shit! You know what's going on over there, don't you? They're targeting soldiers every day. If our grandad told you anything, it was that those Republicans hate anyone in a uniform. Remember he lived there, and he and his mates got fed up with all the hassle. That's why he came here in the first place. Joining the Army in this day and age is like wearing a target on your jumper with an arrow saying 'shoot here'!"

Clive sat down again and indicated for Mo to do the same. He did so reluctantly, feeling wound up by this latest shock to the system. He rubbed his temple in a vain effort to disperse the first throbbings of a migraine.

"I thought this was going to be the easy conversation," said Clive.

"You ain't told the old man?"

"I thought I'd try it out on you first."

"He won't be happy," said Mo. "I know he waxes on about the Union Jack, the royals and sticking up for ourselves, but he doesn't actually want his own kin to take up arms."

"I know," said Clive. "He asked recently if I fancied a job with him. He said I had the brains to help run his business. Me? I don't know where he got that idea from. I've never been interested in that type of life."

"You were always the favourite," said Mo.

"Oh, don't be daft," said Clive. "He just played one off against the other. Still, it shows he knows nothing about me. I ain't a blagger or a thief, and I don't like the idea of violence for violence's sake, hurting some poor bastard just because they stand in your way of a bit of cash. There are more important things in life."

"Like killing people you don't even know?" said Mo. "Anyway, it's OK for you... you're a bright kid, got a few exams behind you and managed to finish your schooling. Some of us were left with few alternatives."

"Don't you see?" said Clive. "That was how I felt about my options after you left home. I got the full lecture from Dad about not letting the family down. It fell on my shoulders to prove the Dolans were up to snuff. He told me if ever the school rang to say I'd been expelled, he'd send me away to one of those strict boarding schools."

"He couldn't handle another me," said Mo. "I was a disgrace, the black sheep, and you had to repair the damage I'd done. Fack!"

"I think it hurt him, that's all," said Clive. "He had high hopes for you... his first born."

"... And all he sees now is a fuck-up."

"That ain't true, Maurice. You've given him two grandkids he adores and if you look carefully around his house pictures of you take pride of place everywhere. You're lucky to find any of me on my own. The trouble is you're too much alike."

"I ain't nothing like that old bastard," Mo protested.

"But you are," said Clive. "You're a leader, someone capable of making their own decisions. You've got the same ruthless streak and the same temper. That's why the old man won't work with you, I'm sure. He doesn't want someone who is going to question him, maybe argue with him about how things should be done. He wants people who follow orders without questioning, pure and simple. That's why he wanted me. I'm one of life's followers, happy doing someone else's bidding." His eyes locked on to his brother's.

"Like a soldier," Mo said, as if the sums had finally added up.

"Exactly," said Clive. "I crave discipline but I don't want to be following an idiot like Dull Dean, the supervisor down the supermarket, all my life. I want to work in a place where what you do actually matters. I want to be part of a team where everyone knows their job and the combined result stands for something... and I want to prove that I can be more than just a two-bit criminal who at one stage or another will be left to rot away behind bars."

"Hasn't happened to the old man yet," said Mo.

"No, but every time there's a knock at the door he has to run around hiding the silver," said Clive.

They both laughed, the tension popping thanks to a telepathic vision shared by siblings.

"Looks like you've thought it through," said Mo. "I guess all I can do is support you and wish you all the best, Monkey. Still, when you get shot up the arse by some left-footer who finds you crawling through his potato patch, don't come crying to me."

"I will," said Clive, his eyes watering up. He rose from his seat and gave his older brother a hug. Eventually they split. "Your support means a lot, Maurice, you know that."

Minutes later Mo was at the front door. "Don't fancy one?" he asked.

"I'll give it a miss, thanks," said Clive. "I could do with a beer but I've got to get into London early tomorrow. They're going to tell me my duties, you know, like the Changing of the Guard. You should bring the boys along sometime."

"Could do," said Big Mo. "Are you going to be the guy who stands in a box, stock still, while schoolkids blow raspberries at him and try to make him laugh?"

"I remember," said Clive, a vision from his childhood giving him a jolt. "Maybe. There's a lot of pomp and tradition associated with the uniform, you know? I'm looking forward to it. My leave runs out tomorrow but first I'm going to see the old man. I wouldn't want him to catch a glimpse of me on TV in all that clobber."

"Good luck."

"Thanks," said Clive, raising his hands to show his brother the fingers were firmly crossed.

IT was half an hour later when Mo fiddled in his pockets for the change to buy a pint in the local estate pub, The Hope and Anchor, that he found the envelope. Mystified, he pulled it from his pocket and opened it. Inside was a short, pencil-written message and the sum of £150 in crisp, new banknotes. In Clive's swirling handwriting, it simply read: "I'm sure you'll find this handy. I've got a little bit spare and I guess I'll only need beer money in barracks. Buy the boys something nice... and, if you're really hard up, sell that bloody Daimler."

Mo smiled, kissed the letter and put it back in his pocket before striding to the bar, a fiver in his hand. "Sell the one piece of luxury which is solely mine, Monkey? Not a bleeding chance mate," he mumbled.

Seven

Christmas Eve, 1981

SERGEANT Max Cooper and PC Cliff Simpson were sharing coffee from a flask and indulging in large portions of Mrs Simpson's Yule log when the call came in. "Damn," swore Cooper. He pressed a button and mumbled into the handset, brushing crumbs from his uniform. It had been a quiet Christmas Eve and both men were hoping it was going to stay that way. They wanted to be at home and the last thing they needed was to be dragged back to the station to write time-consuming reports. "Alpha 38, hearing you loud and clear," said Cooper.

"More than I can say for you, Max," said the woman on dispatch. "You're mumbling. Are you eating something?"

"Sucking a mint, Doris... What is it?"

"Alarm gone off over at Plumpton's Trading Estate in Romford. It's a storage facility used by a number of businesses, as far as I can tell. Something is always setting the damn things off, but I need it checked out."

"Roger that. Over and out." He re-attached the handset to the dashboard. "Just our bloody luck," he said.

"Never mind," said the Constable, whose vast bulk was wedged in behind the steering wheel. He had rosy cheeks and an abundance of white hair which sat on top of his head like candyfloss. "You won't be bothered by this when you're a big cheese on the Flying Squad. I expect someone's just had a bit too much of the Christmas spirit and left the cat on the premises or something. When do you hear about the big job anyway?"

"Straight after the Christmas period," said Cooper. "They said it should be a formality. Don't be jealous now, will you?"

"I've seen all the excitement I wanted to in this job," said Simpson. "Back in the day, y'know..."

"You never moved up, though? No promotions?"

"Like to keep my head below the parapet." Simpson smiled. "There's always someone wants to knock it off. No, I'm quite happy. Don't know how I ended up on traffic duty, to be honest. Still, it's all change for me too in the New Year. Going back to Hackney nick. They offered me the job of jailer and I jumped at the chance."

"Sounds nice and... um... boring," said Cooper, laughing. "Come on then, the sooner we get this done, the sooner we get to go home."

"HERE they come: Jack Regan and his pal George." Mo was peering through the tinted side window of the blue van Handsome Frank had acquired through his 'contacts'.

"You think they're Flying Squad?" said Frank as two uniformed policemen emerged slowly from their car, brushing at their clothes. "I don't reckon that fat one would fly if you pumped 5,000 volts into 'im!"

They laughed. Regan and George were characters in *The Sweeney*, a popular 70s all-action cop show about the police's serious crime unit, the Flying Squad. Mo used to watch it just to take the mickey out of the so-called hard men and bad boys who were outsmarted every week. He'd like to see how The Sweeney would cope with a real London firm.

"Prefer *The Professionals*, me," said Cozza, slumping back in the driving seat and chewing lazily on a corned beef sandwich.

"Yeah, I can see that," said Frank, sniggering. "Professional to the hilt, you."

"Suggesting I ain't?" flared Cozza, sitting up straighter and dropping the packaging at his feet. He wiped his mouth. "I think you'll be changing your tune in a few hours from now."

Frank threw an arm out, making a circular motion with his hand, as if fishing. "Looks like I've caught a big one, Mo! Help me reel him in."

"You won't be laughing when you see what my hard work nets us," complained Cozza.

Mo let them bicker, burying his head in the tabloid daily newspaper he had brought along to pass the time. As was the norm these days, the front page was largely devoted to a picture of the media's darling, Princess Diana, attending the opening of a hospital wing. She was poised to cut a ribbon while wearing that coy smile the photographers seemed to love. Rather than highlight the cause she was promoting, though, the article concentrated on the way she was dressed, the writer speculating how long it might be before the country was honoured with a royal birth. Why couldn't they just give her some peace? thought Mo. The "People's Princess" was young, vivacious and very, very "fit", but surely she deserved a break.

Mo recalled being among the 750million TV audience back in the summer when Prince Charles had tied the knot, people from all over the world lining the route to and from St Paul's Cathedral just so they could say "I was there". Beryl and a gaggle of her mates from the East End had been among them though he didn't really see the point. He had been afforded a much better view from the comfort of his own living room.

Next to Diana's picture was a story about Margaret Thatcher. An opinion poll had revealed she was the most unpopular Prime Minister since the war, and that the relatively new SDP-Liberal Alliance had the support of 50 per cent of the population. "We'll see," he muttered to himself.

"Here we go!" said Cozza. Mo looked up from his paper. A man in cream slacks and a safari jacket ambled up to the policemen. After a brief chat, the more senior officer with the stripes followed the key holder into the building, his overweight mate taking up the rear.

"So we wait for the cops to disappear then we jump this fool, beat the crap out of him and nick his keys," said Frank. "I get it, Cozz."

"Oh yeah," said Cozza, "That method's foolproof, ain't it, Handsome? What is it with you? If we don't beat the crap out of someone you ain't satisfied."

"Never mind all that," snapped Mo. "This is Cozza's operation. We do what he says, OK Handsome?"

The other man grunted.

They fell into silence, Mo considering his partners in crime. While Cozza was a bright spark, Frank could be a loose cannon. A lack of discipline was probably the main reason he never made it to the top level in boxing. His hot-headed approach had its advantages, though, and that disfigured face was enough to scare the crap out of most people.

Cozza broke the spell. "Here they come!" The officers emerged, waiting by their car until the man in the safari jacket joined them. Shaking their hands vigorously, he watched as they climbed into the patrol car and drove away. On cue, Cozza slipped out of the passenger's seat and onto the pavement. He waited for the keyholder to disappear around the corner before the low growl of a powerful car broke the silence. Moments later a red Lamborghini slid into view, taking off at speed in the same direction as the police car. Cozza sidled up to the door of the warehouse and fiddled with the lock. Frank turned to Mo. "What's he doing now, picking the fucker?" he asked.

The overwhelming aroma in the van, left over from the paint and chemicals usually stored within, was making Mo feel light-headed – early signs of a migraine taking hold. "Nah, mate," he said, rubbing his temples to dislodge the fuzzy feeling. "If I know Cozza it involves more brainwork than that. He's been planning this for weeks. Remember, he knows all about locks and stuff... he was obsessed with that Uri Geller as a kid, you know the bloke who claimed to bend spoons with his mind? I remember seeing loads of books in his bedroom, about escapology and the like. He had one about that famous escape artist, whatsisname?"

"Houdini?"

"That's the one," said Mo. "This is Cozza's chance to show off."

They fell silent, watching their mate produce a key, unlock the door and pull it open. He stepped inside briefly, then walked back out and locked it again. As he strode back to the van, the piercing sound of an alarm split the cold night air.

"I don't get it," said Frank as Cozza slid back into the passenger seat.

"Nothing new there then," said the other man with a chuckle.

"Look, if you have the key why can't we just blast in there, grab the goodies and leg it?"

"Watch and learn." Cozza indicated the doorway where a red light flashed on and off above a second-storey window.

Returning his attention to the paper, Mo went to the back page. Chelsea supporters had been banned from visiting away grounds for the rest of the season after causing trouble at Derby. Wankers. He hated them, having found himself on the wrong end of a pasting during his last visit to Stamford Bridge.

The biggest shock to the system, though, was when he studied the First Division table to see Swansea City sitting top, having beaten Aston Villa 2-1 earlier that week. Damn, but that John Toshack had done a good job there. Three seasons earlier they had been scraping along in the bottom division of the Football League. Being above the likes of Liverpool, Manchester United and champions Villa didn't seem credible.

His concentration was disturbed by the growl of the Lamborghini. It parked up and the man in the safari suit appeared at the door again, checking the lock with a baffled expression on his face. A short while later the same police officers arrived. They all disappeared inside.

"This could go on all night." Frank was getting irritable.

"It won't," said Cozza.

"You have a crystal ball?"

"For God's sake, stop it!" Mo had just about had enough of the bickering, the headache getting stronger. Recognising they were on dodgy ground, the two others fell silent, waiting until the officers and the key holder emerged again and drove off.

"That's my cue," said Cozza, slipping from the van and carrying out the same procedure as before. On this occasion when he emerged from the doorway, the alarm remained silent.

"Genius!" said Mo.

"What? What's happened?" asked Frank.

"Our mate Cozza is a real Einstein," said Mo. "He's only got them to turn the bleedin' alarm off, clever cunt! They think it ain't working. Now, let's get in there and fill our boots."

EIGHT

MO felt euphoric even before a drop of alcohol had passed his lips. His migraine had lifted and the night's work had been a success. He entered Room Upstairs, a popular late night drinking den in Ilford, smiling and shaking hands with friends and acquaintances. Pointing Cozza and Handsome Frank in the direction of a free table, he went to buy the drinks.

Tinsel festooned the bar, the counter staff wearing fancy dress. A heavy pall of smoke hung over the room, the smell a pungent mix of tobacco, booze and body odour. A brunette barmaid in a set of reindeer antlers and a daringly short Santa dress approached him. A right sort. From the DJ table in one corner the latest No. 1 was blaring out, a bunch of partygoers on the small dance floor tunelessly singing along with the words, begging each other to answer the question: "Don't you want me, baby?"

"Good, ain't they?" said the barmaid, leaning across and giving Mo an eyeful of cleavage.

"That rabble?" he nodded in the direction of the dance floor.

"No, silly! The group I mean, Human League. No.1 for Christmas." She joined in the singing, failing to see the irony as she mouthed words about working as a waitress in a cocktail bar. He waited patiently for her to finish. "Sorry, darlin', I was getting carried away," she said. "What can I get you?"

Mo gave his order and she loaded shot glasses on a tray, handing it over with a smile. He imagined pulling on her long brown pigtails and taking her from behind. Shit, he thought, a good heist is a better aphrodisiac than a whole bunch of oysters. Perhaps he'd make his move later, but for the moment there was celebrating to be done.

Manoeuvring his way around the human flotsam, Mo noted that many of the customers were a long way down the road to the Christmas Day hangover. He placed the tray on the table then lifted a glass in the direction of the man with greasy long hair and tattoos. "Here's to you Cozza, what a bloody haul!" Big Mo said. "Did you know?"

"About the jewellery, yeah," said Cozza. "The other thing came as a complete surprise. You'd think it would have been better guarded."

"Too right." Mo looked around. "Where's the Handsome facker gone?"

"In the khazi, Mo. Won't be long."

Sure enough, the third musketeer joined them, pushing through a crowd of revellers. He wiped his nose. "Missed a bit," said Cozza, laughing and pointing at his own upper lip. Handsome looked perplexed for a second before rubbing his hand below his nostrils and studying it carefully then licking something from his palm. His craggy, scar-marked face cracked into his best version of a smile. Some kind of private joke between the two of them, thought Mo. The dance floor lights illuminated the ex-fighter's cauliflower ear, known as such because it resembled a piece of oddly-shaped veg, a permanent souvenir from the fight game.

"You're a bleedin' genius Cozza mate, no mistake," said Frank, raising a glass in the direction of the ceiling. "I'd love to see the look on their faces when those mugs realise what we managed to carry off under their piggy noses."

"Me too," agreed Cozza. "So what's this poncey shit we're drinking?"

"Pernod," said Mo, "and it ain't shit, it's got a kick. Gotta treat it with respect. These are doubles."

"Fair play," said Cozza, putting the glass to his nose. "Phwoar, reeks of something, like one of them strange sweets me grandad used to munch."

"It's aniseed," said Mo. "Now let's drink up and start the Christmas festivities. We've got some catching up to do, judging by the rest of the slags in here."

"Come on then, you ain't no member of the magic circle," said Frank as they settled down at the table. "How did you do it, Cozza?"

The other man looked over his shoulder to make sure no one was overhearing their conversation. Most of the people in the room were far too drunk and pre-occupied to notice the three late arrivals.

"Simple really," said Cozza, with false modesty. "I popped along there the other night to case the joint. Pretended I was working at a warehouse nearby, overalls on, the lot. I quickly sussed that bloke with the Lamborghini was the owner, so when he left for the night I inspected the lock and realised it was one of those common five-pronged ones."

"Eh? What's that?"

"Well, each groove in your key fits into one of the prongs and when you turn it the groove raises them and the door unlocks, right?" He saw the other two men were nodding.

"Well, it's a bit tricky and I don't wanna blow your mind with the technicalities, but by removing four of the prongs it means you don't need the exact key. In fact almost any key will push the remaining prong up and spring the lock. To be honest, I used my own front door key tonight. The bloke with the real set of keys wouldn't know anythin' about that. As far as he is concerned the lock is working normally because his key opens it. When he enters the first thing he does is put a code into a panel to turn the alarm off."

"I see where you're coming from," said Mo.

"I don't," said Frank.

Cozza turned to the ex-boxer. "I'll spell it out for you in Jack and Jill terms," he said, referring to a book they had read in primary school. "I turn up tonight, let myself in and trigger the alarm. This brings the bloke running and the cops, too, because when the premises is breached an alarm goes off automatically at the police station."

"Right," said Frank.

"OK. The next thing that happens is the keyholder turns up and finds the door still locked. He goes in with the police and they check around the premises to find everything is in order. Nothing is missing."

"Right," said Frank again.

Cozza continued. "As nothing is missing they leave, only for me to set off the alarm a second time."

"Aah!" The light of understanding entered Handsome Frank's eyes. "So..."

"So they turn up again, go through the same process, come back out only this time..."

"They think the alarm is damaged."

"By George, I think he's got it," said Cozza. "Our boys in blue, no doubt fed up with being dragged out twice on Christmas Eve for nothing, advise the bloke with the keys to switch the alarm off because it is obviously faulty."

"...And how wrong they are about that!" Mo interrupted, a throaty chuckle emerging. Before long, all three men were rolling around, laughing like hyenas. Noticing they were getting strange looks from some of the other people in the bar, Mo knocked back his drink, turned the glass over and thumped it on the table. "Right, Merry Christmas!" he shouted. "Now whose fucking round is it?"

"COMMME onnn, babe," whined Mo. "Open up. Gotta preshunt for you."

"Oh fuckin' 'ell... Mo, is that you? It's half past fuckin' two in the morning."

"Who elsh would it be? Somefin' I should know? You fackin' someone..."

He heard a chain rattle before the door opened quickly, dumping him on the hallway carpet.

"Jeez, look at the state of you!" said Audrey. "You'll wake my neighbours, all that hollering this time of night. What you doing here?"

He grabbed the waist of her knee-length, burgundy dressing robe in an attempt to lever himself up and she had to steady herself to avoid joining him on the floor. "Jussht wanted to see you, babes. I was out with shum of the boysh and I thought... my Aud. I got to have my girl at Kishmash. You fackin' do fings to me, babe."

Slotting her arms around him and managing to get some purchase, she lifted him back to his feet. He reeked of booze as he fell forward, crashing his mouth into hers. "Fuck!" she said, pulling away. "How many have you had?"

He ignored the question. "Look..." he said, fiddling about in the pocket of the sheepskin. "Look, look..." He brought out a small black box and pressed it into her hands. She read the writing embossed on the front. Sterling silver. She looked up at him, her expression one of bemusement then, returning her attention to the box, she opened it slowly. "My God, they're beautiful, Maurice, thank you," she said, smiling. Walking down the hall, she stood in front of the mirror, holding the two hooped earrings to the sides of her face. She felt him press against her, his arms enclosing her chest, a certain part of him rock solid against her buttocks. Pretty impressive, she thought, for someone who had drunk London dry.

"Merry Kishmash!" he slobbered in her ear.

Easing his arms away so that she could turn to face him she said: "And Merry Kishmash to you too, you wonderful lug." He leant in for a kiss but she disappeared and for a minute he thought his advances were being rejected. Then he felt her hands inside his coat, encircling his waist, an arm disappearing under his shirt and up his back. Without him even realising, she had undone the buttons and pulled down his zip. He felt her other hand inside his trousers, grabbing him firmly until he thought the act alone would make him explode.

Looking down he saw her take him into her mouth, her tongue working him expertly. Screwing his eyes shut he conjured up a vision of the barmaid with the pigtails and Santa suit. Should have been her, he thought, losing his balance.

"Shit!" she screamed. "My fuckin' eye! Stings like hell!"

"Shorry!" he slurred, stumbling off into her bedroom and crashing face down, every bit of him spent.

Waking to the overloud ticking of the bedside clock he rolled over, fixing it in his blurred vision. Shit! It was 9.30am Christmas Day. He leapt up and rubbed his temples as the pain registered. He had meant to crawl back to Beryl before dawn. Fumbling around, he struggled for coordination as he gathered his things together. Grabbing a pint of water by the side of the bed, he downed it in one. It didn't have the desired effect. Stumbling out into the crisp, brightness of the day he realised he was right back to square one, at the peak of his drunkenness.

NINE

Christmas Day

MO lost his balance, falling forward as the door flew open.

"Where the fuckin' hell have you been?"

Through bloodshot eyes he saw Beryl looking down on him, her face screwed into a disdainful sneer. "Maurice Dolan, I give you plenty of leeway, but it's Christmas and I thought you wanted to spend it with your family. Look at the bloody state of you! I specifically asked you yesterday if you could help me get things ready and do the Santa Claus bit for your kids. Not only do you fail to come home but I've had to ring your family to make soddin' excuses as to why we're going to be late for lunch. Your dad ain't happy. You know what he's like, Christmas is a huge thing and everything needs to be perfect. Last night I had to make the Xmas pud he loves, plus the pigs in blankets to help ease the workload on Viola, while also getting the boys to bed, wrapping their presents..."

His brain was trying to evaluate the words but failing miserably. Surely, he should be feeling more sober than this? The pint of water he had necked that morning at Audrey's had made matters worse, not better. Beryl's entire diatribe was coming across as a monotonous pounding.

Bang, bang, bang, bang.

He wanted to mount some form of defence but the impulses in his brain weren't connecting, his head clogged with cobwebs. She stood with hands on hips, her face inches from his, waiting for him to say something. When he didn't, she took up the rant again, globules of spittle landing on his face. He finally managed a response, though not one she wanted to hear.

"Shhhh, will ya?" He put a finger to his lips. "Jeshus wept! My head's splitting, doll... I can't cope with this first thing on bloody Christmas morning." He went to push past her but she held her arm out to block his progress.

"That's the whole point, though," she said. "It's not first thing Christmas morning, is it? It's almost midday. Half the day bloody gone and the boys ain't seen their father yet. Where's Chucky's bike, eh? Under your coat? Your sorting that was part of the 'deal'. You insisted you'd be able to afford it and he's got his heart set on it. I don't..."

Bang, bang, bang, bang.

The words smashed at his skull with the subtlety of one of those heavy metal bands he loathed. Fuck! He lifted his arm, desperate to clear a path to the toilet. He was going to be sick, a rare event these days. There was a thud and a squeak. Beryl's face froze in a stunned expression as her head bounced off the wall in slow motion and for a minute he thought she was going down. He regretted his actions instantly, and began stuttering an apology, stopping in his tracks as she bounced back into place like one of those toys Chuck had that wobbled and didn't fall down. As if nothing had happened, she pounded him with both barrels again.

"That's big!" she said. "Punching your wife on Christmas Day. Great! I'm sure that will go down well with your 'family'. The old man would be well impressed, wouldn't he? He always says you're a no good..."

Bang, bang, bang, bang.

Hell, it wasn't even a punch, just a push, and it was her fault. Her assault on his pounding head was relentless, unbearable, and it didn't make any sense in his skewed way of looking at things. This wasn't some gutter-mouthed slut, this was Beryl, his obedient, compliant wife with the sweet nature, who rarely moaned about anything. Salt of the earth, she was. The perfect partner. She never put pressure on him, nagged or cajoled. Some around this way didn't give their fellas a moment's peace, but she was different. Until now when, for some reason, she chose to join the ranks of the screaming banshees, unwired, unpredictable and aggressive like... well, Audrey, he supposed. His feisty, truculent lover was wired differently. She enjoyed a row and gave as good as she got. Sometimes he even wondered if she manufactured a confrontation because their making up was so damned special.

This was his Bee, though, not Audrey. His loving, caring, sweet Bee. He wondered whether someone might have spilled the beans and told her about his bit on the side. Who knew, though? He had been careful to keep that part of his life under wraps. Even Cozza and Frank were in the dark. The guru? He and Beryl had never met, and Bee wasn't the sort to listen to idle gossip from people she barely knew. It had to be someone convincing. Audrey herself?

"Are you listening to me?"

Slap! Now she had clocked him one right across the sodding cheek. His brain was programmed to respond to a physical assault of that nature in only one way, whoever the assailant. Before he knew it he had drawn back his fist and let loose the punch, not a push but a full-blooded jab, causing his wife to buckle like a rag doll and slide down the wall in slow motion, rivulets of blood running from her nose.

"Oh fuck, baby. Bee... I'm sorry," he dropped to his haunches instantly, removing a handkerchief from his pocket and dabbing at the wound. "It's just... you provoked me, babes, and I lashed out. You know me..." What was happening? Tears pricked at his eyes and ran down his cheeks. He brushed them aside carelessly as past images of their life together ran like an old movie through his memory. He heard footsteps in the hallway and saw a small back retreating, a child educating a waddling toddler in the art of the quick getaway. Had his boys seen him at his worst?

"Bee! Bee love! I'm so, so sorry. I love you babe. I love you." He choked on the tears. "I had some business last night, that's all, and I had to get that bike for Chuck like I promised. Did some extra work to raise the cash and I'm picking it up from a mate this morning. See? I was doing family stuff. I wouldn't let Chuck down, you know that. Then I went for a drink with Frank and Paul, just to unwind is all and, well, we ended up on this Pernod shit... knocked me for six. I had a nightcap at Paul's and the next thing I know it's 11am. Totally out of order, I know. I got a banging head, doll, and you pushed me over the edge. Bee, you know I've got a temper, darlin', so when you came running at me you must have known I'd... react. Come on, let me help you..."

She stared at him in a daze, mascara trails running down her face, black hair sticking to her cheeks. His brain unkindly flashed up an image of the rock star Alice Cooper, a singer who dressed garishly as a woman, wrestled snakes and sang about *School's Out* in the 70s. Getting her to balance on wobbly legs he hoped she had a mild concussion and nothing worse. Bending and lifting her into his arms, he carried her like a child to their bedroom. Placing her carefully on the divan, he kissed her and told her how much he loved her again, brushing her hair from her face with tender strokes. Hearing a sniffle from the doorway, he lifted his head to see Chuck and Sylvester standing there, the eldest boy crying. He wasn't sure how to make the situation better, so said the only thing that came into his head.

"Merry Christmas boys! Mummy's not feeling well at the moment so she's gonna have a lie down. Has Santa been? I bet he has! He told me that he was going to leave some bits and bobs in the boot of my car for my precious boys, so let's go and check, eh?"

At first the boys seemed unsure, then Chuck nodded. "Yes please, Daddy. Do you think he brought my bike?"

BERYL ached all over. Lying on her bed, curtains drawn, she felt like a child's ageing rag doll tossed aside. Coughing, the familiar metallic taste of blood coated the back of her throat. Reaching for a tissue she gobbed a huge red lump into it, then dry wretched as the vision of the punch came to her again.

She knew Mo was handy with his fists, and strong, too. She could bear witness to the fact. There had been numerous occasions when his vice-like grip had clamped onto her forearms as he tore her off a strip for a catalogue of mistakes in the home; failing to keep his suits in the right order or forgetting to iron a shirt. To treat her like one of his gangster enemies, though, to pile his fist into her face without reservation represented a new low, even in his skewed, paranoid version of the world.

Had she pushed him too hard? Could it have been her fault? He had let her down when she needed him – there was no getting away from the fact. Yet, if he'd got Chuck's bike that was something and if he was working on a solution to their financial problems she had no right to moan. Of course he had to meet his mates and she would rather not know all the gory details. It was part of the unspoken deal they had struck. He raised the money by whatever means necessary and she ran the house. Expecting him to shift roles and turn up early just because it was Christmas... hell, it had been her fault, hadn't it? She could see that now. Her ferocious verbal attack had been unmerited and had taken him by surprise. He had acted as 'Big Mo' Dolan did when trapped in a corner. He'd lashed out to protect himself.

Pushing up gingerly from the bed she walked to the vanity dresser and peered in the mirror. She looked like shit. There was an ugly graze on the side of her face where her head had bounced off the wall, and her nose was swollen, a splurge of colour spreading like spilt blackcurrant juice across her face to her right eye.

How was she going to explain it away to Mo's old man and his wife? She would have to perform a few miracles with her odds-and-sods make-up collection to appear anything like presentable and ward off the questions that were likely to come thick and fast. Even so, she would need a good back-up excuse. Someone was bound to notice, however good a job she did in damage limitation. Bumped into a door? Wasn't that what all battered wives said? Not that she was branding herself in that category. This was a one-off and she could tell from his tears he regretted it. Big Mo Dolan didn't cry for just anything.

Fumbling about in her drawer for the tools of her art, she came across the small, carefully wrapped gift she had bought Mo for Christmas. She should give it to him now to show there were no hard feelings. Then, maybe, if the boys were playing, she could really make up with him, before they got dressed and hopped in the car for the journey out to Chigwell. A quickie was sure to bring a smile to his face.

"WELL, ain't that a beauty, Chucky, son." Billy Dolan admired his grandson's new bike. "I remember my old man buying bikes for me and the skin 'n blister. He got 'em knock-off from somewhere, maybe even stole 'em, but they were the bollocks."

"Skin and..."

"Sorry son, it means sister... you know, a bit of the old cockney rhyming slang. My sister Joan. Your Great Auntie. Don't get out much these days, poor old gal, got dodgy pins, but in her day she was a right tomboy, a tearaway, and with that bike you didn't see her for dust. Mind you, you could trust your neighbours back in those days. Our parents left the doors unlocked and we were always in and out of each other's houses. Now... well, you wouldn't do it. Too many nonces or darkies looking to steal your stuff. I wouldn't want to take your chances riding a lovely bicycle like that around that playground of yours. Some tea leaf will see it... sorry ... thief, son, thief... well, they'll see it and think, 'I could sell a nifty little runner like that down the market'. Next thing? Gone..."

"You've made your point, Dad," said Mo huffily.

"You know I'm right, don'tcha?"

Mo ignored him. "Anyone fancy a top up?" he asked. "I got the advocaat here or you can have a Baileys with me, nice little tipple it is, or there's sherry." He reached into his pocket, retrieved a cigarette packet and offered the contents around.

"What the fuck are those poncey things?" said his dad.

"Sobraine. They're just ordinary cigarettes, but they come in all different colours. Look, they've got gold filters. It's a bit of fun. A bit of variety for Christmas, y'know?"

"OK, I'll try one. What about you, Arnold?"

His dad always called Clive by his middle name as a tribute to his own father, who had been the last of a long tradition of Arnold's in the family. Billy the Kid was big on tradition and tributes. They were the buzzwords which underpinned every aspect of his life.

"Thanks, Mo," said Clive, taking a mauve one. "Hey, nice lighter! One of those petrol ones, ain't it? Real silver? It looks the dog's bollocks. Ah, what does it say here? *'To my Fozzy Bear, love you so much, your honey Bee, kiss kiss'.* Bleurgh." He pretended to put his fingers down his throat. "You pair of softies! Still, you've always been like that, ain't you? Ever since you were kids."

"Teenagers," corrected Mo, his cheeks colouring. "It's my Christmas present from her." He nodded in the direction of the kitchen, where Beryl was helping Viola wash up. "Forget the soppy stuff, though, the key thing is it works a treat."

Mo took it back and lit his cigarette, recalling the moment Beryl had given it to him. She had been almost back to normal when he returned from collecting Chuck's bike from a mate in one of the other towers. It was as if nothing had happened. She had presented him with the lighter, beautifully wrapped, and then hugged him, pulling him down onto the bed. Apologising for her earlier over-reaction she had covered him with kisses then risen to shut the door and slide a chair under the handle to prevent the boys making an untimely entrance. Then she had unzipped his trousers, hitched her skirt up and climbed on top. She had tried to guide him inside her but for the first time he could remember he had been unable to perform. After that, an air of melancholy had descended and he had left her feeling confused while he showered before ushering everyone into the car.

It must have felt like a rejection to her, but it wasn't meant to be. He had wanted to make things right between them but it appeared the drink had intervened, though he worried deep down it might be something else. He loved her dearly but sex with Beryl was devoid of the excitement instilled in him by Audrey. His mistress was a whore in the sack and he felt no qualms in treating her as such, shaking awake his primal instincts. At her place there was always time to do whatever they wanted, no fears of any kids barging in unannounced.

The boys were a convenient excuse, he had to admit. He knew the sex could never be that raw with Beryl and that was as much his fault as hers. As brother Clive had pointed out, they were a pair of softies together and though they had explored different positions in their younger days, now it didn't feel right. Audrey took sex to a whole new level but that's all it was, sex. He would be embarrassed and even put off if Bee suggested doing some of the things his mistress offered in the bedroom.

"I don't know about a softie, looks like he's wacked seven shades of shit outta her," said Billy, jolting him back to the present.

Mo couldn't believe his ears. "What did you say?"

"Joking, son," said Billy, though his eyes didn't seem to appreciate the punchline. "My you're touchy but I suppose it was bad taste on my part. A seesaw, though? She must have been totally distracted ... and how did it catch one side of her face and break her nose, too. Did she go back for second helpings?"

"You'll have to ask her, Dad – I wasn't there," said Mo. "Now leave it, would you? Look, she's coming back..."

The men fell silent.

Beryl and his stepmother Viola entered, looking around.

"Talking about us?" said Viola.

"Don't be silly, Vi," said Billy. "We're just waiting for it to come on. You know, the Two Ronnies Christmas Special. Those two crack me up. Chucky, we'll let you stay up a bit later but take the bike outside now, we want to watch some grown-ups' TV. I like these Xmas specials. Who's in this one?"

"Chaz 'n' Dave," said Clive, flicking to the appropriate page in the Radio Times.

"Gertcha!" said Billy, rolling around laughing as the others stared at him. He bridled at the rejection. "Well, that's what they sing, ain't it? And that 'Got your beer in the sideboard here'? Reminds me of the old man. He used to keep his pale ale in a big old sideboard. Mum's barley wine, too. Remember Arnold? Grandad used to get you to fetch it. Never would have dreamed of putting it in the fridge in those days."

"Or in a silly contraption that plays music," said Mo, enjoying a modicum of revenge for the earlier jibe. Billy didn't rise to the bait.

"Love a bit of Chas 'n' Dave, I do," he said.

Mo got up, filled a couple of glasses from the sherry decanter and handed them to Beryl and Viola. They sat down, sipping their drinks.

"Well, before we have to listen to Chas 'n' bleedin' Dave, I propose a family toast," said Mo. "It's been a tough year for some of us, but it's nearly over and we've come out the other side. Now, with Monkey taking on a whole new life in the Army, Chuck entering big school and starting football, and me and Dad having a few irons in the fire I just wanted to say Merry Christmas to you all. I have a feeling 1982 could be the Dolans' year."

I bloody hope so, he thought to himself. It's about time our luck changed.

10

December 27, 1981

"NICE Christmas, lads?"

Chief Superintendent Peter Gradel directed a beaming smile across the desk at the two officers. Sgt Max Cooper was surprised how amiable his guv'nor appeared to be. Normally the bloke was a grumpy sod. Perhaps he'd had the present he'd always wanted for Christmas, like a pair of trousers that weren't so tight. "Yes, um thanks, Sir," he muttered, PC Simpson echoing the sentiment beside him.

"Pleased to hear it." The Chief Super paused, looking down at a sheet of paper on his desk. "Would you like to know who else had a very good Christmas?"

"Sir?"

"Not me, Sergeant," said Gradel. "Mine was pretty lousy. No, the people who had a particularly good Christmas were the thieving toerags who got away with 15 handguns, 800 rounds of ammunition, three gun slings, four gun belts, 26 holsters and 3 Remington 870 pump-action shotguns... not to mention at least a grand's worth of jewellery – you know, usual stuff: gold bracelets, expensive watches, silver earrings, wedding rings and all – from a little storage facility outside Romford." He paused, studying the paper in front of him. The unsettling silence washed over Cooper and his partner. "Here it is," said Gradel. "Plumpton's Trading Estate. I should think the buggers who got away with that little lot had a very good Christmas indeed. Laughing all the way to the bank, they were, probably with the intention of robbing it. Been patrolling in Romford lately, have we lads? A little bird told me you might have been in that neck of the woods Christmas Eve."

Cooper couldn't allow the slow torture to continue. He delved into his reserves of courage. "We checked the place thoroughly, sir. Nothing was missing. I don't see..."

"Shut it, Sergeant!" stormed Gradel, his face so flush he had to remove his cap to release the pressure. "I don't like excuses. This is quite simply the most ludicrous piece of policing I have encountered in my 35 years on the force. If you checked for little ratbags hiding on the premises, you didn't check hard enough. I imagine they broke in, found a nice little spot in which to wait it out, watched you two idiots go about your 'job' as quickly as you could so that you could knock off early for Christmas... and then had their pick of whatever took their fancy."

"We went back twice, sir," said Simpson, his voice calm despite the onslaught. He had suffered plenty of bollockings in his time, some of them deserved. Perhaps they had been sloppy but they had searched the warehouse facility high and low without finding any signs of a break-in. "If you ask me, it's the work of a professional locksmith."

"Well, this is a complete disaster," stormed Gradel. "I've asked the owners at the various storage facilities to keep things quiet, telling them it's for operational reasons. I'm lying. It's not for operational reasons – it's because I don't want our bloody noses rammed in the shit by the soddin' press, like incontinent pups. Not on my watch, get it?"

The Chief Superintendent stood, fiddling with the front of his trousers, as if something had crawled down inside them and was playing pitty-pat with his balls. The mannerism had earned him the nickname Grabber Gradel. Cooper was pretty sure he didn't realise he was doing it and those who didn't know about the worrying foible figured the nickname had something to do with the amount of criminals he had "grabbed" during his time on the force. The nickname even appeared in print once when a successful drug bust at Tilbury Docks had been acknowledged by the press. It was the first time Gradel himself had learned of it.

"I want a full report on this," he said. He stopped fiddling and rocked backwards, transferring his arms behind his back. "You'd better go and write it up and make it sound good. Put a bit of fairy dust on it or something because this is going to go down in Met history as one of the biggest bungles of all time. I hope to God there aren't any serious incidents as a result of this – any deaths for instance. I'm praying this is the work of a bunch of chancers and not the IRA. Can you imagine if these weapons got into terrorist hands? Not worth thinking about is it, boys? Go!"

They headed for the exit like two chastised schoolboys, Cooper following Simpson out of the door. As he reached the threshold, Gradel spoke again. "I hear you've been tapped up by the Flying Squad, Cooper," he said. "I'm afraid they will have to hear about this. I'm sorry, Sergeant, truly, but as the senior officer in this debacle I have to hold you chiefly to blame. The PC there is a bit long in the tooth. I guess this sort of thing is why he never rose through the ranks – doesn't know his arse from his elbow. You, though, should have twigged something was up. I know you've proven yourself in the past – some of your snouts have come up trumps and enabled us to bring in some good collars – and that's no doubt why those Flying Squad wallahs want you. I'm sorry, though. If they ask me I can only tell the truth about this cock-up."

Cooper nodded. Of course, you brown-nosed bastard, he thought. A real boss would stick by his officers through thick and thin, particularly the ones who had produced good results in the past. One mistake and this cretin was hanging him out to dry. He wondered what his missus was going to say about this latest turn of events. She had given him a hard time about working in such an all-consuming job and the only way he could placate her was by telling her he was in line for an exciting promotion.

To repair the damage he needed to trace the stolen arms and put those responsible for the blag behind bars. Some of his underworld informants might help in that respect. It was time to make a call.

"OH, it's you."

Cooper recognised the gravelly voice and dropped coins into the payphone. "I need a favour."

"Nice Christmas? Yeah, what about you? Forgotten your small talk, boy?"

"I'm in trouble," said Cooper. "I made a mistake. My Flying Squad place is in doubt."

The other person sighed, as if bored. Cooper smelt frying fish and looked out into a cold, grey afternoon to see a queue forming at the local chippy. He smiled grimly. He felt like a fish. He'd been snared and desperately needed to get off the hook.

"As I always say, you scratch my back..." his informant was saying.

"Know anything about guns?" said Cooper.

"What guns?"

"The stolen variety. A hell of a lot of them. Enough to cause a small war on the streets."

"Nah," said the voice. "Someone break in to an army barracks?"

"A Romford warehouse, actually. Me and a flatfoot were there Christmas Eve. The bloody alarm kept going off so we thought it was a dodgy circuit and told the bloke in charge he should leave it off. Now the Super wants my head on a plate."

"Not surprised!" said the voice. "I'll make some inquiries, see what I can find out. It could take a bit of time, though. I don't want to arouse suspicion. Sounds like some big hitters might be involved. Talking about big hitters, did you see the Kaylor lad at Wembley the other day? Our boy done good."

"Second-round knockout," said Cooper. "Looks handy. Opponent wasn't up to much but you can only beat what's in front of you."

"I tell you, that boy could go all the way."

"Sure. Well, maybe we'll catch up at his next fight."

"Or you can meet me out at the country club," said the informant. "I'll make you my honoured guest. Then perhaps we could discuss any little favours you might do for me, hold on..." He was away from the line for 30 seconds, returning out of breath. "It's my youngest. He's been home for Christmas and I wanted to catch him before he left. He's joined the Army, you know!"

IN the four-bedroom house five miles away, the man replaced the receiver and strolled out of his study.

"Who was that?" asked his wife.

"Just business," said Billy The Kid Dolan. "Arnold left?"

"Why do you insist on calling him that? His name's Clive... Yes, he couldn't wait for you, love, he had to get back to barracks. I'm sure he'll call again soon."

"Hmm," said Billy, his thoughts elsewhere. He went to his drinks cabinet and pressed the buttons on his remote control. He needed a stiff one to help his concentration. Now, who would be interested in guns?

PART TWO

11

March 1982

"GO on, son, put yourself about a bit, like Billy Bonds down the Hammers."

Chuck Dolan looked over at the sheepskin-clad figure standing on the touchline. The familiar tan coat was like a second skin to his dad, reaching down as far as the knees. He wore black drainpipe trousers and on his feet his brogues had been consumed by the clawing mud that he had collected yomping across Hackney Marshes. For as far as the eye could see there were football games taking place on the wide expanse of land, which long ago had been reclaimed from the bogs that gave them their name and turned into a weekend sportsman's paradise.

It had been raining for most of the week and there had been grave doubts whether the game would be on. Fortunately, it had dried up over the previous 24 hours and there wasn't a cloud in the sky now, the pale spring sunshine reflecting off Big Mo's close-cropped head.

Chuck loved his football. He had joined the young Vipers, a team from the Barking and Ilford area run by one of his dad's friends. At least, the old man said the coach was a mate, yet when Big Mo put on a wide smile and grabbed the man in a bear hug, Chuck sensed the show of affection was completely one-sided.

Whatever the nature of their association, Chuck was grateful for it. What he lacked in skill, he tried to make up for in enthusiasm.

His shortage of inches meant he often found himself playing at right back, a role designed to stop the opposition. He wouldn't have chosen it, but there was no way he was going to oust Jimmy Marvin as centre forward. The boy had scored 15 goals already that season and been mentioned in despatches in the *Barking and Dagenham Post*.

Chuck was exceedingly grateful his dad took an interest in his hobby. It meant he could get a lift to matches, and his requests for new boots and kit were looked on favourably. Yet if he was brutally honest, Big Mo's enthusiasm had a counter-productive effect on his performance. He felt slightly ungrateful, even disloyal, for nurturing such thoughts, but his dad was hardly in the Brian Clough bracket when it came to motivational skills. What made matters worse was that his shouting tended to drown out the one voice Chuck needed to hear, that of the coach, whose full name was Ray Parker.

Chuck sensed he was resented by some other members of the team, particularly those sentenced to walk the touchline in temperatures that regularly hovered around the freezing mark in winter. They seemed better players than him but no one said as much. He couldn't fail to notice, however, the whispering that went on in the changing room after the team was announced.

Those who did play had to contend with a constant barracking from the old man, who continually urged them to "Give it to Chuck ... Chuck's free." If they didn't oblige they suffered a tongue-lashing. The strange thing was Chuck would have been happy to take his turn on the bench, but coach Ray wouldn't entertain the idea. Once, when his dad was out of earshot, Chuck suggested to the coach he should be dropped. His request came in the wake of a 7-0 defeat in which he had been "skinned" by the tricky opposition winger. "Son, you're doing fine," said coach Ray, his eyes telling a different story. "It was just one of those days."

"Get rid of it, son... hoof it!" Big Mo's voice shattered his daydream and Chuck looked down to find the ball at his feet. He was poised to carry out his dad's instructions when the more measured tones of Mr Ray intervened. "Look around you, Chuck, Pete's free to your right. Give and go..."

Whump! While his brain was struggling to process the conflicting advice he was tossed skyward like a matador upended by a rampaging bull. Hitting the ground, the air was knocked from his lungs and he ended up face down, dizzy and bewildered. "Fackin' hell, ref, foul ... what the fack?" Slowly coming to his senses, Chuck heard the old man bellowing the case for his defence. As he tried to assimilate his thoughts, there was a loud peep and players from the opposition were running past him, hugging each other, beaming smiles on their faces in response to the goal they had just scored.

"You fackin' blind, ref? That was a foul. That facker almost decapitated my son!" His dad's voice had gone up an octave. "Bleedin' assault it was. You need fackin' glasses you... Hey! You evil little facker, I'll give you somethin' to smile about, assaulting my boy like that!"

Chuck picked himself up and stared open-mouthed as his dad marched onto the pitch, arms gyrating like a demented Octopus. Grabbing the perceived culprit by the shirt he started shouting in the boy's face, the youngster's legs dangling feet from the ground.

"Oi, are you crazy?" Another voice. Chuck and his fellow players were frozen to the spot as a tall, long-haired man in jeans and an Arsenal shirt marched towards the action. "Put my son down, you bully. He's only nine and you're a grown man. Pick on someone your own size!"

Chuck held his breath as Big Mo considered the option then promptly dropped the youngster on his bottom, turning to face a sea of perplexed and angry adult faces. The lad's father had been joined by Mr Ray and the referee, a stick insect of a man who looked like he might blow over if the wind changed direction suddenly.

"What the hell do you think you are playing at?" demanded the other parent. "You owe my son an apology."

"Let's not do anything hasty," said Mr Ray, stepping between the two protagonists. "I'm sure Mr Dolan is sorry for his over-reaction."

"It wasn't a foul," said the referee. "I had a clear view of it. Your son just dawdled on the ball and got caught out."

Chuck knew what kind of response this three-pronged attack was likely to provoke in his father and winced as Big Mo took a step towards them. He was nodding up and down like one of those ornamental dogs in the back of people's cars, a finger pointing in the direction of his attackers.

"Yeah, that's right," he said. "It's all my fackin' fault. Gang up on Maurice Dolan, why don'tcha? Jeez I've seen less serious assaults in borstal! Your boy nearly put my boy in fackin' A and E, mate, and if you don't think that's a foul, ref, you shouldn't be put in charge of a game of tiddlywinks. Christ, Ray, you know what I'm saying, or are you gonna take their side as well?"

"Oh come on, your boy was caught in possession, daydreaming," said the other boy's father, jumping in before the coach could give his view. "You can hardly blame my son if your boy's not..."

Big Mo put his head down and charged, the other man stepping back in alarm. Quick-thinking Mr Ray summoned up all his courage, stepping into the path of the pulsating mass of anger and muscle bearing down on its target. "Go, mate, now!" he shouted over his shoulder. Suddenly realising his predicament, the other parent began slipping and sliding towards the touchline. Bizarrely, the Ref raised the whistle to his mouth and blew, a shrill peep cutting through the chill air.

If it was intended to suspend hostilities – it didn't succeed.

When Hurricane Mo struck, Mr Ray went flying backwards. To a mesmerised Chuck, the coach seemed to hang in the air for an age, his body twisting and turning before it hit the ground with a sickly, squelching sound, mud flying in all directions. Some of it landed on his dad, giving the impression of war paint on the face of a scalp-hunting American Indian chief.

Chuck was aware of a strange, rasping noise and turned to look at the ref, who had fallen to his knees and was gagging in the centre circle. He watched with trepidation, fearing the old man had maimed the official, too. Then, with a mixture of horror and amusement, he saw the figure spit a silver object into his hand. The man in black had almost swallowed his whistle amid the carnage.

Distracted, it dawned on Chuck that he had lost sight of his dad. Peering to the far side of the field he saw Big Mo pursuing his quarry. The boy began sprinting in the same direction, grateful for the advantage of having studs in his boots. He knew that if he didn't do something to prevent the old man meting out his brand of punishment, the repercussions could be devastating for his football career.

"Dad! Dad! Stop!" he shouted, but with the noise from the other pitches Chuck couldn't make himself heard. He was gaining, though, Big Mo slipping and sliding across the mud like Robin Cousins, the figure skater Chuck had watched pirouetting and spinning across the TV to become ice skating champion in the winter Olympics.

On reaching the car park, the other parent was now searching desperately for his vehicle. Finally, he set off at pace across the gravel, forcing Big Mo to adjust his trajectory. The manoeuvre was impossible on the unpredictable surface and Chuck watched in fascination as his dad's legs slid from under him, leaving the old man sprawling on the ground. The vital seconds lost enabled Chuck to close the gap and when he shouted again, a begging quality had entered his voice. "Dad! Please! You'll get me kicked off the team."

Big Mo turned and looked into the pleading eyes of his son, and for a moment Chuck thought his words had registered. Then, as he scrambled up, Big Mo returned his attention to his prey with an unearthly growl that sent a shudder rippling through Chuck's body. "Oi, you cunt! You think you can take the piss out of Big Mo fackin' Dolan? You're dead meat. Keep runnin', I would, but I'll catch you eventually, you prick, and then me wife will be wearing your bollocks for earrings."

Chuck saw the petrified look on the other parent's face as he scrambled to unlock the door of a red Ford Cortina Mark III. It was as if it had suddenly dawned on him the full savagery of the bear he had been baiting. Dropping the keys, he lost vital seconds fumbling on hands and knees to retrieve them from beneath the car.

Big Mo vaulted the metal barrier, his coat now a patchwork quilt of mud and grass. Instead of heading straight for his target, though, he veered in the opposite direction and Chuck knew what was coming. He was heading for the Daimler, a Sovereign Sedan in deep burgundy which he had bought two years earlier and was his pride and joy. When he got to it he lifted the boot and fumbled inside.

Chuck prayed the other parent would take full advantage of the delay and his heart leapt as an engine spluttered into life and he saw the Cortina reversing out of its parking space, the panicked driver crunching the gears before finding the one he needed and putting his foot to the floor. All he needed now was to swerve around the obstruction standing in his way to make a clean getaway.

Unfortunately, he didn't react quickly enough. Chuck's optimism faded as he watched his dad, feet apart, produce Reg from behind his back and bring the weapon crashing down in one flowing arc onto the front of the car. In trying to adjust too quickly, the driver swerved into another parked vehicle, the Cortina's bonnet flying up to obscure his view. Smoke poured out as, in the distance, Chuck heard the sound of police sirens. Someone must have rung them from the clubhouse, but it would be a race against time if they were to prevent the mayhem about to ensue.

Chuck had reached the car park. He tried one last time. "Dad! Please! Don't... you'll get into trouble. The police are..."

Crash! The driver's side window of the Cortina exploded, glass flying in all directions, defenceless in the face of Reg's momentum. Clatter! The sawn-off curtain pole hit the ground, Big Mo needing both hands to manhandle his target, who was hanging limpet-like to the door handle. As his dad's giant, hairy hands worked feverishly, Chuck realised Big Mo's judgment was clouded by anger. It would have been far simpler to reach inside, raise the lock and spring open the door than pull the victim out through the shattered window. The mistake cost Big Mo vital seconds.

Flashing blue lights flooded the car park and Chuck put his hands to his ears in an effort to block out the squealing sirens. An intense smell of burning rubber filled the air as brakes screeched and three cars skidded to a halt in quick succession. Belatedly aware of the new arrivals, Mo bent to retrieve Reg from the floor and turned. He was too late. The last vision Chuck had of his old man was of him disappearing beneath a mountain of blue uniformed bodies. He emerged for an instant, his face screwed up with rage. "Come on then pigs," he shouted. "Me 'n' Reggie will take on the fackin' lot of you!"

12

"YOU OK, young man?" The bear-like police officer patted Chuck on the head as he drove him home. "I'm sorry about all that. I'm sure your dad will be home soon, we just need a chat with him, calm him down. You can call me Cliffy, by the way. My friends do."

Chuck stayed silent. One of his father's favourite phrases was "All coppers are bastards". He'd heard him chanting it at the Hammers, encouraging the boy to join in even though he didn't really know what the 'B' word meant. He'd even seen the letters ACAB spray painted across the estate.

Big Mo said coppers couldn't be trusted, though this cuddly character sitting next to him seemed harmless enough. In fact, the sight of him made Chuck smile, jammed into a car far too small for him, his stomach straining against the seat belt. It put the boy in mind of one of those characters he had seen in *Wacky Races*, a cartoon show his dad had bought him on video at a car boot sale. One of the characters was a giant lumberjack squeezed into a log on wheels alongside his co-driver, a beaver. Rufus Ruffcut was his name and the car was called the Buzzwagon. It had sharp blades attached to the wheels to slice through opposition vehicles.

"You live on the estate?" asked the copper. "I know what that's like. I grew up there me'self. Those flats are due a makeover. I've seen the plans. They're getting a nice paint job, some apartments will get much-needed repairs and the towers are being renamed after famous East End boxers. Great idea, I think. It's a big tradition around here, boxing. Know anything about the sport, kid?" No response. "Don't suppose you do... bit young, perhaps."

Chuck summoned up the courage to speak. "Are you a bastard?"

"What?"

For a moment Chuck thought the policeman might turn nasty. An eerie silence descended. The policeman's cheeks had turned a dark shade of crimson, but it only served to make him look like Santa Claus, and no one ever heard of Santa losing his temper, even with naughty boys. Then the giant figure started roly-polying around. The eruption came from deep within his belly, travelled up through his chest and exploded from between puffed-out cheeks, a loud, guttural guffaw which was so splendidly spontaneous it was infectious. Pretty soon Chuck was laughing, too.

"Oh... ha ha ha... I'm sorry... ha ha... it's just, well, out of the mouths of babes! Do you even know what that means, um, what's your name again?"

"Ch... Chuck," he replied, managing to hold in the laughter as policeman Cliffy patted him hard on the shoulders.

"Short for Charlie?"

"No... just Chuck. After Chuck Norris, my dad's hero."

"Oh, tough guy. Are you a tough guy, Chuck?"

"No," replied Chuck, looking at his feet and feeling embarrassed.

"Well, there is nothing to be gained from it, to be honest," said Cliffy. "You should try to be yourself – the way God made you. Don't let anyone change you."

"Do you know any tough guys?" asked Chuck.

"I know some people who 'think' they're tough guys," said Cliffy. "I've been working here a long time, dealt with a lot of criminals. The Krays, for instance, were twins who thought they were cocks of the walk but they're in prison now because they met someone tougher than them."

"My dad doesn't trust policemen."

"Sure." Cliffy fell silent as if his batteries had run out, only to start up again suddenly. "In answer to your question, I don't think I'm a you-know-what. I'm an ordinary person just like you... ah, here we are. Back on the estate, right as rain." He pulled the car to a halt in the shadow of the imposing tower blocks. "I'd better come in with you. Have a quick word with Mum."

AS he drove away, PC Cliffy Simpson felt a pang of guilt. He liked the boy and, staring up at the bleak surroundings, he was unhappy at having to surrender him to a cruel and unforgiving environment. Part of him wanted to spin the car around and take Chuck Dolan back to his wife Simone, to hide him away and never let him set foot on the estate again. In fact, since his daughter had flown the nest a spare room had become available. She had moved out some time ago, all grown up and ready to test out her independence. It made the house feel empty, though, the echoes of a little girl's excitement fading with each day. He worried about her, as all fathers did, but she insisted she was old enough to look after herself and at least she had been afforded a decent upbringing in a nice environment.

Cliffy knew full well the misery that lay behind the scabby paintwork and condensation-blighted windows of the towers. He had managed to crawl out of the cesspit but others weren't so lucky, finding themselves sucked under, their humanity lost forever. He had been upbeat with the boy, telling him about the planned makeover, but feared things would only get worse. There were new criminal gangs emerging on such estates that threatened to be more troublesome than those twins. At least Ronnie and Reggie were the devils he knew.

Nowadays, ambitious immigrants flooded London, believing the myth that the streets were paved with gold when, in reality, they were covered with takeaway cartons and dog shit. These new arrivals came from Turkey, Greece, the Caribbean, the Balkans, Bangladesh and all points east. When they discovered there wasn't a fortune to be had through legitimate means, they took Prime Minister Thatcher at her word and tried private enterprise. Unfortunately, many of their get-rich-quick schemes were illegal.

What chance for the boy? The word low-life ran through his old man like one of those sticks of rock they sold on the seafront at Southend. Sooner or later he would probably get what he wanted – a son to follow in his footsteps.

"YOU what?" Beryl Dolan furiously stalked the red paisley carpet of the living room. "You ran onto a football pitch and threatened to punch another parent? What were you thinking? And in front of the boy, too!"

"It was because of the boy, for fack's sake! I don't know, first the fackin' coppers give me a grilling, now it's me own family. Jesus!"

"Don't bring him into this... he won't save you! Honestly, you're getting more like your old man every day. Worse even! What are you going to say to the coach now? You've probably lost Chuck his place in the team and you know how he loves his football. Was that your plan? To upset your son?"

"Don't be stupid," said Mo. "You weren't there. This bigger kid nearly decapitated him. Boy could have ended up in the hospital and what would you be saying then? You'd be accusing me of failing to protect my own son, wouldn't you?"

She guessed he had a point and, anyway, Beryl knew her line of questioning was storing up trouble for later. "You eaten?" she asked.

"I'll get pie and mash."

"You're going out?" She didn't really need to ask. It was Saturday night, 6.30pm. In an hour's time he would be settled onto a bar stool at the Hope and Anchor, knocking back the beers and telling his acquaintances about the afternoon's dramas, how it had taken five coppers to bring him down and even then he'd managed to introduce a couple of them to Reg. She was flabbergasted when he had walked through the door with his favourite weapon tucked under his armpit in a plastic carrier bag, bemused at how he had been able to leave the police station with it.

"Stupid bastards!" he had said, a smile creeping across his face. "I told 'em I'd just bought it second-hand and needed it to put up curtains in Chuck's room. Fackin' bought it, they did."

As soon as she had seen him carrying his weapon of choice she couldn't let it go. Finding her sweet little boy on the doorstep with that policeman's arm draped around him, she glimpsed of a future she refused to entertain. She had been forced to say something, even though it would leave her open to reprisals. This, as Big Mo was accustomed to saying, was about family.

The phone rang in the hallway and she used the timely distraction to facilitate her escape. At that precise moment she couldn't stand another minute of her husband's company. She loved him, couldn't help it, they had been through so much together. As teenage sweethearts, they had used each other as sounding boards, railing against the unfair treatment they received from their parents. In those days they thought as one, shared the same dreams and ideals, always on the same page. Sadly, married life had created small fissures in the smooth structure of their relationship, cracks that widened daily.

She recited their phone number and listened to the voice on the other end of the line. "Maurice, it's for you!"

His body filled the passageway, his coat bearing evidence of the day's activity. It was a minor miracle he had escaped an assault charge, though he was scheduled for a day in court over the damage to the other bloke's Cortina. Squeezing past her, he lifted the handset.

"You what?!" Mo's exclamation stopped Beryl in her tracks. "Well, thanks a bunch, you cunt! You was there. You saw it. What do you mean? Oh, so you think if you get rid of my boy then the league will let you off, do you? And what about the fact I was just... Ray, look, it ain't fair on the kid now is it, when others can get away with, well, assault?" She could make out a pleading quality to the voice on the other end of the line, knew the poor bloke making the call was wasting his breath. Mo would never concede ground, believing it a sure sign of weakness. "...And that's your final word is it? Well, see you around 'coach' – though it might be better for you if I didn't."

The phone clattered and when it didn't sit properly on the cradle first time Mo brought it smashing down again, bits of plastic and metal flying around the hallway, small electrical components pinging off the walls like bullets. "We hire that from the bloody phone company, Mo, you plum!" shouted Beryl. "What the..?"

"Shut it!" He held one hairy hand out in her direction like a cop directing traffic. She retreated to the kitchen for a dustpan and brush. Behind her, a door banged open. He'd gone into the boys' room.

"Come on, Chuck, up... now! I'm gonna teach you that no one shits on the Dolans!"

A young child's grating cry added to the brooding atmosphere in the flat. "Oh, now look what you've done," Beryl muttered. "You've woken Sly. Just what I need."

Depositing the guts of the ruptured telephone into the swing bin, she set off in the direction of the bedroom to calm her youngest son. He was a bugger to get to sleep at the best of times and could be so ratty when his slumber was interrupted. Now he would be tired and irritable at the one time in the evening Beryl could usually call her own. Approaching the bedroom, she saw her other little boy stumble into the corridor, his face white, his expression a mix of alarm and confusion. "Mo, please! Did you really need to get Chuck up?" she said. "He's had a tough day and needs his sleep. It's way past his bedtime."

Her husband ignored her, barrelling past with such haste she banged her head against the wall and a chip of plaster went flying, another repair job needed in a flat pockmarked with such blemishes. She could probably go around with a marker pen, drawing arrows and writing underneath exactly what incident had caused each indentation.

"What do you want with that, Daddy?"

Big Mo gripped the boy's arm with one hand while carrying a bag adorned with the West Ham crest in the other. "Honey?" Beryl resorted to sweet talk, hoping to appeal to Mo's better nature. She knew it was lying dormant beneath that tough exterior, it was just much harder to locate these days. "What do you want with the boy's football gear? It isn't his fault..."

The door slammed and father and son were gone, out into the dark of a cold spring night. Beryl kicked a few remaining pieces of broken telephone aside in frustration. Listening at the boys' door, she could hear the gentle snoring of Sylvester and breathed a sigh of relief. He was asleep again. Now she had a new dilemma. Should she swaddle him in blankets and take him with her or leave him to his dreams? Against her better nature, she decided not to disrupt his routine. She wouldn't be gone long.

Grabbing a grey gabardine mac from the rack in the hall, she wrapped a red headscarf around her hair and marched onto the balcony, her nostrils assaulted by a concoction of stomach-churning smells drifting out from neighbouring flats: over-cooked sprouts, poached kippers, frying onions, stewing tinned meat, backed-up sewage, piss and weed. She leaned over the side, staring into the dark recesses where the hit-and-miss street lighting failed to penetrate, waiting for her husband and her eldest son to materialise. No question, Mo had gone crazy this time. Off his head. She had no idea what he was planning to do, but could only hope his natural parental instincts kicked in to calm him down before he went too far.

She was on the horns of a mother's dilemma. Instinct told her to follow, to drag Chuck back to the safety of his own home where she could wrap him in a suffocating embrace and shield him from the harsh realities of their world, but there was little Sly to consider. She couldn't leave the baby a moment longer than necessary. She thought for a second of calling Mo's brother to come over because if anyone could diffuse the situation he could. Then she cursed out loud. "Stupid bitch!" Not only was Clive in barracks, but their phone lay in tatters in the hallway.

About to give up, she spotted them leave by the front doors, Mo out in front, dragging the boy behind him. They were heading for the playground. Maybe that was it! Perhaps Mo felt guilty and planned to spend some father-and-son time apologising on the swings. She had to tell herself it was something like that or she would disintegrate through fear, which was spreading like acid through her veins.

Shutting out the million voices in her head telling her she was as crazy as her husband, she reluctantly turned and walked back into the flat.

13

"WHAT are we doing, Dad?" Tears streamed down Chuck's face, freezing against his skin, making it prickle and sting.

"Sorry, son, it's the only way." Big Mo marched to the wooden bin in the corner of the playground, his first born struggling to keep up the pace. "Stop crying now!" he commanded. "Sometimes in life we have to learn hard lessons. My dad... your grandad... taught me that when I was a nipper and I know why he did. It's a tough life and you'd better get used to it. You're eight now, son, not a baby any more. It's time you grew up."

"But... but that's my Vipers kit, Dad, what..?"

Chuck clammed up mid-sentence as Big Mo unzipped the bag and tipped the contents into the bin. Claret shirt, blue shorts, claret and blue socks, stylish modern football boots, soap, a towel with the Hammers crest on it with a comb to match, some stray sweets... the receptacle overflowed, having had plenty of rubbish in it to begin with. "I want to go home," snivelled Chuck. "I want Mum."

"Hey! What did I tell you? Any more of that and we'll see what Reggie makes of it all." Big Mo sank down and Chuck felt a stubby forefinger under his chin, lifting his head so their eyes met. His dad's voice softened. "I love you son. You know that, don'tcha? I would fight with my last breath to protect you, but I need you to realise that other people can't walk all over the Dolans. Family matters. Maybe you can't see that now, but in time you'll learn. Understand?"

Did he understand? He didn't think so.

"Our family ain't been blessed with much, so we have to take what we can," his father continued. "Once we got it we ain't gonna let go unless it's our decision, right? No one tells us what to do. I was happy getting you into that football team, thought it would be a good thing for you. I didn't mind taking you to matches, didn't even mind slipping Mr Ray a bit of dosh to keep him onside, but in return I expected some fackin' respect. The way they handled things yesterday... these muppets don't deserve my support, them or their shitty football team. Only pussies won't back you when you're in the right. Well I wouldn't piss on 'em now if they were on fire, the way they've treated us. What's worse, Mr Ray says he won't pick you anymore because you ain't any good. I know that ain't true and you know that ain't true, but I won't have people looking down their noses at the Dolans, you hear? I've decided football ain't for you. Watch it all you want, of course, play your Subbuteo and all that, sure, but we're gonna have to find you another sport, something where you can earn respect. Not another second will be wasted on this shit."

Chuck watched his old man dip into a pocket and pull out a square tin. Unscrewing the lid Big Mo poured liquid into the bin. A smell Chuck connected with cars and petrol stations wafted into his sinuses and the odour made him feel lightheaded. When the tin was empty, his dad crushed it and threw it on the top, before taking his lighter from the other pocket. Chuck could clearly see the inscription: *To my Fozzy Bear, love you so much, your honey Bee* xxx.

Dad cherished this lighter more than anything (bar the Daimler, perhaps). On the odd occasion he had misplaced it he would go into meltdown, accusing all in sundry of skulduggery until it turned up, right as rain, in some pocket or other.

"Stand back, son," said Mo, placing his hands on Chuck's shoulders and guiding him to a place a safe distance away. Satisfied, he returned to the bin and, in one casual movement, flicked the lid off the lighter and spun the wheel until a flame emerged. Chuck felt emotion flicker inside him also, forgetting his miserable thoughts for a second to stare in awe at the dancing beacon that lit up the night sky.

The feeling was snuffed out just as quickly, though, as Maurice Dolan shielded the lighter from view, protecting it from the gentle breeze that rustled the trees around them. Bending down, he thrust out an arm and moments later smoke poured from the bottom of the bin, the rubbish having caught alight instantly. Red and orange swirls of flame rose through the slats, gorging everything in their path as they climbed upwards, Chuck's lungs filling with the cloying smell of burning plastic.

Air like icy fingertips caressed the back of his neck as he watched the shadows dance on his father's face, bringing to mind monsters from his story books. Was his dad a monster? Shaking, he became aware he had urinated, his pants hot and wet, clouds of piss-stinking steam rising into the frigid air. He closed his eyes in an effort to hold back the tears. He was overcome with fear, frightened this latest misdemeanour would stoke up his dad's internal fires of rage and he would be introduced to Reg. Shrinking back into the shadows, away from the raging blaze, the darkness provided a perfect cloak behind which to hide his shame.

His father was so distracted with the incendiary ritual he almost forgot Chuck's presence. Only when things started to pop and crackle, presenting a danger to anyone in close proximity, did he rush back to his son, grab his hand and hustle him towards the flats.

In the background the sound of lilting sirens played a familiar London melody.

14

"HEY, darkie, I'm talking to you."

Chuck was playing marbles with his best friend Garry when he heard the shout. Garry's parents hailed from an island a long way away, St Luscious or something, and the two boys had struck up a friendship on their first day at junior school. Turning his head in the direction of the voice, Chuck saw an older boy approaching rapidly across the playground, three mates falling in behind him. Casting a glance over his shoulder to see who they might be talking to, Chuck realised there was no one there and anxiety twisted like worms inside his stomach.

The advancing boy looked familiar. He was older than them, his long, brown hair finishing in a fringe across his eyebrows. It cascaded down the sides of his face and rested in a jumbled heap at his shoulders. His shirt hung out at the back, mocking any idea that school uniform was meant to make kids look presentable. He looked mean and vaguely familiar.

"Yeah, you... Sambo!" said the boy, breaking into a trot, his gaze trained on Garry. Chuck saw his friend bite his bottom lip, fists clenched at his sides. He was whispering under his breath: "Sticks and stones may break my bones, but names will never hurt me!"

Arriving in front of Garry, the older boy afforded him a sinister smile. "Lucky I brought a stick then." He pulled a piece of wood from behind his back and poked Garry in the chest. Hard. Chuck's friend stumbled backwards. "Why don't you go back to where you came from, jiggaboo?!" he taunted.

"What... Ilford?" said Garry. He was telling the truth, but Chuck sensed it was the wrong response. The older boy's facial expression hardened, anger seeping through. He raised the stick like a javelin, his accomplices breaking into a hostile chant: "Nigger, nigger, nigger."

Chuck feared for his friend's safety and thought of his dad. The old man always told him he should stick up for his own. Surely that included Garry. Bravely, he took a step forward, putting his body between his friend and his tormentor. "Leave him alone," he said.

The sounds of a bustling playground disappeared like water down a sink. Faces turned to see what was going on. Without warning, Garry turned and sprinted towards the classroom doors. The gang leader glanced after him then focused scary dark eyes on the new target. Chuck didn't flinch, aware that taking his eyes off the other boy would be interpreted as a sign of weakness.

"What have we here then?" demanded the aggressor, turning to his audience for support. Hefting the stick from one hand to another, he turned back. Chuck stood his ground, nervous shivers shooting to all points of his body. "Nigger lover, eh? He your boyfriend? Your bum chum?" None of the taunts meant anything to Chuck. "Wait a minute!" said the boy, scrutinising his face. "I know your ugly mug. Yeah... you're the wimp who fell face down in the mud when I tackled you in football then got your old man to fight your battle for you. Bloke went Radio Rental, threatened my old man and smashed lumps out of our car. Got nicked by the Sweeney, didn't he? What a wank stain! Still inside, I imagine."

"No, he ain't," said Chuck.

"Well, well, well... he speaks, boys," said the wannabe bully, brushing at his ruler-straight fringe.

"Why don't you do 'im Kev?" shouted one of the entourage.

"Hmm," said their leader. He put his finger to his chin, appearing to consider the proposal. Caught off guard, Chuck didn't see the push coming or notice that one of the other boys had sneaked behind him. As he tumbled backwards he fell over the crouching boy and hit the ground, his clean white shirt ripping at the elbow on contact. Playground grit stung as it embedded itself in his skin. His mum would curse him for getting his new uniform dirty. He saw the boy who had tripped him scamper out of the firing line as the ringleader dived headlong on top of him, a flurry of fists connecting with various parts of Chuck's body.

It was over in less than a minute. The children's faces that had been blocking out the light parted and Chuck found himself staring through painful eye sockets into a cold grey sky, the watery sun partially hidden. Hands grabbed him, pulling him up and planting him on shaky legs.

"Oh dear, it's Mr Dolan, isn't it? I might have expected as much!" An ageing, grey-haired man studied Chuck's face. Garry stood beside him. "Like father like son, I suppose. Miss Lester, can you take young Charles here..."

"Um, my name's Chuck..."

"As I was saying before I was rudely interrupted, can you take Charlie boy here and tidy him up a bit please. Get some antiseptic on that elbow then make sure he is presented in my office, sharpish, in half an hour's time, together with young Kevin Macey." He pointed to Chuck's attacker. "Boys, boys, boys eh? When will you ever learn?" The man, who Chuck knew as deputy head Mr Fazackerley, addressed him again. "You shouldn't be taking on people bigger than you, boy, you might get badly hurt. Guess that's your dad's influence, eh?" Raising his head, he thrust his nose in the air haughtily, holding Chuck at arm's length as if he was a rag used to clean up a particularly pungent mess. "Get him out of my sight, Miss Lester."

As the deputy head walked away, Chuck heard him mutter under his breath.

"Bloody Dolans!"

15

HIS mother's pained expression caused the tears to gather behind his eyes.

"Oh, Chucky," she said. "What on earth's happened to you? Let me see." She turned his face fully to the right so that the ugly purple-black bruise on Chuck's cheek was reflected in the light from the hallway lamp. "Tell me: what happened? Did you fall over, or..."

"It was a fight, Mum." The lump swelled in his throat, making it difficult to talk. "It's OK, though." He tasted salt on his lips as he bit down on them, intent on preventing the build-up of tears escaping.

"It is not OK!" she stormed, her eyes watering, too. "I have half a mind to march up to that school and demand to know what they're doing. This wasn't you, Chucky, I know you. You're a kind, thoughtful little boy. You've been bullied, haven't you? It ain't right. Wait 'til..." She saw the creased envelope he was holding out in front of him. "What's this?"

Snatching it away from him, she opened it to find a note typed on official school letter-headed paper. She read it under her breath:

'*To the parents of Charles Dolan, I am sorry to have to inform you that your son was involved in a playground fight this lunchtime which was very frightening for the other children who witnessed it. As a school we aim to maintain the highest disciplinary standards and cannot condone violent behaviour of this nature. We therefore see no alternative than to issue Charles with an official warning. Any repeat of this action may result in suspension or even expulsion,*

Yours sincerely, JA Fazackerley (deputy head teacher)'

Beryl bit her lip, adopting a steely expression. "Why is he calling you Charles? Your name's Chuck."

"I dunno, Mum, he just does."

"Idiot!" She muttered, gazing at the letter again. "Now, Chuck, tell me, honestly... Is this true? You hit another boy?"

"No, Mum... he attacked us," Chuck said. "Garry and me."

"And has this Garry got a letter, too?" He shook his head. "Why not?"

"Well, they were after him really, because he is black an' all, so he ran off and got the teachers."

"So, you're telling me you stepped in to protect another boy, and when he saw you were in trouble he deserted you?"

"Well, I guess, but he did bring..."

"I see what's happened here, and it ain't right. You were sticking up for someone and got the blame... and your beautiful face ended up... I'm speechless."

"We don't have to tell Dad, do we?" he pleaded.

"It's going to be difficult to keep it from him. I mean... look at the state of you!" She guided him to the elaborate-looking mirror that hung in the hallway. It always reminded Chuck of the cartoon Snow White and the Seven Dwarfs, the magic mirror in which the wicked Queen gazed on her reflection, demanding: "Who is the fairest of them all?" Not me, that's for sure, he thought.

"Come here, I've an idea," she said.

Guiding him into her bedroom, she sat him at the small vanity unit, picked up a round box and opened it to reveal a powder-puff and a pink, talcum powder-like substance. "Maybe if we apply some make-up carefully we might get away with it without dad knowing."

"Knowing what?"

Chuck's heart leapt into his mouth as he turned to see his father's face screwed up in an angry expression. "Not content with letting my boy play with pushchairs and the like, you are going to paint his face like a China doll? What the fack?"

Beryl stepped between Chuck and his dad, intent on preventing him seeing their son's injuries. Mo rushed forward, pushing her aside with such force she fell to the floor, banging her head against the metal bed frame. Chuck watched horrified, then looked into his dad's dark, interrogating eyes.

"What's this?" Big Mo demanded, indicating the wound to his son's cheek.

"He was attacked and beaten up at school," Beryl blurted from her place on the floor. "It's not his fault, Mo, despite the letter."

"What letter?"

"They say he got into a fight and some of it was his fault."

"Was it, son?" his Dad's eyes bored into him like lasers.

"No, Dad," said Chuck, peering at the floor.

"So, you let them hit you? My son's a punchbag for the little scrotes around here? That ain't right."

For a moment, Chuck wasn't sure what to say. Then he remembered his mother's mantra: "Honesty is the best policy".

"Yes, Dad," he said.

Fireworks! A rough hand measuring about the size of Chuck's entire head slapped the side of his face and sent him reeling. His mother had manoeuvred herself from the floor to the bed and, as he dropped, his skull bounced off his mum's knee. "No!" she cried, leaping up and standing in front of her son. "What are you doing?" she demanded of Big Mo. "You don't hit the boy! You never hit the boy! Jeez, he's eight years old and you're a grown man. We're talking about bullies and you're acting like the worst kind!"

Chuck winced and turned away as his dad raised his hand again, the fury blazing in his eyes. "No, love, no... look," yelled his mother in desperation. "Don't turn into your father, you know that ain't the right way. Self-defence classes, that's the answer. You can take him to karate or that Kung fu – it seems to be all the rage these days."

Chuck lay sprawled against the side of the bed for what seemed like ages, his eyes squeezed shut, waiting for an impact that never came. Eventually hands reached down, pulling him to his feet and wrapping him in a suffocating embrace. "Sorry, boy," said his dad. "Your mum's right. It's Saturday tomorrow – the weekend. We got things to do if we are gonna turn you into the real deal. No more snivelling, eh? I'm going to make a phone call. It's time we made a man of you."

Beryl risked a glance at Chuck as Big Mo disappeared out of the door. It was as if he could read her mind. "Sorry, baby, I've tried my best to protect you," her expression said. "It's out of my hands now."

He nodded to show he understood.

16

"THIS is the place," said Big Mo. "You heard of it, Chucky boy? It's legendary round here, produced some great fighters. Everyone I grew up with used to come here, meet the boxers, collect autographs and that. Your Uncle Frank trains here, y'know? He ain't turned out so badly."

Chuck had overheard his dad telling tales of Handsome Frank Purves. He had been in line for a lucrative professional career, only to come crashing down in a British title eliminator against some fighter from the travelling community. There was still an element of mystery as to how such a promising career had been cut short so abruptly. Frank was now involved in the illegal bare-knuckle fight game.

He was a frightening-looking character with a swollen, puffy nose, cauliflower ears and a leaking eye framed by a semi-circular scar, the result of being bottled in a nightclub. When people questioned him about it Handsome retorted: "You should see the other guy." Apparently, he wasn't joking. The story Chuck heard was "the other guy" was in a home for the mentally impaired somewhere outside Gravesend, living out his days in complete ignorance – the brain damage irreparable. Frank wasn't related in any biological way to Chuck, but every one of his mum and dad's friends assumed titles accordingly, as if the Dolans and their pals were one extended family.

Chuck looked up at a sign stretching the entire length of the red brick building: "Wally Molloy's Gym".

"Just down the road from the York Hall," his dad said. "Some of the greatest names in boxing have fought there. Bethnal Green and boxing go hand in hand. It's a noble art and if you do well at it, you earn respect. Who knows? Maybe you'll top the bill there one day. Learn what they teach you, do your best and you'll be fine. It would be great to have another boxer in the family. No little chancers will be trying their luck with the Dolans then, eh?"

"You don't know if I'll be any good, Dad," protested Chuck. "I wasn't at football."

"No negative talk, right?" said Mo. "Course you'll be good. You're a Dolan, ain't you?" he ruffled Chuck's hair playfully. "That means somethin' around here, y'know? Look at your grandad Billy. You've seen his muscles, right? Tough as old boots, me old man, and we're all a chip off that same granite block. My grandad – your great Grandad – was in the Army and won loads of boxing prizes. Your uncle Clive picked up some tricks from him and wasn't bad, either. Then there's me, now you and Sly, who is gonna be a right handful. Just don't be a wuss, right? Show some guts and don't give anyone a break. Strike first and strike hard and if, God forbid, someone starts on you, then you end it... by any means possible."

"There are rules, though, aren't there?"

"In the ring? Of course! But we ain't just talking about a little light sparring on the canvas. These skills will be with you for life." That penetrating stare found Chuck's eyes again. The boy nodded. "OK then, let's meet the blokes who are gonna teach you the ropes. Hey, ropes, get it? Ha ha. You know, the ring is surrounded by ropes." Chuck stared at him, bemused. "Oh, never mind."

He pushed the door open.

THE first things that hit Chuck at Wally Molloy's were the unique sounds and smells. There was the squeak, squeak of rubber soles on floorboards, the pfft pfft of leather gloves colliding with punchbags, the rattle-rat-rat-tattle rhythm of smaller bags being beaten systematically as they hung from chains attached to the ceiling, and the cries, grunts and groans of more than a dozen men engaged in various activities around the room. It was a big space, yet every inch of it was filled with some apparatus or other, all being put to use by a throbbing mass of sweating humanity. The overwhelming smell was that of body odour mixed with the eye-watering potency of various liniments the athletes rubbed on their bodies to ease muscles, repair injuries or just to make them more supple.

In the centre of the area was a boxing ring where people were hanging from the ropes, watching two men dance around each other on the canvas. "Looks like they've pulled Uncle Frank in for some sparring," said Big Mo. Chuck realised the figure under the cumbersome headgear was his dad's friend.

"Steady, kid, he's taken heads off in the past," a spectator shouted by way of encouragement to Frank's opponent.

"He's had his day, Dai. Handsome Frank's only good when he's fighting for pennies on the floor." There was a chuckle and Frank was distracted for a moment, mumbling something beneath his breath and pointing a glove menacingly at the man baiting him. Too late he didn't see the accurate left hook spearing in at his chin. For moments his feet seemed detached from the canvas and Chuck thought he was going down, but he bounced off the ropes and regained his balance. "Good shot, Mark. That's the way. Carry on like that and you'll have that American for breakfast. Well done, though, Frank. Handled like a seasoned pro."

"As I live and breathe..." The words came from behind them and Chuck and Mo turned to face a balding, squat figure, a flattened nose zig-zagging across a heavily lined face, evidence of old scar tissue peeking through bushy grey eyebrows. "This your boy, Mo?" he asked in a heavily accented Ulster drawl.

"Yep. This is Chuck, Wally. Wants you to teach him the ropes, just like Handsome said. That OK?"

"Sure. Got any kit, son?" Chuck shook his head. "Well, we'll sort that out for yous. Yer man, when he arrives, will give you some tips on where to get cheap boots. We normally have some in stock here, but there's been a bit of a rush on. Watching Frank spar, were ye? He's got his work cut out."

"Who's the kid?" asked Mo.

"Name's Kaylor. From Canning Town originally. He's the next big thing if he keeps his nose clean. Fights one of them Yanks at the Albert Hall next, some bloke who thinks he can come here for an easy win to ramp up his rep. He's in for a surprise. Mark's 14 fights unbeaten, stopped nine and had a first-round knockout earlier this year. 'Course, you ask Handsome and he'll tell you the kid ain't up to snuff, but you'll never find Frank throwing around the compliments."

"True," agreed Big Mo. "Kaylor? I'll keep an eye out, splash some cash on the boy if he's any good."

"Oh, he is. Take my word for it."

They stood in silence, watching the boxers in action. Eventually Mo said: "Listen, I've got some errands to run and Beryl's picking the kid up later. What time shall I tell her to be here?"

"We'll ease him in today," said Wally. "I reckon if she's here around one that will be plenty of time to get him started on the basics. I'm waiting for one of my coaches to arrive – pity you missed him actually. He's a good bloke."

"Do I know him?"

"Doubt it. He's not really in your line of, err, business."

"Right." Big Mo sniggered, turning to Chuck. "Have a great time, son. You're in good hands with Wally here. Try your best and you can't go far wrong. Give your old man a hug."

Chuck did as he was told, then watched his dad walk away.

When Mo had gone, Wally guided Chuck to a changing area and handed him a vest top, shorts and plimsolls. Everything was oversized but he got ready quickly, keeping his head down and avoiding eye contact with the boxers on the benches surrounding him. He felt their eyes checking him out. "Doubt he can fight his way out of a paper bag," said one, smirking, just loud enough for Chuck to hear.

Seconds later, there was a choking sound, like someone struggling for breath. Looking up, Chuck saw his Uncle Frank holding the boxer opposite in a headlock. "You know who that is?" he demanded, pointing at Chuck. The other man spluttered an incoherent reply. "Didn't think so, or you wouldn't be so free with your mouth. That's Big Mo Dolan's boy Chuck there and it's his first time, so be nice." Gradually he released his grip and the other boxer sank to the bench, coughing and wheezing. "Sure thing, Frank," he croaked.

"Hope I haven't missed all the fun." Chuck recognised the jovial voice immediately and swivelled towards the doorway to check his ears weren't playing tricks. Entering the changing rooms with a gym bag slung casually over his shoulder was the heavyweight figure of Police Constable Cliffy Simpson.

Handsome gathered his things together and walked from the room. "Not sure he likes me," Cliffy said, standing next to Chuck and peeling off his top. "Can't think why."

"Because you're a copper?" ventured Chuck.

"And we're all..."

"Bastards," said Chuck, smiling.

"Do you know, Chuck Dolan, I think you might have something there. You don't mind me being a cop, though, do you? I hope not, because Wally has asked me to take you through your paces."

"You're my coach?" asked Chuck with disbelief.

"That's right," said Cliffy. "Don't you think I can box?" Chuck let his eyes fall to the jovial policeman's well-stacked midriff. "You cheeky little beggar!" said Cliffy. "I may be big, son, but I can still bounce around the canvas with the best of 'em. Used to box for the Met Police. One of London's finest. Got plenty of trophies at home after teaching those services boys a thing or two. You ask anyone ... they'll tell you Cliffy could mix it with the best. Even thought I might go pro one day, but I enjoyed my job and my grub too much for that. If I get any more cheek out of you though, young sir, you'll be learning the hard way." He smiled, and Chuck smiled back. He had to admit he liked this jolly giant. Suddenly the idea of learning how to box didn't seem so bad at all.

17

"MUM, it was fantastic. They showed me how to avoid a punch and how to throw one and I worked the bag... I even did skipping!" Chuck was bouncing around in his seat, ducking and weaving with his fists held up to his chest.

"Skipping? I thought this was supposed to be toughening you up," said Beryl, laughing. "Skipping is for girls!"

Chuck pouted. "It's quite hard, you know?"

Beryl was unable to keep up the pretence, fearing her teasing might have a negative effect. She was delighted to see her eldest child so enthused about something. Recently it was as if he'd been walking around with the troubles of the world on his shoulders, something that should never tax someone at eight. "I'm teasing you," she said. "All the best boxers are good at skipping. I was hopeless. My friends at school used to laugh at me when we got the ropes out in the playground. Half my school life I was walking around with scuffed knees where I'd messed up and tripped over while jumping to those silly rhymes we chanted. I'm sure it makes you super fit. My legs ached something rotten after just 10 minutes ... I'm so glad you had a good time, though. Who was your trainer?"

"Oh," said Chuck. "There were all different ones. I can't remember their names. Anyway... can we get the boots?"

She turned to face him, her expression unreadable. "Your dad says money is a bit tight but, well, he indicated he had some work coming up and this boxing lark was his idea so... why not?" She found it impossible to refuse Chuck when he looked at her with those pleading eyes, brown and warm as melted caramel. Bringing a smile to his face made her day. Lord knows, they hadn't had much to smile about recently. It was as if they spent their whole existence walking on egg shells. Hell, she remembered when Mo used to smile the way Chuck was now, before life became a constant struggle and he adopted a siege mentality – Dolans against the world. The trouble was that often these days he took out his frustrations on his nearest and dearest. For someone who put family first, Mo had a funny way of showing it.

Looking at Chuck, sometimes Beryl saw the old Mo, the dependable Mo, the one who promised her the earth and all the treasures upon it in return for just one kiss, then one fumble, one fuck and, eventually, her hand in marriage. She knew his whole life revolved around his promises, but he failed to understand that trying to deliver on them was putting him under ridiculous levels of pressure, the part of him she fell in love with vanishing before her eyes.

She was loyal, though, unlike her mother, who ran off with a wealthy customer while working as a barmaid in a nightclub. She hadn't seen the woman for 12 years, the only reminder of her a hastily scrawled letter which did nothing to ease the pain, and though Beryl was a lot older now she was still none the wiser. She saw her mother's actions as heartless and selfish and couldn't envisage a time when she would be able to forgive her. Family life was tough, sure, particularly when you brought kids into the world, but deserting Chuck and Sly was unthinkable.

Beryl's thoughts were interrupted as the bus pulled into their stop. They alighted and were plunged into the hustle and bustle of a busy East End market. Wonderful smells of exotic food accosted their nostrils, the air filled with pungent oriental spices mingling with the more familiar home grown aromas of grilled burgers, hot dogs and fish and chips. Beryl's stomach rumbled to remind her she had missed breakfast that morning, happy to put Chuck and Mo's needs first.

Noise was everywhere, cockney banter dovetailing seamlessly with dialects from the far corners of the earth. She tugged Chuck along behind her and pushed through the crowds, following the directions she had been given. The stall she was seeking was run by Wally Molloy's mate – an Irishman called Patrick Marshall who had won a few amateur fights himself during his younger days. Now, though, he had found his niche, buying and selling sporting footwear at one of the biggest street markets in Europe. "Mum, look... over there, see!" Chuck tugged her towards an impressively decked out stall which had giant posters of a couple of well-known boxers advertising popular sports brands. Staring up at the figures, his mouth formed a perfect O.

"That's Sugar Ray Leonard, son." A smiling man approached and put his arm around Chuck's shoulder. He wore a black leather jacket and denim jeans, hair falling in a mass of brown curls to his shoulders.

"Oh," said Chuck, his knowledge of boxers limited to those he had just seen in the gym.

"They reckon he's the best pound-for-pound boxer in the world right now. Beat Thomas 'The Hitman' Hearns, though there is some debate about whether the judges got the decision right." Chuckling, his face cracked into a maze of laughter lines.

"He's only just got into boxing," said Beryl. "He had his first lesson today and we need to find him some boots. Wally Molloy said to say 'hi'... are you Patrick?"

"Me? Hell, no! That's my dad," said the young man. "Give me a break, would you? I'm Stanley... Stan for short. And you are, darlin'?"

"Beryl," she said, offering a gloved hand, "Beryl Dolan." If the name meant anything to him, he didn't show it. She felt a tingle, though, as his deep brown eyes made an inventory of her face. Reddening, she was unable to remember the last time anyone, including Mo, had looked at her like that. Silly mare. From nowhere, tears sprouted.

"Oh my word," said Stan. "Sorry love. You OK? What's wrong?"

"Mum?" said Chuck, looking at her with bemusement.

"Hey, Azza," Stan called to the young Asian on the stall next to him. "You know your way around this stall as well as I do. The old man will be back in a minute. Look after this lad for a bit, show him the boxing boots and trainers, would you?"

"Sure, Stan," said the boy called Azza. "Don't be long though, eh? We're pretty busy. There's a clamour for Indian dresses with Diwali coming up. Mum's handling it OK, but I don't want to leave her too long."

"We're only going into Kuzey's place for a cup of char," said Stan. "You know where to find me."

Stan led Beryl through a shop doorway and sat her at a table by the window. She thought she must look a right state, and feared her mascara had run. "Two teas, Kuzay," Stan shouted to the man behind the counter.

"Lazy little beggar, come to the counter like everyone else! We don't do table service." Despite the rebuke the cafe owner was smiling, a friendly round face peering out from below tight, dark curls.

"I keep this place open nearly single handed the amount I spend in here, you Turkish robber!" said Stan. "Anyway, can't you see I'm busy?"

"With my own eyes," said Kuzey, turning his attention to Beryl. He winked. "Watch him, love, you don't know where he's been." Too late, he saw the tears. "Oh my, I'm sorry. Yes, you need Kuzey's tea." Moments later he appeared with two steaming mugs.

"You're a mate," said Stan. "Settle up later, yeah?"

"Sure, Stan."

The cafe owner returned to his counter to rearrange pastries in the display cases. Stan leaned over and put his hand on Beryl's. She went to pull away. "What am I thinking?" she blurted. "I should be with Chuck."

"He's fine. Look, we can see him from here." Stan pointed through the window. Chuck was smiling, his attention focused on a boxing boot in his hand. "It's you I'm worried about. Forgive me, but people don't often break down in tears at my stall and... I'm sorry, but I have to tell you, I've noticed you've got a nasty mark on the side of your face." He lent across, placing thumb and forefinger gently under her chin, turning her head to study the part of her face that had collided with the bed frame the previous night. Was she stupid, letting this man handle her so intimately?

"It's nothing!" she snapped, pulling away. She could still feel his gentle touch, though, and imagined his fingers had left an imprint in her face as if her skin was made of putty. "I fell over, that's all."

"Drink your tea..." He handed her the mug, his fingers brushing her hand.

Magic fingers.

Where the hell did that come from? She feared she was going insane.

"He loves me, you know," she said before she could rein herself in. Madness, blurting out private things to a stranger.

"Funny way of showing it," he said.

"You don't know anything about me, or him, or us," she protested. "It's family stuff, nothing to do with you."

"Hey, I'm sorry!" he said, holding his hands up in mock surrender. "But I'm only responding the way any person would to a pretty girl who has obviously been assaulted by a man. You're right, I know nothing of you or your family and it's none of my business, but my guess is you need to speak to someone away from that environment and... well, I'm told I'm a good listener." He paused to pull a packet of tissues from his jacket pocket and hand it over. She looked at it. "It's OK, none of them have been near my big conk."

That made her smile. She took one of the tissues and dabbed at her eyes.

"You're kind."

"Feeling better?"

"Yes. It was silly of me."

"Not a bit of it. Look..." he delved into his pocket and pulled out a scrap of paper. "This is me." He wrote down a telephone number.

"It's the number of a little warehouse we've got. You can get me early in the morning or after 6 when we do a stock take. If I'm not there leave a message. Someone will get it to me. If you need to speak to someone I'll make myself available, promise."

She wondered why he hadn't supplied her with his home number then, reaching for the paper, she noticed the ring. "You're married," she said.

"So are you," he pointed out.

"Touché." Beryl blushed. Had she really said that? All they were doing was having a lunchtime cup of tea and here she was acting like they were in the midst of a full-blown affair.

"We're only here once, Beryl," he said, as if reading her thoughts, jumping in with both feet. "You're a beautiful lady." Those fingers were touching her chin again, raising her face up to look at him. "You don't deserve misery in your life."

"I have to go," she said, standing abruptly, spilling the dregs of her tea as she pushed away from the table.

"Wait!" he shouted. "At least get what you came for."

The words stopped her in her tracks. What did he mean?

Damn! The boots.

"My dad let's me have a certain discount... perks of the job," he said, joining her in the doorway. "Those Adidas boots your boy was looking at – the ones with the two blue stripes and the red one? They're pretty expensive normally but I could tell he really wanted them. There aren't many others they do in his size, him being such a young 'un. I'll give you three quid off, can't say fairer."

Could she do that, put herself in debt to this stranger with the gentle touch and the hypnotic eyes? What would she tell Mo?

"They were in the sale." What? Did he just read her mind again? There were few things that spooked Beryl but this gave her the shivers. She started wondering about his star sign, wanting to know more. Though she normally kept her feet firmly on the ground, she did entertain the occasional little superstition and believed there was such a thing as fate.

CHUCK was beaming as he held his new boots up to the light on the bus, his expression alone telling her she had done thc right thing. It wasn't Chuck's sparkling eyes that were filling her thoughts, though. It was him. She could recall his face, his hair, his clothes and, more than anything, his touch.

Magic fingers.

Another shiver rippled through her, goosebumps making her skin tingle. As ridiculous as it sounded, she was missing him already.

18

BIG Mo was studying his best hand of the morning when his brother pushed through the doors of the Hope and Anchor. Though dressed in a suit, Clive looked dishevelled, his tie askew, his shirt creased, a red stain smearing the collar. Thin red trails criss-crossed his eyes and Mo guessed he had either spent three days without sleep or been on a massive bender. Intrigued to uncover the truth, he willed himself to concentrate on three-card brag. With what he had been dealt he could wipe out his losses at a stroke.

Placing the cards face down, he threw a pound note onto the table. The two strangers opposite glanced at each other, their expressions indicating they thought Mo was bluffing but weren't absolutely sure. After all, he had lost a fair bit that morning and the chances of him going out on a limb with a king or ace seemed highly unlikely. Maybe he had a pair.

To his left, Cozza folded, throwing his cards face up on the table, the Jack of Clubs the best he had to offer. That left the two players he didn't know to make their opening gambits. The bloke sitting opposite him at the small, scarred, dark wood table looked closely at him, trying to see if he could read anything in the crags and crevices that made up Mo's face. Eventually he made a decision. "Two quid blind," he said, having declined to look at the three cards in front of him.

"Brave man," said Cozza. "What's your name? Ain't seen you in here too often."

"Stan," said the stranger. "Stan Marshall."

"You live on the estate?"

"Come on," said Mo impatiently. "This ain't an old dears' coffee morning, it's a serious Saturday morning card game. What's your mate going to do?"

The young Asian who had arrived with Stan picked up his cards, looked at them for the first time then threw them down. "That's me done," he said. "The luck's with Stan this morning. I'm going to the bar. Can I get anyone anything?"

"I'm fine, cheers," said Mo. "See that bloke up there, though, the one in the suit? That's my brother. Tell him I'll be over in a minute, would you?"

"On you, big man," said Stan, refocusing Mo's attention. "Still confident?"

Mo rubbed at the sides of his mouth. This was the key moment, he knew, the one where he would either sell the brag or his opponent would fold. He could carry on putting cash in the pot to gradually build up the fund or he could raise the stakes. He didn't want to prolong the game too much, though. He needed to speak to his brother. He'd seen a documentary about the Falkland Islands and a possible Argentine invasion, and wanted to ask Clive about it. Not that he thought his brother would be involved. He was far more likely to be stomping around a parade ground.

Mo removed his wallet from his inside pocket and dug deep, emerging with a tenner. "Right," he said. "Time to sort the men from the boys." He furtively glanced down, peeling his cards from the table as if to remind himself of their value. "Ten pounds open," he said. "If you wish to carry on blind, son, you'll have to put in a fiver."

"I know the rules," said Stan. "Shit, I've been kicking your arse all morning." If he noticed the cold stare he got in return, he didn't show any sign, scratching his chin and tapping his fingers on the top of his cards like a TV magician about to perform a trick. Finally, he looked Mo in the eye and slowly picked up his hand.

Studying what he had been dealt, he raised his eyebrows. The moment of truth, thought Mo. The greaser type in the leather jacket and AC/DC T-shirt would either lay down his cards, surrendering the pot to Mo, or match the bet and escalate the game of dare. Mo tried to see the cards reflected in the other man's dark eyes but failed.

"Fuck it," said Stan. "It's only money." He threw a £10 note on top of the pile that had accumulated in the centre of the table.

"I DON'T know how the facker did it, but I'd swear on our gran's life he cheated," Mo said, barely able to contain his fury. "D'you know what the cocky bleeder said? 'It's only money'. Fack!"

"Don't know why you're swearing on Granny Dolan's life," said Clive. "The senile old biddy died five fuckin' years ago! Bloody hell, Mo, not everyone is trying to rip you off."

"Look, I had a Queen flush and he turns over a run, on the bounce!" said Mo. "How likely is that? His little Asian mate dealt them. Can't trust them lot, I'm telling you. Those two fackers cleaned me out bruv, and I don't reckon they just got lucky."

"So it's a conspiracy," said Clive. "You don't change! Even when we were kids you had to win; Hangman, Cluedo, Monopoly – even family card games like Newmarket or Rummy; the toys would fly out of the pram if someone pipped you to the prize. Damn, I've still got the scar to show from when you cracked my head open on the door because you claimed I'd gone up a snake instead of down."

"You had, you cheat!" said Mo. "Anyway, I hate being made to look a mug, particularly by some hairy-arsed rocker who acts like God's gift to women. Look at him over there, chatting up that bird."

"Might be his missus."

"Yeah and I'm the Queen of fackin' Sheba. I know his type."

"And I know you should leave the betting alone, mate," said Clive. "It screws with your mind."

"Why the whistle?" asked Mo, changing the subject.

Clive looked down as if he had forgotten how he was dressed. Mo had used cockney rhyming slang – the words whistle and flute meant suit. "Didn't have time to go home and change," he said.

"Copped on, did you?"

"Down the West End," said the younger brother. "The girls were all over us. When they found out we were Army we didn't even have to try. I didn't have the heart to tell 'em that all we do is stand around getting our photos taken with Japanese tourists. This one bird was really into it and, yeah, I laid it on thick, saying we were off to fight for our country and I might never come back." Clive took Mo's expression as criticism. "Why not?" he said. "I'm single, ain't got a girlfriend – never had anything like you've got with Beryl – so thought it was time I started playing the field while the odds were in my favour."

"She the one then?" asked Mo.

"Not likely," said Clive. "Scared the life out of me. Dirty little minx. Put her finger right up me..."

"Shhhhh!" Anxious faces turned towards them and they realised people had gathered beneath a small black-and-white TV set bracketed to the wall just above the bar and were talking in harsh whispers. The brothers glanced over to see what the attraction was. The Prime Minister was standing on the green outside the House of Commons. She was dressed in a Conservative Blue two-piece and had come straight from an emergency session of Parliament.

The hubbub of excitement died, tension filling the void. "What's happening?" someone asked.

"Can't hear what she's saying," mumbled another.

Around Mrs Thatcher a large gathering of news reporters jostled for position. "Shit!" said a voice below the screen, "It looks like there's going to be a bloody war."

Noise levels rose, everyone speaking at once and asking questions, demanding answers. Others tried to "shush!" them so they could hear what was being said. A layer of smoke hovered above as anxious locals sucked greedily on cigarettes, desperate for something to do with their free hand, drink occupying the other. The smell of cooking burgers drifted in from the kitchen.

"Bloody hell!" said a gruff voice, rising above the rest. "What do the soddin' Argies want with some scraps of land off the coast of bleedin' Scotland?"

"What you on about?" asked another.

"I'm asking why we're committing troops to take back control of a place that's famous for ponies and little else."

"You're talking about the Shetland Islands, you prick, not the Falklands."

"Who you calling a prick? You want a war, mate, you can fuckin' have one."

The barman stretched across, trying to keep the warring factions apart. "Calm down, lads," he instructed. "We don't want a fight among ourselves. Let's save it for the bloody Argies."

"Those fuckin' Spurs boys can have it, for a start!" chimed in a voice Mo recognised. Cozza.

"Oh come on!" another voice replied. "You can hardly blame this on Ossie Ardiles and Ricky Villa. They're just footballers. Jeeez!"

"Turn it up, let's all here what she's saying," shouted Clive. "Some of us might have to fight out there."

Mo stared at him incredulously. "You think?"

Clive shrugged. "Who knows? The brass have been getting a bit jittery, though. Told us we're on alert. That's why we went out last night... in case we were suddenly sent off to war."

"They won't require a marching band though, will they?"

"Funny," said Clive, cuffing him on the forearm. "We're trained for other stuff, too, not just ceremonial shit," he said. "We've been on exercises with NATO and last November went to Norway for a couple of weeks getting used to extreme conditions. Can we just listen to what Thatcher's saying?"

The noise in the room died again and the volume was adjusted on the TV set. The Prime Minister looked earnestly into the camera. "The emergency session of Parliament that has just been held was to discuss a situation of great gravity," she explained. "For the first time in many years British sovereign territory has been invaded by a foreign power. After days of rising tensions, Argentina's armed forces attacked the Falklands yesterday and established military control of the Islands, usurping the British governor. There was not one shred of justification for this action and as far as we're concerned it constitutes an illegal act. The people who live on those islands do not want to be Argentine, they wish their homes to remain as part of a British territory. I want people to know, and I want Argentina to know, that a large task force will set sail as soon as preparations are complete with the objective of freeing the islands from occupation and returning them to their rightful British administration at the earliest possible moment." Having said her piece to camera, she turned and, flanked by aides, headed back to the Houses of Parliament, a hundred media voices shouting their questions in her wake.

"Don't worry, Monkey," said Mo, putting his hand on his brother's shoulder. "Someone will come up with a diplomatic solution before our soldiers set foot on those soddin' islands."

When he looked at Clive's face, though, he saw his brother was beaming. "Worry?" he said. "What do you mean? This is what I signed up for. Some bloody excitement in my life. Can't get any more exciting than a war." He turned to look for the landlady. "Hey ... Siobhan... Over here! A couple of pints of bitter please. We've got something to celebrate and I'm not sure when I'll get the chance again."

19

TRAILS of black smoke rolled across the Welsh hillside, mingling with the haze of an unseasonably warm April morning. "Fire! Fire! Come on you lot, let's look lively!" The captain's voice, honed in the Highlands and refined at a private school in Edinburgh, boomed out around the camp. Men dressed in army fatigues and sturdy boots busied themselves inside their tents, collecting various personal items and stuffing them into their rucksacks.

"Well this is going well, isn't it, Jock?" Private Clive Dolan gave his mate Corporal Archie McAllum a knowing look. "Bloody hell, I was just getting nice and cosy. Thought we had done our bit for today, what with that live fire exercise this morning and all. No one said there was going to be another bloody drill this afternoon."

"Too true, Derek," said Archie, a huge fan of the comedians Peter Cooke and Dudley Moore who often regurgitated sketches from their outrageously foul-mouthed Derek and Clive albums. When it came to his buddy in the 2nd battalion, the Scots Guards, he had simply substituted the name Clive for Derek.

"I suppose we're going to need these again," said Clive, lifting his rifle. "Maybe it's an unplanned assault on our position, you know, to see if we are ready for every eventuality. What's this place we are supposed to be fighting over? Falconia? Load of old bollocks if you ask me."

"Too bloody right!" said Archie, his gruff Glaswegian tones booming inside the tent the two men were using as their base during Welsh Falcon, a two-week training exercise based at Sennybridge on the

Brecon Beacons. It was supposed to prepare them for deployment to the South Atlantic. The second battalion had been recruited to the Fifth Infantry Brigade, which had lost some of their main regiments to the Task Force now heading for the Falklands. It was quite a challenge, moulding different battalions which had never worked together into a fully integrated, battle-ready force. Those in charge had already encountered plenty of logistical and operational headaches.

"Everyone knows this is a waste of time," continued McAllum, warming to the theme. "Welsh Falcon? More like Operation soddin' Sheep Droppings if you ask me. It's not as if we're going to do any serious fighting, is it? By the time we get there it will be all over and we'll be asked to bloody babysit the two men and a dog on the islands once the paras, marines and special forces have left with all the glory. I can't see we'll be involved in much fighting unless there is a set-to over who owns which bloody sheep!" He pulled on his guard's beret, lifted his weapon from the floor and headed for the exit, pulling back the flap of the tent. "Christ!" he exclaimed, looking out. "You won't believe this..."

Clive dragged himself to his feet and peered through the gap. There was a full-scale blaze raging around them, soldiers in various states of undress rushing around with buckets of water, tossing their contents on the flames then racing away to fill them again. Others beat at the fires with anything they could lay their hands on, including the jackets of their uniforms. "Jesus!" said Clive. "Are they trying to replicate an Argie air force strike or something?"

"I wish it were that simple, Private," said the captain as they scurried from the tent. "I've been shouting myself hoarse, but you lot took no notice. It's lucky you're not burnt to a crisp! Leave your bags there. They won't be any use."

"But..."

"No buts, Private. Will you listen for once in your damned life. I thought I spoke da English pretty good, no? Then again, I'm not sure you understand the Queen's, being a thick cockney pillock 'n' all!" He leaned over, his craggy, angular face moving up close and personal to

Clive's. "Watch my lips: This... is... a... real... fire. The grass has somehow caught and, in these dry conditions, it's really taken hold. Got it?"

"Yes, Sir." Clive looked suitably chastised though his mind was thinking of ways he could take revenge on the know-it-all Scotsman. The captain seemed to make a habit of picking on him just because he was from south of the border. Still, you had to respect the chain of command. "Sorry, Captain."

"Right, well get over there pronto and see what you can do." He ushered Clive, McAllum and six others out of the tent to join the rest of their company in tackling the blaze. They set off in the direction of the toilet blocks, only to be turned back by another officer. "No buckets left lads. Anyone got their own equipment?"

"We would have, but we weren't allowed to bring our kit," said Archie.

"You left it in your tent? Fat lot of good it will do you there," said the officer. "Never mind, grab anything you can lay your hands on to beat out the flames. That's the best bet."

"How did it start?" asked Archie.

"Fucked if I know," answered the officer, who had a north of England accent. "Bet it had something to do with them bloody Taffies, though."

"Figures," said Archie. The officer was referring to the 1st Welsh Guards, another battalion seconded to the Fifth Brigade with the Scots Guards and the Ghurkas, an elite regiment who were training in a different area of the Beacons, no doubt waving their lethal kukris around and imagining decapitating their enemies.

The two Guards units were unsure what to make of each other. The Scots thought the Welsh were full of themselves, mainly because they had boasted about being battle-ready having spent a period before Christmas on manoeuvres in Kenya. The Welsh regarded the Scots as unfit for combat because they had spent the majority of that year performing ceremonial duties in London.

Removing their jackets, Clive and Archie began beating at the flames which were rapidly encroaching on the camp. "Can't see how this is supposed to prepare us for the Falklands," said Clive, holding his hand to his forehead to protect his eyes from the smoke. The heat warmed his cheeks, producing the same burning sensation as an oven did when you opened the door too quickly. The clogging smell of smouldering dry grass blocked his airways and he collapsed with an impromptu coughing fit.

"Whose bloody idea was it, I wonder?" he spluttered. "Some bloody hoity-toity civvy in the government, I shouldn't doubt. 'I know a good wheeze, let's send those chaps down to jolly old Wales. Spiffing!' Christ. It's got to be 70 degrees here yet I'm told all we can expect in the Falklands is snow, gales and mushy peat bogs. Hardly ideal preparation. They'll probably find some way to blame us for ruining our uniforms after this and reduce our money accordingly... Ouch!" He had let his tunic linger too long in one place, and flames leapt up the arm, catching hold and burning his fingers, forcing him to drop the incinerated garment.

"Well done, mate!" said Archie in fits of laughter as he lifted his jacket above his head and brought it crashing down time and time again. "Laugh, I nearly shat. Haven't laughed so much since Grandma died..."

"... or Auntie Mabel caught her left tit in the mangle. Yeah, all right. This ain't the right time for Derek and Clive really."

"Oh, I don't know," said Archie. "You've got to see the funny side. You're supposed to be putting out the fire, not adding bloody fuel to it."

Suddenly they heard a whumpf followed by a bout of swearing. Recognising the captain's voice, hastily they turned to see what was going on. "Oh shit!" said Clive as he watched flames lick the side of their tent and shoot into the night sky. Suspending their fire-fighting duties they ran back in the hope of rescuing their belongings, knowing in reality it was a lost cause. In seconds, all that was left of their tent was a metal frame.

"THAT'S the twat over there," said Stoney Mason, a tall, sinewy private from a sparsely inhabited area just north of the border. The guardsmen raised their faces to see a tall, muscular man mountain with red cheeks and matching hair enter the canteen area.

"What twat?" asked Clive.

"The twat that started the bloody fire!" said Stoney. "Apparently the bloody pyromaniac was helping to camouflage vehicles with webbing and grass when he came over all peckish. He had brought a temporary stove with him and thought it would be a good idea to rustle up a snack: sausages, beans, egg and something those daft Welsh call Lavabread – apparently, it's a type of bloody seaweed. He got it started then took his eyes off it to have a ciggy, not realising he hadn't allowed enough clear space between the stove and the grass. Next thing you know, blamm!"

"Yeah, the whole place goes up... including our tents and supplies," said Archie. "Twat is right. Shit, he's coming our way."

They fell silent as the giant red-haired man approached. "All right, boys?" he said, arriving at their table with a tray in his hand. "Room for a little one, is there?" Without waiting for a reply he squeezed himself in between Clive and Stoney.

The new arrival's tray was piled high with mash, veg and a large chunk of steak and kidney pie. There was also ice cream, a chocolate bar and a couple of cans of some fizzy substance. Clive couldn't resist a small dig. "I heard you'd eaten enough for one day," he said.

"Aww, you trying to be funny, butt?" For a moment the Welshman pinned him with a glare which caught Clive off guard. He turned his hands into fists under the table. Then a giant hand came clattering down across his back, pushing him forward and nearly pitching him into his dinner. "Oops, sorry!" said the giant. He burst out laughing. "Don't know me own strength. Yeah, you're right. Wasn't the brightest move ever that fry-up, was it?"

Clive straightened up. "You can say that again! I lost my rucksack, my supplies, my uniform... even my soddin' tent."

The red-haired man coloured up again, though Clive wasn't sure whether it was through embarrassment or was just his natural state. "Sorry boys. Truly. You must think I'm a right thick Taffy bastard.

Rest of my platoon do, for sure. They've disowned me. What price loyalty, eh? That's why I've come to sit with you boys. Don't mind, do you? I've got to face the top brass tomorrow over the whole stupid thing, so don't be too hard on me. Where are you from, anyway?" He looked at Clive. "You sound like you hail from a long way south of Glasgow, boy."

"I'm from London; the East End," said Clive, accepting the olive branch. The Taff didn't seem too bad, all things considered.

"Really? I got relatives up there. Well, a sister, actually." He lowered his voice. "Tell the truth we had a lot of trouble in our family. Dad's a bit of an alkie, you know? She got fed up with it, see; ran away when she was 14. Haven't seen her since, apart from one postcard to say she was safe. It had a London postmark on it so I am pretty sure that's where she ended up. I went up there looking for her once, asked around the streets. Walked for miles, but it's a big place, isn't it? Not like Croesybont where I'm from. No luck."

Too much information, thought Clive. He had only known the bloke a couple of minutes and was already getting the life story. He didn't have the heart to ignore him, though. "That's a shame... about your sister," said Clive. "I've got a sister and a big brother. Like you say, London's a big place and it's home to a hell of a lot of runaways. Sounds to me like the girl doesn't want to be found. Anyway, what's your name, mate? I'm Clive, that's Archie on my right and you're sitting next to Stoney."

"Really good to meet you lads," said the Welshman, leaning across to shake each of their hands in turn. "My boys say you Scots Guards are a soft touch, but you look all right to me. I'm Elfin... Elfin Prince. Mates call me Elf... because of my diminutive stature I guess. Not that I've got many mates at the moment. Say, any of you guys play rugby?"

They shook their heads. "Oh, OK," he said, disappointed. "Well, I might not be any good at cookin' but I'm a pretty mean second row. Our company won the Forces Cup a few weeks ago. Smashed all and sundry. We're a well-oiled machine. I win the line outs..." In his enthusiasm he jumped from the bench to demonstrate, his arm snaking up as if reaching for a ball. Unfortunately as he did so a water jug went flying, sending soldiers leaping to their feet to avoid a soaking as others lifted their plates from the table in a vain attempt to protect their food from the dinner-time tsunami. "Oh hell," said the man they called Elf, his cheeks turning crimson again. "Me mam always says I'm a clumsy dufus. Sorry!"

Around him some of the Scots Guards didn't share in the joke, convinced the giant Welshman had been sent over to deliberately cause trouble. Some of the upset soldiers, their faces betraying their anger, moved forward intent on retribution. A giant nicknamed Nessie after the Loch Ness Monster pushed his way to the front, coming nose to nose with Elf. "You got a death wish, son?" he asked.

"Why?" asked the Welshman. "Are you Charles Bronson?"

As Nessie's head crashed into Elf the room erupted, tables and chairs flying everywhere. The Fifth Brigade bonding process had begun.

20

"THERE he is, boy!" Mo ploughed his way through the wellwishers waving flags in the sunshine of a cloudless afternoon in May. A huge crowd had gathered at the harbourside in Southampton to wish bon voyage to the 3,300 troops boarding the 70,000-ton luxury liner the QE2, which had been requisitioned by the Admiralty to ferry forces to the Falkland Islands.

"Oi, that's my foot!" objected one of those Mo had shunted aside.

"Some people... no manners!" muttered another.

Oblivious to their protests, Mo was focused solely on being visible to those boarding the ship. Scooping Chuck up in his muscle-bound arms, he placed the boy on his shoulders. Little fingers grasped his newly shaven scalp as the youngster shouted: "Uncle Clive! Look! It's us!" Mo changed direction, cutting diagonally through the crowd until he arrived at a barrier erected to ensure the progress of the troops wasn't impeded. Next to him a young woman smothered a teen soldier in kisses, holding on so tightly she looked like she would never let go.

"Heyyyy, there he is!" Clive Dolan appeared on the other side of the barrier. "Chucky boy! How is my favourite nephew?"

"Fine, Uncle. Are you going to kick some Argie arses?"

Clive laughed, switching attention to his older brother. "I wonder where he gets that sort of talk from."

"Beats me," said Big Mo, giving his sibling a hug. Splitting apart, Chuck was transferred from the shoulders of one brother to the other.

"How's the boxing, little man?" asked Clive.

"Great, Uncle Clive. You'll have to come and see me when you get back. I'll be ready for my first fight then."

"I'd love to see that, Tiger," said Clive, lifting the boy back over the barrier. He looked at his watch. "We've got a strict timetable," he told his brother. "Dad not here? Not surprised really. He's got enough on his mind."

"Sure," said Mo, "Must be tough running that mansion of his. I heard one of the servants rang in sick."

"Don't," said Clive. They fell silent, the full implications of what was happening taking hold. "We sail at 4," Clive said, breaking the silence. "It's going to be quite an operation stowing away everything we need by then."

"Shit," said Mo. He brushed something from his eye. "I never thought it would come to this. I was sure them Argies would back down. I wish I was coming to keep an eye on you, you soft twat."

"Don't think I'm the soft one, brother," said Clive. "Look at you. I'm coming back you know. It'll be an adventure. It's why I signed up. I could have rotted away in bloody Dagenham for the rest of my sorry life, behind a supermarket checkout or, worse, sorting out the bleedin' stockroom. Now I'll see parts of the world I could never have dreamed of visiting before, and make new friends into the bargain."

"What, penguins?"

They both laughed.

"Maybe," said Clive. "You know what I mean, though. There are some right sound geezers on that boat, Mo. I'll have to introduce you to some of them when we come back... We'll probably get half way down there and they'll turn us around." He smiled, looking up at the imposing cruise liner which dwarfed those gathered on the quay. "See? I would never in a million years have been able to afford to go on the QE2 under normal circumstances, now I get to sail in her for free."

"I know, it's just... I guess we thought we'd won the damn thing when they sank that warship of theirs, The Belgrano," said Mo. "What was that headline in the Sun? 'Gotcha!' There's no doubt when that happened we thought we had victory in the palm of our hand. Then a few days later they sunk the Sheffield, and suddenly it was a real war. Still, you've got to have faith in the Marines and the Paras, don't you? Not to mention the SAS. Hopefully they'll have it won by the time you get down there and this will be a nice little holiday for you."

"Yeah," said Clive. "Shame they've taken off all the sunbeds and plonked bloody great helicopter pads on the front and the back, ain't it? There won't be much time to soak up the rays. There's talk we'll stay on afterwards to form the garrison. I might not see you for a while, so if you could stay out of jail in the meantime that would be good."

"I haven't been locked up in ages," Mo protested. "No danger of that!"

"Hey, Derek!"

Mo ignored the shout, but Clive turned his head.

"OK, Arch? Meet my brother Maurice," said Clive to a new arrival loaded up with kit.

The soldier leant over the fence and the two men shook hands. "Who's this?" The Scotsman pointed at the little boy.

"My nephew, Chuck," said Clive.

Archie dropped to his haunches and ruffled the boy's hair through the fence, then jumped to his feet. "Come on then, let's get on! Baggsy top bunk."

"Not convinced we'll have bunk beds, mate, but if we do you're welcome to it," said Clive. "You might want to swap for something nearer the ground, and the bogs, when those seas get pitching and tossing. Go on ahead and I'll join you in a minute."

Mo and Clive watched Archie disappear up the ramp. "He's a good bloke. One of the best," said Clive.

"Seems OK," said Mo. "Why does he call you Derek?"

"Oh, just a silly nickname. Long story."

"Never did like the Jocks though," said Mo. "Not since their bloody football louts broke the crossbar at Wembley."

"Never one to hold a grudge, are you?" Clive said. "That was five bloody years ago!" He gave his brother another hug then gathered up his gear. As well as the sizeable, heavy rucksack he carried a rolled up groundsheet over his shoulders, a metal case in one hand and a long pole in the other which Mo guessed was his weapon. Before he left he held his arms over the fence and Chucky ran into them. "See you soon, boy. I'll try to bring you back a souvenir. Be good."

"I will, Uncle Clive," said Chuck, smiling. With that Clive Dolan disappeared into the stream of young men heading off to war 8,000 miles away.

"HEY, it's Clive, isn't it? Clive, butty! Remember me?"

Clive Dolan turned from trying to spot his brother and nephew on shore to see a giant, red-haired figure pushing through the crowds on deck, leaving disgruntled fellow servicemen in his wake. "Oh, fuck."

"Don't be like that, man, eh?" said Elf. "Just wanted to say thanks for getting me out of that little scrape. You know, on the Beacons?"

"Yeah, well, you've said it now," replied Clive. "I'm not sure I should be talking to you. It didn't go down well with some of my platoon, that business in Wales. That big geezer, Nessie, hasn't spoken to me since. I'm starting to think you're bad for my health."

The Welshman's roar of laughter was so instantaneous it caused Clive to stumble against the ship's railings. "Bad for your Elf? I get it – good one!" said the Welsh guardsman. "Oops, sorry. Wouldn't do for you to fall in the drink when we haven't left land yet, would it? Still, that was a crazy night on the Beacons, eh?"

Clive nodded. "Haven't seen a good old-fashioned bar brawl like that since those Westerns I watched as a kid. I've got a feeling the scrap we're heading for will be a bit more serious than that."

"Agreed," said the Welshman, nodding. "But look around you." Clive followed Elf's gaze. As far as the eye could see, there were soldiers in uniform, filling the gangways and even occupying the lifeboats swinging from the side of the ship, desperate to get a last glimpse of their loved ones before setting sail for the unknown. The patriotic fervour reminded Clive of the worst excesses of the Queen's Silver Jubilee back in '77 when every street in the neighbourhood threw parties stretching long into the night.

Elf waved a hand in the air, knocking a fellow Welsh guardsman's cap off in the process and drawing an expletive from the victim. He mumbled an apology. "We've got the boys to give them Argies a right bashing," he said. "Cream of the crop here, and once we get together with the paras and marines there'll be no stopping us."

He was talking to himself. Clive stood at the railings, gawping at something on the shore. "Bleedin' Nora," he said. "Would you look at that!"

Elf followed his gaze. "Oh, nooo!" he shouted, his deep, gravelly Welsh voice attracting the attention of those around him. "That ain't bleedin' Nora,mun, it's bleedin' Kerry. Fuck!"

"Who?"

"That bird!" he said, pointing. A buxom brunette had whipped off her blouse and was happily waving a white bra over her head like a knight in armour wielding a mace, her assets on full view to the thousands of servicemen, the ship's civilian crew and the watching spectators lining the harbour.

"It looks like she's feeling the cold," Clive said, grinning. "Got a right pair of raspberries on her."

"Raspberries?" said Elf.

"Raspberry ripples. That's nipples in cockney," said Clive.

"Yeah, well I know about them first hand, you could say. That's my bloody fiancée. Always been a bit of a show-off. I thought she might have reined herself in given the circumstances. No such luck."

As the men on board the QE2 cheered and wolf-whistled, a crane operator intervened, swinging his jib across until the hook was in front of the exposed young lady. With the help of a couple of friends who held her tightly by the waist, she leaned out and hooked her bra on the machine. Accompanied by another rousing cheer the crane operator swung the boom across to the ship, where an eager young soldier removed the discarded piece of underwear.

"Hey!" shouted Elf, "that's mine, that is."

"Suits you," said a comedian in the crowd.

"I mean... that's my bird over there with the... y'know."

Another cheer went up and Clive couldn't contain his laughter as the giant Welshman turned crimson with embarrassment. Gradually, like a finely-tuned logistical operation, the bra was passed from hand to hand until it ended up in the clutches of its rightful owner. Pushing his way to the railing, Elf waved it in the direction of the extrovert Kerry, who had covered her modesty in a fake fur coat. Whether by pure coincidence or because the captain, too, had been monitoring proceedings, the ship sounded its horn three times.

"Five to four," said Clive, glancing at his watch. "It looks like we're loaded and ready to go. Say your last farewells, lads... next stop the Falklands."

21

SQUADDIES poured from the makeshift cinema in the bowels of the luxury liner, a hubbub of noise echoing off the metallic walls. "Wouldn't mind him on our side in a crisis," said Elf who, through sheer persistence, had become an honorary member of their little group.

"We've got enough nutters without Mad Max getting involved," said Clive.

"The more the merrier. An army needs nutters to get things done."

It had been a really good day and the boys were enjoying the banter. In fact, most days had been good ones aboard the QE2. They might have had to endure 6.30am starts, endless daily deck circuits and live firing at rubbish bags jettisoned from the ship, but it was a small price to pay to travel in such salubrious surroundings.

Clive had been given a guided tour of the ship by a volunteer crew member. He'd pointed out where rich holidaymakers usually soaked up the sun on varnished steamer chairs and reclining beds, and spoke of exotic paintings lining the walls. Though the luxury items were now in shore-side warehouses, stored with the expensive crockery and glassware, it helped Clive conjure up a picture of what it was usually like aboard the liner. Below decks, vast rooms where passengers once relaxed, reading books and sipping their gin and tonics, had been turned into troop dormitories, camp beds rammed nose-to-tail. As Clive's boots echoed off resilient, hardboard floors he was told that stretching beneath their feet lay hundreds of yards of luxurious carpet.

After eight days at sea some soldiers grumbled that they weren't allowed to disembark at Ascension, the small, volcanic island which British Forces were using as a half-way base camp. Clive wasn't bothered. It looked like a piece of floating charcoal, hardly the kind of place that served beachside cocktails while you lapped up the rays. He couldn't help feeling Fifth Brigade were far better off than those who had left earlier as part of Operation Corporate.

On only his second day at sea, for instance, he was shocked to discover the restaurant serving smoked salmon. When, at another sitting, caviar appeared on the menu, a commanding officer took it upon himself to enter the kitchen and advise staff their efforts were probably wasted on visitors who considered steak and chips the height of fine dining.

Any early animosity between the battalions washed away as they embraced their new environment. Who needed to fight when you were being treated to the latest films or, if you preferred, organised card evenings? Any friction that did exist was directed at card sharps like Archie for fleecing fellow squaddies. One victim even dubbed Archie "Robber the Bruce" as he casually counted out IOUs he had received from victims. Fortunately, there was a bank on board where they could replenish dwindling funds and for those who enjoyed a tipple, alcohol wasn't a problem. Each soldier was entitled to two beers a day, but one entrepreneurial character had set up his own booze black market and was never short of customers.

Clive and his mates had taken full advantage of this illicit trade earlier that day, standing on the upper deck sipping from cans and laughing uproariously as Elf and another unfortunate were covered in sticky meringue and ducked in the on-deck pool. Squaddies were told it was the way sea-farers paid their respects to King Neptune for ensuring their safe passage across the Equator. The Welshman had been "volunteered" because he was the youngest soldier on board and, watching him undergo the ritual humiliation, Clive almost forgot he was on his way to war. Unfortunately, the carnival atmosphere was cut short by threatening black clouds which forced them to retreat indoors.

It was no hardship. Mad Max 2 was showing on one of the big screens, an offer too good to refuse for the two Scots guardsmen and their Welsh buddy, who joined them after a lengthy clean-up.

Strolling on the quarter-deck after the film, Elf asked: "What are those guys doing?" He was pointing to an area known as the hub, which contained a huge wall map and a schedule of each company's daily activities. It was also the place where the latest news was pinned and Clive and Archie followed the Welshman as he shoehorned his way forward to where a group of other squaddies had gathered. The silence that prevailed instilled in Clive a sense of foreboding.

"Oh fuck! That's not good, not good at all." A platoon sergeant with the emblem of the Welsh Guards on his cap muttered as he started to walk away.

"What's happened Sarge?" said Elf.

The Sergeant stopped. "We're getting news over the BBC World Service. It's The Atlantic Conveyor, Private. They're saying it's been sunk by Exocet missiles. Damn things!"

Horror drained the faces of his audience. For a moment no one spoke. They knew the Conveyor, another ship from the Cunard line, was a key part of the battle group because it carried vital supplies.

Someone broke the silence. "Survivors?"

"Unknown. There was one hell of an explosion."

"What about the helicopters?" asked Clive. "I heard there were Wessexes and Chinooks on board. Harriers, too."

"We don't know," replied the Sergeant. "Hopefully they got them off beforehand. Remember, she left a full month before us. Mind you, losing those choppers would be a massive blow. We need them for disembarking. It could be Plan B now."

"What's Plan B?" asked Clive.

"Swim." The Sergeant turned and walked away. No one laughed.

FOR the next two days the luxury vessel weaved through stormy seas. For much of the time the passengers were shrouded in darkness, a full blackout ordered as rumours spread that they were a major enemy target. The civilian crew had to navigate their way through cloying fog without radar, a perilous job with giant icebergs lurking in the darkness.

As time passed, the weather worsened. Everywhere Clive looked there were soldiers clutching their stomachs and queuing for the nearest toilet. They didn't always make it in time and a cloying smell of puke hung around below decks, the jovial, holiday atmosphere long gone. The relentless rumour mill didn't help.

"The Argies have launched a major air offensive and our boys are sitting ducks."

"I heard a couple of Argie submarines are in this area, hunting for unguarded ships."

"One of the top brass was saying they've sent up spy planes with the specific instruction of finding the QE2 and pinpointing her location so they can sink us."

Morale was ebbing away fast, the soldiers desperate to reach dry land and carry out the duties for which they were trained. Even then, everyday drills were cut short because of the weather, leaving Clive and his friends feeling seriously under-prepared and vulnerable.

"COME on out, boys... it's bloody beautiful out yer." Elf's beaming face appeared around the door, his cheeks redder than usual.

"Looks freezing!" said Archie.

"Oh yeah, it's cold," said the cherubic Welshman. "Don't mind that though, mun, the sky is as clear as day. It's like a fresh winter's morning down the Worm's Head..."

"The where?"

"It's a beauty spot on the Gower peninsular in lovely West Wales."

"Of course it is," said Archie. "Just around the corner from the Slug's Entrails, isn't it?"

Clive followed the Scotsman out, his quilted jacket zipped to his chin and a woolly hat pulled over his ears. Elf's description was spot on. Cotton-wool clouds drifted high in a sky of pure azure, the caw of sea birds reminding Clive of holidays spent in the caravan at Clacton with Dad, Mum, Maurice and Cindy. A watery sun reflected off hills glistening with snow. They had arrived at Cumberland Bay off the island of South Georgia.

"Well I never boys, look; a welcoming party!" Elf pointed down into the calm waters of Grytviken Harbour. "Hello, old mate, how are you?"

Clive and Archie drew up alongside Elf and peered overboard, expecting to see soldiers clambering up the side of the ship. Instead there was a grey seal twisting and turning down below, his nose stuck in the air proudly as if he had saved his display of aquatic gymnastics just for them. "Amazing!" said Clive.

"I'm gonna call him JW," said Elf.

"Why?" asked Archie.

"I'm naming him after JW Owens, one of the greatest Welsh rugby players I ever had the privilege to see. He has the same twists and turns. Reminds me of JW's sidestep."

"Rugby's just cheating at football if you ask me," teased Archie.

"Best game in the world," said Elf. "I'll treat you to a Wales Five Nations game at the Arms Park when we return. England, Scotland, I don't mind. We'll take on all-comers and spank your arses as usual."

A cheer went up around them, the deck having filled rapidly since land was spotted, the mood far better than on previous days. Clive saw a boat was approaching, her whiteness standing out in the clear surroundings. The name Canberra was emblazoned across her hull.

"That'll be our transport," he said. "It's the end of the line for this beauty. As soon as we've cross-decked she'll be heading home. Can't risk her in the battle zone. Imagine if the Argies sunk her? That would be a huge publicity coup."

"I know that bloody ferry!" said Archie. "I cruised the Med in her with the school. I hardly expected to see her in these circumstances."

Above them, a loud speaker crackled to life. "Would all military personnel attend their muster station and report to their commanding officer. Cross-decking will begin at 1500 hours. From the staff of the QE2 and all at Cunard: it has been a pleasure and a privilege to serve you and we wish you every success in the coming weeks. Go get 'em, boys!"

A huge cheer erupted, followed by a round of applause. Someone near the bow shouted: "Three cheers for the QE2 and her crew. Hip, hip..." The "Hurray" in response was deafening. Looking overboard, Clive saw Elf's seal 'JW' twist one final time and head for quieter waters.

"See you JW," said Elf. "You're my lucky charm, you are."

As the three friends headed inside to prepare for disembarkation they failed to notice two figures huddled together on the Funnel Deck high above. The sun's rays glinted off the sniper rifle one of them was holding. "Right, son, pretend it's an Argie machine gun operator. Better still, you've got General bloody Galtieri in your crosshairs and this shot wins us the war. Take a breath, steady yourself, that's it... now, take him out." The pfft sound could have been caused by anything, the silencer doing its job. Where the grey seal had been, a red sheen now spread out across gently lapping water.

22

WEIGHED down by equipment that seemed determined to force him from the webbing, Clive carefully placed one foot after another as the ship rocked on an increasingly temperamental tide. All around him men similarly burdened clung grimly to nets, negotiating their passage to the minesweepers and tugs below. As a kid Clive had loved going wild at adventure playgrounds where the reward for his determination and perseverance was a nasty collection of scrapes and bruises. Those family adventures were conducted in pleasant, warm sunshine during the summer holidays. He would leave his brother and sister far behind as he swung across nets, ropes and zipwires, making it look so easy it was why Mo had given him the nickname Monkey.

At no stage had he attempted this kind of feat in below-zero temperatures, however, and all feeling had left his fingers long ago, his backpack seemingly weighed down with lead. His ability to balance wasn't helped by the heavy weapon he was carrying, along with the ammunition and temporary bedding strapped to him. Clive let his mind drift, thinking of alternative scenarios where he might have been warm. It would have been far easier to clamber on and off a helicopter, but that option had been sunk along with The Atlantic Conveyor. Now the two Guards battalions were being asked to cross-deck to the Canberra with the help of rigging and smaller boats, the Gurkhas following a similar procedure in making their way to the North Sea Ferry Norland, anchored somewhere on the other side of the QE2. It all seemed so primitive in this era of modern warfare.

A scream and a thump fractured the repetitive soundtrack of the cajoling wind. Someone had fallen. Clive prayed they had hit the deck rather than disappeared through the gap between the vessels. Anyone falling into the sea risked instant hypothermia and the chance of being crushed.

For Clive, bobbing around like a spider clinging to its web in a hurricane, the alarming sound served as a wake-up call, persuading him to focus more intently on his task. From above him the first snow fell. He peered skywards, marvelling at the beauty of nature as dazzling white flakes illuminated the blackened sky, only to be reminded of its perils when the frozen water crystals hit his face like sharp needles, impeding his vision. Looking down, he vaguely made out the lights of the tug he was trying to reach, the blanket of south Atlantic mist closing around him snuggly.

It was tempting to laugh at his predicament. Weeks ago he would never have envisaged a scenario where he would be clinging to a makeshift rope ladder attached to the side of one of the world's biggest cruise liners, in gathering gloom and temperatures well below freezing on the edge of the Antarctic Circle.

What would Maurice say? "You stupid sod. You said this was going to be fun. You need your fackin' head read." Distracted, his foot slid from an increasingly wet rope and for a second he hung by the fingers of one hand, the heavy rucksack coaxing him to surrender to gravity. He told himself to stay calm. After all, his refusal to let things faze him was supposed to be one of his biggest strengths. Perhaps life had been preparing him for just such a moment. Willing his pulse rate to remain steady, he swung rhythmically around until his right boot made contact with the rope, his free hand regaining a grip. The danger was averted.

He continued to progress down the webbing and, after what seemed like hours, hands guided him onto the deck of a minesweeper. "Sit over there soldier, take a breather, and wait for the rest of your company," he was told. Ignoring the instruction, he walked to where two medics were attending a groaning man. Clive could see his leg bent at an awkward angle, something glaringly white protruding from the shin. With mounting horror he realised it was a bone. One of the medics was telling the patient: "Look on the bright side, there'll be no yomping across minefields for you. It's broken, son. Before you know it you'll be back on the QE2 with your feet up, heading back to your loved ones. What did you say your name was?"

The injured man mumbled something.

"Oh, that's right. A few months and you'll be right as rain, Stoney. It may not seem like it at the moment, but you're one lucky bugger. You'll never have to point a gun at an Argie and your family will never have to welcome you home in a body bag."

The final leg of Clive's journey wasn't plain sailing either. Bouncing off the walls below decks he cursed, rubbing his arms as ugly bruises formed. Close by, hidden objects banged and crashed, the symphony conducted by gale-force winds using huge breakers as batons. The Canberra was better equipped for gentle climes like the Caribbean and the Med and didn't take kindly to being tossed around like a grain of crystal in a child's kaleidoscope. The mild weather that had greeted the soldiers on their arrival at South Georgia had lulled them into a false sense of security. Out on the open sea they were fully exposed to the worst the south Atlantic could throw at them.

"Bloody 'ell," said Elf, surveying the demoralising sight of ranks of soldiers laid low by sea sickness, moaning and groaning as they were pitched and tossed at the height of the storm. "We'll be lucky to reach the bloody war zone at this rate," he said. "What if we bump into one of those bloody icebergs, eh? It would be like the Titanic all over again... and that story didn't have a happy ending."

"Cheery soul, ain't you?" said Clive. "All I can think of is that with your track record we're lucky you aren't steering. How did you get here safely from the QE2?"

"Sea King," said Elf, "Very pleasant it was, too. Only took us a couple of minutes. Mind you, there was nowhere to sit and we had to hold on for dear life. I was lucky I didn't fall out of the door!" Clive nodded. Those alongside Elf had been far more fortunate to escape unscathed given his track record, he imagined.

The boat bucked, sending the Welshman tumbling, his size-13 feet scrabbling for grip. Clive watched helplessly as his friend clattered into a bench where another Guard was sitting, head in hands. The impact of a 6ft6in, 18-stone Welshman colliding with his shins wasn't welcome. "Fucking hell, mate!" Clive recognised the voice of the monstrous Scots Guardsman Nessie. Uh oh, he thought, more trouble. He needn't have worried. Nessie's immediate concern was bringing up the soup he had ingested when he first arrived on board Canberra. The bigger they are, the harder they fall, thought Clive, recalling the words to one of Big Mo's favourite records.

"YOU'LL be all right, boys, I'm sure of it."

"What about you?"

"Oh... you know..."

Clive didn't. The Welshman had been an endless source of amusement and positivity over the previous two months but seemed to be having a low moment.

"Come out on deck, mate... get some air. I want to have a look around at this prime piece of real estate we have vowed to protect."

"OK."

Clive pushed through the doors into a misty, rain-filled morning. Despite the weather, what he saw filled him with awe. Big ships, both Royal Navy and civilian, stretched for as far as the eye could see. Some near the mouth of the wide stretch of water known as Falkland Sound were warships, their guns primed to defend the Battle Group. "Now what's up, mate?" he said to Elf. "Still sea sick? Bit of a bumpy ride that."

"It's not that butt," said Elf, pausing as if unsure whether to share his thoughts. "It's just... well... I had a vivid dream last night. Spooked the hell out of me. I was on this boat see, and there was fire raging all around. It was baking, man, and I couldn't find a way out."

"Like the Beacons," said Clive, smiling.

"No mun, far worse." There was no trace of humour in Elf's eyes. "These flames wouldn't be beaten down. I tried the doors but there was no escape. It was scary. I hate fire. For the first time it got me seriously thinking... what if I don't return to Kerry?"

Clive studied the Welshman's face, ghostly pale and gaunt. "Don't talk like that," he said. "You'll be fine. You're a survivor. There aren't many would have escaped the fury of an entire battalion of Scots Guards."

Elf allowed himself a grin, though fear was still evident in his eyes. "I guess," he said. "Do me a favour, though, would you? See my Kerry if I don't make it. Tell her I was my usual happy, whacky self 'til the end."

"Tell her that yourself, mate," said Clive. "You'll be OK... don't forget your lucky charm."

"JW. Sure. It's just a seal, though." Elf undid the top buttons of his uniform, pulling out two rings on a chain and removing them from around his neck. He pressed them into Clive's hand. "They're our engagement rings," he said. "We agreed I should carry them into battle as a symbol she was by my side. I need you to look after them ... give them back to me in Stanley if I make it."

Clive pushed them back in his friend's direction. "This is stupid," he protested. "There's no guarantee I'll be any safer than you are, mate."

"Just humour a crazy Welsh boy would you, butt? If you drop them overboard by mistake I'll forgive you, no problem. I might expect a little, um, compensation but that will be the least of my worries, won't it? Giving them to you just makes me feel better."

Seeing his mate with a smile back on his face, Clive decided not to press the point. He slipped the chain over his neck. "Can I wear them like this?" he asked. "It seems best."

"Fine," said Elf. "Just fine."

23

June 5

"IT'S a shambles Jock." Clive stared down at the surf thrown up by the gently rolling waves. An eerie phosphorescent glow spread out from somewhere below HMS Intrepid, providing the only source of light in the darkness, a blackout in force to conceal the warship from enemy eyes.

"Nothing new, Derek," said Archie, putting an arm around Clive's shoulders and shaking him. "Always rely on the top brass to fuck it up."

"Yeah, but this is a war... you'd think if they were ever to get their act together it would be now."

"Mate, let me tell you something," said Archie. "I was told this ship was going to be sold off just before the war... to the Argies! That's the level of fuckwittery we're dealing with here. These people sit in their little bunkers with a drawing board in front of them, some pins and some coloured flags. It's like pin the tail on the fuckin' donkey – and we're the donkey's arse. Shame about Elf."

"Yeah," said Clive. "One minute he was coming with us, the next they changed their minds and kept the Welsh Guards on shore."

"Shambles is the only word." Archie looked to the skies as if British Battle Group headquarters was situated among the stars. "It wouldn't have been a problem if the ship was taking us all the way but someone blocked that, too. Decided this hunk of metal was too 'valuable' to risk."

"It's a bleedin' warship and we're at war," said Clive. "Surely this is the sort of job we brought it here for! We should be steaming full speed ahead to wherever we are needed, backed by air support, big artillery, the works. I'm sure the marines weren't treated this way."

"Too bloody right," said Archie. "Get what they want, that lot... cos they're Navy, I suppose."

"You know what narks me? Our leaders tell us they can't win the war without us then leave us to the mercy of the Argies. If we were needed that badly they would be making sure we got there pretty damn quick. How are we supposed to reach our destination?"

Clive noticed the twinkle in Archie's eye and instantly knew what was coming. "Jump, you fucker, jump... into the blanket we are holding..."

"... and you will be all right," Clive joined in, the words of the Derek and Clive tune embedded in his memory from the numerous times his Scottish pal had sung them. "He jumped, hit the deck, broke his fuckin' neck..." Shouting into each other's faces, they sang the pay off: "There waaaas no blanket!" Rocking with laughter, the humour helped Clive ward off a creeping sense of unease. There was something poignant about the words to the comedy song. They were about to jump off into war and there was no safety blanket in sight.

SOLDIERS crammed into four landing craft on the tank deck of the destroyer, faces locked in grim determination. The atmosphere was one of anticipation mixed with unease, none of them sure what they would face once the dock gates opened and they were jettisoned into open water. Wedged between sweating, jostling bodies, Clive almost gagged as a taste as strong as ammonia hit the back of his throat, the fishy scent of sea water overwhelming in the darkness. It was like being trapped in a moving, living straitjacket.

"If I could reach my rucksack I'd have a drink," he muttered in a vain attempt to break the tension. "Fuck, I'm knackered, feels like I ain't slept for weeks. Don't half miss the old QE2, even if it did mean sharing a dorm with 200 farting, snoring twats. Better than stealing a couple of minutes shut-eye here and there, waiting for someone to call you to arms. What time is it?"

Archie found just enough room to shrug his shoulders. "Must be four in the soddin' morning," he said. "No one should be awake at this time. Not us, not the Argies."

"Someone must be, though," said Clive. "That siren..?"

"Air raid red," said the Scotsman. "A false alarm I guess. I didn't see any planes, did you?"

"No," said Clive, allowing himself the flicker of a smile. "We all hit the deck quick enough, though, like a bunch of German footballers seeking a penalty... If it had been a Mirage or something we'd have been dead in the water."

Suddenly, the landing craft jerked violently and Clive grabbed his friend's arm to steady himself. "This could be it, Derek," said Archie.

In front of them the huge metal doors began opening, allowing sea water to flood in. Intrepid's engines were silent, her aft low, weighed down by 7,000 tons of water. Clive's stomach lurched as the swell increased, raising the landing craft higher and tossing it like an excited adolescent's bath toy. The four craft bashed against each other playfully in the confined space, Scots Guards and assorted other troops struggling to keep their balance. They were crammed together in the central well, each tasked with looking after specific items of equipment.

An officer began addressing them and they strained to make out the words amid the creaking of the craft, the slap of the swell and the wind grumbling in from open water. "This shouldn't take long," he said. "You've all got your life jackets? It's time to say goodbye to HMS Intrepid and do what we came here to do – kick the Argies off this island!"

There were murmurs of approval as Clive's craft bobbed through the dock gates and out into the eerie darkness. He could make out the silhouette of an island on one side of them and the hulking, awesome presence of the Intrepid on the other. He felt insignificant, small and vulnerable. There was no going back, the battalion now on their own, trapped in a tin can exposed to the unpredictable whims of nature. It was like being one of those crazy people who went over Niagara Falls in a barrel. The silence weighed heavy, others sharing the same worrying thoughts.

The low rumble of the Intrepid's engines cut through the silence and soon it was heading away, back to San Carlos water to rejoin the main battle group before dawn broke. In its swell the landing craft bumped against each other more vigorously. Pretty soon the warship was a dot in the distance and slowly the craft fell into line, forming an ugly convoy. Clive hunkered down, seeking protection from the bitingly cold wind. When the first icy breaker slammed against the side of the vessel, shooting up and over the well-packed deck, he gasped in shock. There was little time to react before the next one arrived, then the next one, the assaults becoming faster and more violent. It reminded Clive of an episode from his childhood when the dotty old bat who lived on the corner of their east London street unloaded a bucket of cold water over him because he had kicked his football against her wall.

An elbow clattered his ribs, an unsteady foot crunched down on his toes. In any other situation he might have fallen to the floor, but he was wedged solid in the over-populated can. It took mere seconds for him to become soaked through, icy tentacles wrapping themselves around his skin and squeezing the breath from him, his backpack dragging him down with the extra weight of the water. He heard gasps and moans, nature sapping the morale of his battalion quicker than any enemy could hope to do.

A thunderous rumble cracked the night air. Heads turned skywards and someone shouted "hit the deck". Clive ducked, wrapping his hands around his helmet, but no sooner had the mystery aircraft invaded their airspace than it had disappeared.

"I suppose a brew is out of the question?" said a fellow Guardsman in an attempt to break the tension. Clive longed for a warming cup of something to thaw his insides. He needed to sit down and unload the weight of the bergen, but there was just no room.

"What the hell?" He recognised Archie's voice, even though he had lost sight of his close friend amid the swaying, ducking and diving. "Blimey!" A cockney accent joined in. People were pointing to the sky where a pyrotechnic light show had burst into life, water fountaining into the air a few hundred yards away. "Shit! Argies?" asked a voice.

"Has to be," said another. "That or something set a mine off. We're the sole British presence in the area; the only show in town. There aren't supposed to be any of our ships, aircraft or land forces for miles around."

Like the aircraft, the explosions soon died, another mystery on a night full of such things. Plunged into darkness, the soldiers edged upright. "Hey, who's this?" said a voice to his left. Clive saw a body clamber over the side into their craft. He shuffled forward, pinning his ears back in an effort to glean snippets of information.

"Bloody radar's gone," the new arrival told the colour sergeant at the helm of their vessel. "I hold my hands up, it was my fault. I was turning it on and off to pinpoint our position and it just died. Any thoughts on the firework display?"

"Nah," said the colour sergeant. "The good news is we're roughly on course, but we've picked up these couple of blips, Major. Four miles astern."

"Heading our way?"

"Yes, and crossing the water pretty fast."

"Let's play possum," said the Major. "Head for Dangerous Point on the north east of the island. Lots of shadows. Dark and craggy. Probably our best and only chance."

"THIS is turning into an eventful night." The captain on the bridge of the type-42 Destroyer was the master of understatement. He looked at the four small blobs on his screen. Having just blasted an Argentine aircraft out of the sky with a Sea Dart missile, he was feeling chuffed with himself. "Any of our boys supposed to be around here?"

"Not that I know of," said his second-in-command. "It could be an Argie landing party planning a surprise attack. Should we take them out?"

"Let's get a bit closer."

"They're nearing the shoreline, Sir. Could be heading for Choiseul Sound. We'll catch them, though, they're only doing nine knots."

"Reel them in then, Number One. And let our pals on the frigate know what's happening. They might like to join in the fun."

"We need to make a decision pretty soon, though, sir. Those inlets aren't particularly deep. We don't want to snag her."

"Understood. Get the missiles ready. Just in case."

"WHOEVER this is they are coming at a rate of knots!" whispered the Colour Sergeant as the snub-nosed landing craft thrashed about on the unsettled sea. "We can't outrun them. They're bloody warships, unless I'm very much mistaken, and if what we have been told is correct they're going to be Argies. I'm at a loss..."

He tried to keep his voice down but the words were picked up by the nearby Guardsmen. Chinese whispers quickly spread around the 600 soldiers in the flotilla, with each reacting by reaching for a weapon and fitting a magazine. It was a hubbub of frenzied and uncoordinated activity.

"Nice knowing you." A hand gripped Clive's shoulder. He turned to see Archie, staring intently at him from under bushy black eyebrows. Clive grabbed his mate's shoulder in turn. They looked at each other for a few seconds, no words needed. Then the craft lurched again and a giant wave fell across them, breaking the contact. Focusing on his weapon, Clive was acutely aware of the absurdity of the situation. Would their guns even work after such a battering from the elements?

"This will be as useful as curling tongs at a skinhead convention," he whispered, looking down at the machine gun. If anyone heard, no one raised a chuckle. It might have been flippant, but most would acknowledge an element of truth in his remark. To fire a weapon in those conditions, with the rampaging sea tossing them about like balls in a bingo machine, would put those nearby in far more danger than the enemy.

THE bizarre nature of what he was about to do didn't register with the captain of the Destroyer. This particular war was so unconventional it made even the most hare-brained schemes seem logical. His gunnery officer stood with one hand held out in front of him, a coin nestling on the thumbnail. "Heads," muttered the captain.

The other man flicked his fingers and they watched the coin spin circles in the air, reflecting the lights from the control panel. It seemed to hang forever before landing back in the open palm of the officer, who closed his other hand over it with a slap.

"Give me the bad news then," said the captain.

"Tails, sir," said the Gunnery Officer.

"Remind me what that means again?"

"Illumination, sir."

"You're sure?"

"Yes, captain. If it was heads you said we would let them have it with the 4.5-inch guns; tails and we were to give them a warning."

"Hmm," said the captain. "We could do best of three, I suppose, but that would be wasting time. Let's pray we've got it right."

ABOVE the Guardsmen, six bright stars flashed against the charcoal background, then erupted. Some of them ducked for cover, while others kept their attention fixed on the sky, fascinated by the light display.

"We may be in luck," said the Colour Sergeant tersely.

"How's that?" asked the Major.

"They've sent us a message."

"Yeah, so how do you know..?"

"It's in English, sir. It says: 'Heave-to'."

"Might be a trick," said the Major. "I imagine a few of the Argies speak the lingo."

"He's just sent another. 'Friend' it says."

"Yeah, but friend to who?"

Silence crowded in around them as they waited for the warship to elaborate on the signal. Nothing happen. Minutes passed, the breath catching in Clive's throat as he strained to pick up any hint of what was to follow. The next firework display would probably be the last he would ever see.

A broad, Highlands accent broke the silence. "They're turning back, look! They must have been our boys all along."

A huge cheer went up, soldiers patting each other on the back as if by their willpower alone they had turned the heavily armed intruders away.

They would never know they had been saved by the toss of a coin.

24

June 8

"FOUND the perfect place," said Mo, shifting on the upturned crate. Around him lay boxes jam-packed with the proceeds of the Romford raid at Christmas. They had managed to offload some of the smaller merchandise like the jewellery, but the guns would take longer. None of them had the kind of contacts needed to move them and Mo's main hope was his old man might help once the heat had died down.

"Where?" said Cozza.

"Me and the boy went for a little trip around Kent and Sussex after we saw Clive off from Southampton," said Mo. "Tunbridge Wells looks good. I got talking to the locals... Hey, you listening?"

Head down, Handsome Frank was fiddling with the rifle in his hand, fascinated with his new hardware. Mo cuffed the ex-boxer around the head.

"Hey!" Frank protested, lifting the gun in a knee-jerk motion. Mo swept it aside, confident in the knowledge the weapon wasn't loaded.

"Don't ever point a gun at me again!" he said. "Jesus, Frank, it's not as if you're trained to use one of those. A few hours every weekend taking pot-shots at beer cans in a disused quarry doesn't qualify you as a candidate for Sniper of the Fackin' Year. If you were any good you would be in the Falklands with my brother. You ain't Rambo."

Frank glared at him. The ex-boxer's quick temper was legendary and had been on a hair-trigger since the day he lost his "good" looks.

Mo waited anxiously to learn if he had poured cold water on the flames or lit the blue touchpaper. Finally, with a sigh, his partner in crime put the weapon down. "Sorry, Mo," he mumbled.

"OK then," said Mo. "So this is what I learnt. Me and the boy went into this average-sized post office just outside the centre. It was quiet and the old postmaster had time to talk. He was quite taken with our Chucky, wasn't he boy?"

Mo looked over to where his youngest son lay on the floor in his school uniform, flicking small ceramic figures around a green cloth marked out like a football pitch. "Hammers are winning, Dad," the boy said. "Brooking scored."

"Good stuff." Mo returned his attention to his two colleagues. "Mad about that game he is, ever since the Hammers beat Arsenal in the FA Cup final last year. Our Clive took him to the Ipswich game down the Boleyn not so long ago, fackin' loved it, he did. Before he went away he gave Chuck his old Subbuteo game and the boy hasn't stopped playing it since. "

"Shame he missed football's golden age," said Cozza. From East End Jewish stock, Cozza's father had fled Austria before the Nazi Anschluss in the second world war. He could remember the outpouring of joy when he was a kid in 1966. It brought everyone in the East End together and beating the Germans had a special resonance for him. "The Hammers won the World Cup on their own: Moore, Peters, Hurst..."

They murmured agreement. "Sure," said Mo. "Forget football for now, though. So this postmaster bloke, right, he makes a right fuss over Chuck, gives him free crayons and a colouring book. We were shooting the breeze, talking about families and such, and he asked where I came from. I told him up St Albans way and he bought that. Then I told the geezer I was fed up with London because of all the fackin' immigrants and wanted out, so was thinking of moving the family down that way, grandad and all. I asked about all the normal things: Schools, house prices, pension days, social payments..."

"What was the feeling, Mo?" asked Cozza.

"The day they have most money on the premises is Wednesday, and that's perfect for us..." The other two looked blankly at him. "Oh, come on boys, wake up! What's happening on that Wednesday?" Still no response. "Football! England's first game in the soddin' World Cup, that's what."

"Rules that out then," said Frank. Mo's brow furrowed in confusion. "Well, we can't do the job and watch the game, can we?"

There was a moment's silence before Mo exploded. "For fack's sake! Are you really that thick? The idea is we do the job when the game is on. Everyone will be pre-occupied with the match – even the filth, hopefully – so we stroll in there and take 'em by surprise." He looked at their faces. Slowly a light seemed to go on behind Frank's eyes.

"Oh, I get you!" he said. "It's a plan I'll grant you, but I was really looking forward to that game."

"Right," said Mo. "Shall we do it on a day which suits you better? When can you turn up, Frank? Are you free Friday or are you doing your hair? Come on! I love my football, too, but surely you can see the merits. The 'compensation' for missing the match will be pretty substantial, and we can always watch the highlights."

"Probably miss them, too," said Cozza. "You know what London traffic's like?"

"That's the beauty of the thing," said Mo. "We ain't coming back to London... at least not for a while. I've been asking the old man's advice on this one and he's come up with a good idea. I've rented somewhere not far away, little place in Hastings. We can switch vehicles and lie low, wait for the heat to die down."

"Yeah?" said Frank.

"It becomes a family holiday," said Mo. "Take the birds down there, and the kids, and act like normal people, enjoying an English summer holiday. The key, though, is to be in and out fast, lose any unwanted attention. So we'll need a couple of vehicle swaps – cars left in certain places on the big day. Then we stash the gear, dump the guns and off we go: sand, sea, cold beers and, hopefully, a bit of sun."

"Don't push it," said Cozza. "This is England."

They laughed.

"Right," said Mo. "So Frank, we need more than one vehicle – and one of them needs to be legit."

"I'll borrow our Barry's," said Frank. "He's my cousin. Owes me a favour."

"We've got plenty of guns." Mo swept his arm around the room. "Cozza it'll be your job to plan the route. You'll need to work out where to park the cars so they don't attract busybodies. Also you need to find us somewhere to stash the goodies. Oh yeah, and you'll be the driver."

"I get it," said Cozza. "You two have all the fun while muggins here sits in the car like a neglected bloody dog. Hope you'll crack the window."

"You're the best driver Coz, you know that," said Mo. "They won't even give Frank a licence due to his eye injury. We need someone on lookout and I don't wanna bring strangers in... too dangerous. Plus, of course, you're carrying a bit." Out of the blue, Mo poked his friend in the stomach, sending him toppling off his crate. "I wouldn't fancy your chances of a quick getaway on foot."

"Bloody hell, Mo!" Cozza pushed himself up from the floor.

"Stop moaning... you're like an old bloody fish wife. One final thing..." Mo looked at each of them in turn. They were wary about what was to come, eyebrows raised, faces drawn. "Where are we bloody drinking?"

The tension in the room popped like a balloon, the three men erupting with laughter. On the floor, Chuck looked up from his game and wondered what the adults found so funny. Probably that TV show they all liked but he was never allowed to stay up and watch. What was it called again? Something to do with donkeys?

No, horses, that was it.

And fools.

THE three men rounded off the day in the 3 Wishes. It had a late music licence on a Thursday, the landlord Tommy Fordham fancying himself as a talent spotter keen to give up-and-coming performers their lucky break. The level of his success could be measured by the fact many of them were still headlining at the pub ten years later, though Tommy did boast one of his 'finds' played occasional session guitar for Rod Stewart.

The pub was busy, with no sign of the New Romantics who had caused Mo so much grief. Hot, sweaty bodies jostled for position at the bar, but gave Handsome Frank a wide berth when he approached.

"He's so ugly he could part waves," said Cozza.

Mo nodded. "We'll have to keep a close eye on him," he said. "Frank's on a short fuse and his lively temper could give us all sorts of grief."

"Sure thing, boss," said Cozza. "Is there any way..."

"We can do the job without him? Not a chance! Let's face it, that ugly mug's an asset. One look from him and even the toughest postmaster will give up the combination to his safe. He's good at blagging cars, too. A few contacts he made in the fight game help him out."

"He frightens me at times," said Cozza. "He ain't the full shillin'."

Mo checked Frank was still out of range. Reassured by the sight of the fighter deep in conversation with the landlord, he said: "Look, he's one of ours. He's like family. We went to school together, got into scrapes: hell, remember those detentions? Frank setting fire to the bloody library? We did everything for each other bar wipe each other's arses. We can't just ditch a mate because he's struggling."

A series of full-blooded guitar chords interrupted conversations everywhere. There was a whine of high-pitched feedback. The two men looked up. A guitarist, bassist and drummer were squeezed onto the small stage, bookended by amplifiers. The audience gave wolf whistles and shouts of encouragement. Mo vaguely recognised the song. It had been a hit for that punk group Blondie and their sexy minx of a singer Debbie Harry. He'd always had a soft spot for her... or maybe hard spot was a better description.

Frank handed Mo his pint of pilsner snakebite, a mixture of strong lager and cider. Standing, Mo turned to face the stage and nearly spat out his beer. The band had been joined by a fourth member, all blonde hair, heavy make-up and ripped black stockings, the outfit topped off by knee-length leather boots. Spellbound, he watched Audrey snarl menacingly at an enthralled audience. He didn't think she had noticed his presence until her finger pointed in his direction, her heavily rouged lips spitting out a message just for him. "One way or another... I'm gonna getcha, getcha, getcha, getcha."

"Bloody hell, that bird fancies you," said Frank. "And the feeling might be mutual... put your tongue back in fella."

"Eh?"

"I don't think it will reach from here... know what I mean, Coz?" The third member of their group rose to his feet. "I'd give her one!" he said.

"Shut it!" Mo's angry glare took them by surprise.

"Woah, sorry boss!" said Cozza. "I didn't know..."

"You don't know nothing, right!" said Mo. "I'm just enjoying the band is all."

"OK, OK," said Cozza. "Another?" He indicated Mo's pint glass, three quarters of the snakebite having already disappeared.

"Sure, OK." Calming down, Mo watched the band. Audrey was now on her knees, the guitarist standing over her thrusting his instrument back and forth, simulating oral sex. Mo could feel heat rising within, overcome by a strange mixture of anger, lust and jealousy. "It's just a performance, that's all," he told himself. "She's yours, but not yours, and that's the way you want it. That's what makes her so desirable." It took all of his willpower to refrain from charging the stage, grabbing the guitar and breaking it over the spiky-haired cunt's head.

"DO you always take your work home with you?"

Mo stepped out in front of Audrey as she walked arm in arm down the lane with the spiky-haired band member. They were chatting so animatedly about the evening's performance they hadn't noticed him.

"Oh," she said, stopping in her tracks. "Mo, meet Dan. He's..."

"I know who he is," said Mo, his voice a low rumble. "I'm just wondering where he thinks he's going."

"What's the problem, man?" said the guitarist, letting go of Audrey and stepping forward. He was a thin bloke, his stringy figure wrapped in drainpipe black jeans and a ripped vest-top, the words Siouxsie and The Banshees spewing across it in anarchic type. A leather jacket hung from his finger, resting over his shoulder. Mo could smell marijuana. He stepped forward to meet the challenge, one fist cocked, Reg hanging at the ready by his side. Before he could strike, Audrey stepped between them and turned to address the musician.

"Fuck off home, Dan," she said.

"What?"

"You heard."

"You're going with..."

"You wouldn't understand. I'll give you a bell, yeah."

"Oh fuck you very much," he said. "See you around."

Turning, he headed back in the direction of the pub.

"So?" said Mo.

She punched him. Hard. In the face. He felt the blood dribble from his nose. Wiping it away slowly with his hand, he took time to gather his thoughts. Fuck! It made him horny.

"What's it got to do with you?" she stormed, raising her voice. "He's a friend and you've just fuckin' damaged our relationship and the band. He's a good bloke and all you want..."

"Are you fuckin' him?" He wiped the blood on his jeans.

"What?" There was a moment's hesitation before the question sank in. "No! We're mates like I said. I can't expect you to understand that."

"Maybe not, but I know blokes and unless he's a raving homo I'm pretty sure his sole intention is to get inside your knickers."

"Not everyone's like you, Mo," she spat. "You're a bloody animal."

He charged. "Animal, am I?" Grabbing her by the hair, he pulled her head back and clamped his mouth on her exposed neck. She groaned and pulled his head away before clattering her mouth against his, the blood dripping again as his nose clashed with her cheekbone. His hands grasped her buttocks and she lifted a leather boot, clamping it to his hip. His fingers drifted up between her legs, finding the sweet spot where thigh and stocking met. Lingering there for just a second, he moved on quickly to rip away her pants, biting her ear to illicit a yelp, then a gasp. The sounds made him hard, so hard.

"That's right!" she wheezed, breathless. "Go on then. Take what you fuckin' want. You always do." He heard the zip of his fly, then a cold hand grasped the heat of his inflamed libido. "Fuck me bastard!" she shouted, wantonly pulling him into her.

"PUT the TV on if you want... I'm going to bed." The words were delivered coldly as Audrey disappeared into the bathroom. She was still upset with him, though the sex had been electric. Afterwards, she had continued to hound him over his actions. If he really wanted her exclusively, she said, it was about time he showed it. She deserved better than to be treated like a cheap tart, the easy lay he could forget once he had shot his load. Couldn't he see? For all the shit he gave her, she loved him. She couldn't help it.

The revelation kicked him in the solar plexus, winding him in a way few street brawls had. It reminded him where his priorities lay. He should be home with the family. This was new and dangerous territory.

He was toying with the idea of calling a cab when she re-entered the room dressed in a nightie with a cute Disney character on the front. The contrast between hot rock chick and vulnerable young girl reinforced his guilt. "By the way, you left these," she said, throwing a small bundle at him. A pair of socks.

"Oh... thanks."

The bedroom door slammed, Audrey leaving without a goodnight kiss. He would let her brood. He had lost control and needed to get it back. She was messing with his head, and he sensed it was deliberate. He opted to drown himself in the banality of late-night television.

Twisting the switch on the 18inch portable black and white set, for a while nothing happened. Then a picture slowly emerged, plagued by interference, the sound muted. Mo played with the attached aerial, wiggling it until he obtained some sort of picture. As the snow cleared and things came into focus, a muffled voice emerged from the white noise.

Peering at the screen through the murky effects of six or seven snakebites, Mo thought the figure on set looked like the strait-laced headmaster who had expelled him from Barking Comprehensive. The civil servant-type had become a familiar figure on TV with his black hair severely parted on the left side and those large, square National Health specs balanced on his ski-slope nose. His deadpan monotone suggested he was delivering the shipping forecast rather than announcing issues of life and death.

Mo remembered him imparting news of Britain's first major war casualty, HMS Sheffield, in the same way he might read a shopping list. So many dead, so many injured, how many missiles fired, how many hit the target. The bloke was a Ministry of Defence lackey named McDonald and when he first talked mundanely about Exocet missiles, little did Mo know the phrase was soon to become one of the most used in the English language. When Beryl had informed him some of her mates actually "fancied" the bloke, Mo was amazed. He had asked her what fun they thought they would have with "a bloke who could send the speaking clock to sleep". She had shrugged, saying there was no accounting for taste.

Mo realised he was missing the point of the story and his mind switched to his brother. He turned up the volume as the MoD man handed over to a military general with a chest full of medals.

"At 2pm local time today in Port Pleasant, just off Fitzroy on the East Falkland Island, Royal Fleet Auxiliary ships the Sir Galahad and Sir Tristram were attacked by a formation of Argentine Sky Hawks. At the time the ships were unloading troops, many from the Fifth Infantry Brigade, including a substantial number of Welsh and Scots Guards. Two bombs struck the Sir Tristram and failed to explode but caused enough

damage to produce fires and extensive damage. The Sir Galahad was struck by three bombs, all on the starboard side and, though some again didn't explode, the ship was severely damaged. It is with deepest regret that I have to tell you that we have established 22 people were killed in these attacks, and we are expecting the number to rise as more information becomes available. There will be further bulletins throughout the night."

Mo turned off the TV and stared at his reflection in the screen. For the first time in his life he was scared out of his wits. Once again, he was in the wrong place at the wrong time and, though he didn't have a religious bone in his body, he said a silent prayer. Maybe God would forgive his misdemeanours and keep his brother safe, if it wasn't too late. "I warned you, Monkey, you stupid sod," he mumbled to himself. Reaching for his coat, he threw it over his arm and headed home.

25

MOUNTAINS of impenetrable black smoke blotted out the sky, jagged flames ravenously licking at their base. Clive stared down on the vision from hell, a symphony of detonating explosives assaulting his ears.

Minutes earlier he had been standing in the same spot, high on the hillside, appreciating the idyllic scene as the weather belatedly took a turn for the better in the south Atlantic. A pale sun had emerged, the sky bright and decorated with wispy clouds, bringing to mind carefully crafted drawings on an infants' school wall. Below him the Royal Auxiliary ships Sir Galahad and Sir Tristram bobbed on the gentle swell of Port Pleasant Bay as those on board began unloading their equipment.

His thoughts had been disturbed by the buzz of angry insects and when Clive looked over his shoulder, he spotted five black dots on the horizon. As they filled out, he realised they weren't insects but aircraft approaching at surprising speed. When a voice shouted "Take cover!" The full horror of what was about to happen struck him. He jumped into a ditch as the buzz grew to a roar, his ears assaulted by the sounds of low-flying Argentinian A4 SkyHawk jets homing in on their target.

As they passed overhead, soldiers rose to their feet around him, letting loose with machine gun fire, but it was too little, too late. What they really needed was one of the imposing anti-aircraft Rapier guns, but a series of technical glitches had put them out of action.

Clive emerged from his hiding place in time to see the enemy skim the shore, rise up then swoop on the unsuspecting ships like angry birds from that famous Hitchcock movie. A series of dazzling flashes were followed by booming explosions, resonating around the hills. Clive held his breath, hoping the jets would now return to base, but they circled around for a second attack.

This time the Sir Galahad erupted in flames – the smoke spreading like an ink stain on blotting paper sky, obscuring the ships from view. Clive put a hand to his throat and gripped the wedding bands his friend Elf had passed into his care. Hope and prayer was all he had left.

BELOW decks on the Sir Galahad, Elf and his platoon were squeezed onto the narrow tank deck, making a final inventory of their gear, when the planes struck. The Welsh Guards were grouped around piles of ammunition, backpacks, rifles and webbing stored higgledy-piggledy in the centre of the confined space. Bored with being cooped up on ships far longer than they needed to be, they had been doing their best to amuse themselves. To his left Elf had heard the shout of "get in" and turned to see a dark-haired lieutenant jumping to his feet, waving his cards in the air.

"Air Raid Red!"

The alert burst from the tannoy just as a huge fireball pierced the outer casing of the hull and rolled at incredible speed through the deck. Elf flung himself to the wall, making as thin a target as possible. Heat singed his eyebrows and penetrated his skin and, looking down, he was stunned to see his jacket in pieces on the floor, flames lapping its edges. Jerking his foot into action, he stomped them out, a futile gesture when the entire area was ablaze.

There was a series of staccato pops and whistles and he stood mesmerised as a bullet flew out of the ammunition dump and buried itself in the eye of the card game winner. Elf saw the look of stunned disbelief on the lieutenant's face before his head collapsed in on itself and his body fell in slow motion, disappearing beneath thick black smoke. Sounds guided Elf now: the fast-paced ping, ping, zingedy ping of bullets hitting the metal walls, the reverberating thump of igniting grenades, the falsetto screams of soldiers stripped of arms and legs and other parts of their anatomy which made them uniquely human, the dull thud of torsos hitting the deck. He choked on the savage aroma produced by a strange concoction of gunpowder, paint fumes and cooking meat. Moving quickly lest he lost the ability to breathe, he covered his mouth with his girlfriend's bra, which he'd been carrying in his pocket for good luck. He smelt the intoxicating aroma of her favourite brand of perfume and for a moment felt calm.

Everything was surreal and random. Those with whom he had trained, eaten, slept, argued, played rugby and, on occasion, fought, were being picked off by their own ammunition. They were suffering terrible injuries and, in many cases, horrific deaths. He knew that if he didn't move quickly he would join them.

As the smoke cleared, a ghostly figure beckoned to him from a doorway. Relief flooded through him as he saw an escape route from the burning carnage. Before stepping through the gap, though, he caught sight of another figure, frozen in shock against the bulkhead. It was the giant Scotsman Nessie and, realising every second was vital for survival, it was only his in-built sense of fair play and honour which made him hesitate.

"Nessie, boy... come on, mun, Nessie!" His pleading seemed to fall on deaf ears. Looking into the pale blue eyes, he feared the man's mental faculties had deserted him so, reaching out, he grasped for the figure in the same way he would a fellow rugby forward in a scrum. Nessie refused to move. "Fuckin' 'ell, mun, come on!" he urged, yanking more sharply. "Shit!" The full enormity of Nessie's plight registered. Elf almost puked. It wasn't that the soldier wouldn't move it was that he couldn't, the paint on the bulkhead having melted and glued his head, hair and skin to the metal like napalm. Finally, his eyes locked with Elf's, desperation writ deep, and the Welshman knew there was nothing more he could do.

Turning to escape the floating torture chamber, an arrow-shaped piece of shrapnel which had once been part of a grenade ploughed into Elf's chest with such force it pierced his heart and exited his back, exposing blood, guts and gristle to the outside world. Mouth frozen in the shape of an O, his final breath departed with a rush from his lungs. He was dead before his body hit the floor, his girlfriend's undergarment still clutched in his fist.

CLIVE spent all day at the hastily constructed medical facility in Fitzroy Community Centre, watching the Sea Kings drop off survivors. He saw sights that would remain scorched on his memory forever. Burn victims, their faces unrecognisable, flesh hanging off them, screamed as the morphine failed to mask their pain. Others missing arms and legs drifted in and out of comas, as yet unaware of the impact the injuries would have on the rest of their lives. Screaming, bleeding survivors littered the floors, having to wait while medics prioritised cases. Hard-looking infantrymen cried out for their mothers while others stood dazed, having walked up from the shore after being delivered by boat. On the edge of the room, figures stood with their burnt hands in drums of cold water. Clive noticed one casualty, his mind a jumble of conflicting thoughts, walking around with his hands in the air, as if he had been captured by the enemy.

At one stage when Clive was helping to carry a stretcher, a voice croaked, "I know you" in a Welsh accent, but when Clive whispered the name "Elf" there was no response. By the time night fell, Clive had sought out every victim, asked questions of most medics and officers, and still hadn't found his friend.

Despite the lack of daylight, down in the bay the brave helicopter pilots continued risking life and limb, diving beneath thick blankets of smoke and materialising some time later with a swaying figure dangling from a winch. Each time Clive's optimism rose only to take a dive when he discovered Elf wasn't among them. When the captain of his platoon turned up and told him he was needed back at base he was forced to abandon the search.

"We've just had our orders and I need to go through them with everyone," the captain explained. "It seems we're going to play a major role in the liberation of Port Stanley."

26

June 13

THE womp, womp, womp split the freezing air, helicopter blades beating out their rhythm from the top of the isolated ridge. The tension sat on Clive's chest like a dumbbell, his breathing shallow, wisps of vapour escaping his mouth as he ducked low and ran for cover. This was the moment of truth, and every one of the second battalion of Scots Guards knew it; A moment that, when you joined the Army, you wondered whether you would ever see.

Clive had daydreams about playing the hero, storming an enemy position and firing a machine gun from the hip. It was during the night that his subconscious played him the alternative scenario, his cold body lying alone, dead in a ditch on these Godforsaken islands. Often he woke with his blankets saturated in sweat which, for a brief moment, he imagined was blood. He had been trained to kill and told in no uncertain terms the alternative was to be killed. Here, in this bitter wilderness, he and his fellow guardsmen would put that training to the ultimate test.

The Lieutenant-Colonel had given them a rousing speech before despatching them to battle, reminding them what they fought for and why. "This regiment has a proud tradition," he had said. "Many of you have fathers, uncles, grandfathers, even great-grandfathers who proudly wore the uniform and beret of the Scots Guards. At home, you can be sure that everyone is praying for you to succeed.

The people we are here to liberate have families just like yours. They consider themselves British to the core and their lives have been turned upside down so that some gung-ho South American Generals can make a political point. They expected us to shrug our shoulders and carry on. But the British aren't like that and Her Majesty's Forces aren't like that. We will defend our own and fight tooth and nail for the right of these people to determine their own destiny.

"We are a family. We live together, sleep together, eat together and train together. Tonight, we fight together. It is that camaraderie and kinship that will see us through. And, of course, our training. If you find yourself paralysed in the moment, fall back on what you have been taught and it may save your life. Remember, you're fighting for the people of the Falkland Islands, Her Majesty The Queen and the reputation of the Fifth Battalion and the Scots Guards. Leave nothing on the battlefield."

Comprehensive instructions had been issued to each platoon as they were despatched by Sea King or Chinook helicopter to the thick of the action. Now Clive and Archie sat under a small shelter below a craggy and barren hillock, waiting for the order to advance onto Mount Tumbledown. On the higher crags lay a crack squad of Argentine Marines who had been dug in for three months, determined to provide an impenetrable final barrier to Port Stanley. "If you come across any soldiers you don't recognise, the codeword is 'Hey Jimmy'," the Lieutenant-Colonel advised them. "You say 'Hey Jimmy' back. The Argies struggle to pronounce the letter J so you should be able to establish who is friend or foe by the reply."

NIGHT folded around them as dark and restrictive as a body bag. The first snow tumbled from the darkness, nature's syringe injecting ice into their battered souls. The distant rumbles of fire-fights surrounded them, seemingly taking place in a different world from theirs. Clive secretly hoped the Argentines would surrender before his company advanced, then inwardly admonished himself for his cowardice. Though he knew he would be risking everything to raid enemy positions, the alternative was to return home a sham, a spectator who had sat on his hands and done nothing as others died. He turned to his best friend. "What would you be doing at home now, Jock?"

"What day is it, anyway?" asked Archie. "Not that it matters back in Pitlochry. Nothing ever happens."

"It's Sunday."

"Och, in that case it's easy," said the Scotsman. "I've friends at a nearby hotel – get lots of English in there plus a few Yanks, Aussies and Kiwis trying to trace their Highland ancestry. Normally they have a quiz night on Sunday, and all the locals turn up to take on all-comers."

"Bit like here then," said Clive, smiling. "What do your folks do – for work, I mean?"

"They own a salmon farm. Provides some of the best fish you can ever imagine. Just landed a big contract with one of the supermarket chains so there's gonna be money in it. They've asked me to play a part when I get back. They aren't getting any younger and want someone to keep the family business going. As a kid I loved salmon fishing, used to go out into the rivers in these bloody great waders..."

He fell silent, his mind drifting.

"Sounds great," said Clive.

The two men made a token effort at warming themselves, blowing on the tips of their freezing fingers. "No quizzes where I live," said Clive. "Someone would be on their toes, stealing the prizes before the final question! To be honest, I'd most likely be down one of the local boozers with my brother playing cards, brag or something... or maybe shooting pool. Just a normal, quiet ..."

"Right lads!" the bark came from a Major who appeared in front of them, his face back-lit by the pyrotechnics of war. His eyes gleamed with manic intensity as he affixed a bayonet to his rifle. "This is the big one. Get as much ammunition as you can carry – make sure your rifles are loaded and be careful. On my command you will follow me onto Tumbledown."

There were murmurs and nods of assent. Clive and Archie joined the queue waiting to cross the white tape affixed to the rutted ground, like the starting line on an athletics track. The battle was about to commence.

"DOWN!"

Clive buried his face deep in the peaty earth, unaware of the reason for the warning. The shout had come from up front as his platoon clambered over rocky crags towards the summit. Lying flat, he was suddenly assaulted by clumps of grass and clods of earth concealing missiles of jagged stone. Gravel pebbledashed his helmet, then something hot seared into his shoulder, a burning smell alerting him to the fact his uniform was on fire. As his lips formed in prayer the world turned dark and beside him a faint cry of anguish reminded him he was still alive. The fetid air carried clogging smells of cordite, earth, smoke and human excrement.

The mountain shook as if a huge, angry monster had awoken beneath the surface. From other directions came more cries, moans and the odd, teeth-jarring scream. Slowly, Clive lifted his head and rolled over to extinguish any lingering flames. He saw trails of colourful tracer painting patterns on the blackened canvas above until there was barely a spot left untouched. Even when he shut his eyes the images remained, stored on his retina. Bangs and blasts rendered giant cracks in the night air, reminding Clive of a moment in his childhood when a thunderstorm shook the family home so badly the lights were extinguished, only to come back on when he was nestled safely in the bed of his older brother. Off to his right there were more explosions, mortar fire raining down from on high, while the chatter-chatter-chatter of gossiping machine guns competed with the deep-throated boom-boom of the artillery support provided by Royal Navy frigates HMS Yarmouth and HMS Active, stationed off the coast to pound the Argentine positions with their 4.5 inch guns.

Putting his hands over his ears to protect them from the assault on his senses, he caught sight of Archie lying face down. His friend wasn't moving and a feeling of dread settled on Clive's shoulders. Then he saw an arm paw the ground and, lifting his rifle, he raced across the rocky terrain, keeping his body low. "Mate, mate... Jock ... you OK?"

"Would you look at that bloody thing, Derek!"

A mixture of joy and relief flooded through Clive to hear the sound of his friend's voice. Where Archie was pointing he saw a large piece of strangely shaped metal poking through the earth's surface, like a whale's tail after breaching. "Is that..?"

"Bloody mortar shell. Too right. Nearly did for me, pal. It's only this soft earth that stopped it from exploding. Fell about 6ft from me. If it had gone off I'd be a goner."

Both of them fell silent, reflecting on the lucky escape.

"Come on lads, keep going," said their platoon captain, sweeping past them and heading up the hill. As they watched, staccato machine gun fire burst out again and, simultaneously, the captain fell. It was such a theatrical dive both men laughed before realising he hadn't moved. They were about to clamber after him when they were forced to cover their heads for protection, a new form of death-inducing horror heading straight for them.

It wasn't an explosive, though. It was a leg. It tumbled foot over stump towards them, army boot still firmly affixed, though the clothing covering it had been ripped to shreds. Blood splattered Archie's face as it hurtled between them at speed on its way down the hill. Eventually losing momentum, it hit one of the crags and keeled over.

"Fuck!" said Clive.

Ahead of them they heard a plaintiff cry. The injured captain was wheeling around in frantic circles. "My leg, where's my leg? Help me, help me, anyone seen it? I can't find my fuckin' leg."

Clive voided the contents of his stomach. Looking up, he saw tears mingling with the blood splatter on Archie's horrified face. Around them, the cacophony of battle was unrelenting.

FOR three hours, Clive and his company were pinned down by the onslaught. They moved forward by inches only to retreat by feet when the next round of incoming fire arrived. To make matters worse, the fire laid down by their own side sometimes fell short, representing as much a danger to them as the enemy shells.

"Gather up anything you can, men," said the Major. "We need every weapon we can get our hands on. Some machine guns would be nice, also bullets, grenades. Don't leave anything we can use on the battlefield. I know some of your mates have fallen, but they would want you to win this war so if they have anything of use don't stand on ceremony."

"Sir?" The interruption came from a second lieutenant.

"What is it?"

"Up on that ridge," said the second lieutenant, pointing. "There's a sniper giving us real problems. He's dug in on the higher ground but I reckon a small team could get to him."

"You volunteering?" asked the Major.

"Yes, sir," said the Second Lieutenant.

"OK, pick some men."

He made his selection, leading a small group off to his left.

Clive rubbed his arms vigorously, attempting get the circulation flowing. The South Atlantic winter was now at its most fierce. "What's the time, Jock?" he asked.

Archie lifted his sleeve. "Three in the soddin' morning," he said. "If we don't move soon it will be dawn, and God knows where that will leave us... we'll probably have to do it all again tomorrow."

"Shit."

They looked grimly at each other, waiting for something to break the stalemate. Time lapsed. Another ten minutes, 15, 20.

"Eh English pigs, you pigs, we turn you into sausage, pigs."

They whirled around, grabbing their weapons, looking this way and that, trying to establish the source of the voices. There was the rat-tat-tat of laughter, the person responsible sounding like he might have a bronchial problem, the slither of footsteps on wet grass. "We slice you in two, motherfucking bastards," said a voice from a different direction. "We fuck your mothers, too! We rape your fucking sisters. Las Malvinas son Argentinas!"

It was pretty obvious what the last chant meant: The Argentines called the islands The Malvinas. Their abuser was claiming that the Falklands belonged to them. Clive felt rage burn inside him. Not content with forcing him to travel 8,000 miles to endure appalling weather and live in conditions unfit for the most resilient animal, the bastards were now taunting him. He wanted to stand up, rush the Argentine trenches and make the arrogant wankers pay for their disrespect. He pushed against the wet grass, only for Archie to pull him back by the shoulder.

"Don't you see?!" he said. "That's what they want."

"It's what they are going to get: Bastards!"

"I know, but wait. Listen."

"I don't hear anything," said Clive.

"Exactly. No machine gun and no sniper fire. I reckon those boys have done it."

There was a whistling sound overhead and a mighty explosion in the vicinity of the Argentine trenches. It was followed by another and another, deafening noise shredding the night air again. There was the sound of retreating footsteps, urgent, their Argentine tormentors making for the high ground and what they hoped was cover. In front of the Scots Guards fires were burning and around them came the sound of screams but no return fire. After another two salvoes, the big guns fell silent.

The Major stood facing his men, legs apart, rifle held across his chest. "Are you with me, Jock?" he shouted at the top of his voice to make himself heard. There was a brief, uncomfortable silence, then Archie stood. "Aye, sir, I'm with ye!"

"Me too," said Clive. "With you all the fuckin' way, sir!"

Within seconds, everyone was shouting back.

"Let's do this, then," said the Major. "Fix bayonets, lads!"

Clive and Archie looked at each other, their eyes reflecting each other's anger and determination. Signalling for them to advance, the Major charged the hill, the two friends close behind. One of the first soldiers to reach the Argentine trenches lit up the scene with a phosphorous grenade before plunging over the side. Breathing heavily, Clive leapt the crag in front of him and plunged into the narrow drop, his boot connecting with a face, though he had no idea whether the victim was friend or foe, alive or dead. "Madre!" came a shriek from below and as the smoke cleared Clive saw a gun levelled in his direction. Finger already on the trigger, he shot the man then lunged forward, spearing another helmeted soldier in the chest with his bayonet, pleading eyes going dull as life ebbed away.

Without warning, a hand closed around Clive's neck and he felt a sharp point in the small of his back before the pressure eased and there was a splash. Turning, he saw Archie giving him the thumbs up, a dead soldier at his feet. "I just saved yer wee life, Derek!" he said.

Clive followed the Scots Guard in front, rising up and out of one trench into the biting wind and swirling snow, running across craggy rocks and tufted grass before diving into the next, smoke obscuring his vision as grenades exploded in front. Around him the noise continued unabated; the rat-tat-tat of guns, the screams, pleading voices and menacing declarations. "Take that ye Argie bastard!" The Guards tore through the trenches, momentum carrying them forward, no time to stop and think. Clive punched a man, shot a man, stabbed a man; everything was happening at breakneck speed, no end in sight. He didn't know how long it had been going on: seconds, minutes, hours.

Sucking mud dragged at him as he pulled himself from another trench, every muscle aching from the effort. Then he stopped abruptly. There were lights in the distance and trucks visible on the road below. Bedraggled, silhouetted figures tumbled down the hillside and away from the fearsome fighting and the wrath of the maniacal bayonet-wielding Scots.

With relief, he realised the Argentines were retreating in the direction of the flickering lights of Port Stanley. "Fuckin' hell, mate," said Archie, climbing up to join him. "I think we've bloody won! Jump you fuckers..."

"Jump," said Clive. The two men hugged, tears leaking from their eyes. They had been tested beyond human endurance but they had come through, looked the enemy in the eye and conquered him. As they parted, Clive stumbled backwards. "What the..?" He regained his balance and looked down.

"It's all right," said Archie. "Looks pretty fuckin' dead to..." He didn't finish the sentence. The body on the ground span onto its back, raising a gun and firing. Archie, face frozen in shock, dropped to his knees.

"Engleesh pig!" spat his killer. Clive's bayonet went straight through his eye, the steel making a squelching noise as he withdrew it then plunged it down again, this time spearing his mouth. "Scottish, you bastard... he's not English he's fuckin' Scottish," shouted Clive, a tidal wave of anger sweeping over him. He was unable to breathe, think or coordinate his functions. Struggling to pull the rifle free again, he stamped down on his victim's head, held his foot there and yanked, ripping the gun clear, the bayonet snapping in the process. Dropping to his knees, he grabbed the broken piece and plunged it again and again and again into the heart of an enemy who had drawn his last breath some moments earlier.

Behind him, Corporal Archie McAllum's lifeblood drained away into the crumbling soil and knotted grass of Tumbledown Mountain.

27

June 16

"YOU heard from the kid?" Cozza took his eyes from the road briefly, hoping he wasn't stepping out of line. Mo had been pretty volatile since the whole Falklands business kicked off.

"Got a call last night," said Mo. "Just a few seconds but Clive's OK. Lost a few mates, though. The line wasn't good, but he said the people of Port Stanley had been welcoming and he and some of the guys have been put up in the house of a local vet. Other than that, he seemed strange. Had no interest in the football...and you know how he loves his football."

"Give it time, Mo."

A head poked through from the back of the van. "Did I hear you mention the football?" asked Frank.

"We were talking about the Falklands. Frank."

"Oh, that. Fuckin' result, eh? Stuck it to them Argies good and proper... done and dusted in seven weeks. Walk in the park."

"You can't say that, Frank." Cozza checked the road was clear up ahead and looked over his right shoulder. "We took a few casualties. What about them poor boys at Bluff Cove?"

"The Taffs?" Frank wrinkled his mouth, trying to remember something. "Yeah, bad luck that, but you get that in war. Hell, the last two big wars took four years. We should be pretty grateful this one was so brief eh, Mo? Clive OK?" Mo nodded, not wanting to go over old ground. "Anyway, on to the next overseas battle, eh? Against the French. I've got a good feeling about it. They've called up Butch in midfield. He can make a difference."

"You're kidding, right?" said Mo, slumping back in his seat and peering over his shoulder at Frank, who was hunkered over a wheel arch in the back of the van, wincing every time they hit a bump in the road. "Butch Wilkins ain't fit to lace our Trev's boots. I tell you, if they don't get him fit soon we are out of this tournament before we've started."

"I gotta disagree," said the bare-knuckle boxer, a fervent Chelsea fan. "Butch is one of our own. He started out playing at Wanstead Flats for that Senrab bunch. The Blues picked him when he was 16. Now he's doing the biz for United, too. They wouldn't have paid 800 grand if he was no good."

"He's a crab," said Mo, making pincer movements with his fingers.

"Maybe, but he keeps the ball." Frank paused to crack his knuckles. "They reckon it'll be in excess of 100 degrees out there in Bilbao. Our boys ain't used to that... it's about retaining possession."

"Hark at Alf fackin' Ramsey!"

"Come on boys, what does it matter?" asked Cozza. "At least we're in the thing. Remember listening to them crowing sweaties at the World Cup four years ago – Ally's Army and all that bollocks?" The term sweatie was a derogatory term for the Scots, sweatie socks meaning Jocks. The other two nodded in agreement. "Hopefully we'll have Brooking and Keegan back before long, fresh as daisies and ready for action. I'm excited about the game today. Pity we can't watch it."

"Oh don't start that again," said Big Mo. Then his eyes brightened and his face became more animated. "I've got a good idea. For your benefit, Cozza, we'll ask the fackin' postmaster if he can pop the box on for us. Then we'll come and get you and you can sit in front of the game while we rob the fackin' place. We'll try not to let any stray bullets interfere with your enjoyment."

"Give us a break, Big Mo, I was just saying."

There was silence for a moment, each man consumed by his own thoughts. Finally Big Mo spoke. He rarely conceded ground but he didn't want anyone sulking, it was bad for business. "Thanks for driving anyway, Cozz. You're the best wheel man I know."

"Can't go wrong, Big Mo," said the driver, seizing the olive branch. "Vauxhall Astravan. All the rage. Only a year old. It handles real beautiful. Where did you get it, Frank?"

"Sitting around a yard in Newham it was. You would think these bloody workmen would keep an eye on their tools. Quick switch of plates, bit of a paint job and Bob's yer uncle, Fanny's yer aunt."

"Better if no one gets a look inside though, eh? If we're supposed to be Wilson's painters and decorators there is a distinct lack of paint and ladders in the back."

"Oh, I don't know, Mo," said Frank. "We can tell the Old Bill this is a paint gun." He held up a sawn-off. "Where are we, Coz?"

"Around Sevenoaks way. Won't be long now," said Cozza.

"Take your time," said Mo. "No point in getting pulled for speeding. You know what them traffic cops are like."

"Sure. Maybe we should take a break," said Cozza. He pulled up his sleeve to scratch an ugly welt that had appeared over his tattoo of the crossed Hammers, the ink symbolising his affection for West Ham. "...You know, stop for lunch. When I dropped the cars off there was one of them Little Chefs around here."

"Whaaat!" Big Mo erupted. Cozza glanced sidewards, warily. "Fackin' 'ell Coz I got a better idea. Why don't we just stamp our names and addresses on our foreheads and be done with it? Perhaps we could even make it slightly easier for the filth by finding a phone box and tipping them off. What part of total secrecy don't you get? We don't want people to know we've even been here."

Mo fell silent, aware they were all feeling the tension. It was always like this on a job, and this one made previous escapades look trivial. As a crew, they had started off with simple street muggings, then graduated to shop raids and house break-ins, which had netted them a tidy sum. Big Mo reasoned that if people chose to live in posh places like Hampstead and Holland Park and publicised their good fortune in hoity-toity magazines like Harper's Bazaar or The Lady they only had themselves to blame. In a way his gang were on a par with Robin Hood and his merry men. Rather than redistributing the wealth, though, they kept all the "liberated" goods for themselves or got friendly antique dealers to fence them abroad. The important thing was to look after your own.

"We need a break," said Frank, acting as peacemaker. "Let's pull over somewhere off the beaten track, like in one of those lorry stops. I'm dying for a piss anyway."

"Guess we can do that," said Mo.

"Keep your eyes peeled," said Cozza. "Some of these little slip roads take you by surprise. A secluded little picnic area would be just the ticket."

TEN minutes later, they clambered out, shielding their eyes from the brightness. "Hot!" exclaimed Cozza.

"Yeah, and this ain't nothing like those footballers will have to put up with," Handsome Frank pointed out.

"Give it a rest," said Mo, scanning their surroundings. They had driven down a winding gravel track to a rest area hidden from the road by dense trees. There was only one other vehicle, a delivery truck with foreign plates. To the right was a squat brick building marked with the universal signs for gents and ladies. "You need a wazz, go for it!" Mo told Frank.

The boxer waved a hand and headed off. "Two minutes," he said.

Cozza pulled out a pack of cigarettes. He ripped off the cellophane and shook one out for Mo.

"John Player Special?" Mo's thick eyebrows arched. "Why the fack did you buy them?"

"Sorry, your Lordship. Not to your taste?" said Cozza.

"Don't get cute. It's just... they're my unlucky fags."

"What?"

"They're unlucky... well, they've always brought me bad luck."

"What do you mean?"

"Going back a few years when I first started smoking I bought a pack of these and me old man caught me with them," said Mo. "There was hell to pay, gave me a right slap, he did, then grounded me for a week. Next time I had me mitts on some was a couple of years later. I sneaked behind the counter in the Offie while the bloke was helping some bird select a bottle of wine. I grabbed the nearest packet... them." He indicated the black packet with the gold lettering. "Would have got away with it, too, but I went arse over tit at the doorstep and they fell out of my pocket, right in front of the bloke. I tried to escape, dropped the nut on him, but he held firm and a mate of his called the cops."

"Fuck! And you blame it on these?" Cozza held up the packet.

"What's that?" Handsome Frank was back.

"Mo says these fags are unlucky."

"Don't they say that about all fags? They kill you in the end, apparently." Frank put his hand in his pocket and removed it again quickly, opening it as if he was presenting a magic trick. "Ta ra! What about these though?" He smiled. "They ain't unlucky are they?" In his hand he held three elongated, hand-rolled items, which had been pinched closed at the ends.

"What the..."

"Bit of the old Mary Jane," said the ex-boxer. "Ma-ri-ju-ana. You know... dope. I got us a spliff each. Found 'em under your Shaun's bedside table when I stayed last night, Cozza. Let's just say I confiscated them. He and his bandmates think it's the in-thing to do, I bet, as if no one has been there before. Ain't they read up on Jagger and Richards? Anyway, I thought it might ease the tension... oh don't look at me like that Coz, you must have had an idea. Anyway, your Shaun's hardly gonna accuse you of nicking them, is he? He ain't supposed to have them in the first place."

"Do we look like a bunch of hippy wankers?" asked Mo.

"It will relax us," said Frank, fighting his corner. "We're wound up like springs... and once we've calmed down I got this." He pulled a medicine bottle from the other pocket of his bulky donkey jacket with the leather elbow patches.

"Oh right, let me guess. Aspirin for the headache?" said Mo.

"No, you plum!"

Handsome Frank realised his mistake when a close-cropped head crashed into his own. The bottle flew from his hands.

"No one calls me a fackin' plum!" roared Mo. "You out of your tiny mind, bringing this shit to a robbery?"

Frank clenched his fists and advanced, Cozza moving quickly to stand between the two antagonists. "Look, boys, we're on the same team, right?" he urged. "You know, like Ron and the boys out in Spain. I know you're old school, Mo, but there are plenty of ways to skin a cat. Maybe..."

"He's a bloody header!" stormed Frank, rubbing his brow.

"Calm down, Handsome, it can't spoil your looks." Cozza kept his attention fixed on Mo. "Why not try Frank's way, Mo? Just a few puffs, what harm can it do?"

"That's my point," said Frank.

"Shut it!" said Mo.

The two jostled against Cozza again.

"Look at it this way, Mo," Cozza pleaded. "it's only tobacco with a tiny bit of the wacky stuff in it – it's not like acid or anything."

"And what's in that?" asked Mo, pointing to the small white bottle Frank had retrieved from the ground.

"Speed," the former boxer replied. "I've had it before. It don't do anything bad, just heightens your senses, makes sure you're up to the mark. It's no bad thing when you consider what we're attempting."

"My God," said Mo, shaking his head. "Have you learned nothing from your mistakes, Frank? It was this sort of shit that cost you that British title fight and your career. You went on a three-day drink and drug bender when you should have been training. Not only did you lose but you got tested and banned. I don't get you sometimes." He sighed. "If I end up in jail because of this... mentalness... then I'll be looking for you two on the inside. Come on then, back in the van."

AN hour later Mo had his arm wrapped around Handsome Frank, planting a kiss on his forehead. "Love you guys," he said. "Always been there for me... like family – and I don't mean my old man. Frank, I don't even care that you're so ugly that when you were born the doctor took one look at you and slapped your parents." There was silence for a moment before laughter roared through the enclosed space like water bursting through a dam. Cozza doubled up in a coughing fit, banging on the side of the van, while Mo and Frank put their foreheads together and shouted, phlegm speckling each other's faces.

"Turn that up!" shouted Frank, recognising a familiar tune on the stereo. Cozza leaned into the front seat. "This is more like it!" he said, bouncing up and down.

"I like this lot," said Mo. "What are they called? Madness? Yeah." He started moving his arms up and down then broke into song. "Baggy trousers da, da, da, da, da."

The other two joined in with the moves, the van rocking as they let off steam, hammering fists into the roof and singing along to the chart hit. When the music petered out they calmed down again. "What time is it?" asked Mo.

Cozza looked at the clock on the dash. "Shit, it's getting on for half past two. We got a way to go yet."

"No sweat," said Mo. "Should be perfect if we leave now provided the traffic ain't too bad."

"Can I travel shotgun?" asked Handsome, waving the sawn-off around. Cozza clambered past the others and threw the doors open, coming face to face with a burly, balding figure in a leather jacket.

"Hey," said the stranger, his voice betraying the trace of a foreign accent. "You all OK in there? I heard..."

Kaboom! The man looked down to see a dark patch spreading over his stomach, staining the white jumper he wore under his jacket. Drained of colour, his face bore a perplexed expression. Sinking to his knees like a footballer in a slow motion replay, he fell backwards onto the gravel, eyes fixed on the blinking sun that flickered through the idyllic glade.

It seemed like minutes before anyone reacted, Cozza breaking the silence. "Fuck!" he said, staring at Frank, who was holding the still-smoking firearm so tightly his knuckles were white.

"He surprised me," said the former boxer.

Big Mo took control. He pulled on a pair of gloves and grabbed the metal barrel, feeling the warmth permeate his fingers, the smell of gunpowder invading his nostrils and lodging in his throat.

"Relax Frank," he said. "Have some of my spliff... here, I got a bit left. Just give me the shooter." The fighter did what he was told.

Smash! The stock of the gun crashed into Handsome Frank's ear. "You dumb cunt!" shouted Mo. "So this is what your fackin' drugs do, is it? Relax us? Well, if that's an example of you relaxing I'd hate to see you highly strung."

"He saw our faces," said Frank, his expression confused, as if an irritating fly had buzzed him. He stared passed Mo at the dead trucker. There was a brief movement, the body trying to crawl across the gravel in the direction of the lorry on the other side of the parking area.

"Oh, that's all we need!" said Mo. "He's still alive. Brilliant."

Jumping out, he stood over the victim, placing a sturdy brogue shoe on his back. The trucker fell flat on his face. "Well, come on!" he shouted to the others. Cozza followed him but Frank remained frozen to the spot.

"Get his keys!" ordered Mo.

"What?" said Cozza.

"Get his fackin' keys. Come on! We'll lock him in the truck. Hopefully no one will find him for days."

"Shit! He'll bleed out in there. You can't..?" Cozza had turned white, the high the dope had provided dissipating in a second.

"What's your suggestion?" Mo crowded Cozza's private space, their noses almost touching. "Leave him here for all to see?"

"You can't let him die like that," said Cozza. "You got to put him out of his misery."

"What a fackin' mess," said Mo.

Behind them, Handsome Frank finally emerged. "What was I supposed to do?" he asked.

"You could have left the gun alone for starters," said Mo. "Sitting in the back, playing with it like it was a toy."

The fighter held his hand up like a one-armed man surrendering. "I know, I know. Maybe it did us a favour, though. The bloke looked straight at Coz, could have easily picked him out of a line-up; them tattoos are a giveaway. And he saw into the van. We don't know what he clocked. The bags, the masks, the guns... shit, he could have heard us planning. Our names. We don't know how long he was there. In effect, I took care of business."

"Yeah? Well you better finish your business then, cos the facker's still breathin'," said Mo.

The faint rumble of traffic on the nearby A21 was the only soundtrack to their thoughts, each one wondering if there might have been another way and realising Handsome Frank was right. Once the trucker had seen into the back of the van, he had to disappear. The bare-knuckle boxer turned his back on the other two and unscrewed the medicine bottle, popping two small white pills into his hand. Throwing them into his mouth, he swallowed them dry before climbing into the back of the van. Grabbing the shotgun, he cracked it open, loaded it, snapped it shut and jumped back out.

FRANK felt sharp and alert. He could hear the chirrup of birds in the trees, the roar of a faraway jet transporting holidaymakers to luxury climes, the click, clacking sound of his boots on the gravel like that breakfast cereal that went snap, crackle and pop. Smells pushed their way into his consciousness, the intoxicatingly pungent aroma of petrol mixing with that of fragrant wild flowers, both competing with disinfectant and urine from the nearby toilet block. Running his hand up and down the cold metal cylinder of the gun, he blanked out all thought apart from the mission itself.

Dragging the trucker behind him he was aware of the other two watching, open mouthed. At last he heard Mo mutter: "Make it count."

Frank disappeared behind the toilet block and moments later a loud "crack" split the air, sending birds erupting from the trees, their messages of alarm loud and clear to the countryside's fellow inhabitants.

28

IT was a loose thread that brought Beryl Dolan's world crashing down. She was in the bedroom, packing for the holiday and she considered it her "duty" to ensure Maurice had suitable clothes for the week ahead. She had grabbed his army surplus duffle bag and was placing things inside with care, knowing how he prided himself on organisation. Everything had to be compartmentalised, socks in one place, T-shirts in another, trousers on top to prevent creasing, pants rolled up and grouped together rather than scattered willy-nilly.

Most of his life was ordered in this way. His vinyl record collection was stored alphabetically in a glass cabinet, spines facing out so that the names of album and artist were clearly visible – and woe betide anyone who put a record back in the wrong way or in the wrong place. She had learned her lesson the hard way, receiving a severe tongue lashing when a Rory Gallagher album was slotted in ahead of Beggars Banquet by the Rolling Stones. Was she so stupid she didn't realise it should be stored under G for Gallagher rather than R for Rory?

Throwing open the wardrobe she took out suits. They were all colour co-ordinated, lined up from darkest on one side to lightest on the other. He had an impressive collection, 15 in total, and was careful to restock when he had money. Black, dark blue, purple tonic, dark green, red... she struggled to remember whether grey or beige came first so had to resort to writing the order down in a notepad so she didn't forget. He would need a varied selection while they were away so he could decide which was best for a visit to the local restaurant and what might be preferable for a night club visit. Beryl kept them in dry cleaners' bags to prevent them creasing or picking up stains. A small unidentified mark on a sleeve was the sort of thing that would send Mo's temper into the stratosphere.

She would laugh if the consequences weren't so damn serious. It was strange that he didn't appear to follow his own rules. She had lost count of the times he had got involved in a ruck and she'd had to ask the dry cleaning woman to "work her magic" on some tell-tale smudge or other. On occasion, the clothes were beyond saving and he'd whisk them away, destroying the evidence so that it didn't return to haunt him later.

Suits bagged and placed tidily around the room, she at last felt she could relax. Earlier that morning, while Chuck and Sly were eating breakfast, she had ironed five of Mo's favourite button-down shirts, white and black, Ben Sherman and Brutus, and hung them in the kitchen. With all that out of the way, packing the bag promised to be easy in comparison. She was so glad there were no distractions. Sly had gone down for a morning nap and Chuck was at boxing, fitting in a last training session before a week of playing 'happy families' in Sussex with the Cohens and the Purveses. In all honesty, she wasn't keen on either but, being the dutiful wife, she had gone along with it. She considered Cozza a lech. He often eyed her up or gave her a wink when his common-law wife Bev wasn't looking. Their son Shaun was stroppy and incommunicative while daughter Wendy was downright needy, always demanding attention. Bev was so out of it on prescription pills she failed to notice.

Handsome Frank gave Beryl the creeps. With that awful scarred face and weeping eye, he was like something out of a horror movie. She hadn't met his latest "conquest" Marsha but had seen a grainy picture. She was no stunner. Going away with them would be like holidaying with the Munsters, the ghoulish family from the comedy TV programme she'd watched during her childhood.

It was the first time the Dolans had been away as a family and Beryl thought it would have been nice to escape on their own. Frank and Cozza might be Mo's closest friends, but she suspected there was more to the surprise trip than met the eye. Mo never discussed business with her – for her own sake as much as anything – but she sensed something big was going down. The previous fortnight she had been walking a tightrope with Maurice, aware any small shift in atmosphere could bring things crashing down on top of her.

Crossing to his bedside drawers, she pulled out seven pairs of pants – one for every day of the week – then grabbed an eighth pair in case of emergencies. Rolling each pair, she placed them neatly into one of the pockets in the bag, returning for socks. She counted out two pairs of black, four assorted pairs and four pairs of white, rolling each pair into a ball. Noticing with alarm that the thread had come loose on one of the white pairs, stringy elastic poking out of the top, she imagined there would be hell to pay if Big Mo had come across them. It was her job to detect such flaws before they came to his attention. Throwing them to the floor to bin later, she grabbed a replacement pair... and froze.

There was a piece of paper, folded up, inside one of the socks. She felt her heart flutter. When you lived in the kind of environment where everything had its rightful place, there was no room for imperfections. Luckily, she had found it before Mo unless, of course, he had placed it there. She screwed it up and was about to throw it in the bin when a small voice inside her head persuaded her otherwise. Sitting on the bed, she grabbed her black-framed spectacles from the dressing table and unfolded the mysterious item.

It was a bill, a normal household electricity bill. Not that strange really, because Mo took care of all the finances. Recently he had been a bit lax, and she had noticed some final reminders dropping on to the doormat. This particular bill wasn't a red letter, though. In fact, it wasn't even addressed to them. The person it belonged to lived at Flat 17, Princess Court, Dagenham. Backlit against the window, she noticed something had been handwritten on the other side.

Hands trembling, she turned it over to find a note in a childlike scrawl. Chuck? Whoever had written it, the spelling was atrocious.

"You sexy man, yor mi wurld. Thees last months have bin grate. I cant stop thinkin about you, yor bodie yor mouf + yor massif cock... fanx four last nite. Cant wait for you to spend evry nite in mi bed. I'll suck you dry wen yor bak, luv you, Aud xx"

Beryl sat frozen to the spot. Inside, her brain began a mantra, her inner spirit whispering to her numbed physical being...

How do we handle this? What do we do? Confront him? Confront her? Follow him and spy on him? Rip her head off? Stab her eyes? Cry? Shout? Scream? Slit our own fucking wrists? Hey, that's an idea. What would Maurice do then, eh? How would he respond to that? You took all of me, wanted to own every bit of me, so here I am emptied out in front of you, Mo. Want my blood? Here it is ... I've done it for you. Want my guts? Here they are. No need for you to wound me now... anything you do to me can't be worse than this, this... betrayal, this assault and battery of the heart. After all I've been through with you, you do this to me? Knowing you loved me was the one thing that kept me going. Nothing's left.

Pushing herself from the bed, Beryl's legs turned to pipe cleaners, her balance all over the place. She repeated the sentence over and over in her head until it became fact: "My husband is having an affair", "My husband is having an affair", "My husband is having an affair". If she was entirely truthful with herself, she had always harboured suspicions but buried them deep, making excuses on his behalf. She had reasoned with herself that the two nights or so a week that he slept away from the marital bed were due to the fact he was working late, or had fallen asleep during a late game of cards at a mate's, or because there had been an impromptu lock-in at a local boozer and he'd dozed off on one of the sofas. Quite often, she had been relieved he hadn't come back. It was better than the alternative. She hated him falling into bed at 3 in the morning, stinking of booze and fags then rubbing himself against her ass, begging to hump her. When she finally awoke and did her best to encourage him, he would nod off in the middle of the act, leaving her pinned beneath his dead weight. On other occasions, she lay awake, waiting for that tell-tale rattle as he mastered the intricacies of fitting his keys in the front door lock. When it didn't come she was almost grateful. A night spared.

When he turned up the next day, he had no need of well-rehearsed excuses because she had made them up for him. "Lock-in down the Hope, was it?" she would say when he sauntered in the next morning for a shower and a change of clothes, the ones he was wearing rife with sickly, cheap scent suffused with tobacco smoke. What of it? She would tell herself it belonged to some other bloke's girl or an over-friendly barmaid who had helped him on with his coat because he was worse for wear. It was easier for her to imagine these things than to think Maurice Dolan, the only man she had ever loved, was regularly sleeping in another woman's bed, lavishing on her all the attention he had been withholding from Beryl.

She had never wanted to be one of those jealous wives who accused their husbands of all and sundry, eventually forcing them to go out and have an affair to justify the haranguing. In her case, things went far deeper. If she acknowledged the truth about Mo's 'other' life it would be tantamount to owning up to her failures as a wife, something she could never do for fear of becoming a carbon copy of her mother.

The sound of crying interrupted her thoughts. Sly was awake and grizzly, his body clock telling him it was lunchtime. Damn! Where had the time gone? Chuck would be back soon, his coach volunteering to drop him off after training, and she still had to pack the kids' stuff. Shaking her head in a bid to clear her mind, Beryl wondered how the hell she was going to go through with the pretence of enjoying a happy family holiday. It was the last thing she needed.

Tucking the note into the back pocket of her tight-fit jeans, she looked in the mirror to wipe away a tear, pushed the sides of her mouth up with her fingers and painted on a smile. "Coming, Sylvester dear!" she said through gritted teeth.

WITH her youngest sitting at the kitchen table, face coated in runny egg, she opened the front door to see if there was any sign of Chuck.

Walking onto the balcony, she peered down on the car park. A small blue mini was pulling into one of the spots and she suspected it was him. She wiped her eyes again. Chucky couldn't know she was upset.

Putting her foot on a rail she climbed up to get a better look, her frazzled mind suddenly relaying images of her standing on top of the wall, over-balancing and nose-diving to the unyielding tarmac below, leaving another stain on an estate bleached with despair and sorrow. The suicidal thoughts immediately dissolved. Selfish cow. There were the boys to consider. Her mind flashed forward, picturing how they might grow up in the care of their philandering father or, worse still, with his illiterate girlfriend teaching them right from wrong and helping them with their homework.

She jumped a mile when a hand touched her shoulder. "Careful, you don't want to go too close," a familiar voice said.

"You!" shouted Beryl, spinning towards the source of the words. "You scared the bloody life out of me."

Stan Marshall stood there with a boyish grin on his face, pushing his wavy, shoulder-length hair back behind his ears. "I'm sorry. For a minute there I was worried you were going to..."

"Don't be daft! With my boys relying on me? That ain't going to happen."

"You're crying again."

"What? No! It's the wind," she said. "It's blowy up here, made my eyes run. What are you doing here, anyway? It's a bit creepy, if I'm honest. Are you stalking me?"

"I could ask you the same question."

"Don't tell me you live here?"

"Next block, actually. I was just visiting a mate to ask if he could open up for me. I'm seeing a band tonight in a pub in Dalston: they're pretty good. Hey, I don't suppose you fancy it? You look like you need a good night out."

She opened her mouth to say "no", but the word stuck in her throat. At any other moment on any other day she would have shot him down straight away, told him he was taking his life in his hands asking out the wife of Big Maurice Dolan. Yet this wasn't any other day. This was the day she had found out the truth, that her marriage was a sham and that the man who professed to love her was sneaking around behind her back with some skanky trollop from Dagenham. Was this meeting the fate she read about in magazines?

There was certainly a mutual attraction, and the fact he lived in the same town, on the same estate, and had bumped into her when she was at her lowest ebb – no Mills and Boon plot could rival it. Should she seize the moment or walk away and spend a night at home with only her intrusive thoughts for company?

29

THEY sat in silence, Cozza's mouth set in grim determination as he folded himself over the steering wheel. Handsome Frank hadn't said a word since completing his mission. He held the shotgun in one hand, a rag in the other, rubbing it up and down repetitively against the steel as if he could wipe away his memories as well as the fingerprints. No one had the heart or courage to lean over and take it away from him.

"Maybe we should call it off now," Cozza said, breaking the ice.

"No," said Mo. "We came here for a reason. This doesn't change anything."

"Look at him, though," said Cozza. "The guy's in some kind of trance."

"I'll do it on my own if needs be," said Mo. "Christ, Cozza, I've been banking on this one. We need the dosh. I promised our Bee all sorts of stuff, the boy needs a new uniform, the baby causes us no end of expense and she wants more fackin' kids. We've been living off that Hampstead job and the jewellery from the Romford heist for too long. We can't shift them guns because they're too hot, which doesn't help."

"We could get proper jobs," said Cozza. Big Mo looked at him vacantly for a second before spotting the smirk and cracking a smile, too.

"Fuck that! Look, Thatcher's got it right," he said. "You got to work for yourself, be entrepreneurial, know what I'm saying?"

"Not a clue," said Cozza, laughing. "Last chance. Let's just turn around, go off on holiday..."

"What with? I'm up to my neck in debt just paying for that bastard 'retreat' – this job can solve all our problems. Right?"

"Course," said Cozza, knowing there was no leeway to argue.

"I am here, you know," said Frank, interrupting. "You don't have to talk around me. I'm OK." As if only just noticing his fanatical polishing he threw the rag to the ground. "Like you said, it has to be done. I need the wedge as well. Down to me last shillings, I am."

"Sorted," said Mo. "No more shooting though, eh? Nice clean job, in and out and have it away on our toes. Should be easy pickings."

"It's all planned to the letter," said Cozza. "You really OK, Frank?"

"Yeah," said the fighter, swigging from a bottle of Dr Pepper. He wiped his mouth. "It ain't a nice thing to do, kill a geezer you don't even know, but he should have minded his own business. Right?"

The other two nodded.

Frank pulled a fur coat from the bag at his feet and placed it over his shoulders. From his pocket, he withdrew a rubber mask and held it to his eyes and nose, pulling the attached elastic over his head to keep it in place. Dipping back into the bag one final time, he pulled out a long blonde wig and put it on his head, adjusting it with the aid of a small hand mirror. Crossing his legs dramatically, he said: "It's all in the best possible taste."

Mo took in the fur coat, bearded mask and blonde wig, finding it hard to believe it was Frank peering out from behind the mass of curls. "Fackin' 'ell," he said. "We've brought Kenny fackin' Everett with us. Or should I say Cupid Stunt?"

The others laughed. Cupid Stunt was an American porn star with flowing blonde locks, an alter-ego invented by DJ and TV personality Everett. She crossed and uncrossed her legs in a manner which was supposed to be provocative, but the fact she had Everett's beard made the whole thing look bizarre. Frank had introduced his new persona with Cupid's trademark catchphrase.

"Hope you don't expect me to dress up like that, you bloody nonce," said Mo.

"You're OK. I knew you wouldn't go for anything like that, so I got this one." He threw a latex mask across. Mo looked down at it, trying to make out who it was meant to be before pulling it over his head.

"Brilliant," said Cozza. "Terry bloody Wogan. Can you do the accent?"

"To be sure, to be sure," said Big Mo. "Potatoes. Fiddle-de-de and all that."

"Thought you might appreciate being Tel, with your love of the Irish," said Frank.

"Cunts!" exclaimed Mo, but he was smiling. "I wouldn't fancy being the sub-postmaster and his missus, though. I mean, who wants to admit to the shame of being robbed by the cream of BBC Radio One's light entertainment. Where did you get them?"

"The masks? Walthamstow market, of course," said Frank. "Don't worry, I'm sure they're untraceable."

Mo studied Handsome Frank, who had removed his mask and was holding it limply in his hand. "You sure you're OK?" he asked. "I need you at your best. I know I said I could do it alone, but that ain't true. I just can't have you throwing a wobbly in there. Let's be calm, OK? Professional."

"Don't worry, Mo. I may seem a bit off my game, but that's just the speed. Truth is I can't wait to get started."

NO ONE on the High Street paid any attention to the man with the ugly-looking girlfriend who crossed the street in the direction of the post office. Hidden behind his Terry Wogan mask, Mo pushed the door open then turned to his accomplice. "Shit!" he hissed.

"What is it..?"

"Don't say my name!"

"I wasn't going to."

"You were," complained Mo. "Bollocks. We've got a problem. They brought in some of them soddin' anti-bandit screens. The counter was open when me and the boy paid a visit."

"You want to call it off?"

Mo hesitated for a moment. "Nah!" He charged in. "Right, shit-for-brains!" he said to the man behind the reinforced screen. "This ain't no candid camera and there ain't no bloke hiding around the corner, gonna spring out and tell you it's some kind of joke." He pulled the shotgun from under his coat. "This ain't a toy. It's a loaded gun, right? We've already killed one person today just for serving us lukewarm tea. No room for heroes, understand? All the money and valuables in this fuckin' bag!" He placed a hessian sack on the counter and looked around. Four elderly customers were cowering in the corner, held hostage by Frank in his Kenny Everett mask.

"I can't," said the sub-postmaster.

"What!?" The gun went off, blasting a hole in the roof and bringing plaster down on top of them. "Don't be a cunt all your life, son!"

"It's the Royal Mail's new security measures. I can't open up and let you have the money. It isn't possible."

"Is that right?" said Mo, dark eyes pinning the postmaster to the spot. "Don't piss up my back and tell me it's raining. Maybe I should start shooting your fackin' customers, see if that helps you rethink the problem." Striding across the room, he grabbed an elderly man in a beige cap and overcoat, lifting him from the floor. The pensioner was shaking uncontrollably. "What about this one?"

"No... please," said the hostage. Mo backhanded him across the face, sending blood spurting from his nose. Pushing him to the floor, Big Mo stood over him with the gun.

"Fuck this for a game of soldiers," shouted Frank. "I got a better idea."

He raced off, disappearing for a minute behind a stand of post-cards and stationery. Mo was feeling edgy, alternately looking at his prisoners, then searching for his partner. Just when he thought Frank had lost it again a shout came from behind the counter. Mo turned to see Cupid Stunt looking out from behind reinforced glass, gun tucked under the postmaster's chin.

"How the fuck..?"

"They have to get the parcels in here somehow, don't they? Found the 'atch and crawled through. No bother." He slammed the butt of the gun against the side of the postmaster's head, the Royal Mail employee crashing out of sight, squealing with pain. "Now, like our good friend Terry Wogan says, you don't wanna play the hero, do you?" Handsome Frank's blonde wig flopped over his eyes. Pushing it back, he played with one of the curls. "Just give us the money and we'll be out of your hair... Oh, and don't forget the parcels, I like presents."

TWO of Kent's finest were still celebrating as the red van passed them at a ridiculous speed. They had pulled to the side of the road to listen to England's opening World Cup game against France on a portable radio. PC Briggs had located the wavelength just in time to hear England's captain Bryan Robson put Ron Greenwood's team ahead.

"Someone's in a hurry!" exclaimed his partner PC Nash.

"Yeah, always thought Robson was capable of that. Just 27 seconds after the kick off – must be the fastest-ever goal at a World Cup finals."

"Not the football, you div. That bloody van! What do you reckon?"

The radio on the dashboard crackled to life. "All cars, all cars... robbery at Five Ways sub-post office on Grosvenor Road. Criminals escaping in red transit with Wilson's Painters and Decorators on the side. Two men plus driver. Be careful... they're armed and extremely dangerous. Repeat, armed and dangerous. Don't play heroes. Call for back up."

"Always some low life that has to spoil it," said PC Briggs, turning his transistor off. "We'll miss the rest of the match now." He turned the key in the ignition, the Ford Granada Mark II bursting into life.

"WE got ourselves a police escort," said Cozza, eyes fixed on the rear-view mirror.

"You'd better lose them then!" said Big Mo, removing his mask. He sat in the back opposite Frank, who was wearing a manic smile. One leg jiggled up and down as he cradled a shotgun in his arms, the wig flopping over his face.

"Maybe you should put that down, mate," said Mo. "We don't want any more little accidents, do we?" He leaned across for the weapon, but the fighter turned away from him.

"Hold on!" said Cozza, swinging the car to the right and forcing a vehicle travelling in the opposite direction to screech to a halt, narrowly avoiding a collision.

"Shit, mate, let's get there in one piece!" shouted Mo.

"Damn," said Cozza. "They're still there."

He was negotiating a winding B road, quaint terraced houses flashing by on both sides, pretty window boxes boasting flowers of all different shades and hues. Normally, the setting would be idyllic but on this occasion it was shattered by the wail of a police siren. Two cars travelling in the opposite direction pulled to the side of the narrow road, startled faces peering out through windows, trying to establish whether it was a real live cop chase or some stunt being filmed for TV.

"He's a good driver," said Cozza. "Pretty persistent." He threw the car to his left, into another country road.

"How far?" asked Big Mo.

"Another two miles, there's a derelict barn not far from here. I found it on my little scouting mission. We'll need to lose these guys first, though."

The road became narrower, bends looming up more frequently. Cozza couldn't see the police car in his mirrors, which meant they couldn't see him either. Mo held on for grim life as bags of cash, parcels and mail slid around, their contents spilling onto the floor of the van. "Looks like you're losing..."

Just as the words came out, Cozza slammed on the brakes. A herd of cattle blocked the road ahead, wandering aimlessly. "Fuck!" Cozza pounded the horn relentlessly and some of the animals turned to see what the fuss was about while chewing boredly.

The siren was getting louder and through the back window Mo saw the police car screech around the corner then slide to a halt.

Before Mo or Cozza could register what was happening the back door banged open and Handsome Frank disappeared with the shotgun. A boom echoed around the leafy countryside, startled birds shrieking as they took to the air from surrounding fields. Mo saw the police car's windscreen shatter and its two occupants dive for cover, the one in the passenger seat springing back upright, his face covered in blood. Within seconds the police car was backing away at speed down the lane, its tyres slaloming for grip on a surface slick with cow dung.

"Frank, you fackin' header!" Mo emerged from the van in an effort to coax his mate back inside. The bare-knuckle fighter had other ideas, though, turning and charging in the other direction, firing over the heads of the cattle. They stampeded, smashing into fences and climbing onto the backs of each other in their desperation to escape.

One of the animals, panicked by the chaos in front, turned back and ran straight at them, rearing up, its eyes wide with fear. On its way back down the man in the blonde wig let out a blood-curdling war cry, stepped forward and unleashed an uppercut which connected flush with the cow's jaw. Stunned, it shook its head, teetered, then turned in the opposite direction and ran, bellowing a warning to the rest of the herd.

"Get in! Come on!" shouted Cozza through the driver's side window. "This is our chance. I reckon we can get through now."

Big Mo grabbed Frank by the collar of the fur coat. "You fackin' head the ball," he shouted in his mate's ear. "You just punched a cow!"

The former boxer's eyelids flickered and he came back to life like a toy with its batteries recharged. "I did, didn't I?" he said, tossing blonde curls back over his shoulder, his face full of wonder. "Shit, if I'd have produced that sort of shot in the ring I'd be world champion now."

30

"SHE'S very ill, you know?" The landlord of the Crown and Sceptre leaned forward, whispering behind a cupped hand. Like a talentless ventriloquist trying to con an audience at a working men's club, the words tumbled from a gap at the side of his mouth.

Big Cliffy Simpson scanned the interior of the East End boozer. It wasn't as if it was full of spies or Special Branch informers. There were just a few lonely losers dotted about, too busy examining the racing form guide to bother about the publican's tittle-tattle. Possibly the last person Trev Breaks should have been passing information to was a copper, but he didn't see one of his favourite customers as part of the thin blue line.

Cliffy was hardly thin for a start, a state of affairs not helped by the fact he always had a packet of pork scratchings on the go. They sat on the bar now so that he could occasionally dip in for a nibble. Cliffy had been coming here for decades, often stopping off on his way home from Molloy's gym around the corner. It was rare he gave up secrets himself, just enough juicy morsels to encourage Trev to do the same. In fact, most of Cliffy's revelations could easily be discovered by studying the 'Who's in Court' section of the local paper.

The landlord was as synonymous with the East End as pie, mash and liquor. He knew everything and everyone and Cliff made it his business to keep his ear to the ground, even when out of uniform. It was what good cops did. He felt it was his duty to the community, even if it did mean risking life and limb in an old boozer which paid scant regard to the health and safety of its customers. Peeling, faded wallpaper gave it a neglected air and it smelt of damp, hops and an unidentifiable strong chemical that made the eyes water.

"Who are you banging on about now, Twiggy?" Cliffy asked. The pub manager had earned his nickname because he was as skinny as an undernourished tree branch. Any stranger entering might have thought he had stumbled onto the set of a Laurel and Hardy remake. Cliffy added to the comedic value by perching precariously on a bar stool straining to cope with his weight.

"Her!" said the landlord, as if only one woman merited discussion in that neck of the woods. "Vi... Violet Kray. If she pops her clogs they'll break out, mark my words... and they won't be happy. They loves their mum. Which reminds me, you coming to our charity do?"

"What? To line the pockets of two of the nastiest crims I've ever had the misfortune to encounter?" said Cliffy, raising his voice. "You know they skim off the top, don't you, Twiggy? This ain't about helping some poor kid get an operation in the States, it's so that Reg and Ron can swan around in Parkhurst, Broadmoor, or whichever sorry institution they are in at the moment, wearing expensive clothes, new trainers, sophisticated after-shaves and whatever else their hearts desire. Look, I'm sorry for the lad and all, I've been around to see his mum and slipped her some cash myself, but this fundraiser ain't some act of great 'benevolence' by the Krays, mark my words."

"Shhhhh!" said Twiggy, his face turning the same shade of purple as his nose. He flicked wisps of greying hair back across his exposed scalp. "Mr Simpson, you can't say that around here. They still have 'pull' in these parts. You don't want to be in their bad books when they get out, Mr S."

"You're deluded, Twiggy," said Cliff, wagging a podgy finger in his direction. "They won't ever get out. They're the best guarded prisoners in the country. However much respect they think they had on the outside, once those bolts slammed behind them it vanished as quickly as a pickpocket in the West End. There are new criminals filling the void, just as nasty, dangerous and greedy. I heard Reggie got beaten up inside by some little fuckers out to prove themselves. Those twins will be carried out in their coffins, sooner or later."

"Oh, you don't..."

"Don't what?" said Cliffy, cutting off the landlord's train of thought. "Don't know them? I certainly do and I tell you what: when they were out, I wouldn't give them the time of day. People have rewritten history for these blokes, painted them like the Robin Hoods of this manor. Robin Hood? Robbing bastards is what they were. Robbing, murdering bastards. Ask the families who suffered at their hands, loved ones killed or maimed."

"Shhhhh!" said Twiggy again, jumping around as if desperate for a toilet break. "It was that sort of talk that got Cornell off'd. I was just sayin'..."

"Listen, Twiggy, I sympathise with your position. They drank here, or at least some of their firm did, and you had to pander to them... but I'm a cop and a straight one. Strange, I know, with all the shit being said about The Met, but I didn't join the force to line my own pockets and be in hock to the likes of them two. I know Vi well. Lovely woman, and it is a shame she's ill. I can't help thinking, though, that if she had been stricter with those two boys they wouldn't have grown up the way they did." He paused momentarily. "I had a fight with Reg once, you know?"

The landlord was genuinely shocked. "Yeah?"

"They put him in the ring with me down the gym. To be fair, he wasn't a bad boxer. Bit too headstrong, like many around here. Not disciplined enough. When he hit me he thought he could finish me off, went for it hell for leather and left himself exposed. I tagged him flush on the chin. He wobbled a bit, didn't go down though. Then his brother started shouting insults from the sidelines. He looked like he wanted to climb in, too, so the trainer called a halt early."

Twiggy was speechless. Breaking eye contact, he walked to the beer pump and filled one of the mugs with Cliffy's favourite tipple. "Fair play," he said, plonking the beer in front of the policeman. "You deserve a pint for that. On the house. Not sure you should have done it, but still."

Typical, thought Cliffy. Twiggy shared the mindset of the majority of the people in the area. If a few more of them had stood up to the Krays they might have found it slightly more difficult to build their formidable empire. Mind you, times had been tough around there after the war and it was no wonder many explored alternative ways of earning a living. Crime was arguably the most lucrative profession in these parts.

As Cliffy took a sip of his beer, the warped door behind him scraped open, its jarring noise putting his teeth on edge. He turned to see Max Cooper sauntering in. "There you are!" he said, greeting Cliff with a smile. Charging forward, he stopped abruptly, peering down at his brand-new brogues. They were swimming in dirty brown liquid. "What the..?"

"Toilets flooded, guv. Sorry about that," said Twiggy.

"Again? Shit! These were new on today, you fucker. I've a mind to sue over this, Twiggy."

"You won't get anywhere," said Cliffy. "The beak will just say it serves you right for coming here in the first place."

"Don't know why you do it, Cliffy," moaned Cooper. "Place is a shithole. They haven't even got the TV on. England were 2-1 up last I heard. Thought I'd be able to watch at least a bit of the game here. Robson's just scored his second."

"Flood's fucked the electrics," said Twiggy. "You're lucky we got any beer on."

"Not sure that's lucky," said Cliff.

"Well, if my beer ain't good enough you can give it back." He went to snatch the pint, but Cliffy moved too quickly.

"Got to be faster than that Twiggy, to get Cliffy's pint off him," said Cooper. "You know he's a trained boxer? They used to call him Speedy Simpson back in the day."

"Oh yeah," said Twiggy. "Only time he shows any speed these days is if someone tries to nick his scratchings." The two men laughed as Cliffy gulped back the remainder of his pint. "Oh, and he can finish one of them pretty sharpish, too... I've known him neck five pints during *Coronation Street*, then drive home!"

Cliffy ignored the taunts. "Fill it up, Twiggy... and one for Max here; if he is prepared to slum it in our company without a TV, of course."

"Just a quick one," said Cooper, dragging up a stool next to Cliff, its legs making a squishing sound as they sunk into sodden carpet. "It stinks in here... is that the flood or the beer?"

"Bit of both," said Cliffy. "It's piss from the toilets and piss in the beer, too, I wouldn't be surprised. What brings you here?"

"I've got good news," said Cooper. "It's finally happening... Flying Squad; joining in a couple of days. It was a bit touch and go after that business with the guns. Grabem didn't help. Bastard set me back six months. Luckily my snout gave me a couple of decent tip-offs and they paid off. That swung it."

"Congratulations!" said Cliff, thumping him on the back. "You always fancied yourself as Regan in the Sweeney, didn't you?"

Cooper didn't bite. "Looks like I could be pretty busy, too. They want me on a firearms course. Speaking of which... hear about that business in Kent?"

"No. What?"

"Armed robbery of a post office... Tunbridge Wells," said Cooper. "Got away with 15 grand... carrying shotguns."

"Who'd run a post office?" said Cliffy. "There's one of these every day it seems. Kent you say?" His brain gave him a nudge. During his coaching session at the gym that day he'd had a chat with young Chuck Dolan, who had told him he wouldn't be around the following week.

"We're going on holiday," the Dolan kid had told him, a beaming smile on his face. Cliff was surprised. He didn't think the family had two pennies to rub together.

"Anywhere nice?" he'd asked.

"By the seaside my dad says. We're going to be staying in a cottage right on the beach. Place called Hay Stings."

When Cliff asked him if he had been there before the boy shook his head. "Nah, well, I did go with my dad when he booked it. It's nice. Uncle Frank is coming too and another friend of dad's... my uncle Paul. Dad took us there after our uncle Clive sailed for the Folk Lands. He said he had a bit of business to attend to first and took us to some other place – the man in the post office gave me a sticker book. It was called something bridge? – didn't see no bridge, though."

"Tunbridge," said Cliff.

"That's what I said." Cooper looked confused.

"Sorry, thinking out loud," said Cliff. Up until now, he thought Maurice Dolan and his pals were pretty small time, though he could imagine they had aspirations to move up in the world. By all accounts, Maurice's old man was a bit of a criminal mastermind, though no one had ever been able to pin anything on him. It wouldn't be a big stretch to see Handsome Frank and Mo Dolan graduating to armed robbery, though, given their backgrounds. It was certainly a coincidence that Big Mo was away on business in the Kent area with Handsome Frank Purves and another pal on the same day a post office had been blagged... and Cliffy didn't do coincidences.

31

"THE good news is he'll live," said the boss of Kent CID. There was a murmur as those in the squad room digested the news. "Just bashed his bonce rather badly, apparently, trying to dodge out of the way when the shooter let rip. It looked serious for a while. He thought he'd been shot and we thought he'd been shot. There was a lot of blood, but no bullet wound. The cut on his head was caused by a collision with the sharp angle of a transistor radio. I don't need to tell you he shouldn't have had that with him on patrol, he could have poked his bloody eye out with the aerial. These rules exist for a reason. Anyway, enough said for now."

A loud chorus of muttering broke out, the overall feeling one of relief. For a few hours, officers at East Kent police headquarters had been desperate for news on their colleague, PC Bob Nash. A newcomer to traffic patrol, he had a wife and two young kids at home. His colleagues had pledged violent retribution if his wounds proved fatal. The problem was catching those responsible.

"Our blaggers are gone with the wind," said DCI Royston Paige, confirming their worst fears. "We tried to pick up the trail, put the helicopter up and made inquiries locally, but this was planned with military precision."

"Are there descriptions, boss?" asked someone from the floor.

"Yes, but they're not very helpful. It appears we're looking for a bearded blonde in a fur coat and a Terry Wogan lookalike."

"About time someone locked Wogan up – that *Blankety Blank* he presents is a crime!" shouted one wag, who elicited sniggers from his colleagues.

"Yeah, all right," said the DCI, making calming motions with his hands. "Anyway, we found the van dumped in a barn, but no clue as to their escape vehicle. We've had forensics there all evening, examining the evidence, but there were no tyre tracks and little else to go on." The news was greeted with disgruntled murmurs.

"In other news, I'm told the Flying Squad are stepping in." There were boos and hisses from the crowd. "I know, I know, but they're in-the-know when it comes to organised gangs like this and they're convinced it has all the hallmarks of a London firm. I've no reason to doubt them. They'll be checking their files for similar raids over the last few years and drawing up a list of suspects. They also believe the van was stolen from a builders' yard in east London recently. We've agreed to help them as best we can."

As the level of chatter rose, the gathered officers failed to notice the female PC enter the room and hand something to the DC. Reading it, his face took on a grim expression.

"This, uh, situation has just escalated," he announced, raising his voice to be heard. "A body has been found stashed in the back of a lorry at a truck stop off the A21, riddled with gunshot wounds. I know we shouldn't jump to conclusions, but it's difficult to imagine a scenario where two armed gangs are charging around this part of Kent on the same day at roughly the same time. These bastards could well be murderers as well as armed robbers."

"WHERE have you been all my life?" Cozza hauled Handsome Frank onto his lap. They were in a Jacobean cottage in Hastings Old Town. Full of character and rustic charm, the three-bedroom property was a couple of minutes' walk from the seafront.

The fighter, blonde wig reinstated, had been mincing around to a Madness tune blasting from the radio. "My girl's mad at me," he wailed drunkenly, taking a glug from the expensive bottle of fizz they had bought to celebrate their success. Combined with the drugs still flowing through his system and the natural effects of the adrenaline comedown, it was an intoxicating mix. Just as he was getting into his stride, though, the music came to an abrupt halt.

"What the..."

Big Mo stood in the doorway, face like thunder. "Are you fackin' mental?" The two men stared at him as he marched across the room, pulling curtains as he went.

"Come on, Mo, we gotta let our hair down a bit." Cozza sniggered, lifting off Handsome's wig in an attempt to lighten the mood.

"You think?" Big Mo ripped it from his hand. "So we use this, do we? The exact fackin' wig he wore in the raid. Damn. You should be destroying evidence, not prancing about in it like you're Debbie bleedin' 'Arry. Hell, if they extracted all the electricity from your brains, you two wouldn't have enough to make a lightbulb flicker."

Frank was still trying to think of a witty response, something about being better looking than Blondie's glamorous lead singer, but Mo's furious expression made the words catch in his throat. "You OK, Mo?" he asked instead.

"I will be when I know we got away with this, but until then we keep our heads down," said Mo. "We shouldn't be sticking them above the parapet wearing things like... well, this." He held up the wig. "Maybe it's time we had a little bonfire. There's a wood burning stove out in the kitchen, I suggest we file it away in there."

Silence descended on the cottage, Cozza breaking the spell.

"Anything else troubling you?" he asked. He had known Mo a long time.

"Nah, fine."

Mo wasn't going to tell them that he had just spent 15 minutes trying to get hold of Beryl on the phone. She had known roughly the time he would ring and the fact she hadn't answered was an item out of place in his meticulously organised brain. She should have been waiting by the phone table, literally at his beck and call. He hoped she was all right, though he wasn't overly concerned about his family's welfare. The thing with Audrey had been playing on his mind, her declaration of love a worrying escalation and he wouldn't put it past the crazy tart to stir the pot, maybe visit Beryl and reveal details of the whole sordid affair.

Audrey was younger than Bee, more headstrong, and he had no doubt she worshipped the ground he walked on. It fed his ego and was almost certainly the reason he had started up with her. That it had continued was down to the fact she had no limits when it came to sex, and he did things to her his wife would never countenance. Come to think of it, he wouldn't want Beryl doing things like that. She was the mother of his kids after all.

Respect couldn't rein in a man's urges, though. Audrey satisfied his dark, carnal side. He had wanted to end the affair almost from the day it started, but had been drawn deeper and deeper into a labyrinth of excitement. What made Audrey appealing to him was also what made her dangerous: call it off and who knew what she might do?

Younger women were different these days, more independent. Audrey wasn't a girly girl. She preferred dressing in dark colours and plastering on garish make-up, like some of her music heroes. While his wife wouldn't dream of going out in ripped tights, it was almost compulsory for his lover. She challenged everything he had been brought up to believe about a woman. Her style shouldn't have worked, but it did. The girl oozed sex. She even instigated it.

Perhaps it was the punk scene that inspired women of a certain age to challenge the natural order – singers with bizarre names like Polly Styrene, Siouxsie Sioux and Becci Bondage, who spat out defiant lyrics about previously taboo subjects, parading their individuality without fear. Or maybe their freedom of expression was down to the fact that for the first time in British political history a woman sat at the head of government – a woman whose strength made powerful men look weak by comparison. The modern female seemed to think that if they were bold and brave enough they could achieve anything. Big Mo wasn't afraid of much, but this scared him.

"Fuck it, give me some hooch," he demanded of Cozza.

"Now you're talking... let your hair down, Mo. God knows, there have been few chances of late."

"Too fackin' right." He swigged from the bottle and wandered out through the kitchen into the small garden area, lighting a cigarette and blowing smoke into the warm evening air. He made a mental note to ring Beryl later. Heaven help her if she didn't answer then.

32

"IT'S a bit loud!" Beryl stood on tiptoe to whisper in Stan's ear. He wore a pristine blue leather jacket, turned-up jeans and Converse baseball boots. Underneath the jacket, his T-shirt bore the band's name: Dr Feelgood.

"I hope you weren't expecting The Carpenters," he said, leaning into her so he could be heard. "You ain't seen the Feelgoods before, babe?"

"No!" she shouted.

"You ain't lived," he said. "That manic one on the guitar? That's Wilko Johnson. He always jerks around as if someone pumped him up with live electricity. He can really play though. Listen to those riffs, man! Hey, you like Quo? My..."

"Your what?"

"Nothing." Even in the dark she could tell he was blushing.

"You were going to say your wife," she nudged him playfully.

"Sorry."

"It's OK. We're both adults. Where is she, anyway?"

"Sheila?"

"Why, how many wives have you got?"

"Only one," he said. "She's at home with a mate."

"I get it. She didn't want to come, so you brought me as a substitute." This was fun, thought Beryl. He was so easy to wind up. Strangely, even though she was on a date with a married man, she felt in control, something she could never claim with Maurice. It was liberating that for one night, and one night only, she had no kids to worry about having taken them for a sleepover at a friend's on the estate, explaining she had lots to do before heading off on holiday. It meant she had no need to be home at a certain time and wouldn't be lying awake nervously awaiting the rattle of keys in the lock.

The music changed and Stan beamed, bending to whisper in her ear, brushing her skin gently with his lips as he did so. "I love this one!" he said. She smelt the musk on him. Oh please! she thought. Hai Karate? Mo had stopped wearing it years ago. Even so, a tingle passed through her, an urge to get up close and personal with her 'date'. It reminded her of earlier times with Mo, but she told herself to stop thinking like that for fear of killing her buzz.

The singer leaned over the audience, shouting something about wanting to hear a girl moan after getting her home, only to find out she had been leading him on. A prick tease, the boys at school had called that type of girl. She had known girls like that who had promised to "put out" for boys, milked them for whatever they had, then laughingly waved them goodbye without fulfilling their end of the bargain. She felt a degree of sympathy for the singer, her in-built moral compass telling her that a woman acting like that was wrong.

Without warning, Stan swung her around, dancing extravagantly as he belted out the chorus along with hundreds of other Feelgood fans.

"She's a wind up, wind up!"

God, he loved life, she thought. He acted as if he didn't have a care in the world. He was everything Mo wasn't and she wasn't just thinking that because of what she had learned earlier. Mo had his good points, sure, but she would never describe him as a fun person. His strongest attribute until now had been his loyalty. Once that had been shown up as a myth it was hard to find anything left to love.

The band closed out the song and announced they were taking a short break. Beryl blew at her fringe in a pointless attempt to cool herself, brushed her perspiration-soaked forehead and pulled at her vest top to prevent it sticking to her skin. She hoped Stan couldn't smell her body odour. Gross. She remembered a line her mother used to say: "Men sweat, dear, ladies glow." She sniggered. Some lady her mother had been.

"What now?" she asked.

"Let's find some seats in the pub next door," said Stan. "We can have a drink and a chat. Gigs are great fun but they're a conversation killer."

"I'm not very good at conversation," she said.

"Oh, I think you'll be fine once you get started – it's a case of warming you up."

She was flirting, but couldn't stop herself. "... and how do you propose to do that?"

"Alcohol helps. It can melt even the most frosted-up vocal chords. Come on!" He grabbed her hand, leading her through crowds of excited fans still talking about the band. When they found a cosy corner of the pub to their liking she sat down while he headed for the bar. She furtively cast around for any faces she might recognise, wondering how many times Mo had parked his slag in a discreet corner of the pub. What did the little tart drink? Probably some awful fizz meant to appeal to those just out of school. At least Beryl was in Dalston, an area she doubted anyone would recognise her. Mo carried out his liaisons right under her nose, his contempt for her nauseating.

"Here," said Stan, placing a half of cider in front of her. He took a swig from a pint of bitter and settled in opposite. "Aaaah, that hit the spot," he said. "You OK? You look deep in thought."

"Oh... it's nothing."

"Let's not hide stuff from each other," he said. "We'll get nowhere, babe."

Usually, she hated people calling her "babe". It was something that lech Cozza always did it and it made her want to kick him in the balls. With Stan, though, it felt natural, almost flattering, as if he really did think of her as a babe, like one of those models in the glossy magazines. It brought a smile to her face.

"I propose we tackle the elephants in the room straight away," he said. "I'll start. My wife is called Sheila. She works at a bakery in

Barking. We got hitched very young, I was 16 and she was 18... Have you seen *The Graduate*?" Beryl nodded. "She was my Mrs Robinson."

Beryl burst out laughing. "Oh, please!" she exclaimed as heads turned in their direction. She put her hand up to conceal her face, leaning over and lowering her voice to a whisper. "There's only two years' difference between you! If she 'seduced' you it wasn't as if you were young and naive and she was the experienced 'older' woman. You're such a comedian!"

"Shhhh! They'll be demanding I do an impromptu stand-up act next," he said, putting his hand on hers. She didn't pull away. Only now did she notice the spark in his dark, chocolate eyes. She ought to have been embarrassed, looking at a relative stranger that way, but felt comfortable in his company. He was different from any man she had ever met, not that she was experienced in relationships with the opposite sex. Most men she knew were unpredictable and, in some ways, frightening. She didn't feel the least bit scared in the presence of witty Stan Marshall, who obviously thought he was a real catch for the ladies.

"So, once you got married to this much older woman...?" she prompted.

"For a while things were great, you know, the honeymoon period before life takes over. We couldn't keep our hands off each other. Then everything settled down and I realised we had little in common. You know what they say? Marry in haste..."

"Repent at leisure. Yeah, I heard that," said Beryl. "You sound like you were on the same wavelength in your musical tastes, though?"

"Absolutely! But isn't that the sort of thing that brings people together in the first place. Though I hate to say it, there is a lot more to a relationship than enjoying the same bands."

"You're not happy?"

"Sheila's a nice, sweet girl. A bit bullish, but sometimes I think we've gone as far as we can. I'm not sure about divorce, we're both Catholics, but it's been a loveless marriage for some time."

"No kids?"

He paused. "No. It's never happened for us. Maybe that's it. Little chance now, though. She's moved into the spare room and we haven't slept together for ages. She has her own problems, a bit of a troubled background to be honest. I don't think she understands my, um, needs, though. I'm a pretty intimate person, I require closeness and love. It's like she's shut me out and I feel trapped. That's all there is I can say... on my part. What about you?"

Beryl thought. Where to start? She wasn't used to blurting out personal secrets, even to close friends. If Maurice knew he would rip her limb from limb. Sod him.

"Maurice is the only man I've ever been with," she admitted. "He rescued me from an unhappy childhood. My parents split up early and my mum disappeared, ran off with a well-paid footballer, would you believe? Dad never got over it. He did his best bringing us up but he wasn't the sort of bloke to dole out emotional support. He drank heavily, too. It was left to us – me and my twin brothers – to muddle through. They were OK I guess, but they had enough on their plate looking after each other and Dad."

"Your mum abandoned you?"

"That's about the size of it." She felt the tears prickling at the back of her eyes, the memories flooding back. Taking a drink, the fruity taste of the cider turned sour on her tongue. "She wrote me a letter, trying to explain it. I've only really been able to understand any of it since I got older. Even so, I couldn't imagine upping and leaving my kids. Cutting all ties and never seeing them again. It takes a special kind of bitch." She realised she had raised her voice again. He gave her hand a squeeze, prompting her to carry on. "When something like that happens to you, you try to piece the story together – look for the spanner that was thrown into the works to make the whole thing grind to a halt. From the way I understand it, they had once been very much in love. Dad was reasonably well educated and worked as foreman at one of the big print works in the city. He met my mum, Shirley, when she worked behind the bar in one of the Docklands pubs. She was attracted by his generosity and his flash car and they married after a whirlwind romance... like you and Sheila, I guess."

He nodded. Those eyes, she thought. He was like a priest in the confessional, teasing the truth out of her without saying a word. "I came along a year later, followed by Kevin and Keith a year after that. My dad, Albert's his name, invested in a house out in Hainault. We loved it, plenty of open space to ride our bikes and not as claustrophobic as where we live now. Me and the boys were sent to a well-regarded school and everything seemed perfect. I guess we were buffered from reality and too pre-occupied with our own lives to notice what was going on around us."

"Most kids are like that, I think," said Stan. "If you asked me about my mum and dad, and the way they really were with each other, I wouldn't have a clue. So when did you realise it was going wrong?"

"When I found the note on my pillow. I was just 13. I came home from school and it was lying there. I read it three times before it made any sense. She said she'd felt trapped for a long time, and that she wasn't suited to the role of stay-at-home mum. A few months before she had taken a waitressing job at a country club in order to 'rediscover herself'." Beryl took another glug of the cider and realised her glass was empty. Had she really drunk it that quickly?

"I've heard about this rediscovering yourself lark before," he said. "What a cliché!" he patted her hand encouragingly. "Don't stop though, babe, you're a dab hand at this conversation lark."

Beryl smiled. "In the letter she told us that we should never think she didn't love us, but Dad was stifling her. She didn't mention her head being turned by a wealthy footballer who lavished champagne and presents on her... I only learned about that later, hearing the old man ranting drunkenly down the phone at her." She paused and pulled out her purse. "Look," she said, wiping her eye. "It's my round now, let me..."

"I wouldn't think of it. Wait there!" He was out of his seat straight away, leaving her to her thoughts. When he returned, he had a tray with another half of cider, a pint of beer and two shot glasses. "We needed something stronger," he said. "I told you alcohol warmed the vocal chords." He sat down, handing her a shot glass. "On the count of three..." He banged his glass three times on the table, counting as he did so, then let his head fall back and swallowed the liquid down in one, grimacing. "Aaah..." he said, "Now your turn."

"Oh, I don't know," she said, "I need my wits about me tomorrow."

"Tomorrow is another day. Live for the moment, Beryl. Come on, it's a great night, we're having fun and exorcising some demons in the process. A little Dutch courage can't do any harm, can it?"

She thought about what Maurice might say then remembered it was his fault she was here in the first place. Copying his lead, she banged the small glass on the table and downed the contents in one. Nice. Not too sharp. A slight burn at the back of her throat there to remind her it actually contained alcohol. "Wow!" she said.

"Tequila. It's Mexican."

"Never had it before. I could get used to it, but maybe not tonight. Cheers." She lifted her cider in his direction. For a moment he looked perplexed then realised she wanted to clink glasses. When he reciprocated, she said: "Thank you for everything. Tonight has been really nice. I've enjoyed myself."

"It's nice to see you smile," he said. "You've got a beautiful smile. You need to smile more."

"Easier said than done," she murmured, sinking back into her thoughts. They sat there in silence for a moment.

"So why are you here?" he asked, catching her off guard. "Has he hit you again?"

"No, no, nothing like that. To be honest he isn't all bad, Maurice. Like I said, he rescued me."

"The last time I saw you, he'd hurt you. Call me old fashioned but I don't believe a man should ever hit a woman."

"Well, you don't understand all of it... our relationship."

"Explain then," he said.

She sat back in the booth, took a deep breath. "Things really started to change when my dad lost his job," she said. "The twins invented a world for themselves and I felt excluded. Because Dad was no longer on the same money he had to sell the house and we moved to a smaller place in Barking. I got in with the wrong crowd and Dad was so wrapped up in his own self-loathing that he barely noticed. They were a bit older these kids, fancied themselves as rebels, drinking, smoking, hanging around near a rank of shops and terrorising the locals at night. The police often turned up to move us on, asking where our parents were, but we just gave them lip, then legged it."

"Maurice was one of those kids?"

She took a drink. "Hell, no... he came later. One of the places we used to go if we had a bit of pocket money was the local disco. One time, I think I'd just turned 15, I bumped into this well-dressed skinhead: perfectly ironed white shirt, red braces, faded blue bags and Doc Marten boots. He was cock of the walk, his mates in awe of him. They called him Big Mo. At first, I felt really intimidated. He was so full of self confidence and I was the opposite. He had this air of danger about him, different from anyone I'd ever met."

She paused, reflecting on the moment. "When he came over to talk to me, I was tongue-tied. Somehow we hit it off, though. I guess we had things in common. We were both pissed off with our home life for starters. He told me his dad ruled their house with a rod of iron. I told him about my mother, and the story made him angry. I felt for the first time since she'd left I had a real ally. To cut a long story short we went for a walk on the local field, me wrapped in his olive-coloured bomber jacket..." Her mind wandered, inhibitions disappearing as rapidly as the tequila. "He took my virginity that night. There... on that field, under the stars. It was fumbled and quick, but being in his embrace made me feel safe and protected for the first time in years."

"So when did you marry?"

"A year later. I left school at 16 – he had finished some time earlier – and discovered I was pregnant with Chuck. Before it started to show he whisked me down to the local register office and we tied the knot. I didn't even tell Dad or the twins, the only witnesses being his best mate Cozza and my friend Mary Beth. Because I was pregnant we were given a council flat on the estate and, well, here we are seven years later, two kids and..." She looked off into the distance, the hint of a smile on her lips.

"Why does he hit you?" The question rocked her like a Big Mo uppercut.

"He doesn't, not normally. He isn't a bad man. Once or twice his temper has got the better of him."

"How big are you? Five four at best? And he's... what?"

"Six foot five."

"Well, if your boy Chuck got bullied at school by a kid a lot bigger and heavier than him, you would be outraged."

"Of course."

"I don't see the difference. Look, you can't go on like this. These things escalate and a leopard doesn't change its spots. Leave him."

Bam! There it was. Straight talking from a person she barely knew. She stood abruptly.

"I should go," she said. "This was a mistake."

He continued to hold her hand, though, and she didn't pull away.

"Sorry. None of my business," he said. "Be honest, though, if you were happily married would you be here with me?"

The tears sprouted. He was looking at her earnestly, those magnetic eyes demanding an answer. She sank back into her seat.

"I can't," she said. "Leave him, I mean."

"Because he'll come after you?"

"No, not that, though I don't think he would just let me go," she said.

How could she explain it to him? She knew exactly how it would pan out. If she told Mo she was walking out, he would have the perfect riposte. She could imagine him saying it. "You're just like your mother." If anything was likely to make her turn her anger in on herself it was the mere mention of that woman. Ingrained in her psyche was an all-encompassing fear that she might have inherited the same values as the person who had abandoned her and her siblings.

"You're nothing like her... your mum." Damn! How the hell did he do that? He had read her mind again. She was still trying to work it out when she realised he was still talking. "It is obvious to anyone you adore your kids. You were made to be a mother. Do you feel stifled by them...? Not a bit. I bet half the time we've been here you've been thinking about them. They're with a friend tonight, yeah? When I brought the tequila and you said you had a busy day tomorrow... you were thinking about them." She nodded. "So it's not the same... nowhere near," he continued. "If anything, to walk away would be saving your kids, making sure they weren't growing up in a hostile, violent environment. It could be the best thing you ever did for them."

"They love their dad," she protested, tears streaming down her face. All the time, though, she was asking herself the question: "Could I really leave Maurice?"

"I'VE had a fabulous night. Wonderful. Thanks so much." She held her hand out and he shook it, both of them feeling the gesture was not enough, an awkward silence descending between them. They had left Dalston shortly after 11, Stan flagging a taxi down then talking animatedly to the driver. He seemed to know everyone. While she could count the number of people who were genuine friends of Maurice on the fingers of one hand, it seemed Stan was on first-name terms with half of London. She accepted that some of it could be attributed to the inner confidence a person needed to run a successful market stall, but it was more than that. He had an easy going charm, a warmth that had made her instantly bond with him.

Standing outside the door of her flat, she glanced at her watch and noted it was quarter to midnight. She knew she had missed several calls from Maurice. The two pints of cider and three shots had deadened any fears she might have of the consequences. In fact, she felt empowered, happy to let Maurice stew in his own juices. She could get back to the normal humdrum, fear-infused routine of her life tomorrow.

Suddenly she realised Stan was walking away. She watched the sway of his shoulders, his lithe, well-proportioned body moving in a fluid rhythm as if interpreting some internal music soundtrack. She couldn't stop herself, the words flying out of her mouth before she considered the consequences. "Wait!"

He turned, a smile playing on his lips. Slipping her shoes off and placing them neatly by the door, she felt cold air invigorating her tired feet. Then she was running, her short black skirt flapping around her thighs as she closed the gap between them. Reaching up, gripping his neck beneath his hair and pulling his head down to meet hers, their lips clashed in a fusion of hops, apples, tequila, smoke, aftershave and perfume. She looped her fingers in the wiry brown curls, pulling him closer, drinking deep of the intoxicating brew and only wrenching herself free when she needed to come up for air.

Breathless, dishevelled, invigorated and dizzy she stood there, her hands on her knees, looking up at his startled face. At last, she was able to whisper the one word which would change things forever, allowing it to escape before it could be snatched away on the warm summer night's breeze.

"Stay."

33

"BLOODY hell, Chuck! There's sand all over the shop," stormed Big Mo. "What did I tell you about bringing it into the Daimler? Put a towel down, I said. Beryl! Look what your son's done now, he's got sand all over my fackin' car."

"Funny, Chuck always happens to be 'my' son when he's done something wrong." Beryl peered in through the passenger window, her expression devoid of humour.

"Don't fuckin' start, love," said Mo. "Christ, you've been in a funny mood since you bloody got here. Some people are cryin' out for a nice holiday, and here's you with a face like a slapped arse."

"Don't have a go at me because your posh motor has got a bit of sand in it!" Beryl was in the mood for a fight. "I told you at the time it was a risk buying a nice car like this while the kids were young. These things are bound to happen. You wouldn't listen, though. Never do."

"What's got into you?" he asked. "You on the blob?"

"What?" she wrinkled her nose in a disbelieving sneer, looking him in the eye. "Oh, that's great that is! Just because I feel a bit under the weather and ain't going around with a big smile plastered all over my face like a demented zombie, you reckon it must be my time of the month."

"No?"

"No," she said, calming down. "I told you. I don't feel myself at the moment. Bit of flu or something."

"Flu? It's the middle of bloody summer. Hottest weather in a long time."

"You've never heard of a summer cold?"

"Can't say I have," he admitted. "Anyway, it's not bothered you in the past. We're husband and wife, in case you've forgotten. For better or worse. You should..."

"Is this about sex?" she demanded a bit too loudly. "I should have guessed. Do you think I should open my legs at your beck and call? Lie back and think of England? Fuck you, Maurice Dolan!" Immediately the words were out of her mouth she regretted them. She never swore in front of the children, but too many unsavoury thoughts had been festering inside her head since she'd uncovered his adultery. She knew a volcanic reaction was coming, just wasn't sure when. No one shouted at Big Mo Dolan like that and got away with it, particularly not his wife and particularly not in front of his 'pals' and their partners. He would consider it a mark of mutinous disrespect.

Moving away from the window, she held Sly close and waited for the fireworks to start. He was too young to realise it, but her youngest son was an unwitting contributor to her uncharacteristic flare-up. He himself had been feeling poorly and a local doctor had diagnosed tonsillitis. His miserable wailing had robbed her of sleep. At least it had been an excuse to interrupt any ideas Maurice had on the sexual front. By the time she had settled Sly down most nights, the alcohol had taken its effect and her cheating husband was in a snore-ravaged coma. Better that than him passing on a sexual disease from his little tart.

During the day, it had been easy to steer clear of the bastard. Sly was far too unwell to venture into the sea so most of the time she had stayed at home with him, allowing Mo and Chuck valuable bonding time. It wasn't that she didn't want to spend quality time with her eldest boy, too, but letting him wander off to the beach or park with his father was the lesser of two evils.

On the occasions Big Mo tried to kiss or cuddle her, Beryl gave in because it was the easiest thing to do. She questioned his motives, though. The way she saw it, he just wanted to give his friends and their partners the impression that his marriage was in perfect working order and his wife firmly under his control. In the recesses of her mind, she still harboured dreams of leaving him. How would that play out in the world of Big Mo Dolan?

When she wasn't thinking of how to extricate herself from their sham of a marriage, Beryl's subconscious was saturated with images of Stan Marshall. He'd been such a considerate and adventurous lover – their intimacy so completely different from that which she had experienced with her husband.

It was weird. Their entanglement seemed to last forever that night, yet when she woke in the morning it was as if it had all been a weird hallucination. She vaguely recalled Stan slipping from her bed sometime around 3am, whispering goodbye and kissing her on the cheek, but the image was lost in a haze of alcohol. When she did drag herself out of bed she felt like shit as she packed the car and collected the boys.

She couldn't believe Mo had let her drive the Daimler on such a long journey. Usually she was restricted to ferrying him home from the pub on the occasions he was too drunk to walk, but that was about the only time he let her behind the wheel. It was ironic that the first time he entrusted his pride and joy to her, she was still drunk from the night before and had managed just a few hours sleep. He would have gone ballistic had he known.

She had a car full, too – her kids plus Cozza's daughter Wendy and wife Bev. Cozza's son Sean had headed off to an open-air festival, thankfully, and Beryl was also grateful Frank's woman Marsha had chosen to take the train. The sight of that woman's distorted face in the rear mirror would have made her throw up the concoction of tequila and cider that sat uneasily on her stomach. It was bad enough having to make stilted conversation with Cozza's bint when your head was shrouded in an alcoholic fug, let alone experiencing a close encounter with that monstrosity.

"In the car, boy!" said Mo, wrenching Sly from her grasp. His whimpering lasted seconds before the door slammed.

"What are you...?"

Too late, Beryl saw the curtain pole in Mo's hand. "Come on, you've obviously got issues," he said. "Perhaps Reg can help iron them out."

"Wha..? No! Don't you..." Slap! Her eyes fixed on the heavy lump of scarred and stained wood, she had missed the open hand careering towards her face from the opposite direction. It stung like perfume in a papercut and she screamed, legs buckling beneath her. Scraping her knee on the shingle driveway, she had no time to reflect on the pain. She felt herself being dragged along, her feet scuttling for purchase in jelly sandals ill-equipped for the purpose. Aware a couple of buttons had dislodged and her short, white summer dress with the red flowers was billowing open, to her utter consternation and disbelief she caught sight of Cozza leering at her. Jeez! She thought. He's got the same in-built homing instinct as one of those fucking pigeons he keeps in his allotment shed.

"Do something Paul, love," whispered Bev at his side.

"Stay outta this!" blasted Mo, wheeling on her, his eyes bloodshot from the week's booze binge. "Keep your missus in line, mate, or..."

Cozza grabbed Bev's hand and tugged her protesting towards the house. She looked over her shoulder, fear and puzzlement chiselled on her face.

The scrape of the gate informed Beryl she was changing scene. She was now in a narrow passageway which ran alongside the cottage, her knees bumping against wood and concrete to add new grazes to her collection. Her mind was thinking desperately of a way to extricate herself from the situation, but she knew once Mo had started he was impossible to stop.

Things rarely went this far, however. For the most part Beryl found ways to extinguish the flames of his fury before they leapt out of control. Since the incident in the hallway at Christmas there had been the occasional open-handed slap, a subtle knee to the thigh, and a more blatant kick to the shin. When Reg appeared, though, she knew things had elevated to a new level.

In the past, Maurice had always regretted these outbursts; his apologies tended to be whole-hearted, complete with sobbing, as he handed over a huge bouquet of flowers or some expensive item of jewellery as compensation. For a short while, he would be extra thoughtful, gentle and tolerant until some new 'crime' of hers pushed him over the edge into violence again.

She wondered if he would have been the same if the children hadn't arrived. Mo obviously loved Chuck and Sly but, as parents, they had contradictory views on the way the boys should be brought up. He wanted them fully prepared for a dangerous, unforgiving world while her natural instinct was to shield them from such realities. These differences of opinion had widened as Chuck grew older, the dispute running parallel to the increased strain on their finances.

Mo's answer when the pressure built was to escape to the bookies or one of the local public houses and seek the support of his mates. It was on one such occasion he came across Reg, and it had quickly been promoted to his weapon of choice. Now here she was, splayed out on the back lawn of the cottage, her dress up around her waist. Mo was pounding the wooden pole against his hand, the click of the wood beating a frightening rhythm against the selection of gold sovereign rings on his hand, like a clock ticking down to her destruction.

"You wanna get lippy with me?" he demanded, kicking her in the side of the thigh to add another purple welt to the collection. "Do you? Fuckin' 'ell, the things I put myself through for this family. What reward do I get? My wife embarrassing me in front of my crew. You don't know the half of it, you don't, Beryl... You don't know the risks I take just so you and the kids can have a few decent things. Well maybe it's time you learnt."

He hefted the club again, shaking his arms and revolving his head on his neck until there was a cracking sound like a gunshot. As he pulled his arms back sharply there was a shout of "No Dad! Leave Mu..." followed by a blood-curdling scream. In her blurry line of sight she saw Mo's eyes open wide before he span and sank to his knees. "Fuck!" he shouted, his head tossed skywards. "Fuck!"

She summoned up all her remaining strength to push herself into a sitting position, trying to focus on the drama in front of her. Mo was cradling something in his arms, blood soaking his top. It took a fraction of a second for the message to pass from her eyes to her brain. When the full horror of what she was seeing sank in she launched herself forward, oblivious to her own pain.

"Chuck!!!" she screamed.

PART THREE

34

"HE'S a very lucky young fellow."

Maurice and Beryl Dolan listened to the man in the white coat while peering over his shoulder at their son, sleeping peacefully in a hospital bed, his head cocooned in bandages. "There's a lot of swelling and he's going to have two shiners to show off to his mates at school, plus an array of stitches, but fortunately the only thing broken is his nose," said the doctor. "Keep an eye on him. If he is sick or anything you need to take him straight to your local hospital because he could be suffering from concussion... hopefully nothing worse. When it's a head injury we take extra care. We have a lot of kids come in after holiday accidents – they fall off climbing frames and the like and break an arm or a leg. If they bump their head things aren't so simple. The brain can't be patched up with plaster and bandages."

Mo offered his hand. "Thank you, Doctor. I'm sure he's learned his lesson: Don't stand up on a moving swing, eh Beryl?"

Her face partially hidden beneath a headscarf, she had done a good job disguising her injuries. They were mostly superficial cuts and scrapes, though a big chunk of her hair was missing at the back where Mo had pulled her along. She imagined it was noticeable, but was an expert these days in damage concealment. "Yes, Maurice. I'm sure he won't do that again," she murmured dutifully.

"Hopefully, you'll be more careful, too," the Doctor told her. "I know you were trying to rescue him, but you could do without getting a kick in the face for your troubles. That's a serious bruise on your cheek. Still... this is what's going to happen now. When he wakes I'll give him another few tests, just to make sure he's OK. Then I'll ask the pharmacy to issue his drugs..."

"Drugs?"

The doctor acted quickly to ease Mo's concerns. "Painkillers, mainly. He's likely to feel pretty rubbish over the next few days until the swelling subsides. What I'm prescribing is fine for kids, provided you stick to the right dose. Now, if you don't mind, I have to get on. You can sit with him until he wakes... no problem."

"Thanks."

Mo watched the doctor stroll off down the corridor then perched on a visitors' chair, his eyes focused on his son. He was still for a moment, Beryl spotting the tears streaming down her husband's face, dropping from his chin to his white T-shirt. He put a hand up to block their path, squeezing his nose in an effort to stem the flow. Pulling a chair up beside him, she rested an arm across his heaving shoulders.

"What have I done?" A drop of spittle fell from his lips before his whole body gave way to grief, the control that so dominated his life deserting him at his lowest ebb. She had never seen him weep in public and it made her forget briefly why they were in hospital. All she saw was Mo as he had been in the early stages of their relationship.

"Look," she said. "He'll be fine, I'm sure. It was an accident... where Chucky was concerned, anyway. But you know this has got to stop, don't you? For the boys' sakes. We can't go on fighting the way we have. We've got responsibilities. We're the adults here but sometimes we act like the kids. It's time we both grew up."

He turned his head to look at her, his eyes rheumy from the crying and heavy drinking sessions which had dominated his week. It was as if he had been on a mission to get cirrosis of the liver in record-breaking time and she had an uneasy feeling she was being kept in the dark about what had happened in the days leading up to the holiday. Maurice was always edgy when he had "a bit of work come in", yet she had never seen him so wound up. His reaction over a few grains of sand had been totally out of proportion. For the first time since she had known him, he appeared to have lost control of what was going on around him.

Perhaps his brother's absence was having a bigger effect than she could have expected. The two were close, but Mo had heard before their break that Clive was fine and that, if anything, should have made him more relaxed; his younger sibling had survived without injury and was staying on to garrison the Falklands until August, when no doubt he would return to a hero's welcome.

Her mind drifting, she was aware of Mo pushing himself to his feet and looking down at her. "Sorry, Bee, truly I am," he said. "You don't deserve this. I know I'm a bastard to you at times but I'm gonna try harder... promise. I just get so shaken up, like a bottle of fizzy pop. All it needs is someone to unscrew the lid and I explode."

She touched his arm, but didn't say anything. She was hearing the excuses and apologies too often these days. What she wanted was real evidence he could change. "We've got to pack our stuff," he said. "We have to be out of there this morning. It must be about 6am now. You wait with the boy and I'll race back, pack the car, collect Sly from Bev and return to take you home."

She watched him weave his way past a couple of beds surrounded by screens and disappear into the corridor.

Shuffling her chair forward, Beryl took Chuck's hand.

MO removed the cigarettes from his leather jacket pocket. The black packaging with the gold lettering made him shiver. JPS. Fucking hell! What didn't Cozza understand about them being unlucky? "Didn't have your brand," Cozza had explained on his return from the shop. "These were the next best thing."

"Not to me they're not!" he had argued.

After loading the car, Mo said goodbye to the others and told them he would see them back in London. The other two would stop off to pick up the post office haul from a lock-up Cozza had rented just outside Battle.

Back at the hospital, Mo quickly popped in to tell them he was back then waited for Beryl and Chuck in the short-stay car park. He didn't want to risk leaving the car in case an officious parking attendant turned up. Chuck was awake but groggy and when Mo made a fuss of him there didn't seem much response. He couldn't blame the kid. He probably hated his father right now for what he had done. The thought of hurting his own family – particularly his first-born – brought back the tears. He had to get a grip. Leaving Sly asleep in the back seat he strolled to the hospital entrance, pulling out a smoke and fiddling in his coat pockets for his lighter. When he came up empty, he thought he'd just missed it somehow, so turned all his pockets out. He always kept it in the inside pocket on the left-hand side of this particular jacket, but perhaps the shock of the last day had made him forgetful.

This second search was more meticulous and he pulled out tissues, a couple of chewing gum wrappers, a handful of coins, his wallet, but still no lighter. Tentacles of fear began to wrap themselves around him. Where the hell was it?

A bloke hobbled out of the hospital entrance, his foot in a plaster cast. "All right?" he asked, seeing Mo patting himself down. "You want a light?" He waved a flame under his nose but Mo shook his head and walked back in through the entrance doors to the hospital, intent on retracing his steps. If he had dropped it what were the chances some little punk had picked it up and had it away on his toes? The feeling of unease morphed seamlessly into anger. Despite his earlier chat with Beryl the trigger movements were so ingrained in him there was no easy way to stop them. It was as if one of those TV hypnotists had whispered a word in his ear to set off a chain reaction.

Storming onto the ward, his nose was instantly assaulted by a cocktail of disinfectant, urine and vomit. Beryl was alarmed to see him. "What's wrong?" she asked.

"My fackin' lighter. You seen it?"

"No, hun, have you looked in..?"

"Course I've fackin' looked! Everywhere. It should be in my pocket and it ain't."

"Maybe it fell out in the car?"

Without acknowledging the suggestion, he turned on his heels, feeling Beryl and Chuck's eyes drilling into his back. In his heightened state of paranoia he wondered whether they were plotting against him somehow.

The smoker with his leg in plaster was walking back through the sliding doors as Mo barrelled out, knocking him into a coffee shop run by the Women's Royal Voluntary Service. Cups and saucers went flying. "Hey," said the victim, straightening himself. "You should learn some manners, mate!"

The door buzzed open again and Mo stormed towards him, fists clenched. The old ladies behind the stall retreated from the line of fire. "What did you fackin' say to me?" Mo demanded. The smoker cowered, hands protectively covering his face as he sought to make himself as small a target as possible. "I should tear your fackin' arms off and beat you with the soggy ends, you piss-taking cunt."

"S... sorry." The smoker screwed his eyes shut and waited for his punishment. One second... two... But Mo was gone, charging away, thumping parked cars like a rugby player handing off opponents.

MO removed Sly's car seat, parking the boy on the floor beside him. He pushed his hands down the side of the seats, coming up with discarded crisps and half-sucked sweets, cursing himself for letting Beryl drive scummy Bev and her daughter down to Hastings. The truth, of course, was his own kids were responsible for most of the detritus, but it suited his purposes to vent his wrath on others, his own family deserving a free pass after all that had happened. He checked the floor, lifting rubber mats and finding a kids' colouring book, an Ordnance Survey map of the south of England, an escaped tampon from a woman's handbag, some pens and a toy car. For a second he thought he'd struck lucky, only for the crushing weight of disappointment to fall when the square metal object he held in his hand turned out to be another of those batteries required to power one of the children's toys. He thought of the posh bloke who had told him to move his car all that time ago. "Twat!" It still made him angry.

Switching to the front seats, he found a bag of opened barley sugars – Beryl's favoured cure for travel sickness – and a couple of Bazooka Joe bubble gum wrappers in the passenger's glove compartment. He pictured Bev blowing bubbles so large they popped and spread across her face. God, she was gross. It probably wasn't the only thing she liked exploding in her face, the slag. One of Beryl's women's mags rested against the passenger door, but that was it. With a resigned sigh he realised he would have to go back to the holiday home.

HE saw the police car as soon as he turned into the street. "Shit!"

A tall man with CID written all over him was talking to someone Mo could only assume was the owner of their rented cottage. He smacked the walnut dashboard so hard he regretted it immediately, fearing he might have caused some damage. The CID officer looked up as if hearing the noise and Mo had to duck out of sight, aware he could be recognised from a police mug shot further down the line.

What could he do now? If the police instigated a search of the premises, they might find the lighter. With modern-day fingerprint techniques and the giveaway inscription it wouldn't be too much of a leap to tie in Big Mo with the Tunbridge Wells job. The cops having tracked down their hideaway so quickly suggested someone, somewhere had tipped them off. If there was one thing Mo hated more than anything, it was a sneaky, double-crossing grass.

"IT'S a lovely spot," said the Detective Sergeant.

"It's all yours," said the cottage proprietor, digging into the pocket of his tweed jacket for the keys. "There were a couple of families and their kids down here before you, but they left this morning. Give me time to make sure everything is spick and span. Let me change the bedding and that, then from Monday it's yours. That OK with you?"

"Great," said the officer. "Now, I really must go. Me and Phil, the driver, are supposed to be making house-to-house inquiries about a post office robbery in Tunbridge Wells. The neighbours see us parked here and they'll think something major is going down." He chuckled. "I'll drop off a cheque at the shop first thing in the morning."

"Splendid."

If Big Mo had heard the conversation his stress levels would have plummeted. Unfortunately, he hadn't. He was now breaking all speed limits on a headlong charge back to the Royal East Sussex Hospital, swerving around the narrow streets of Hastings and causing other road users to brake suddenly. Oblivious to the horns sounded in protests, he was only concerned with picking up the rest of his family and getting as far away as possible.

He would piece it all together later.

35

"GOOD Scotch here. Don't know why you settle for that gnat's piss." The old man took a gulp then leaned forward and tapped his companion's glass.

"I'm on duty later," DS Max Cooper raised his half pint of lager and took a sip.

"I hear you've made it," said Billy The Kid Dolan. "Flying squad now, ain't it? Congratulations."

"Cheers," said Cooper. "Been there a couple of weeks. I should be thanking you. You've been a big help."

"Sure," said the older man. "Maybe you'll return the favour sometime. Listen, I hope you don't mind if we make this brief. My son's supposed to be ringing."

"The one who went to the Falklands?"

"Yeah, that's right... Arnie."

"I thought his name was Clive."

"Sorry, that's him. I've always called him Arnie. I wanted him named after my dad, but his mum insisted he was named after her old man. Arnie is his second name, a compromise. I was soft in those days. Appropriate, though, because Dad doted on the boy. He was in the Army, too, and from the minute he could walk my lad wanted to follow in his footsteps... well, march in them. You should have seen him on them kiddie assault courses."

They broke into gentle laughter, easy in each other's company.

"Why isn't he back? A lot of them are."

"His boys, the Scots Guards, have been asked to defend the Islands from further attacks – hence why I can't afford to miss his call. I won't see him for six weeks."

"Talking of wars, any luck with those guns?" said Cooper.

"I may have something for you, but you'll owe me big time... and I don't just want some piddlin' charity hand-out from the CI fund," said Billy, referring to money the police set aside to pay confidential informants... "Also, I need a guarantee from you."

"Oh?"

"Let's face it, you just want to get those guns back and make an easy arrest, don'tcha? I got this from someone pretty close to me. He's got to be kept out of it."

"Do my best," said Cooper. "It's a prickly subject, though. Those weapons can be linked directly to a murder; some lorry driver down in Kent. Also, some bullets were removed from the ceiling after a post office raid down that way the same day. They match the ammunition stolen in the Christmas raid."

Billy fell silent. This was news to him and he was supposed to be the one with his ear to the ground. "You're sure?"

Cooper took a sip of his pint and looked around at the deep, oak-panelled walls of the country club. "Yeah," he said.

Billy stiffened. "I can't tell you anything."

"Oh, come on!" said Cooper, leaning forward, his temper rising. He felt the old man was deliberately teasing him, throwing him a bone then snatching it away as soon as he got excited. Here was Billy The Kid Dolan sitting in luxurious surroundings, his membership paid for by various acts of villainy, and he was clamming up.

"Now, hang on!" said Billy. "Don't get the 'ump with me! I've given you plenty: the security van heist and the warehouse robbery. It doesn't mean you can treat me like a mug!" Nostrils flaring, he leaned forward, getting in Cooper's face. The detective could see the capillary lines shooting across the whites of his eyes. Previous meetings between the pair had always been civilised, their relationship stretching back to a police-sponsored charity boxing event in the East End three years earlier. Introduced by a mutual friend from Molloy's Bethnal Green gym, they had talked about the sport for ages. Since then the relationship had flourished, information passing one way then the other with Billy Dolan benefitting financially from the relationship.

"I warn you," he said, wagging a finger in Cooper's face. "Don't fuckin' push me. I ain't no tinker, tailor, soldier, grass like out of one of them Le Carré books. If I do something for you, I expect something in return. It's been pretty one sided lately. Oh, and let me just say: 32 Endsleigh Park Road, Harrold Hill, Essex."

"What?" Cooper felt the blood drain from his face.

"Nice little bird you got stashed away there: what's her name again? Julie? Your missus know about her?"

"Hey don't you..!"

"No, son, don't you!" stormed Billy, moving so fast that he surprised Cooper, grabbing him by the tie he wore to comply with the country club dress code. "I ain't some limp-dick mongrel allowing the Old Bill to scratch his belly and throw him a bone now and then! I'm a fuckin' rotty and the truth is you don't want to know how bad my bite can be. I could put a few bits of information in the hands of nice old Mr Gradel, your former boss, and maybe he would find a way to cut short your promotion. More to the point, you could find yourself on the wrong end of criminal proceedings. That won't help you, the wife, the lover or that little sprog of yours... what's his name? Christopher?" He let go of Cooper's tie and the detective sat back down. It dawned on him he had underestimated the old man. Billy Dolan might seem like a gentle old grandfather to the outside world, but he wouldn't be treated like lord of the manor if he didn't possess a ruthless streak. Some of those sitting around the room resumed their conversations, occasionally casting furtive glances in their direction.

"Sorry," said Cooper, knowing that to prolong the animosity would do him no favours. If anything, the altercation re-enforced Cooper's belief that he had a top-level informant on his hands.

"Well, is there anything you can tell me about those guns?" he asked, straightening his tie.

Billy sighed. "All I can say was that I was offered some. I'll give you a name, right? The guy's an expert locksmith... that's all I'm saying."

"OK."

"You'll need to put the rest of it together and it's up to you to make sure there are no traces of this leading to anyone close to me: shut it down, quick and simple. Also, when you make the bust, I would appreciate it if some of the, umm, booty might just go missing at some stage and turn up on my doorstep. Comprende?"

Cooper didn't speak Spanish but the message was clear. He was being asked to do a deal with the devil. He could walk away now and, in his own mind at least, he would remain a clean copper. Trouble is he could hear his wife's voice nagging him about the house not being big enough and how the area was unsuitable for bringing up a child. Not to mention the fact he had to keep his tart in the lifestyle to which she had become accustomed.

He leant across the table. "Tell me about the locksmith," he said.

36

HANDSOME Frank and Cozza were throwing handfuls of paper money at each other when Mo entered via the inconspicuous side door. "I heard you were a cheap date!" Cozza was saying.

"Not that bloody cheap," said Frank, throwing a wad of cash back.

In front of them were three burlap sacks, bulging with the proceeds of the post office raid. Mo watched them silently until it registered with the two men they were not alone.

"All right, Mo?" asked Cozza. The big man didn't answer as he stepped further into the room, the dim lights casting a shadow over his face. Peering into a sack, he hefted it, trying to gauge its weight. Heavy, but Mo was a strong man. He lifted it from the floor and hurled it in the direction of his two accomplices. They dodged out of the way as money scattered everywhere.

"Woah!" said Frank. "What's your problem?"

Mo closed the distance between them quickly, Reg hanging loosely at his side. "Who left the cottage last?" he asked.

"We left together," said Cozza.

"Yeah... and you checked everything thoroughly? Crawled under all the beds? Left nothing behind?"

The two men looked at each other. "We did as much as we could mate, honest," said Frank. Without warning, Reg connected with his right knee, sending him crashing to the floor. "Fuck!" he squealed, looking up in shock as he nursed the injury. "What was that for?"

"That's for being fackin' careless!" stormed Mo. He turned to Cozza, who put his hands up defensively. Mo wasn't bothered. The

Jew was a big target. He swung the club in the direction of his former school mate's gut. Cozza made the mistake of moving his hands to defend himself, then screamed as the weapon caught him across the wrists. There was the clicking sound of bones breaking. He let out a high-pitched scream and nursed his hand. Mo bent down, grabbed him by the collar and pulled him across to join Frank, who was groaning in agony.

"You're mental," said Frank. "What do you mean, careless?"

Mo patted Reg against his palm. "How often did I remind you to keep a low profile?" he said.

Cozza answered. "Every day, Mo, and we did. Honest. We didn't do anything..."

"Why then, when I went back to the fackin' cottage, were filth swarming all over it?"

Frank shrugged. "Nothing to do with us." He hauled himself into a sitting position, staring at Big Mo defiantly. "Maybe some of the neighbours called them in after your little exhibition – beating up your wife and kid." It was a provocative statement, bound to bring a reaction. Mo didn't disappoint.

"You pair of fackin' losers!" he stormed. He raised the weapon above his head and Frank balled his fists, psyched up to defend himself. Instead, Mo took off, charging around the room, battering crates and other inanimate objects, Reg warming to the task. Bits of wood and plastic flew through the fetid air of the warehouse, the men on the ground ducking for cover. "...Or maybe," said Mo as he kicked a packing crate into the air, "just maybe, someone saw you two larkin' about, you with that stupid wig on, Handsome. Thought of that? If I ain't with you, it seems compulsory for the two of you to fack about. This is a perfect example. Look what I just walked in on..." He picked up a bundle of notes lying on the floor. "Does this stuff mean so little to you that you can throw it around?"

"Come on, Mo," said Frank, struggling to his feet, relying heavily on the leg which had escaped injury. "That wig thing. That happened on the first day. We burnt the bloody thing after that – on your orders! Don't you think the Old Bill would have been around a damn sight quicker if they had been alerted to that?" He left the question hanging in the air. "Nah, there's something else going on here, I can tell. What is it?"

Mo lifted the club again, smashing another box. Ammunition scattered, proceeds from the warehouse robbery. The two men covered their heads again, fearing one explosion might be followed by another. "What is it?" Mo said, pointing Reg in their direction. "I'm fed up to the back teeth with having to nursemaid you cunts, that's what it is. You're bloody amateur hour, the pair of you. You with your fackin' drugs, Handsome, getting off your tits when what is needed is a level head, shooting innocent people – turning a robbery into a fackin' murder hunt – punching fackin' cattle... for fack's sake, do you think the top blaggers act like that?"

"Give him a break, Mo," said Cozza.

"And you, you fackin' cunt," Mo growled, pointing Reg at Cozza. "It's all one big laugh with you, ain't it? You humour this facker when you should be setting an example. If I wanted a comedy double act I would go up the West End on a Saturday night. Christ, I don't want us to be labelled a gang of jokers, I want us to be thought of as the ultimate professionals, big hitters. I want some fackin' respect! How do I get that when I have to deal with a clown and a drag queen?"

"A drag queen with a gun."

There was a deathly hush. Handsome Frank was now pointing a shotgun in Mo's direction. "Shit," said Mo and Cozza at the same time.

"Steady on, mate," whispered Cozza. The bare-knuckle fighter ignored him.

"We all know what you want, Mo," said Frank. "You want to be your fuckin' dad. You want to get some respect from him, because all he's ever done is treat you like a cunt. We get that. Honestly we do. But that doesn't mean you have to pass it down the line and treat us the same way."

Mo recovered quickly from the shock of seeing the gun. He looked his mate in the eye.

"You see?" he said. "Amateur hour. What if that gun went off, Frank? We'd have London's finest, from Marylebone to Upminster, surrounding this place within a couple of minutes. To be fair, Cozza and I should be really worried. The last time you shot someone you didn't even mean to pull the trigger. It was a complete fack up, like most of the things you do. We don't want another of your 'accidents', Handsome, eh?"

"Oh, that's good," said Frank. "Great way to talk to a man with a gun. You should be showing me some respect. Me and Cozz have been with you all the way, Mo, never shirked when you've asked us to do things for you. By your own admission, the three of us are a tightly knit crew. You want to fuck that up just because you got a bee in your bonnet?"

Cozza was standing too, now. "Frank's right," he said. "This is about more than a few Old Bill at a holiday cottage, ain't it?"

Mo stood still, swinging Reg gently at his side.

"My lighter."

The two men looked at him incredulously. "What?" said Frank.

"That's why I went back to the cottage. I couldn't find it. What I did find was the Old Bill."

"Ahh, so you lost your lighter!" said Frank, his eyes glinting below the overhead strip light. "Christ, call us unprofessional and yet it's you who may have given the soddin' game away."

"I'm just saying," said Mo. "It's probably in the car. I ain't checked it thoroughly since I got back. Or did you pair decided to hide it from me as a little joke?" He studied their expressions carefully, looking for tell-tale signs. All he saw was confusion. "Hell," he said. "I've got to get out of here. You can bag that money up in your own sweet time. Let me know when it's done and I'll come collect my share. I can't be around you two mugs anymore."

Ignoring the gun, Mo walked to the door. The others watched, stunned, unable to fathom what had just happened. They were both wondering if their association with Big Maurice Dolan had come to an end.

MO pulled up outside the 3 Wishes, parked in the street and ran the short distance to the pub. It was a busy Saturday night, customers three deep at the bar. He pushed his way to the bar, ignoring the protests of customers who had been waiting longer. "Hey Tom! Tommy!"

"Oi, wait your turn," said a youngster with a crew cut. He looked barely 18. Mo dropped the nut on him, blood spurting from his nose. The crowd moved backwards.

"Anyone else got any issues they want ironed out?" said Mo, his hand cupped to his ear. The pub fell silent.

Registering the commotion, Tommy strode towards him. "Fuckin' 'ell, Mo, not again! Any more of that I'll have to bar you. You're gonna lose me all my best customers."

"Seem to be doing all right."

"You mean the queue?" said Tommy. "One of my barmaids called in sick."

"Who?"

"Audrey."

"Shit, she OK?"

"Won't be when I get hold of her. From the way I hear it she had a night on the tiles yesterday and can't be bothered to show her face today." He turned his attention to the glass in his hand, running a cloth around it. "It's happened a couple of times this week... Mo?" When he looked up, the publican realised he was talking to himself.

WHEN Mo got to Audrey's flat he just sensed that something wasn't right. It was rare for her to take time off work. He had a terrible feeling that this might be more than a few too many the previous night. He remembered Beryl going through the same thing. She hadn't been able to leave the house for a fortnight it affected her so badly. Morning sickness. Without really knowing why, he picked up Reg and headed for the flat. Rapping loudly on the door, he got no reply. Funny. If she was sick, she wouldn't be out. He knocked again and thought he heard something so put his ear to the wood panel.

There it was again. "Shhhhhh!" Strange. Who was she talking to, the cat?

"Aud, it's me, Mo," he shouted. "I'm back. You OK? I bought you something darlin'." A lie, but she was a material girl. "Come to check you're all right. Tommy at the pub said you were sick. Come on girl, open up!"

He heard shuffling and bolts drawn back. He was through the door as soon as the final latch was turned. "Jeez, Mo, hang on! Damn, you broke one of my nails."

"What's wrong with you?"

"Tummy bug, that's all. Been throwing up all day. I thought it might be something I ate, but now I'm not sure. Look, it's best you weren't here. You might catch something. You don't want to pass it on to your kids. You'll spend the next two days mopping up puke."

"You sure you ain't...?"

"What?" He looked at her stomach. Nodded. "Pregnant?" she raised her eyebrows. "Don't make me laugh! I'm on the pill. I've been on the pill since long before we met. I ain't stupid, you know? What would I want with a sprog? Particular one fathered by a married man?"

He didn't know why, but the words hurt him.

"Not good enough, am I?"

"It's not that," she said. "It's the fact you wouldn't be here for me or the baby. You wouldn't leave Beryl and your kids to look after mine and I understand that. Look, come back tomorrow and we'll have a proper talk. You seem wound up at the moment. Pop in about six, I'll cook you dinner."

As he turned to go something caught his eye; something that was out of place in his girlfriend's flat. A pair of winklepicker-style shoes, partially hidden under the telephone table. Too big to belong to a female. He whipped back around to look her in the eye. "Who is he?"

"What?"

He shoved her and she fell backwards, head connecting with the hallway mirror, which cracked like a car windshield hit by a stone.

From behind the bedroom door he heard a scurrying sound. He tried it but it wouldn't budge. Walking backwards a few steps, he launched himself with a flying kick. Crack! Grabbing Reg, he smashed the enforcer into the area of the handle, once, twice...

"Mo!" Audrey screamed. "Don't wreck my flat, for fuck's sake. What's got into you?"

"Who is he?" he demanded a second time.

She put her hand to her head then pulled it away to survey the damage. "I'm bleeding," she said. "Look, I never said you were the only one, did I? Christ, you can't have your cake and eat it. It was a bit of fun. You love your wife, you told me that, so there was no future in this anyway. Why don't you just go home before you do something you might regret?"

"It's the bastard in there who's gonna regret it." He glared at her then turned his attention back to the door. Another kick to the lock area and it burst in on itself, the bottom hinge breaking. The top of the door had buckled and he could see inside. He took a quick inventory of the scene. Bed sheets bunched on the floor, ashtrays overflowing, some kind of white substance smeared across the drawers... a man in the corner desperately pulling on pants.

"I don't fackin' believe this!" Mo smashed Reg into the top of the door time and time again until there was little left and he could climb through the wreckage. The rings on his fingers sounded their familiar metronomic rhythm as he swung Reg against them. The figure in the corner was as tall as Mo but thinner, more sinewy. His blond hair rose up on his forehead like a wave then flopped down over one eye, gel keeping it in place. In his ear there was a hoop. "I thought I removed that for you once before," Mo said, pointing Reg.

The barely dressed figure was the New Romantic that had caused him so much grief that time in the 3 Wishes. "Yeah, I needed stitches and everything," said the boy. "My ear has only just recovered. Still, Audrey's been looking after me. Aud! Call the police, would you? Someone's let a lunatic out of the asylum."

Mo needed no other provocation. He leapt forward, pulling the bed out of the way, his bloodshot eyes fixed on the target. Without a moment's hesitation, Reg joined the party.

37

"YOU can't come here!" Beryl was frantic.

"Too late, I am here. What's he done now?" said Stan, putting his hand gently under her chin and turning her face to the light. The bruises and scrapes showed up clearly, despite the lack of lighting on the balcony. "My God, babe, you can't let this go on. Leave him... now!"

"Shhhhhhhhhh! The kids are in bed and the neighbours will hear you. You don't know what you're dealing with... what I'm dealing with. He would bloody kill me if he knew you'd called round."

"Look," he indicated the white box under his arm. "I've thought of that. I've just called to show you those boxing boots you were interested in, that's all. Good excuse, don't you think? He should buy that one."

"I doubt it," she said. "He's in a strange mood."

"Anyway, I'm here because you called me."

"I know, but..." Her voice trailed off into the night air.

A smile crept across his face, the small dimple revealing itself at the corner of his mouth. "You missed me! Ha! That's why you called, because you missed me. Do you know, I haven't stopped thinking about you since the moment I left here. I haven't felt like this, ever!"

She blushed, patted his arm. "Oh, shut up," she said. "What about on your wedding day, when you were making plans with Sheila?"

"No," he said. "It was like we were both in a coma. We thought it was love because we knew no different. It wasn't real... like this."

"This isn't real," she said. "It's a dream. You know it. I know it. I'm sure if we took it any further a few months down the line it wouldn't feel the same. What's the word? Infatuation."

"Yeah, you're infatuated with me." She punched him on the arm, her fist barely making an impression. The grin was stuck to his face. She felt weak at the knees. That dimple.

"So..." she said, not knowing whether to tell him to go or keep him talking for a few minutes. She didn't want to part so quickly but knew that an appearance by Mo would kill the mood completely. She had only contacted Stan out of a fit of pique. The journey back from Hastings had been terrible, miles and miles of silence as Mo brooded over his loss. Hell, it was only a lighter. Then when she had offered to make him tea when he got home, he just grabbed his coat and said he had to go out, telling her not to wait up.

That was a good indication he was going to see his tart, but he was so unpredictable these days he could easily return unannounced. Seeing the situation on the doorstep, she doubted he would take to it kindly. He would take action first then ask questions later. It was what he did. He was a destroyer. He had done his best to destroy them, Chuck, everything. Sly would be next if he got the chance.

It dawned on her like a religious epiphany. She had reached a crossroads; turn one way and she would have to lie in the bed she had made forever, turn the other...

"Look," she said. "You don't want to get me in any more trouble, do you? I'll meet you. Tomorrow. Chucky will be at school and I'll have the little one but if you can get out of work for a while…"

"No problem," he said. "My mate will look after the stall."

"Where, though?"

He thought for a moment. "Let's go into town. The South Bank? Can't imagine Mo or any of his cronies get south of the river too often. Take the District Line to Blackfriars and I'll meet you. We can wander across the bridge and have a stroll down by the river. There are some nice little pubs down that way. We can talk."

"OK," she said, aware of the giant step she was taking. "Now go."

He saluted, the grin fixed to his face. She watched his purposeful walk and the swing of his hips, marvelling at the natural confidence he displayed as he disappeared around the corner in the direction of the lifts.

MO had beaten the living daylights out of the kid. His face was unrecognisable, both eyes swollen shut while dark, oily blood matted his hair to his scalp. His arms were battered and bruised, his left wrist hanging at a strange angle. Mo had been unrelenting, swinging and slashing and poking and prodding, sucking energy from a pool of hate formed deep inside. It was only when Audrey jumped on his back and wrapped him in a bed sheet, making it physically impossible for him to swing his arms properly, that the victim was able to crawl to safety. Even then, the younger man received a powerful kick in the solar plexus that left him struggling for breath. Audrey felt sure that Mo's heavy, black brogue, delivered with such force, must have caused internal damage.

Holding on for dear life, she rode Big Maurice Dolan like a rodeo star might a bucking bronco. When she heard the door slam, she breathed a sigh of relief. The boy had escaped, possibly with his life. Now, hopefully, he would call for help.

She felt so guilty. What had seemed an exciting conquest the previous night had turned into a nightmare, her latest lover possibly maimed forever. It was her wanton desires, her inability to go without a fuck for more than a few nights, her continual need to test her allure on members of the opposite sex, which had put him at risk in the first place. When she set eyes on him in the club, instead of being warned off by their previous encounter she saw a challenge in front of her, the opportunity to test fully her seduction technique; to see if it was strong enough to conquer any lingering animosity. Before he knew what had hit him she was dragging him home, sharing his drug stash, then calling in sick the next day as she recovered from their furious lovemaking and over-indulgence.

From what she could remember, which admittedly wasn't a lot, the sex had been good, maybe because he gave as much as he took, or maybe because he was young and pliable and didn't treat her like a cheap whore. It had been fun, all ruined now because the mistake she made was bringing him to her home, leaving him vulnerable to her fucked up, demented part-time lover. How could she be surprised at Mo's reaction having seen his worst excesses first hand?

Her mind in drug-induced overdrive, she realised too late that she had relaxed her grip. "Calm down, Mo, come on," she pleaded. "Let's talk about this..." She sensed some of the fight drain out of him, and whispered an apology in his ear, hoping to dilute his rage further.

Too late she realised he had only been storing up his energy for the next assault. It happened so fast. Reaching back, he gripped the sleeves of her black silk dressing grown and threw her, judo-style, over his shoulder. She sailed through the air before her velocity was checked suddenly by a chest of drawers. Slithering to the floor, pain exploded throughout her body. She tried to stand but her legs reacted like those of a novice at an ice rink, refusing to obey commands. Her vision impaired by the crack to her head, she could see two blurred images of Mo, moving monstrously into the light. She felt her hair being pulled as he threw her across the bed. Rolling straight off the other side, she cracked her head again, this time on the parquet floor. The lights went out.

WHEN she came to her senses, the first thing she did was scream. It felt like she had been turned inside out, shaken, then put back together the wrong way. She looked down to see blood pooled on her bed linen around her aching legs, leaned over the side of the bed and wretched stringy bile from an empty stomach.

The noise of the doorbell made her jump. Shakily, she tried to stand up, but her legs gave way. Crawling into the hallway, she was wary Mo might have come back for seconds, but knew she had to take the chance. She hauled herself up the door, leaning heavily against it and listening intently for clues.

"Hello! Are you in there?" A familiar voice, Not Mo, thank God.

"Gurgh." She couldn't talk, blood having poured back through her nose and congealed in her throat, leaving a bitter taste.

"Come on, lovely, open the door. I've had a call from the station. A young man reported that you were in trouble. One of my mates recognised the address and called me."

Summoning her last reserves of strength, she grasped the handle and eased herself around. Seeing his shape through the glass reduced her to unrelenting sobs. She couldn't remember the last time she'd seen him, although inevitably it would have been in his role as peace-maker, trying to smooth things over with her mother.

She slid back the bolt and pulled the door open. "Hi, Dad," she muttered shamefully through blood-soaked teeth.

"Oh my good Lord," said Constable Cliffy Simpson, rushing to catch her before she hit the ground.

38

CHUCK didn't want to go back to school, convinced everyone had it in for him. His teacher Miss Lester hadn't been the same with him since that playground fight while the deputy head still insisted on calling him Charles and directed an unpleasant scowl in his direction whenever they crossed paths. Even the dinner ladies on playground duty paid him special attention, ready to reprimand him at every opportunity while others got off scot free.

His mum said school should be the best years of your life and told him a good education was vital because it was so hard to get decent jobs these days. He thought about answering back, telling her that Dad seemed to do just fine, but knew that would earn him another finger-wagging lecture. There had been plenty of them since that day he returned home with the deputy headmaster's note.

His only respite came at the boxing club. At school he was a target and at home there were tensions, but at the club he could be himself. Coach Cliffy had become like a second father, someone he could go to with his problems. He had been toying with the idea of telling Cliffy about the "accident" on holiday, but knew Dad would hit the roof if he discovered his son was revealing "family secrets". Still, something told him that Cliffy would look after him and make sure he didn't come to any harm – inside and outside the ring.

"Come on, Chucky, we'll be late," said Mum. "Have you eaten your breakfast?" He nodded. "I'm talking to you boy. Cat got your tongue?"

He swallowed a mouthful of snap, crackle and pop. "We haven't got a cat, Mum," he said.

"Don't be silly, it's just an expression." She entered the kitchen, looking really nice in a yellow summer dress decorated with brightly coloured flowers. Her arms were bare and he could see her boobs and legs, while on her feet were her favourite black high-heeled stiletto shoes. It surprised him because she usually threw on jeans or track-suit bottoms for the school run. Completing the new look he noticed her hair tied in bunches with pretty butterfly bobbles.

"You look nice, Mum," he said.

"Thank you, young man." She did a curtsy then busied herself mopping the counter where he had splashed milk. "You had enough, lovey?" she asked. "You and Sly are eating us out of house and home. Always hungry, the pair of you. Sometimes I wonder if you have a worm, Chuck Dolan."

"What's that Mum?"

"Never mind, just an expression. Done your homework?"

"Didn't have time, Mum, you know, after hospital."

"Well, if your teachers ask..."

"I fell off the swings," he said. "I feel silly saying that. It makes me sound like a kid."

"You are a kid," she said, then mumbled, "Better than the alternative."

It reminded him of something. "Where's Dad?"

She was silent for a moment too long, indicating to him she was about to lie. As he got older, he could read the signs. "With Uncle Frank and Uncle Paul," she said. "They had work things to sort out after the holiday."

Better not to ask questions, he thought. It would only prompt more lies and the more she told him the angrier she would get. His dad was a mystery and he would just have to put up with it.

Mum stepped through to the hallway, strapping Sylvester into his pushchair. He was getting too big for it. "I want sweets Mum, sweets," he was saying. Chuck wished he was spending the day with his mum, too.

He walked out to join them, taking his bag from her and putting it over his shoulder. "Where are you going?" he asked, wondering why the question made her face flush red. It wasn't a hot day, not like the week they spent on holiday.

"What do you mean?" she asked.

"Well, you're all dressed up like it's some kind of special occasion."

"It is... in a way. I'm taking Sly on a little trip into the big city."

"Can I come?" he asked. Even though they lived so close to the sights of London, he had only really been "up West" once, and that was to see his Uncle Clive marching around to celebrate the Queen's birthday. He had looked very smart in his red uniform. The memory brought a pang of longing. He hadn't seen his uncle since they had waved him off to war from the dock at Southampton. He had cried afterwards and his dad had patted him on the head. "Don't worry, he'll be back before you know it," Dad had said. Another lie. It was ages since he had seen his favourite uncle.

"You know you have to go to school, love," said mum. "It's the law. Mummy and Daddy will be in trouble if you don't."

"Like when Dad was arrested by those policemen?"

"Well... not quite but... gosh! Is that the time? We'll be late. Let's go." She ushered him towards the front door, following with the pushchair out in front of her and Sly repeating the familiar chorus: "Want sweets, Mum."

"WHAT happened to your loser mate, then?" The prod in the back came as Chuck was walking out through the school gates.

It had been another miserable day, Miss Lester barely hiding her contempt when he gave her his excuse for not doing his homework. He was still fuming about the unfairness of it all when he heard the jibe and swivelled quickly, balling his fists at his sides. "He deserted you has he, your special friend?" The boy was goading him and had three of his gang for back up. "What was his name? Garry? I heard he left for another school... didn't like it here for some reason. How come you ain't gone with him? Bet he's missing his homo mate." He glanced over his shoulder to see if he had raised a smile among his crew.

Chuck knew he should ignore the boy, but he'd had enough of keeping his mouth shut. It got him into more trouble than it was worth. His right hand shooting out, Chuck caught his tormentor flush on the nose. There was a sharp, cracking sound and the boy's hand shot up, a look of disbelief on his face when he brought it back down to see it was covered in blood. Mistake number two: He'd left his chin unprotected. With his left, Chuck produced the perfect uppercut, his victim buckling at the knees and sinking to the ground. Chuck stood there, bouncing on his toes, admiring his handiwork. The other boy's eyes were vacant beneath the ruler-straight fringe, a puddle of blood blotting his white school shirt, his shoulder-length hair spread below him like a fan. My first KO, thought Chuck. Boy, it felt good.

"Who else wants some?" he asked, maintaining his boxer pose: side on, left foot in front of right, one fist leading, the other raised to protect his chin.

"You're all right," said a slightly chubby, squat boy with fair hair, taking the lead as his mates stepped back. "Great punch, geez. We were getting fed up with that idiot bossin' us around. It was Kevin Macey this, Kevin Macey that... like he was the bees' knees. You really put him in his place. You live over on the estate, don't you? We're from there, unlike him. He's from the posh houses down by the park. Hang around with us if you want, reckon he'll be on his own from now on."

He held his hand out and Chuck thought it might be a trick. To prove the offer was genuine, the boy turned and kicked the Macey kid just as he was coming to his senses. He groaned and fell backwards again. "I'm Jimmy, these lads are Phil and Dunny," said the chubby boy. "Shake?"

As Chuck clutched his hand, a familiar voice cut through the air. "Right, Mr Dolan, you've really gone and done it now."

Looking up, Chuck saw the deputy head cutting through the crowd of onlookers. "I should have known it would be you at the centre of all this commotion. You're in big trouble." He grabbed Chuck's left ear and squeezed.

"So are you," said Chuck, twisting away and balling his fists in front of him. "Keep your fucking hands off me or I'll spark you out, too!"

39

THE pain in his neck jolted him awake. Rubbing ferociously at the spot, he slowly twisted his head from side to side, hoping the damage wasn't serious. There was a strong, sickly smell in the air. He recognised it as a particular brand of alcohol and rolled his eyes at his stupidity. Taking his bearings, he realised he had been sleeping in the back of the bloody Daimler, somehow folding his body into the restrictive space. On the floor was a bottle of Southern Comfort, a small splash left in the bottom. Shit, he thought. No wonder he felt bad. They should rename it Southern Discomfort. There was something hard and unyielding jabbing him in the back. He manoeuvred so that he could fit his hand down between the seat and the backrest and retrieve the source of his irritation.

Reg.

One look at the curtain pole brought back memories of the previous night. There were dark, encrusted blood stains along its length, telling a story that his mind was reluctant to recall. He'd lost it. All the way. No half measures. It had been like driving a fast car with no brakes. Mo had gone headlong into craziness.

Maximum force had always been his doctrine; people out to do him damage were met with such force they were rendered incapable of carrying out what they had intended. Yesterday had been different. Audrey wasn't a threat and neither, to be honest, was the young bloke with the stupid hair and even sillier clothes he had beaten to a pulp. It was all done out of some ridiculous sense of pride and what was it they said? Pride comes before a fall.

Audrey had taken the piss it was true, and if there was one thing he couldn't handle it was someone taking the piss. By finding another, younger lover, the implications were that Mo didn't measure up in the sack and once he reached this conclusion pangs of insane jealously ripped through him. It wasn't that he wanted her, not really, he just didn't want anyone else to have her. To explain that rationale you had to look deep inside him, to the route of his paranoia. He had never felt comfortable with sex, believing lovers' intimate secrets should be locked away, the key buried forever. Deep down, he feared his performance was not up to scratch and that once he was out of sight women laughed at his lack of ability between the sheets and the size of his manhood. He thought he was reasonable proportioned down there, but how did you measure up? The only comparison he could draw was with his brother, and Clive seemed a lot bigger.

Of all his fears, the one that troubled him most was that women might discuss his failures as a lover, comparing and contrasting him with other men and awarding marks accordingly. This was what he imagined had been going on when he discovered his mistress test-driving a younger model. Had they laughed together about him as they performed feats of sexual gymnastics throughout her compact flat? Even if that had been the case, he now realised his response had been completely out of order and could backfire on him.

There had been a series of explosions the previous day. Volcano Mo put them all down to seeing that copper outside the holiday home. The image had burned away inside him, gathering fuel as the hours ticked by. When the violence came it was Frank, Cozza and Audrey who suffered the consequences. There was every chance his lover would report him to the police, which could lead to much worse things than charges of grievous bodily harm and criminal damage. With the spotlight thrown on him, what was to stop the Filth digging deeper and uncovering the armed post office raid, not to mention the murder lying at the bottom of the whole damned, stinking heap.

Smashing his fist into the back of the front seat in frustration, Mo shook his hand vigorously as pain erupted across his knuckles.

Studying them he saw they were red raw, skin peeling away, crusty, embalmed in dried blood. On the back of his hand was a neat semi circle, the perfect imprint from a set of teeth; Audrey's last desperate act. He wondered whether crime investigators could use those teeth marks to convict him. They identified corpses by their teeth so why not? Throwing the car door open, he vomited onto the gravel then lifted his head in an effort to establish where he was. The sizeable car park was empty save for one wrecked old Corsair. After that, there were football pitches as far as the eye could see. He was back on Hackney Marshes, where his son used to play football.

Pushing himself up and out, he realised the mental and physical pain wouldn't get better on its own. He needed help fast. It was time to call the guru.

HE was about to pull into a vacant parking space when a car shot across the road and veered into the gap, leaving its boot exposed to on-coming traffic. A few manoeuvres later and it was hardly better parked. "Who are you, Reginald fackin' Molehusband?" Mo shouted through the open window. A tall Asian in an expensive suit stepped out of the vehicle and came over to him. "Who?"

Christ, thought Mo. Only a bloody foreigner wouldn't know the name of the terrible driver from the old public information films designed to encourage people to reverse park. "Come on, move it, Paki!" he said. "I was here first."

"Fuck you, mate," said the other driver. "You're a racist scum. I'm Indian, not Pakistani. You want a fight? You look like you do. Come on out!"

Mo had one hand on the door handle and one hand on Reg when the rage unexpectedly died within him. It was this sort of knee-jerk reaction which had caused his current strife. He revved the car and the other man jumped out of the way. "Fuck you, too!" he shouted, pulling off and driving around the corner to the public car park.

Twenty minutes later, he pounded up the steps leading to the guru's surgery, fearing he was late for his appointment. As he pushed the door open another figure stepped out, almost bumping into him. "Sorry, mate," the man said, disappearing down the staircase. Mo watched him go, a flicker of recognition tugging at his brain.

"Aaaah, Mr Mo!" A smiling Sunil Prabhakar ushered him through the door. "You're feeling stressed? Suni sort it for you."

"Thanks, Suni," said Mo.

"Normal routine, put on the robe then lie face down on the bed. We see if we can get you feeling better in body and soul."

Mo went behind the curtain. "That bloke, Suni; the one who just left here... Who is he?"

"What, Max? I call him Mad Max." He chuckled.

"Why?"

"Because of the film," said Suni. "You not seen it?"

"Not really into films," admitted Mo.

"Oh." Suni sounded surprised. "Anyway," he said, talking to Mo through the screen, "Mad Max is this kind of law unto himself in the future when there's been a big nuclear explosion which has wiped everything out. It seemed highly appropriate."

"Why? What is this Max, a nuclear physicist?" asked Mo.

"Of course not," said Suni. "He's a copper. Just been promoted to the Flying Squad."

Mo didn't answer. It was all fitting into place. The man he had seen leaving the guru's office was one of the policemen who had been there on the day they broke into the warehouse. The tension began flowing through his body again.

"Ready?" asked Suni. Mo emerged, a white towel wrapped around his waist. "Face down on the bed, Mr Mo, please. You have a sore neck? We'll make it good as new. What happened to your hand? Looks painful. You haven't been ten rounds with that Larry Holmes? See his fight with Gerry Cooney? Great White Hope they were calling Cooney. Great White Dope if you ask me. Holmes battered him."

"Didn't see it," said Mo.

"Silly me, you were in Hastings. Do the damage to those knuckles on holiday, did you? Or is the injury work-related?"

"Hey," said Mo, raising himself onto his elbow just as the little Indian Masseur was about to start working the shoulders and neck. "What do you know about Hastings?"

"Lie flat please, Mr Mo, I need to..."

Mo grabbed the guru's wrist. "Answer the bloody question!"

"Let go, Mr Mo... that hurts!" shouted the guru. "I need my hands to give good massage. Why you ask me that as if your holiday was a secret. You told me on your last visit. 'Going away, Suni,' you said. 'Not able to make it next month, I'm taking family on holiday', you said. I asked you where and you said..."

"Hastings." Mo cursed under his breath. How did he have the right to chastise Cozza and Frank when he'd been just as unprofessional?

"You didn't tell him anything?" asked Mo, still gripping the guru's wrist.

"Who?" Suni stared into Mo's face, trying to read his mind.

"The copper," said Mo. "That Max bloke. You didn't tell him that I went away to Hastings did you? Because the only reason I tell you stuff, Suni, is because it's confidential."

Fear ran in a deep groove across the guru's forehead. "I'm not a doctor, Mr Mo," he said. "There's no patient-client privilege, but why would I mention your business? You don't know each other so there's no point."

Slowly, Mo relaxed his grip. "He doesn't ask about me?"

"I doubt he even knows who you are, Mr Mo. All he does is talk about work and his family, out in Essex. He is chuffed about his new job, though. They let him have a gun! He was boasting today about investigating some weapons that were stolen. Says he's cracked the case. He's full of shit, though. What copper is going to tell you about an investigation before it's over?"

Mo pulled him forward so the Indian's nose was level with his own. "Well, if there's nothing confidential in all this, I want to know exactly what he tells you on his visits," said Mo. "There'll be a nice little bonus in it if you do; a pony for starters and a lot more if it's really helpful."

"Sure," said the guru, Mo releasing his hand. "It doesn't sound very exciting, though. Some stolen guns, hand grenades and ammunition. IRA I expect, don't you?"

Mo didn't answer. He was too busy thinking he needed to warn the boys.

40

SILENCE hung heavy like fog over the flat and Mo knew instantly no one was in. He picked his way around bicycles and other assorted junk in the hallway, cursing that their home wasn't big enough for a family with two growing boys. Perhaps he had been spoilt by the holiday cottage where there were a number of outbuildings in which you could store stuff.

He sighed heavily. The guru had eased his aches and pains, but had failed to dissolve his underlying tension. He had popped into the Hope for a couple of pints thinking that might do the trick, then strolled to the bookies to place a quick bet. Pocketing a tidy ton thanks to a 20-1 shot racing home unopposed, he thought it strange that when you had money, it seemed to attract more money, yet when you were skint it steered well clear.

Despite the stroke of good fortune he felt uneasy, as if something was about to go badly wrong. The fact the police hadn't been lying in wait for him at the flat or two of his favoured haunts eased his concerns slightly, suggesting neither Audrey nor the floppy haired twat had reported the previous night's incident. Perhaps she really did love him and was giving him another chance. Unlikely. He had holed their relationship below the waterline and had to accept she would hate his guts forever.

Strolling into the kitchen, he filled the kettle then took a box of matches from his pocket, reflecting sorrowfully on his lost lighter. It was as he put a flame to the gas that he noticed the handwritten message on a spiral notebook by the sink. '*Mo, I've taken Sly to town.*

He needs some new togs and there are summer sales down Oxford Street. Do me a big favour please and wait in for Chucky to get back from school? Won't be long. I'll sort tea out when I get in, love Bee x.'

Strange. Since when did Beryl go to town? There were plenty of bargains in the local shops. It was another sign that things weren't right. If he thought about it more deeply she had been acting odd for a couple of weeks. Was this the warning signs of a marriage going stale; he having an affair while she constructed a more independent lifestyle? There was no time to pursue the idea. In the hallway, their new phone started ringing just as the kettle whistled to inform him it was boiling. He turned off the gas ring and went to answer the call.

"Mr Dolan?" The voice was vaguely recognisable.

"Yeah?" Police? "Who's that?"

"Mr Fazackerley, the deputy head at your son Charles' school."

"Chuck," he corrected, breathing a sigh of relief.

"That's the one," said Mr Fazackerley. "I'm sorry to have to tell you he's been misbehaving again. This afternoon outside the school gates he punched a boy..."

"Was it a good one?" asked Mo.

"Sorry?"

"The punch. Was it a good one?"

"Well, that's not the point... I'm afraid to say he knocked the other boy out cold."

"So it was a good one? Well done, Chuck."

"I don't think you understand," said the deputy head. "We are suspending your son until further notice. You have a right to appeal against this punishment, but there is a good chance the school will decide that Charles, sorry Chuck, will be expelled."

"OK," said Mo. "And what's happening with the other boy?"

"Oh, um, it's difficult to tell. He's gone to hospital for a check-up."

"I didn't ask how the facker was!" said Mo, his voice a low rumble. "I asked you how you are planning to punish him. I know my Chuck, and he wouldn't react like that unless he was provoked... he's a trained boxer, Mr Fazackerley. They are taught discipline. Can I suggest, therefore, that you get your fackin' facts right before ringing up here with your hoity-toity threats?"

"I'm sorry you feel the need to swear, Mr Dolan," said the deputy head. "You don't seem to have grasped the seriousness..."

"You remember me, don't you?" Mo interrupted.

"Pardon me?"

"You taught me, Mr Fazackerley, years ago. We called you Fuck-zackerley, because you were such a nasty bastard. You always had your favourites: those whose mums and dads volunteered to help out at everything from school sports day to Harvest Festival and readily contributed to school funds. The rest of us were constantly picked on. Our parents weren't so well off and some of them just took no interest in school activities. We didn't need to have the additional punishment of being treated like shit by you, we were treated badly enough at home."

"Well, really!" The deputy head was indignant.

"Apology accepted," said Mo. "Now when can I pick up my bloody son?"

AS Mo opened the hallway door and prepared to leave for school the phone rang again. Snatching it up, he heard another familiar voice. "Frank," he said coldly.

"I need to talk to you, Mo. This is important."

"Shoot."

"Not on the phone, at the boat house."

'The Boat House' was their code for the Wapping warehouse. It briefly crossed his mind that Frank and Cozza might be planning some sort of revenge on him for the previous day. He attributed the idea to his overpowering feelings of paranoia.

"I've got to pick the boy up first," he said. "I'll be around at about 4.30. OK?"

"Sure."

"And Handsome?"

"Yes, Mo?"

"You'd better not be facking me over."

"You know me better than that." The line went dead.

"ARRESTED? When?"

"This morning," said Frank. "His missus rang. They raided the house at 5 in the fuckin' morning. Sweeney-style. Bev thought they were after Shaun for drugs, but they marched straight past his room and hauled Cozza off in his keks."

"What have they got on him?" said Mo.

"No idea," said Frank. "I don't think it can be the post office, though. If it was an eye-witness account he was driving and had his head down most of the time. He never went near the premises."

"Caught on hidden camera for the arms break-in, perhaps?"

"That's what I thought," said Frank. "I'd be surprised, though. He was adamant there were no cameras and he took every precaution. Also, they would have come for us, too, and a lot sooner."

"He's got a reputation as a locksman, mind," said Mo.

"Sure, but others are just as good. Remember, we never told a soul, but I heard through the grapevine that a security guard stumbled across someone 'mending' the locks just before Christmas."

"Cozza."

"Who else could it be? The guard couldn't describe him, luckily," said Frank. "If they had come up with the perfect artist's impression he would have been banged up months ago."

"Grass?" said Mo, thinking out loud.

"Who though? Who knows?"

There was the rattle of a lock and both men froze. Frank lurched across, picking up a gun that had been leaning against a crate. Mo grabbed his arm. "Don't be a lunatic," he hissed. "This is bad enough without you sparking a shootout."

A small head poked around the door. "Dad?"

"Hell, Chuck!" said Mo. "I thought I told you to wait in the car? Get in here, boy, and shut the bloody door behind you! Frank, put on the padlock would you? What do you want son?"

"Need a wee, Dad," said the boy.

"Over there then... behind those crates. Stinks enough in here as it is, your piss can't make it any worse... but don't touch anything!"

The boy shuffled off, desperate to empty his bladder.

"He all right?" asked Frank. Mo nodded. "So what do we do?"

"We get young Cozza a bloody good lawyer," said Mo. "Then we pray like hell he doesn't rat us out."

"WE'VE got you your own little parade lined up," said DS Max Cooper. "Be nice that, won't it, Mr Cohen... or can I call you Cozza?"

Cozza said nothing.

"Have it your way. Doesn't bother me. We've got enough to go on without a peep from you... unless you feel like making it easier on yourself. Accessory to murder can carry quite a sentence."

"Murder?" Cozza looked alarmed.

"So, he does speak!" said Cooper. "Yes, Mr Cohen, murder. To be precise, the murder of an innocent driver in a truck stop just off the Tunbridge Wells bypass. Hear about it?"

Cozza shook his head.

"Really? Well, I've been talking to my forensics boys and according to them bullets you stole from Sharpstone's Warehouse in Romford on the night of December 24, 1981, killed that poor trucker – and others were found in the ceiling of a post office in Tunbridge Wells after a robbery. There's also the small matter of a police squad car being shot up. This should sound familiar because I'm pretty sure you were there. And if you weren't, you know who was."

The detective noticed a twitch on the left side of the suspect's face just below the ear. He loved things like that. However much a crim wanted to conceal something, their body was always happy to undermine them. "No matter," he continued. "We've a security guard coming in to take a look at you in a line-up of suspects for the warehouse robbery. Anything you would like to say for the record, Mr Cohen?"

Cozza sat still, mouth closed... his twitch growing stronger. He resembled a junkie doing cold turkey. Got you, you fucker, thought Cooper, remembering the humiliating dressing down he had been given by the chief superintendent at Christmas time. The prisoner would lawyer up, of course, but sometimes the evidence was stacked just too high.

41

CLIFFY knocked quietly, not wishing to disturb his daughter if she was asleep. Audrey needed all the rest and recuperation she could get and he would make sure she got it now she was 'home' and he could keep an eye on her. A tear squeezed from his left eye and he wiped it away with his hand.

"Who is it?" Her voice was barely a whisper, croaky from the small amount of pain-free sleep she had managed.

"It's Dad," he said.

"Oh... OK."

Pushing the door open, the strong smell of iodine made his eyes water, but he swore by it. He had seen enough wounds patched up during his time on the job to know the bluish-black liquid was a terrific sterilizing agent. The last thing Audrey needed now was an infection. He had dressed the visible wounds as best he could. The hidden ones would take longer to heal.

"She wants to see you," he said.

"I'm not ready," croaked Audrey. "I don't think I can handle her saying 'I told you so'."

Her attitude annoyed him. "Whatever you think, your mother loves you and only wants the best for you," he said. "She's worried sick."

"How do you know what she wants? You were never here!" She became animated, her face creasing in pain as she manoeuvred herself into a sitting position. "That's why I had to leave."

"Trouble is, you're too much alike," he said. "You're as bloody stubborn as she is."

It had been two years since Audrey left the family home and Cliffy wouldn't admit it, but he had worried every day. Never in his worst nightmares, though, could he have imagined this scenario. She was a headstrong girl, always had been, and as she grew older and tried to assert her independence, the clashes came. Her mother Simone had been such a stickler during Audrey's younger days, nagging her over her abysmal school grades. When they didn't pick up her mother's idea was to load her with more and more "home" work, but none of it did the trick. Cliffy tried to intervene but, as Audrey pointed out, he wasn't around much, spending a lot of his time working night shifts in those days.

Eventually, at 16, Audrey rebelled. All her friends were talking about their boyfriends and their exciting lives outside of school and she felt deprived. With her personality, though, she couldn't just be one of the crowd. She had to go one step further to create an impression and ingratiate herself with her peers. Her mother wanted her to carry on in education and conquer her problems, but Audrey was adamant. School had made her life a misery.

When she met Daniel she saw him as her passport to freedom. Skinny as a rake, he dressed in what could only be described as a black bin bag with holes for arms; tight black jeans with safety pins all over the place, spiky hair on top, shaved around the ears, he was like some British male equivalent of the Statue of Liberty. Extremely polite, mind you; a few years older than Audrey and a university student doing a degree in sociology. Cliffy didn't approve of his dress sense, but hoped Dan's academic leanings and desire to better himself would rub off on Audrey.

Pretty soon Cliff's daughter was dressing in similar vein, creating her own style, rather than looking like a younger version of her mother. Joining Dan's punk band served to bolster her confidence and helped to establish her 'new' identity. None of it sat well with Simone Simpson, though. "You look like a bloody tart," she said rather unkindly in one heated row, Audrey coming downstairs wearing thick black eyeliner, bright red lipstick and ripped fishnet tights.

"Well, maybe you've turned me into one!" Audrey responded. Cliffy almost applauded before realising his job was to stay neutral. In quiet moments, though, he did try to persuade Simone that all she was achieving with such comments was driving their daughter further away from them. Then came the day when, arriving home from work, he found Simone sitting alone in a dark front room, silent and brooding. When he asked what had happened she told him Audrey had walked out after another row. Cliffy was convinced their girl would return when she became hungry or needed some money, but as the days passed both parents realised things had gone a lot further than in previous spats.

After putting feelers out at work, he discovered that Audrey, now 17, had moved into a squat near Battersea with Daniel and some other punks. He wasn't sure slumming it would suit her, though, knowing how she treasured home comforts and, sure enough, she soon tired of the 'rock 'n' roll' lifestyle.

She got in touch through a former school pal who had taken up boxing and after an exchange of messages they met on neutral ground, The Crown and Sceptre in Bethnal Green. He told her he understood her need for independence but wasn't happy with her living in the squat. He suggested she needed her own place but she argued that renting in London was too expensive, even though she had found part-time work at a greasy spoon during the day and in a pub at night.

Cliffy said to leave it with him and a couple of weeks later the golden opportunity came along. A police colleague informed him that he had bought a flat in Dagenham as an investment and needed a tenant to help with the mortgage and upkeep. Cliffy agreed to pay a regular 'retainer' himself, and Audrey moved in a week later. It was perfect for what she wanted and she soon settled, only contacting him on occasion to inquire after his health.

The first he knew there was a problem was when a PC mate had phoned him. He said a young man had contacted the station to inform them of an on-going, furious 'domestic'. He had fled the scene reluctantly and feared for the safety of the young lady in question, whose bloke had gone "off his head". He didn't know the man's name, just that he was a nasty piece of work who sometimes went in the 3 Wishes in Dagenham. When the PC learned the name of the girl he immediately got in touch with Cliff, who jumped in the car and shot across to the estate where he found his daughter unable to walk, delirious and nursing a catalogue of injuries. First, he wanted to cry, then he wanted to go out into the street and find the son of a bitch responsible, but neither of those actions would have helped Audrey in her predicament. Contacting the emergency services, he travelled with her by ambulance to nearby Oldchurch Hospital where they patched her up as best they could. When they asked if she wanted to be examined for rape, though, she shook her head.

That morning he had picked her up and taken her back to the family home, installing her in her own room, Simone having kept it exactly the same since the day Audrey left. Seeing her lying on her bed, head pressed to the window, buried deep in her own thoughts, he decided it wasn't the right time to quiz her about her ordeal.

Now, having given her a few hours respite, he felt he couldn't leave it any longer. "Are you going to tell me what happened?" he asked, perching on the side of the bed.

"Do I have to?"

"No, but this man shouldn't be allowed to get away with what he's done. What if there are other women facing the same threat from him? He could kill someone. Do you want that on your conscience?"

"He won't," she said.

"You know that for certain, do you?"

"He isn't a bad bloke," she said. "He's just got a short fuse."

"What? Have you seen yourself? Any person who can do that to another human being – girl or boy – is a monster who should be locked up for good."

"It was my fault," she said, her lip wobbling as the tears came. "I virtually flaunted another bloke in front of him. What's more, I did it on purpose, Dad. Part of me wanted him to find out because I was hoping he might see what he was in danger of losing and it might give him a nudge to leave his wife."

"He's married? He has kids?" She didn't answer, just buried her face in her knees. "Christ," he said. "What if he carries on like that at home? His kids are in danger... you have to tell me who he is."

She looked up defiantly. "Oh, don't worry," she said. "He loves his sodding kids, wouldn't do a thing to harm a hair on their heads. He tells me all the time."

His bear-like arms wrapped her in an embrace. "Oh, love," he whispered, "You don't understand. I love you and it's unconditional. I created you. I was there from day one when you were born... so was your mother." She wanted to protest but he put his finger to her lips. "It might not seem obvious to you but your mother loves you so much it hurts, which is why she was so reluctant to let you go. This was exactly the sort of thing she was trying to protect you from."

"Protect me?" she sniggered. "You really don't know, do you?"

"Know what love?"

"Never mind."

"Well, whoever he is, this man will never love anyone like he loves his kids, and I speak as a fellow father. It's a worry, though. The things they see and hear might colour them for life. Help me help them. Tell me who he is."

Her breathing was shallow now, relaxed. He could feel the beat of her heart next to his. He loved her more than anything in the world. What monster had made his child suffer like this?

"I'm sorry, Dad, I can't," she said. "You'll only try to do something about it yourself and you aren't the young and fit bloke who used to drag me down the boxing gym when I was little. Anyway, I was pretty horrible to him. I left a note in his clothes, intending his wife to find it..."

"Stop making excuses for him!" he stormed.

"I'm just trying to explain why it happened," she said, deep in thought. "If she found it then I can understand why he came back from Hastings all wound up. He probably came around to tell me they'd split... then found another man in my bed."

"Hastings?"

She fell silent.

"You said Hastings," he repeated.

"Yeah, his family holiday," she said. "What of it?"

"Last week?"

"Yeah," she said.

"I know him."

"No... no, you don't... you can't! Loads of people from around here go to the south coast for their holidays, particularly in the current climate. It could be anyone. You're not a detective, Dad."

"How many kids? No, don't tell me. Two boys. Aged about 4 and 8. Am I right?"

She buried her face in her hands again. Extricating himself from their hug, he got to his feet and walked from the room.

"WHAT the fuck time do you call this?" Mo was in the hall, tapping Reg against his open hand. She wheeled the pushchair inside, undid the buckles and picked up Sly, who had started to cry.

"Don't, honey, I'm tired and so is he," said Beryl. "Go in the front room and sit down and I'll put him to bed. Then I'll make your tea and tell you all about our lovely day." She leaned in to Sly, whispering in his ear. "All right baby. We did have a lovely, lovely day though, didn't we, my precious?" Sly was having none of it, his cries increasing in pitch. She walked towards the bedroom.

"I asked you a sodding question." Mo blocked her way.

"Look, we did a lot of shopping. Remember, until this recent job you landed we hadn't been able to kit the kids out properly for ages, so it seemed a good idea. Then the flippin' Tubes weren't running properly. I was stuck at Mile End for ages waiting for a connection. Where's Chuck?"

"In his room."

"Bit early for bed, isn't it?" she said. "What's wrong?"

"He's been suspended."

"Oh, bloody great. Chuck!"

"Leave him," said Mo. "He's OK. We've had a chat."

"Oh fuckin' hell, Mo, you haven't..."

"Haven't what?" His features hardened. "Oh, for Christ's sake, you think I would hit him? After the last time? It was an accident, you know that! God, you still blame me, don't you? I thought we were supposed to be sorting this out, cutting out the rows, and then you act like this... swanning off into London and neglecting your responsibilities."

"So you haven't got any responsibilities?" she said, raising her voice. Sly's crying reached a crescendo, adding to the poisonous atmosphere. "They're your kids as much as mine. We talked about this. It's hardly a hardship to wait in until Chuck comes home from school. And why have you got that... thing... out?" she indicated Reg. "Gonna give me a good slap with it, were you? Not content with sending Chuck to school with bumps and bruises, you are ready to do it all again. Out of my way..."

She pushed past him, clutching Sly close. She had figured he wouldn't do anything while she was holding the child. Relieved to be right, she entered the boys' room. Chuck was on his bed, flicking through a boxing magazine. "Hi honey, you OK?" she asked. "Where did you get that?"

"Dad bought it," he said. "As a reward."

"Reward?"

"For sticking up for myself and sparking out Kevin Macey."

She was flabbergasted. She placed Sly on the bed and was about to ask another question when pain reverberate through the back of her legs and they gave way, sending her crashing across the four-year-old's bed. It was by luck alone that she avoided landing on top of her youngest child. Twisting, she saw Mo staring down at her, his eyes seemingly aflame as they reflected the boys' night light.

"Think you can just give me a mouthful and get away with it?" he stormed. "Where's the respect, eh? You owe me that. I keep a bloody roof over our heads, risk life and limb at times, give you money for your little shopping expeditions, and you talk to me like I'm a piece of shit. I hold this family together, you got it?" He raised Reg again.

"Don't!" The cry came from Chuck, putting down his magazine and bravely standing in front of his raging father, protecting his mother from another battering.

"Out of the way, Chuck," said Mo.

"No, Dad. I don't want you to hurt our mum. Please?"

Mo looked into his son's eyes, saw Sly crawl over and brush his little fingers through Beryl's hair, as if trying to smooth away her pain, then lowered Reg, turned and walked from the room without another word. With perfect timing, the phone rang. He ignored it and walked off down the hall to the front room. Struggling to her feet, Beryl stumbled out into the hallway, still feeling the effects of Reg clattering against the back of her knees.

"Hello?" she said into the receiver. There were some clicks on the line then another voice took over. Moments later, she was shouting down the hall. "Mo! Mo!" she said. "You'll want to take this. It's Clive. He's coming home!"

42

AS the Daimler sped along the A40 towards RAF Brize Norton, Chuck was shouting out the things he saw in the Oxfordshire countryside. Mo shared the excitement, his eagerness to see Clive again tempered by a nagging sense of trepidation. His brother might have been gone for just two months but so much had happened at home and abroad in that time he couldn't wait to bring Clive up to date.

From their brief call, Mo understood Clive and the rest of the 2nd battalion, Scots Guards, were aboard a transport plane on an 11-hour flight back to Britain. They would land at around 4pm, giving Mo plenty of time to be in place to greet his brother as he stepped back onto British soil. Would his brother's appearance have changed much? Two months was plenty of time in which to grow a beard, for instance, and he didn't imagine grooming products were easy to come by where he'd been. The Army were sticklers for tidiness but in the middle of a war zone did anyone truly care whether you had a skinhead or a mullet? Perhaps Clive would climb from the plane with a full bush of facial hair, his fringe flopping down over his eyelids. It would be an interesting development.

Mo couldn't help but speculate. In the brief phone call they had shared, Clive had told him precious little. The usual warmth in his voice was missing, but Mo put that down to the fact he was probably exhausted from early mornings and late nights guarding the islands from another attack. Either that or he and his Army buddies had been on the piss every night since liberating Port Stanley, something quite understandable in the circumstances.

PRIVATE Clive Dolan, in full Scots Guard dress uniform, waited in line behind the rest of his platoon, eyes focused on the door. His rucksack hung heavy on his back but he barely noticed it, his mind trapped in a turbulent storm of thoughts and memories, the overall emotion that of overwhelming sadness. Since leaving Port Stanley, he had been filled with a sense of guilt, as if he had abandoned close friends. When he thought about it a while longer, that was exactly what he was doing. How he had dreamed of making this return trip alongside Jock, and later sharing a reunion with Elf, perhaps at that international rugby game the Welshman had rattled on about. They could have shared a few beers and swapped memories of the day they liberated the islands from slavery.

Without them, the victory felt hollow. His mind rewound the moment Archie McAllum had fallen constantly, different scenarios filling his head. Had the gunman aimed a fraction to the left, Clive and Archie would have made the triumphant walk into the Falklands capital together. Had that shot been a few feet to the right and it would have been Clive experiencing scorching, agonising pain as the high-velocity bullet tore through flesh, bone and brain, splattering him inside out on the rocks of Tumbledown.

Fighting in a battle of that magnitude had been like betting your life on the roll of a dice or playing Russian roulette with your mates. There was a scene in one of Clive's favourite films, *The Deer Hunter*, when Robert De Niro's character Michael and Christopher Walken's Nick sat facing each other, taking turns to put a loaded gun to their heads and pull the trigger. Though the film carried a strong anti-war message, when Clive saw it on its release in 1978 it only strengthened his resolve to join the Army, perhaps because of the camaraderie, close friendships and loyalty shared by the main protagonists. Honour and duty were the words that stuck in his mind, the film reinforcing war stories his grandfather had told him.

Grandad Arnold hadn't sugar-coated them particularly, but while he mourned the friends lost on the battlefield he told positive tales involving his band of brothers to such an extent that they outweighed the negatives in a young Clive's mind.

The final few weeks in Stanley had flown by in a blur. Shortly after the Argentine surrender, he had seen the full devastating toll the war had taken on the small community. Bedraggled, worn-out enemy conscripts were wandering the streets like ghostly apparitions, their faces encrusted with filth, their uniforms ruined, their feet bare after surrendering their army-issue boots to the liberators, many of whom were battling the effects of trench foot. The further he ventured into town, the more locals he encountered, their gestures suggesting welcome, their expressions indicating they just wanted to return to normality, free from occupation by friend or foe. While they appeared defiant, Clive knew the events of the previous two months would colour the rest of their lives.

Warned there might be pockets of resistance from Argentine fighters unaware the war was over, the soldiers trod carefully as they entered buildings, knowing that one wrong step might trigger a booby trap or cause a hail of bullets to rain down on them. What they found was far more upsetting. Houses which islanders had once called home had been horrifically redecorated, wallpaper festooned with bloody fingerprints, furniture replaced with piles of human waste, dirty toilet paper spread wall-to-wall across the floor instead of carpets. The smell was cloying, unrelenting. The longer you stood and surveyed the scene, the more it stayed with you – the obscene stink latching onto your clothes, your hair, the insides of your nostrils and even settling under your nails. It was as if it was a permanent addition to your body, seeping into your arteries and veins by osmosis, kicking out all memory of the pleasant smells that had gone before: wild flowers, cut grass, summer barbecues, purified air after a rain shower. Every nook and cranny, every orifice, was coated now by this pure reek of destruction and degradation, as if you were traipsing through an endless river of shit. Perhaps hell was like this.

It didn't get any better at night when he bedded down with other troops in a sheep shed where the rancid smell of faeces, puke, blood and something unidentifiable like burnt meat hung in the air. The syncopated, ear-bashing sound of exhausted soldiers snoring was only broken up by the odd wail and scream emitting from those revisiting their worst memories of the trip to the south Atlantic. Often there were fights, Para against Marine, Guard against Para, Guard against Marine, Para against Para. This was the way winners reacted when fuelled by enough alcohol to numb the senses. If you set an all-fighting, all-killing war machine in motion you couldn't just hit the off button at the end of the game and expect everything to return to normal.

A couple of days after liberation there was a church service, the Army chaplain reading out the names of those confirmed dead. Archie was among them but not Elf, who was still labelled missing. Chances were they had found no evidence of him aboard the wreck of the Sir Galahad, his body incinerated in the floating furnace. He fingered the rings attached to his throat but no tears would come. His body was an empty vessel, still moving by muscle memory while the soul had lapsed into coma.

"...ANYWAY, I reckon we might do OK this season. Brooking is still on top of his game and Bondy will lead by example. The World Cup could have gone better... we showed too much respect to the fackin' Germans again. I blame Don Howe. He's a negative coach and I reckon he had too much influence... Ron Greenwood is far more adventurous. Must be all those days Howe was with the Gunners. Boring, boring Arsenal. That Rumenigge was a good player to be fair, but the other krauts... you should have seen how they got through to the final. Scandalous. Their keeper came rushing out and clattered into the French fullback Battiston, who was clean through, knocking him into the back of next week and didn't even get sent off. Instead, he saved a penalty in the shootout. No match for the Eye-ties, though, that German side... anyway, I've got you a ticket for the first game of the season. Should be a corker... Forest at home ... you don't look very pleased. Thought you would be made up. We can go as a family. I got three: Me, you and Chucky. Mad Hammer since you took him to..."

"Fuuuuuck!"

The ear-splitting scream almost forced Mo from the road. He straightened the wheel and looked warily at his brother. "Did you forget something?"

Clive collided ferociously with the dashboard, his forehead coming back bloody. "Fuck! Fuck! Fuck!" He went to bang his head again but Mo shot out a hand, holding him inches from connecting. There was blood all over the immaculate walnut dash.

"Mate, calm down... my car! I can see you're upset but remember Chuck is here, won't you?"

"Mo, please... shut... up!" said Clive. Mo was shocked. They were the first words his brother had spoken with any conviction since emerging from the bowels of the big transport plane into the bright sunlight of an English summer afternoon.

"Sure." It was all he could think of to say.

They were on the outskirts of the picturesque Buckinghamshire town of Marlow when Clive spoke again. "Sorry. I'm just... not myself. It's been a long flight. Can we stop? I could murder a pint."

Mo smiled. "Shit, of course! Why didn't you say? Great idea. I mean, I was going to drive us back and maybe pop in the Hope for a few, but if you've been on a plane 11 hours and haven't had a proper British pint for, well, however long it is, you must be gagging, son." He glanced at his brother who sat stock still, blood haphazardly smeared across his face. Pulling onto the slip road, Mo drove through the quaint, narrow streets and crossed a bridge before entering the car park to an inn resplendent with hanging baskets, the beer garden at the back overlooking the River Thames. "Will this do you?"

"Thanks," said Clive.

Mo leaned into the back seat. "OK, Chucky, best behaviour now boy, please. Uncle Clive has something we call jet lag, I think. He banged his head accidentally and we need to get him cleaned up. What he is really looking forward to, though, is a pint of good British ale. We can't begrudge him that now, can we?"

CHUCK ran off to watch the fishermen in action as the two men settled at a table in the garden. It was the perfect English setting. Clive took a mouthful of beer and stared up at the blue sky. He whispered something under his breath.

"You what?" asked Mo.

"Just saying a prayer," said Clive.

"Fuck, you going all religious on me?" Clive didn't answer, just gazed out over the river. "Sorry," said Mo.

They sat in silence, sipping occasionally at their drinks.

"I need to go to Wales," said Clive, out of the blue.

"OK," said Mo. "We'll fix it when we get home. I'll phone Paddington and see if we can book you on a train."

"No," said Clive. "I need to go now."

Mo couldn't hide his surprise. "Seriously?"

"Yeah."

"Well, it's a few hours away but you don't ask me too many favours, and you are a war hero, so how I can refuse you? I'm not sure what our Bee will say, though. I'll give her a bell. She'll probably give me a rollickin' for keeping Chuck up... Why Wales?"

Clive played with the chain around his neck.

"I have to see someone."

"OK," said Mo, drawing out the syllables. "Girl? Boy?"

"A woman, but it's not like that. I've got something to deliver on a friend's behalf."

"We can't be travelling all night," said Mo. "We'll turn around here and get on the A40. I'll book us somewhere to stay overnight."

"Sure", said Clive, nodding slowly. Mo walked into the pub in search of a phone. While he was gone, Chuck came racing back, a beaming smile on his face. "That man just caught a big one," he said, pointing. "He said it was a Chub and he had tempted it with some mashed bread. I've never been fishing, have you?"

"No," said Clive.

"I'd like to have a go. Apparently you don't keep them. Once you have beaten them in a fight you throw them back."

Clive nodded, his mind elsewhere.

"Uncle, can I ask you a question?" Chuck wrapped his arms around Clive's midriff.

"Sure," said Clive.

"You know when you were in the war; did you catch anyone in the fighting then let them go, you know, like in fishing?"

Suddenly, Clive heard the gruff voice of the Lieutenant-Colonel, clear as day, giving his battle briefing. *"It's kill or be killed. We haven't got the facilities or the manpower to be taking prisoners, understand? I repeat, no prisoners."*

Clive looked down at his nephew. "No."

"Did you kill anyone?"

A figure loomed up behind them. "All right, Chuck, that's enough questions," said Mo. "Your uncle's tired and he doesn't need a full-scale inquisition. He'll tell you all about it later. Now, who's for a nice adventure?"

Chuck raised his hand in the air. "Me! Me!"

"OK then," said Mo. "We're all going to Wales!"

43

A SURGE of excitement raced from Beryl's brain to her toes, born of anticipation mingled with fear. Either someone up there liked her or they were playing nasty tricks. Lifting Sly, she danced an impromptu jig in the hallway.

Mo had just called, telling her he wouldn't be home that night. He and Clive were heading for Wales and would book into a hotel so that Chuck could get a good night's sleep. She put up a token protest because that's what he would have expected, but secretly she was already planning ahead.

Earlier that day Mo had marched Chuck out of the door with just the briefest goodbye, still holding a grudge over her tardiness the previous day. His absence had given her more time to think. He had barely said a word since smacking her around the back of the legs with that stick. Despite Chuck's intervention on her behalf, she had been expecting repercussions until Clive's phone call saved the day. After that, everything went on the back burner as he rushed around the flat preparing for the trip, even though it was a relatively short journey. She felt she had dodged a bullet.

Beryl prayed Clive's homecoming would have a positive effect on her husband. Things certainly couldn't get much worse; she was starting to think it was too late for her and Mo. The wonderful day she had spent on the south bank of the Thames with Stan, indulging in ice creams at one of the little riverside cafes, then going on a boat trip and finishing it all off with tea and scones in a posh London hotel, had given her a glimpse at an alternative life.

Even Sly seemed happier for the experience. Stan had made a real fuss over her youngest son, going through his repertoire of funny faces and bringing the best out in the toddler. The child's tantrums were legendary, but Stan pacified him with just a few well chosen words and some well-intentioned bribes, never raising his voice. Beryl couldn't help thinking he would make a wonderful dad.

During the day they had talked, and talked, and talked. She had probably shared more intimacies with Stan in one afternoon than she had in a lifetime with Maurice. He was a completely open person, giving her a warts-and-all history of his marriage, including the fact he was convinced his wife loved the Status Quo musician Rick Parfitt more than she did him. She laughed so much she thought she would never stop.

After they parted, it dawned on her she had forgotten all about her carefully rehearsed alibi. At a time when she should have been on the way home, she found herself racing hell for leather up Oxford Street to grasp a few bargain children's clothes. When her husband had been waiting for her in the hallway, tapping that bloody club against the collection of rings on his right hand, her stomach dropped to her boots.

Did she really have to put up with things the way they were? She had vowed never to give up on her marriage, intent on proving the motivations that drove her mother weren't genetically passed down the family tree. Yet wasn't this an entirely different scenario? Her mother hadn't endured a regime of mental and physical torture. If anything, she had been the strong one which, to Beryl's mind, was a key reason the marriage broke down. Her dad just wasn't tough enough to fight for what they had. Worse, deep down perhaps he didn't want it either, but painting himself as the aggrieved party earned him the sympathy vote in the jury of public opinion.

When she looked at things that way, she started to see things from her mother's perspective. Everyone had a right to be happy, just as Stan told her. Thinking of him now, she tingled. It would be just her luck if he wasn't around tonight but as her mother used to say: "If you don't ask, you don't get."

Beryl dialled the number.

CLIVE nervously twirled his Guards cap in his hand as he stood in front of the neat little terraced house. He heard voices coming from inside and saw shapes through the patterned glass window. The street was on a steep hill, each house identical except for individual little quirks. Some of the little boxes had their brickwork painted in different shades, a light blue or a bright pink interrupting the regimental uniformity. Like soldiers, he thought. They all looked identical if you lined them up on parade and placed a hat on their heads, but once you got to know them they all had their different foibles. Elf the joker, Archie the sarcastic king of the one-liners and singer of comedy songs...

"Help you, butt?" The accent brought Clive crashing back to the present and for a minute his heart leapt, thinking it was his mate Elf standing there, somehow having miraculously survived. The bloke in front of him had the same ginger tinge to his hair, though it was longer and a reddish moustache crawled across his top lip like an exotic caterpillar. A close relative, obviously.

"Is Kerry there?" he asked.

"Kerry!" The Welshman's booming voice echoed around the small hallway. Over his shoulder Clive identified the busty brunette he had last seen waving her bra above her head on the quayside at Southampton.

"Who's there, Owen?" she asked. "Not the bloody council is it? I told them..."

"No, it's a soldier," replied the man called Owen. "Sorry, what's your name, mate?"

"Clive Dolan. Private Dolan. I'm with the Scots Guards."

Kerry pushed Owen out of the way and planted herself in front of Clive. "I've heard all about you," she said. "Hi!" A hand thrust out and Clive took it. "Elfyn told me about that pickle you got him out of up on the Beacons, you and your mate."

"Archie."

"Yeah," said Kerry. "He not with you?"

"He's dead."

"Oh," she paused. "Well, sorry and all. Looks like the Lord took all the good ones, no offence." He didn't reply. "Anyway, what can I do you for, lover? Tsk! Where are my manners? Put the kettle on, Owen... make our visitor a cup of tea. While you're at it how about making a start on them steaks?"

"You're OK," said Clive, not wishing to intrude. "My brother and nephew are in the car. I only popped in to give you something."

"Oh." She looked confused.

He reached for his neck and removed the chain with the rings on it. "Elf gave me these for safe keeping in case... well, he told me about your wedding plans; said that if anything was to happen to him I should give them to you."

She looked at them, twisting them in her hand. He wondered if she might cry. Instead she placed them back in his palm. "You're his friend, you have them," she said. "To be honest, he was a bit of a dreamer... Wedding plans? No. He hadn't asked me, anyway. He was away with the fairies most of the time, which is another reason we called him Elf. I know I did that little exhibition for him down the Docks but to be honest that was for all you boys."

"But you..."

"Passed my bra over. Yeah, well... only a bit of material, isn't it? It doesn't mean nothing."

His forehead creased, the tumblers refusing to roll into place. He nodded his head in the direction of the kitchen. "That's..."

"His older brother, Owen, I know. It's all a bit complicated, but we've been helping each other deal with our grief and, well, we've kind of got together. We comforted each other and things just went from there."

Clive's body stiffened. The smell of meat cooking wafted from inside the house, mixing with an underlying stench of something rotting in an overflowing bin at the side of the building. A thick, black cloud passed overhead in the gloomy evening and he was unsure whether his mind was playing tricks. He could smell the cloying smoke, detect cordite in the air. Without warning, a rocket shot overhead, exploding right above him.

"Hey," she said, putting her hand on his shoulder. "Are you...?"

Suddenly Clive was barrelling through the house, knocking Kerry to the floor as he headed for the kitchen. Elf's brother turned, spatula in hand, a comedy apron wrapped around him, the image that of a man's six-pack, cock and balls. The punch caught him flush in the face, his expression turning from surprise to alarm as he dropped the frying pan and flames shot up, oil pouring onto the gas cooker. The smell of cooking meat was overpowering now, images flickering through Clive's mind like a cine projector on fast forward; bodies being carried from the ships, men walking around arms out wide reciting prayers, melting flesh hanging from them in clumps, one particular soldier with a face all but obliterated by fire, just one eye peering out, pleading for someone to end his misery...

"Hey, what are you bloody doin', coming in here causing a scene?" Kerry had recovered quickly from her fall and was charging towards him. "Leave him alone, would you? Christ, haven't we had enough to deal with? I'm sorry right, sorry for Elf, sorry for all them boys who lost their lives but... well, life goes on, doesn't it? Elf would have told you that. He would say, 'Live it to the full because you only have one'. You're one of the lucky ones. You should be grateful."

A figure appeared behind her. "Clive?" said Mo.

Kerry turned. "Are you his brother? You need to get him out of here. He's cracked, mate... a fuckin' looney. He's just punched me boyfriend and..."

Mo gave her a slap across the face. "No one talks about my brother that way."

"Oh," she said, recovering quickly. "Two loonies, is it? Christ, go and get your own asylum and leave us in peace."

Mo grabbed Clive's arm and started talking to him gently until a glimmer of recognition flickered across his face. Taking the rings from his pocket, Clive threw them onto the counter and stalked out of the house, Mo following. "Do what you want with them," he shouted over his shoulder. "I promised to deliver them and that's what I've done."

Back in the car, Mo said: "You want to go home? I know we were going to stay but they could call the police and we might find ourselves with a bit of aggro." Clive shrugged.

"Home it is then," said Mo.

44

THE room was spinning. Beryl reached down, wrapped her hands in his thick, rebellious hair and tugged. What was he doing to her? It was like there were three of him, kneading, fondling, licking, stroking all at the same time. It had never been this good. Never!

Somewhere beneath the pounding waves of pleasure she thought she heard a phone ring, but couldn't stop now. She couldn't! What if..? What the hell! The intervention just made her feel more acutely aroused, excited, out of control. Approaching the plateau she pushed her pelvis down towards him, rolling his head in her hands, directing him to her most receptive spots as if he was the joystick on a computer consul until... GAME OVER. She imagined her high-pitched scream could be heard blocks away, cities away, even countries away; all of her sexuality, her being, her pent-up frustrations being released in one powerful, intoxicating moment.

"Steady on," he said. "My turn now..."

She laughed freely, but it didn't disturb his concentration. He rolled her onto her front and raised her hips, her head flat against the pillow. She felt the soft hairs of his legs brush against the back of her thighs as he slid in behind her, kissing her shoulders while running his hands tenderly over her erect nipples. Sliding further down, his fingers grasped her hips and she waited with anticipation, hearing his breathing slow. She felt as if they were locked in a time vacuum – waiting, waiting – and she wondered whether his moment had passed. Completely still, she was aware of everything: the ticking of his watch, the dripping of the bathroom tap, the gentle rhythm of his breath on her neck. Then, at the height of her anticipation, he thrust into her so deeply that she thought he would pierce her very soul. The glorious ride began again. It seemed to go on forever...

"NO answer, probably in bed," said Mo. He had pulled in at a road-side phone box so he could tell Beryl they were coming home early. Climbing back into the driver's seat, Mo briefly checked on Chuck, sleeping soundly in the back.

"Poor lad," said Clive, climbing in the other side. "Still, he'll be OK sleeping in here. It's not like this is some old jalopy is it?"

"Only 20 miles to go," said Mo. "We might as well get on with it."

BERYL heard the faint mumble of voices outside as she got a glass of water from the kitchen. She looked at the clock on the wall and realised it had gone 1. It was probably some latecomers returning from a lock-in at The Hope. Even so, a knot formed in her stomach as she tiptoed back to the bedroom.

Stan was putting his trousers on as she entered. "You're leaving?" She couldn't mask her disappointment.

"I've got to get back. Sorry." He pulled his T-shirt over his torso, still glistening from their love making. "Work tomorrow and I am supposed to be in early."

"Take a shower here. I mean, won't she..."

"Sheila will be fast asleep now. She takes a pill. The dead could rise and she would sleep through it. As much as it's tempting to drag you in the shower with me I can honestly wait until I get home. It's not like I'll be doing anything unusual. Sometimes I work late at the warehouse and need to wash the day's grime off when I get in."

She rushed to him, enveloping him in her arms, pressing her fingers into the small of his back and pulling him towards her, hoping she might reignite the fires of passion inside him. It wouldn't be a difficult task. He was pretty insatiable. An hour ago her hand had simply brushed against him and she had been amazed at the reaction. "You're hard again," she had said in disbelief.

"Incredible, isn't it?" he had pulled her to him as her fingers traced the contours of his erection. "You do this to me, no one else," he said. Same here, she thought, disappearing under the sheets to heighten his pleasure.

Her mind was brought jolting back to the present by the sound of a key rattling in a lock. They both froze. "Shit!" Acting on instinct, she grabbed his socks and shoes from the floor then pushed him into the cheap, flimsy wardrobe in the corner, throwing the articles of clothing after him. "Hey!" he protested.

"Shhhhh! It must be Mo!" she said. It was like a scene from a slapstick comedy but neither of them was laughing. On the contrary. She was petrified. "Sorry!"

Shutting the door, she raced around in a desperate attempt to find something with which she could defend herself. From under the bed she pulled a child's cricket set she had bought for the boys to use on holiday, only for her brain to become so scrambled over the letter from Maurice's tart that she had forgotten to pack it.

She slipped her hand inside the plastic packaging and removed a stump. It was hardly a match for Reg, just 2ft long and weedy by comparison, but at least if she poked him in the eye she might be able to facilitate her lover's escape. Whatever happened, she was determined to put up some sort of resistance. The future was at stake – the one she and Stan had mapped out together. The last few hours had strengthened her resolve to leave Mo and when her lover had revealed he was ready to split from Sheila it just about sealed the deal. She didn't want to waste the rest of her life as a convenient punch bag for a man who had lost all sense of reason. She told herself she wasn't doing this just for herself, but for the kids, too. Growing up in an environment where violence played such a central role could only do them harm.

Climbing into bed, she pulled the covers up over her head and closed her eyes tightly, willing the problem to go away. For once, she actually hoped Mo was drunk. It would numb his sense of smell and prevent him noticing the musky scent of her lovemaking with Stan. She would have to pull her husband onto her and endure his fumbling crassness until he fell asleep. That way he might wake in the morning, believing the smell was down to his own antics in the night. She shivered at the very idea of it, particularly with the new love of her life listening from the wardrobe.

She heard movement in the corridor followed by a rustling coming from the boys' room next door, Mo putting their eldest son to bed. She cursed him for keeping Chuck up so late. When he had spoken to her on the phone earlier he had assured her they would book into a hotel so the boy could get a good night's sleep. Pulling the covers back she looked around, trying to gauge whether anything was out of place. Damn! How could she be so stupid? Throwing herself across the bed she quickly extinguished the light, hoping Mo hadn't seen it below the bedroom door. The only way this deception could work was if she feigned sleep. Once he spoke to her she was convinced his internal radar for trouble would kick in and he would sense her betrayal.

Squeezing her eyes shut, she heard the door open and sensed his penetrating gaze pass over her. The seconds he stood there felt like minutes. She kept the fingers of one hand crossed for luck while the others tightened their grip on the cricket stump under the pillow. Goosebumps ran chaotically across her naked torso.

The door cracked wider, light spilling in from the hallway. He would be able to make out her shape under the sheets now. "Bee," he whispered. "You awake?" Should she answer? If she did maybe she could take the conversation out into the corridor, offer to make them a sandwich and give Stan time to make his escape through the small bedroom window which led out onto the balcony. "Bee!" Mo's whisper was more insistent as he stepped further into the room.

"Mo?"

Another voice. Clive's.

The creak of the floorboards stopped for a second, then Beryl heard her husband pad back in the direction of the corridor.

"Mo!"

Hell!, What if Clive had found something to indicate another man was in the flat?

Then she knew the game was up.

Stan's combat jacket.

It was hanging over a chair in the living room.

CLIVE sat upright on the sofa, waiting for his brother to return with blankets and a pillow so he could bed down for the night. The room was in darkness apart from the light spilling in from the corridor. Lost in thought he scanned the room to let his eyes adjust. Eerie shadows lurked in every corner, the clock ticking away the seconds on the mantelpiece, feeding an unnamed fear. He had slept in many strange places over the last few months, so it wasn't his surroundings that troubled him. It was the fear of sleep itself. When it came, so did the ghosts.

He could make out the television, a record player, a footstool and Mo's favourite armchair. He froze. Draped across it was something so out of place fear crept like a colony of ants up his spine and across his scalp. He saw a camouflage jacket, discarded, thrown carelessly across a chair. He'd seen an identical one on the battlefield. The owner was a private he'd got to know aboard the QE2 and on this day had removed his jacket while working on a trench. The two of them had been sharing a joke before Clive was called away to help Archie with their own shelter. Without warning, he had been catapulted forward by an explosion. Looking back, there was just a grey, expanding cloud and a huge hole where the trench had been. From amid the acrid smoke an unrecognisable figure stumbled, both arms shorn off, a large, shadowy hole gaping where the right eye should have been, the mouth stalled mid-scream. The other glassy, unseeing eye latched on to Clive for a second, accusing. Then the body keeled over.

This jacket was resting at an identical angle – left arm lying crookedly across the top of the chair, right arm hanging loose. It proved too much for Clive. Pushing himself from the sofa, he raced into the hallway. "Mo?"

No answer.

"Mo!"

"Shit! What now?" His brother's voice came from a room deeper inside the flat. Clive couldn't move in that direction, petrified he would encounter more harmful spirits. Breathing heavily, his body trapped in the strait-jacket of a panic attack, he composed himself long enough to say: "I can't stay. Sorry! Got to get out, need a drink ..."

Finally overriding the invisible shackles, he broke into a run, stumbling over a kid's tricycle in the corridor, his mind flashing back to the crags he negotiated on Tumbledown. When eventually he freed himself, he reached for the front door latch and dived out into the comforting familiarity of the chill night air.

BERYL listened intently to the drama kicking off in the hallway. "Shit!" Mo whispered under his breath. "OK, wait up! I'm coming."

She said a silent prayer of thanks as she heard the echoing sound of footsteps retreating down the hallway. "Stop! Clive, stop!" Mo was pleading. "It's OK. I know a place. Opens late. We'll get that drink."

The sound of the door slamming was almost as loud as Beryl's heartbeat in her ears. She threw off the covers and padded naked across the room, peering tentatively out into the hallway, the cricket stump still in her hand. She feared Mo might be fooling her, hiding around the corner ready to pounce. There was no one. Standing at the front door, she heard running feet beat a tattoo on the concrete, fading into the distance.

When he gripped her from behind, pinning her arms to her side, Beryl thought she would have a heart attack. A kiss was planted on her neck, the mouth lingering longer than necessary, sucking at her skin until she pulled away. "Stop it, you nutter!" she said. "That would be a great idea, wouldn't it, giving me a bloody love bite?"

She twisted, turning to face Stan, who was wearing that infectious smile, dimple to the fore. "Oh, you fucker!" she shouted, thumping him hard on the arm. "You actually enjoyed that bit of drama, didn't you?"

"It was fun," he admitted, rubbing his back. "Wouldn't want to go through it every day mind you, that cupboard's a tight squeeze. Shall we..?" He indicated for them to go back into the flat.

"No!" she said. "No, you mad bastard, of course not. He's gone but he could be back any time. We've been lucky. Let's not mess it up. You'd better go."

He nodded, disappearing back into the flat for his combat jacket. Returning, he wrapped his arm around her and kissed her hard on the mouth. Her body tingled but she pulled away before temptation took a grip. "I love you, Beryl Dolan," he said, stepping past her onto the balcony. "I want to be with you forever."

She watched him walk away, a quiver passing through her. The things they had done that night. "Love you, too," she whispered, just out of his earshot. Returning to the flat, she shut the door, leaning with her back against it, head resting against the coolness of the white painted wood, letting out a breath she seemed to have been holding forever. She said it again out loud to herself, just to convince herself it was true. "I love you, Stan Marshall. I really fucking do!"

45

IT had been a tough night and Mo arrived home sometime around midday. Beryl was sitting at the kitchen table drinking a cup of coffee and he thought about confiding in her about his worries for Clive. He would normally have kept such things bottled up but the guru said a problem shared was a problem halved. He hoped Suni didn't adopt the mantra personally; who knew what 'problems' he might be sharing with the local CID? He stalled, though, seeing the dark shadows around her eyes and realising she was tired. Perhaps Sly had given her a tough time the day before.

As if she could read his thoughts, Beryl said: "You're worried about Clive, Mo, I can tell. Did you two come in last night then go straight out again? Is he OK?"

"It... it's like the bond we had is broken," said Mo sadly.

"Give it time," she said. "He's hardly going to be laughing and joking, is he? He's lost some close friends."

"I know, but he can't be allowed to forget he's got friends here, too ... I was thinking about a homecoming party."

"It's a good idea," she said. "Maybe a bit early, though. Let him settle in. His birthday's in November, isn't it? Why not wait until then?"

He shrugged his shoulders and walked to the kettle, filled it and joined her at the table. Despite her fatigue she looked better today. There was some colour to her cheeks and the bruises had faded nicely, thank God. What the hell had he been thinking, giving her such a torrid time? She was his rock and he sensed he was losing her. Not physically, of course. She would never leave him. Mentally, though. Sometimes it was as if she was in the same room but her mind was elsewhere. He had to do better, put the relationship back together. Now Clive was back...

"Here he is," said Beryl. "Here's my beautiful boy. You had a nice sleep, lover?" Chuck moved into her open arms, resting his head on her shoulder.

"Bit of a late one wasn't it, old son?" said Mo. The boy nodded.

"What we going to do, Mo?" she asked.

"About what?"

"Him, of course," she nudged her head in the direction of the boy.

"In what respect?"

"In the respect that he hasn't got a school to go to. I mean..."

"I don't want him going back to that one."

"What?" She was stunned.

"They don't respect him there," said Mo. "They don't respect us! Hell, you heard what he said – that deputy-head – going on about how he 'expected' trouble from a Dolan. Well, he's gonna get some if he..."

"Come on, love," she said. "Violence isn't the answer." He fell silent, pouting like a school kid. "Look, I'll ring the school today. They go back next week. I'll tell them he has learned his lesson..."

"Lesson?" Mo's fury boiled to the surface. "It wasn't his fault, Bee! The other kid attacked him. He was doing what he should do in the circumstances... defending himself. Ain't that right, Chuck?" The little boy whispered to his mum. Mo sensed Chuck was deliberately avoiding eye contact with him. "What did he say?"

"He doesn't want to leave," she replied. "He's met some new friends."

"Well..." Mo took a deep breath, calmed himself, the way he had been taught by the guru. He'd seldom known it work. Once he felt comfortable he spoke again. "Maybe I should leave it to you, honey. I'm no good at this. That school just drives me insane. Always had it in for us Dolans, I tell you. Even Clive got treated crap there, and he was a right goody two-shoes. Still, if Chuck wants to stay..."

It was a concession. Mo wondered if he was going soft in his old age. He poured hot water into his West Ham mug and took a sip of his coffee. "Make sure you sort it, Bee," he said. "Or I will."

THE headmaster Mr Pullin agreed to lift the suspension after a long discussion. He was relatively new to the school so she explained the background and said she felt there was a clash of personalities between Chuck and a member of staff. Mr Pullin agreed to take a personal interest in the matter.

After the phone call, she found Chuck watching TV. She recognised the show. It had been on every summer since she was a kid. It was about a boy called Sebastian and a big, hairy dog called Belle, who lived in a village half way up a snowy mountain. The villagers thought the dog dangerous but the boy protected him. It was a mystery to her why Chuck wanted to look at snow when the sun was beating down outside. "Where's your dad?" she asked.

"Bathroom," said Chuck.

"Well, I've got some good news," she said. "Mr Pullin says you can go back to the school again, but that you have to keep your fists under control in future. It's your last chance."

"Thanks, Mum," he said, then as an after-thought: "When can I go back to boxing?"

She hated to burst his bubble, but saw no option. "The doctor said that you had a nasty blow to the head. You can't go back until you're absolutely, one hundred per cent mended. A couple of weeks should do it."

In truth, she wanted the wounds to fade before he resumed the sport to avoid the embarrassment of having to lie when people asked questions.

"But, Mum – that's not fair!" he protested.

Moving over to sit on the arm of the sofa, she gently stroked his hair, making a mental note to get it cut before he resumed school. "Life isn't fair, son," she said, repeating one of her father's favourite phrases. "Life isn't fair."

46

"YOU found it yet?" asked Handsome Frank, whispering to Mo as he grasped him in a bear hug.

"What?"

"Your lighter."

"No... no," said Mo hesitantly. "It's a pity. It's got sentimental value, a present from Bee. I must have dropped it when we were out on the piss. Look, I'm sorry I had a go at you... I flipped. We got to stick together with Cozza inside."

"I can understand you criticising us for being slapdash. We were throwing around those sacks of cash after all, but I assure you we cleaned up real thorough," said Frank, hitting one boxing glove against another. "We took that cottage apart, bit by bit, making sure there wasn't a trace of us left behind. I'm sure you would have approved if you had been there."

"Well, you know... circumstances," said Mo.

"Course. How is he?"

"Fine." Mo looked down and rubbed Chuck on the head. "You're all right aren't you, son?" The boy nodded, but didn't say anything. "A few little cuts and bruises of course, but he couldn't wait to get back here. We kept him away for a few weeks because the doc said there was a danger of concussion, but he seems fine now – can't wait to get the gloves back on." His inquisitive eyes passed around the room. "Which one's his trainer?"

"Not here yet," said Frank.

"Well, I'd like to meet him... shake his hand," said Mo. "You do realise that our kid punched a school bully's lights out the other week, do you? All down to the sessions he's been having here."

"I suspect he won't turn up for a while," said Frank. He seemed nervous, but Mo put it down to the uneasy atmosphere between the two of them. He allowed himself to be ushered towards the door. "You could meet him another time, yeah?" said Frank.

Mo shrugged. "I'm in no hurry. You sort that cash situation?"

"Bagged up and ready for you to collect. We did it ages ago, but weren't sure when you were going to turn up. We can go down there later if you like."

"Nah. No rush." Mo put his hand around Handsome Frank's neck and leaned in, lowering his voice to a whisper. "Perhaps we should give the lock-up a wide berth after what happened to Cozza. Old Bill could be watching us. You heard from him?"

"I saw Bev," said Frank. "She's upset. I said we'd look after her and the kids... told her to let Cozza know he doesn't have to worry as long as he keeps schtum. Trial's scheduled for around Christmas."

"Merry fackin' Christmas," said Mo. "Good work, Frank. It's in his interests now not to grass us up. Not that I think he would."

He pulled away and bent down to talk to his son. "OK, I'd better go, Chucky," he said. "Keep up the good work and you'll be a proper boxer in no time. Just imagine, now your uncle is back he will be around to see your first bout!"

"Clive back, is he?" said Frank.

Mo stood up, pulling his friend close again. "He's been back since August, but to tell you the truth he's all over the place, mate. I've been a bit reluctant to take him out to any of the old haunts."

"Header?"

"What do you think?" said Mo. "I know we're all a bit nuts but Clive was the sane one. War has done something to him, and no mistake. Still, he's a hero and he deserves a welcome home party. I've had a word with Sinead down the Hope, and with it being his birthday soon, too, she said she would put on some nibbles and such.

It won't be a big crew because I don't want to spook him... Me, you, Wally and his boy, Tommy from the 3 Wishes... a good old East End knees-up. I'd invite the old man, but I doubt he'd come. Doesn't like venturing into the 'wilds' of Barking now he's got his country pile. Cunt."

"Parents, eh?" said Frank.

"Yeah." Mo rubbed Chuck on the head, shook his friend's hand again and walked out.

CLIFFY SIMPSON had just removed the boxing bag from the boot of his dilapidated Ford Escort Mark II when he saw the big man exit. Normally a placid person, Cliffy's fists clenched automatically. Looking down, he saw the tyre iron and thought how simple it would be to pick it up, march over and cave in the shaven-headed thug's skull. The days Cliffy had gone toe-to-toe with the likes of Reggie Kray were long gone, though, and there was no point in starting a fight you might not win. He sensed violence was a way of life for the man across the road from him.

He could make an arrest but that would cause difficulties. Audrey had insisted she wouldn't press charges. He sympathised. Too often young ladies like her were treated like criminals themselves under cross examination by worm-like defence lawyers. It would be as if she was enduring the ordeal all over again.

There had to be a way to get justice. From the moment Cliffy had seen the horrific injuries suffered by his little girl he had set about learning all he could about Maurice 'Big Mo' Dolan. He was sure the man was addicted to criminality and it was a matter of time before he slipped up. Though it was frustrating to play the waiting game, experience taught Cliffy that sooner or later nasty pieces of work like Dolan had their comeuppance.

Slamming the boot down, the police officer crossed the road.

MO looked at the badly out-of-shape man approaching, swinging his boxing bag in one hand and his gloves in the other. Surely, this old codger didn't come here to punch bags and mix it in the ring with East London's finest? He could imagine that a minute bobbing and weaving around the canvas with someone like Handsome Frank would leave the bloke red-faced and blowing from every orifice. The thought made him chuckle.

Mind you, if that fatso wasn't a boxer, why would he be entering Molloy's gym? They were barely feet from each other now and he seemed to be giving Mo the hard stare. Unbelievable! Now even granddads wanted a pop. There was something familiar about the bloke, too, like he'd seen him before. Maybe they had swapped words on a previous occasion.

The doors swung open and the old geezer entered. Mo heard a familiar voice just as he was about to head back to the car. "Hi Cliffy!" His son was greeting the old man as if they were close pals.

"Well, well, well," said the man called Cliffy. "If it isn't my favourite pupil. How are you, Chuck? Enjoy your holiday? You seem to have picked up a couple of bruises. What did I say about keeping your guard up?"

Electrical charges connected in Mo's brain. "Unbelievable!" he said out loud. It had come to him suddenly. The fat guy was one of the coppers they had seen on the night of the Romford warehouse robbery. It seemed he was also Chuck's boxing trainer. Surprises came in many shapes and sizes.

Taking a few more steps towards the Daimler, another memory stopped Mo in his tracks – four or five Filth dragging him into the local nick and taking him down to the cells. Another bloke shouting instructions. "Put him in No 4, that's free..." It was the same copper. He was the jailer at Hackney nick.

Turning, Mo raced back into the gym. "Chucky! Chuck!" The boy was about to disappear in the direction of the changing rooms but looked over his shoulder at the last moment. "Come here!" shouted Mo. When the boy saw the look on his father's face he headed back. The old copper watched from the changing room doorway.

"Yes, Dad?"

"You ain't doing boxing no more," said Mo.

"What..?" Chuck's mouth hung open, his expression a mixture of confusion and anger. "Why? You said I was good at it."

"I don't think you're mixing with the right people here," said Mo. "Your coach. He's a copper."

"I know," said Chuck. "It's OK, though. He's really nice."

"What have I told you?" said Mo, grabbing the boy's arm. "All coppers are bastards."

"Let me go!" shouted Chuck. "You bloody ruin everything, Dad!"

"Whaaat!" Mo exploded, dragging his son towards the exit. At the last moment Chuck wriggled free and ran back inside. Mo realised everyone was watching him, other boxers closing in to see what the fuss was about, the copper walking in his direction, a fierce look on his face.

Let him try.

"You took my football away from me and now you're going to take my boxing? That isn't fair!" His son was shouting at him from a distance. What the fuck? "Cliffy is a great teacher. He's shown me how to look after myself, how to stand up to bullies. It's called the art of self defence and it's all about discipline. You said yourself that you were going to thank my trainer for teaching me how to punch properly. Well, here he is..."

Mo couldn't handle it. He felt the walls closing in, ready to crush him. There were three or four boxers in close proximity now, primed to act. He didn't want to make himself look a fool.

"We'll talk about this when you get home." He fixed his son with a glare. "The way you've just spoken to me suggests this boxing lark has made you too big for your boots. I think you should say your goodbyes when you finish here today, because I'm pretty sure you won't be coming back."

He turned and stormed out, aware of the eyes on his back. For some reason he could feel the old copper's stare more intensely than any other, burning into him like a laser.

He should have punched his lights out.

Just for the hell of it.

47

BERYL almost fell as she jumped from the bus. Her desire to see him again was bordering on ridiculous. The humdrum routines of ordinary life had consumed them both in recent weeks, leaving them little time to discuss their plans. In her case, it seemed Mo was always around these days, the late night absences a thing of the past. She could only conclude he had split from the floozy.

She'd only seen Stan once since he had gone on a couples' holiday with Sheila. Beryl had felt pangs of jealously when he told her what he had planned, but immediately scolded herself for her hypocrisy. She was hardly in a position to take the moral high ground when she and Mo had been away with the kids earlier in the summer.

Holidays were part of the deal and if Stan and Sheila's marriage was true to type, their time alone together had probably driven the wedge further between them. There had been an article on the subject in one of Beryl's magazines. New research suggested holidays were a major cause of couples separating, annoying habits being amplified by so much time in each other's company. She felt wicked for thinking that way. She wasn't a malicious person, but it showed the spell he had cast over her.

The one time she had seen Stan since his return was when Mo spent the night at his brother's. Beryl had raced to a nearby phone box to call her lover, begging him to spend the night, and was shocked by his negative reaction. He said he was uneasy about going to her place, not wishing to tempt fate after their previous lucky escape. Instead, he suggested a liaison at a flat on the estate he was looking after for a mate who was visiting family in India.

Beryl didn't hesitate, arranging for a neighbour's 16-year-old daughter and her boyfriend to babysit for a few hours while she crept around the estate like a spy, moving from one tower block to another with her coat collar pulled up to hide her face. The moment Stan saw her it was as if they had never been apart. He had whipped off her clothes and taken her fast and furious in the passageway with her back forced up against some cheap framed painting. When she cried out, he thought she was enjoying it so much he thrust harder, only for her to punch him in the back and shout into his ear: "You bastard, that's hurting, my back's in agony!"

With his pants around his ankles, he manoeuvred her into the front room. She couldn't help laughing as she imagined how the scene might look to an outsider. Throwing her onto the sofa he thrust into her roughly, whispering dirty words in her ear, a new development in their blossoming sex life. His actions were urgent and inflamed, his naked lust for her clearly evident. Spent, he lay getting his breath back as she squeezed from beneath him, collecting her coat, grabbing her keys from the coffee table and making her way home, face burning from the sheer audacity of the brief encounter.

It was only when she got back to the flat she realised the keys weren't hers. Worried Mo might come across them and interrogate her, she hid them in a tampon box in her closet, a place he would never dream of looking. When she was tidying up the previous day she noticed them and realised they presented her with the perfect excuse to visit him at the market. Leaving Sylvester with a neighbour, she had set off for the bus stop with no plan and no excuse should Mo ask where she had been.

Perhaps this was the day she would break it to him. "I'm leaving you. I'm in love with someone else." She had practised hundreds of variations in the mirror, but at no stage did the words feel comfortably in her mouth. Thinking about that impending confrontation sent lightning bolts shooting around her insides and goosebumps up her legs. Excitement, mixed with a large dollop of fear. Humming *Jumping From Love to Love*, a Dr Feelgood song from the album Stan had brought to her flat while Mo was in Wales, she thought how poignant the title was given her situation – not that there had been many signs of love in the Dolan household of late.

In Walthamstow, it was a chilly and bright autumn day. The stalls were inundated with people looking for weekend bargains on food and clothes. Pop-up stalls were selling fireworks at knockdown prices in preparation for Bonfire Night while the sights and smells of frying meat, exotic curry sauce, ripe fruit and fresh herbs combined to make her stomach rumble. There hadn't been time for breakfast that morning. All her concentration had been focused on getting Chuck ready for his first day back at the gym. She hoped to satisfy her appetite by stealing Stan away for lunch.

Pushing past mothers with pushchairs and kids in tow, she watched teenagers loitering at the computer game stalls while old women eyed up summer dresses on offer. Men hovered around DIY exhibits, burying their heads in reject bins to find items to help them with their weekend running repairs.

"Hey, sister, mind where you're at!" shouted a woman of Caribbean descent when Beryl accidentally trod on her toe.

Turning, she gave the woman a beaming smile. "Oh, I'm so sorry, love, just in a bit of a hurry," she said. "I'll be more careful." The woman had been readying herself for a good old London street row, so the pleasant apology caught her off guard.

"Yeah, well," she stammered, "Make sure you do." She flounced off in the other direction, pulling one of those tartan shopping bags on wheels.

At last Beryl reached her destination, the stall for shoes, trainers and sporting boots. A man in his 50s was serving a young Asian, a queue stretching out behind him. Bobbing and weaving to get a better look, Beryl saw no sign of Stan. Maybe his father had given him a lie-in or, worse, the day off. She felt jealous. If only she had those options, but with two kids it was mission impossible.

Pulling level with the stall she took the plunge. "Excuse me," she said, trying to attract the stallholder's attention.

"There's a queue, lady!" shouted one of the punters in the line.

"Sorry!" She smiled, gesticulating with her hands. "I'm not trying to jump in or buy anything, I just need to ask a question."

Placing colourful baseball boots into an unmarked white box, the stallholder collected the cash before looking over. "Is it me you would be wanting, darlin'?" he said in a broad Irish accent.

"Uh, no... well, yes. Are you Patrick Marshall?"

He looked at her suspiciously. "Who wants to know?"

She held out her hand. "Sorry, my name is Beryl... Beryl Dolan. I came down here to see you a while ago about getting my son some boxing boots."

The handshake was accepted. "Ahhhh, Molloy sent you, did he?"

"Yes, anyway..."

"Good customer, Molloy – knows I always get the best stuff at a decent price."

There was a murmur from the crowd, a burly bouncer type having arrived at the front of the queue with a pair of plimsolls dangling from his hand. They would never fit him, thought Beryl, chuckling nervously, the footwear obviously meant for a child. "Bloody hell! Come on Patrick, I ain't got all bleedin' day," the man protested to murmurs of agreement.

Blushing, Beryl apologised again. The store owner stepped in. "Won't be long, Mac," he said. The bouncer waved dismissively. "What is it, darling?"

"Well, when I came here I saw your son Stan and he was very helpful. I was hoping to speak to him about something else we discussed." She made a show of looking around. "He's not here?"

"Sorry, love," said Patrick. "He's got an appointment this lunchtime. Had to nip off. Should be back soon, though. Can I help?"

"Not really."

"OK well I'm sure if you come back later he'll be here. He's only nipped to the hospital." He noticed her concern. "Don't worry, he's fine. Tell you what, why don't you go and do your shopping, then come back in about half an hour. Shall I tell him Beryl was here?"

She thought about it. It would make her sound needy. "If I see him, I see him," she said. "It's not urgent."

"I'll leave it with you then, love." Patrick turned to the bouncer, took the plimsolls from him and placed them in a carrier bag.

THOUGH Patrick had told her not to worry, Beryl couldn't help it. What if Stan had an awful ailment he hadn't told her about like cancer or something? It sounded selfish, but it would be typical if she rearranged her life only to have happiness snatched away at the last moment. Then a worse thought popped into her head. What if he had one of those diseases that were passed on sexually: syphilis, gonorrhoea or chlamydia? There was even that deadly one that had appeared from nowhere, Aids. The rumour mill was full of theories about how it started – everything from the idea it was passed on by African monkeys to the crazy notion it was a biological weapon one of the world's super powers had released in error. Stan couldn't have Aids, though. She had read it only affected homosexuals.

She chastised herself. What the hell was she doing, thinking such nasty thoughts about the man she loved? Maybe it was something minor, like a muscle pull or something. He was always lugging boxes around. She sniggered. Maybe he had picked up the injury during their last encounter, something so embarrassing he was struggling to tell the doctor what had happened.

"Doc, I think I may have damaged my tongue."

"How did you manage that, Mr Marshall?"

She walked up to one of the fast food outlets then checked herself at the last minute. Why give these places her custom when local people would benefit more? She recalled the sympathetic Turkish cafe owner from her first meeting with Stan. If she went back there it would be easy to keep an eye out for her lover.

She turned, retraced her steps and was about to enter when she spotted Stan sitting at the table they had shared. Opposite him was a woman with jet black hair and a peach winter coat. They sipped tea, looking comfortable and happy in each other's company, the woman – who looked about Beryl's age or perhaps a bit older – speaking animatedly while Stan listened.

A knot formed in Beryl's stomach. Might it be true that Stan was the sort of Lothario the cafe owner had jokingly warned her about? No, it wasn't possible. They had something special, didn't they? She paused, mid-thought. How much did she really know about him? He'd supposedly opened up to her about his marriage, but people lied all the time. She had read a million stories of gullible women being duped by Romeos who had run off with their life savings. Was Stan a conman?

As she watched, the other woman stood up. Beryl lay flat against the wall to avoid being spotted. Stan's companion was taking off her coat, resting it across the back of the bench. Oh... my... God! Beryl gasped out loud. The woman with the black dyed hair had a little bump sitting comfortably under a pair of swelled breasts.

"Ahh," said Patrick, approaching from behind. "Looks like you've found him. The two of them look very happy, don't they? So am I. I'm going to be a grandaddy! I can't wait to know what Sheila's having. Blooming, isn't she? Radiant. I reckon it will be a boy meself. All the signs are there, if you believe my wife who fancies herself as a bit of a clairvoyant. Imagine that? Another..."

Beryl had tuned out at the word grandaddy, thoughts tumbling, her mind grasping for an alternative explanation, coming up empty. Her memory navigated its way through her entire history with Stan, flipping moments over like index cards in a librarian's binder. Surely, she had missed a clue, something she should have spotted at the very start. There was nothing. He'd been clever, a master of deception, his trail of lies told with the smooth assurance of a person well versed in the business of selling dreams. Christ, he'd done it with Chucky on their first-ever meeting, showing him pictures of boxers and telling him that with the right gear he could become a Tyson or Sugar Ray; with Sly, too, promising him the earth on their trip to the South Bank. They called it patter or, given his Irish background, blarney.

"You all right, darlin'?" asked Patrick. She didn't answer – couldn't. The bile rose in her throat, a nauseous feeling spreading through her stomach. She stumbled away, leaving the old man open mouthed. The warmth of the sun added to her dizziness, making her feel a bit delirious like the time she had food poisoning on a school trip. She bumped into a rack of cards outside a newsagents, sending it crashing to the ground, but didn't stop to rectify the damage, plunging on through the pressing crowds, a living, moving straitjacket from which she couldn't escape.

"Beryl! Wait!" The voice came from somewhere behind her. Twisting, she broke off the heel of one of her favourite stiletto shoes and crashed to the ground, grazing her knees and the palms of her hands. The tears were flowing thick and fast, passers-by showing concern, unaware her crying was not as a result of the fall. Then he was there, sinking to his knees and looking into her eyes, pleading: "Let me explain. It's not what you think."

She scrambled for her bag, pulling out a tissue and blowing her nose, wet blotches on her cheeks burning like angry insects biting her skin. "What is it then?" she snapped. "Did you just fall over and accidentally stick your dick in her, eh, this wife you claim you don't sleep with anymore? Maybe it got trapped inside her when you rolled over during sleep or, I don't know, she caught it off the toilet seat. You're a fucking bastard, you know that? I was making plans around you – real, solid plans. More fool me for being sucked in by your lies. How could I even think to leave Maurice for someone who cheats on their pregnant wife? I must be so, so stupid."

The surrounding crowd were enthralled at the drama taking place. It was like a soap opera being filmed in an East London market square. Perhaps she should pitch the idea to TV bosses. He reached out, but she shrugged him off. "Don't!" she said through the tears. "Don't touch me. Everything hurts. I fuckin' hurt."

"I know." Studying him for the first time, she saw he had tears in his eyes, too. "Look, I meant what I said it's just, well, Sheila's always wanted a baby and I... how could I deny her? She had a pretty rough childhood..."

"Sympathy fuck, was it?" she said cuttingly. "Well that's all right then! How were you going to break it to her? I'm leaving you for another woman but you'll be OK because I've given you the baby you wanted?"

There was a scuffling sound, the crowd parting. "Stanley!" A woman's voice. Shrill, irritable. Beryl looked up to see Stan's wife staring down at them, shaking a child's car seat in his direction. "I thought you were going to help with this? It's bloody heavy and in case you hadn't noticed I'm three months pregnant. What are you doing down there anyway? Who's this?"

"This lady had a nasty fall," said Stan sheepishly. "I was worried she might have done herself an injury."

This lady. Like there was absolutely nothing special about her. Beryl was desperate to puncture the cosy relationship between Stan and his wife. Instead, she sat dumbstruck on the floor, letting her tears flow like a silly schoolgirl.

Stan pulled out a handkerchief embroidered with his initials. An intimate gift from the wife? She pushed his hand away. "I'm fine, thanks." An undercurrent of bitterness. "You run along. You shouldn't leave your wife having to carry that heavy burden."

"I meant what I said." He lowered his voice to a whisper. "You have to make the break and I promised I'd help. I will. I owe you that. You can't stay with Mo."

She chuckled. "He's not so bad," she spat. "He couldn't hurt me anywhere near as much as you have."

Sheila broke in, having caught snippets of her sentence. "Yes, well, sorry you've hurt yourself, girl," she said. "Glad you're on the mend. Now, if you don't mind, I'd like my husband back."

"Sure." Beryl made a dismissive gesture. "With my pleasure... and good luck with the baby."

Her knees a mess of cuts, her pretty yellow dress stained with dirt and gravel, Beryl watched Sheila pass over the child seat then drag Stan back through the market. As the crowd dispersed, their lunchtime entertainment over, it started to rain.

"Good luck, Sheila," Beryl said out loud, getting glances from passers-by. "You're going to fucking need it."

48

"I NEED to speak to you."

The sentence sent a shiver through Beryl's battered body. For most couples, those six simple words would be the prelude to a sensible discussion. In the Dolan household, it was foreplay to a full-scale row and, though she couldn't see him, the tone of Mo's voice told her he had an axe to grind. She was relieved to peer around the door and find he wasn't in the hallway. Reg was there, resting against the wall behind the bikes, which at least convinced her that her husband hadn't been loosening up with a few practice swings.

"Where are you, love?" she asked, keeping her voice level, aware he would detect fear like a tiger shark smelling the blood of a wounded seal.

"In here." The voice came from the kitchen. "At the dining table."

Backing into the hallway, she pulled the pushchair behind her. "Sly's fallen asleep," she said, picking up the boy. "OK if I put him down for a nap? Did the boxing go OK?"

He grunted, neither confirmation nor denial. Was this the reason he needed a chat? Chuck's sporting activities rarely merited a family conference, though that football issue had been a bit more dramatic than necessary. Plenty of other things were more likely to wind up Maurice Dolan, and any one of them could escalate his temper drastically in seconds.

Firstly, there was her affair. She was positive she hadn't left any clues around, covering her tracks with almost forensic zeal. After Stan's last visit she had moved every piece of furniture in the flat, any hint of her lover's presence being sucked up into the vacuum cleaner. She'd checked for coins around skirting boards and buttons underneath bedside tables, just in case something had popped off at the peak of their lovemaking. Even the wardrobe in which Stan had hidden had received a thorough polish, all clothes removed.

The thought brought to mind her second fear; had she put his suits back in the right colour-coordinated order? Were his pants and socks neatly folded? Had the kids been playing with his record collection again? In sharp contrast with most couples she knew, Maurice had more storage space than she did. It wasn't that she had no interest in trending fashions. She liked to look presentable but put her needs on the back burner, giving priority to the three men in the family.

Sly gave a groan as she tucked him in bed, but turned onto his side and was away with the fairies again instantly. Taking a deep breath, she walked into the kitchen. "Fancy a cuppa?" she said cheerily. "I do, I'm parched. Been..."

"Give me a minute, eh?" he said calmly. It was good that he was in control, though she knew that might be a ruse to put her off guard.

"Everything all right?"

He tapped the table, commanding her to sit opposite him. Sinking into the chair, she remembered her dress was damaged and she had a new collection of bruises. Damn! She had meant to go straight to their bedroom to change. Now Mo would notice her dishevelled appearance, which would inevitably lead to questions.

"No, babe, I'm not all right," he said, worry lines creasing his big, imposing forehead. "I've been a right cunt."

She tilted her head, not sure she had heard correctly.

"I said Clive was losing it, but his troubles have put mine into perspective," he continued. "I got stuck in traffic on the way back from the gym and it gave me time to think. I've been a bastard to you and those boys, and I've been the same with my mates, too. The other week I flew off the handle, went crazy at Cozz and Frank, took Reg to them. What on earth was I thinking?"

He genuinely looked remorseful and confused. "Now Cozza's in custody and I can't make it up to him. Jeez!"

This felt different from his normal tearful apologies. Genuine.

"Do you need your guru?" she asked.

He thought about it. "Maybe... no. I'm not sure. I've got to sort this out myself and the first thing I have to do is be honest with you. You're my wife and we've been through so much together."

An uneven flutter started up in her heart. Mo admitting he was in the wrong? It felt weird, almost as if he sensed how close she had been to leaving him. On the bus she had thought about what Stan had said, about how she should leave Maurice anyway. Where was she going to go? Her pursuit of happiness had been a far-fetched dream. She was awake now.

This was her life.

Her lot.

"It's fine, Mo," she said calmly, putting her hand on his. "You've just had a lot on your mind."

"You don't understand!" He became more animated.

"OK." She pushed herself up. "If this is going to be a long chat I need tea. I am gagging."

She took the kettle to the sink, filled it up. He used the opportunity to lift his cigarettes from the table, his thick, pudgy fingers extracting one from the pack. "You want one?" Beryl rarely smoked, except when she felt it was "sociable" to do so, mingling with friends and relatives at Christmas. On this occasion, she needed the nicotine in her lungs to calm her.

"Please," she said, returning to the table. She took one from the pack, put it in her mouth and bent over to meet the flame from his disposable lighter. Behind her, the kettle whistled. From the shelf above the sink, she pulled down a tin with London scenes on it, a red bus, a guardsman, Big Ben. Levering off the lid, she shovelled three heaps of brown leaves into the silver teapot, poured on water and covered the pot with a knitted claret and blue cosy bought from the West Ham gift shop.

The silence gnawed at her as she let it brew, raising herself on tiptoe to retrieve two mugs from a cupboard, the clock winding down the seconds: tick, tick, tick. Job done, she returned to the table, handing him a cup, even though he hadn't asked for one. "Thanks, Bee." He blew on the hot liquid. "I cheated on you."

Shit, shit, shit! It was 'this' type of confession. He had just blurted it out, opening up fully like a gambler laying all his cards on the table and hoping it would be enough. This was an honesty session, but to reciprocate would bring a whole heap of unnecessary trouble down on her shoulders. Putting her hands over his again, she said: "I know."

That stumped him. "You do?" he said, eyebrows rising to meet the worry lines on his forehead. "How?"

She went to the counter, retrieved her purse and opened it, taking the piece of paper from inside and placing it in his hand. Reading it, his brow furrowed. "How long have you had this?" he asked.

"Since before the holiday. I found it when I was packing."

"Aaaah."

"What does that mean?"

"It explains a lot," he said. "Why you were so off with me, flinching away when I tried to touch you, starting rows for no reason, refusing to go to the beach even though Bev was quite happy to keep an eye on Sly. And the fight..."

"Yes," she said. "I was angry. You destroyed everything I believed in... your loyalty and commitment to your family. I was furious. I couldn't help it."

"I was a fool," he said. "I wasn't thinking straight. I know it sounds weird, but I needed to believe I was someone else. I had all this anger bubbling inside me..."

She nodded. "It didn't work, did it? It made things worse."

He frowned. "The guilt, I guess."

"It's over?"

"Yes. I finished it just after we got back from Hastings."

"Promise me it won't happen again," she said, feeling every inch the hypocrite.

"Promise," he said. "Scout's honour."

"You were never in the bloody Scouts!" she said. They both laughed nervously as she reached for his hand again, drawing circles on his coarse, weathered skin. She traced the lines of his scars, each telling a story she would rather not know or remember.

"What brought this on?"

He sighed. "Chuck, I guess," he said. "When I took him to boxing today I met his coach. He's Filth. I had no idea. Big bloke, you may have met him. He brought Chuck home after that incident at the football."

She nodded. "He seemed all right."

Mo shrugged. "Maybe he is, maybe he isn't," he said. "All I know is he's a copper and you know what I think about them."

"There are exceptions to every rule."

He was silent for a second, taking in her words.

"Anyway, I lost it today," he finally admitted. "I told Chucky he would have to give up the boxing and, do you know what? He stood up to me, big time. I know he's been getting a bit chopsy, but this was full-on confrontation. I actually felt quite proud of him. He told me I ruin everything for him... do I?"

"No," she said. "Of course not. You take him with you places, do all sorts with him... hell, it was you who got him into the gym in the first place. I'm sure he knows that what you do is in his best interests. He was just letting off steam."

"I felt awful." He wiped an eye. "What made matters worse was these big fuckin' bruisers started coming over, crowding around me as if I was some nonce or kiddy fiddler, the kind of bloke who beats his own kids. I couldn't get out of there fast enough. Now he hates me."

"Chucky? He doesn't!" Beryl got up and moved around the table, putting her arm across his broad shoulders. She saw a tear fall into his mug, breaking the surface. "Chucky worships the ground you walk on," she said. "This is him growing up, testing the water, becoming an individual. You have to give him his own space. Stop him doing everything he enjoys then, yes, you will make him an enemy. You can't control his life. His boxing coach is a copper? So what! The question is does he coach Chucky well, and does our son enjoy it? The answer to both questions is 'Yes'."

"But what if, you know, he is using Chuck to get to me," said Mo. "He gave me this tough guy look today as if I was the shit on the bottom of his shoe. I worry he might plug Chuck for information."

"You need to have more faith in your son," she said. "Perhaps you need a man-to-man chat, explain to him that he mustn't divulge family 'secrets'. If he agrees to that I see no reason why you should stop him doing what he loves. As for this bloke having it in for you: What reason could he have? Perhaps you just caught him on a bad day. We all have them."

He nodded. "Guess so."

She knelt beside him, pulling his face down to look at her. His eyes were bloodshot and moist. She felt strangely protective, as if he was one of her kids. Sometimes it felt like he was. She planted a kiss on both eyelids, tasting the salt of his unhappiness. Maybe this was the watershed in their marriage. They had both been tested, failed and needed to come out the other side stronger. So many young couples gave up at the first hurdle these days. Divorce seemed to be a first resort, rather than the last one.

It felt like they had been together forever, though, and plenty of people had tried to drive a wedge between them: His father, her mother, her brothers, that bloody floozy... even fucking Stan. She was angry and wanted to do something that would hurt him, her lover, something that would fly in the face of his 'advice'. She kissed her husband on the mouth.

"Take me to bed, Maurice," she said. "Do me like you did her."

49

THE boozer crept out of the early evening gloom, the estate tower blocks flanking it like sentries. With winter approaching, it appeared even more dreary and uninviting than usual. The landlady Siobhan had been planning "refurbishments" for as long as Mo could remember, but the Hope and Anchor hadn't received so much as a lick of paint, the yellow exterior the colour of nicotine on the fingers of a 60-a-day smoker. The sign hung loose, and always made Mo smile. Someone with the agility of an acrobat or cat burglar had clambered to the top of the pole and sprayed a W in red paint in front of the word anchor.

Having spent a couple of hours inside the pub earlier that day with Siobhan and her ridiculously overweight teenage son Phil, Mo knew what awaited them. As he pushed open the door he felt a tingle of anticipation, unsure of how his brother would react. Clive didn't give much away when he saw the giant banner pinned to the apron of the bar. "Welcome Home, Clive, our Falklands hero", it said and was flanked by two large Union Jacks. In fact, Mo had ensured there were patriotic flags of varying sizes in every nook and cranny of the large room.

Seeing his handiwork now, Mo's chest swelled with pride. It wasn't just that he had achieved the transformation in such a short space of time, but while preparing everything it had dawned on him exactly what his younger brother had achieved. Clive deserved every accolade he would get from those who'd stayed safely at home while he fought their battles for them. At that moment Maurice Dolan's respect for his younger sibling knew no limits.

The pub was filling nicely. It would be a traditional Friday night booze-up in the East End, just as Mo had intended. Everyone from the estate seemed to be out, determined to fritter away their social security, dole money or meagre wages on one big night to take their mind off the crushing pressures of everyday life. Mo wanted Clive to feel this was where he belonged. He may have been thrust into an extraordinary situation but now things had to go back to the way they were, for sanity's sake. Around here, nothing had changed, not the surroundings, the pub, the decor or the clientele. Mo spotted some recognisable faces while he stood at the bar waiting to collect their "complimentary" drinks. That idiot Shooter was still walking with the aid of a stick, and the Irish bloke who fancied himself as a card sharp was there, the one who had beaten him at brag on the day Clive got his orders... Stan something. He seemed to recall the bloke sold trainers from a stall in the market.

In the corner by the smaller side entrance, Mo was shocked to see his guru in conversation with the copper who trained his son at the gym. He wondered if during all the time he had been receiving treatment, the masseur had been fraternising with the enemy and telling tales about his less law-abiding clientele. He shouldn't be surprised. The person who had put him onto the guru in the first place worked for "the other side", a doctor employed by the prison authorities. It stood to reason he would recommend someone who could keep an eye on Mo. Finally, in the opposite corner, he saw some exotically clad youngsters and recognised the New Romantics he had clashed with in Dagenham. No sign of the bloke he had discovered in Audrey's bed, though, thank God.

Pre-occupied, only now did Mo note with alarm that Clive was in a trance-like state. Fortunately, help was at hand, Handsome Frank Purves marching through the door along with gym owner Wally Molloy and his professional gambler son Patrick, Lilly Lacey – a girl that Clive had held a soft spot for at school – and his brother's best friend from his supermarket days, Ricky Masters. They converged on Clive, shaking his hand and telling him what a great job he and his fellow soldiers had done, Lilly giving him a hug and a kiss before whispering, "You've always been my hero". It shocked them all when Clive wrestled his way clear, pushing out and connecting with Ricky, who fell backwards into a couple of builders enjoying an after-work beer. "Watch it, pal!" one objected aggressively.

"Yeah, and what are you gonna do about it?" said Handsome Frank, stepping forward. One look at the fighter's deformities and the two men decided it wasn't worth the hassle. They held their hands up in surrender and wandered off to another area of the bar, muttering their displeasure. Mo caught up with Clive at the exit and bundled him through.

Outside, a chilly drizzle was falling, the hot days of summer a thing of the past. In the sporadic street lighting, Clive's face looked pale and haunted. "I..." he made a false start and tried again. "Mo, I can't do this."

"Of course you can!" Mo grabbed his brother by the forearms. "These people are your mates. You've known them years! They all want what's best for you and are proud of you for what you have done. Protecting our country..."

"It was hardly that," said Clive, the rain getting heavier, dribbling down his face like tears.

"What do you mean?" said Mo, pulling up the collar on his leather jacket.

"The Argies," said Clive. "They weren't planning to come up here and attack us any time soon. They live thousands of miles away and when they invaded the Falklands they were fighting for something they believe in. When we left Britain to take them on we didn't even know where we were going. Most of the boys thought the Falklands were off the coast of Scotland! I've been thinking about it a lot... I'm not sure we should even have been there in the first place."

"Nonsense," said Mo. "Those people down there... they are as English as us. Maggie said..."

"Screw Maggie," spat Clive with venom.

"Hey, steady!" Mo gave him a stern look. He didn't like anything said against the country's awe-inspiring leader.

"Listen," said Clive. "Many of those Argie conscripts were kids, sent out to do a man's job after just a couple of weeks' training. Your Maggie and her fucking government didn't have to look them in the eye... I did. They were in poor condition, and I had to fuckin' kill them, Mo, do you understand? I had shoot them in the head, or stab them through the heart. Do you know, I was stumbling down the hill towards Stanley after the main fighting was over and I tripped over something. I looked down and it was a body, an Argentine soldier, spread-eagled and nailed to the floor. Still alive. I couldn't believe it. When I met some of the Marines they said they had found similar. These guys were being punished by their own superiors for running away from battle! The guys we were fighting, they had families and friends waiting at home for them, just like you were waiting for me. Mums, dads, brothers, sisters... the difference is many of them won't be going home, ever... I'm responsible for that, you know?"

Mo shook his head. "No," he said. "They were the invaders, not you! I understand you have regrets, mate, but they would have done the same to you, given the chance. It's about survival, just like on these streets."

"No, you haven't a clue what it's like really," said Clive. "You've spent your life around here. To understand what I'm saying, you had to be there."

Mo grabbed his brother by the shoulders, leaning in gently so their noses connected.

"Look," he said. "When you signed up no one told you it was going to be easy, did they? You even told me yourself, you didn't want it to be easy. You'd heard all grandad's stories, the good ones and the bad ones, and you decided it was the life you wanted and the tougher the better. You knew he had lost people close to him, but it was your ambition and though I tried to persuade you differently, your mind was made up."

"Well, I've lost people too now," said Clive. "Close friends. Hell, you met one of them when we left Southampton. That Scottish guy I introduced as Jock. His real name was Archie and he was a great bloke; helped me settle in when I joined the Battalion. He didn't come back, though, and I did. Why? The bullet he took could so easily have been mine, we were feet apart. So why am I here, Mo, eh? Tell me that. Why am I here?"

"You're here because you're my brother and I need you," said Mo, his voice cracking with emotion. "I couldn't cope without you. If you knew what it's been like these past few months, how I have struggled to keep a lid on things... You've always been good for me, mate. You know how bad my temper can get and that I have the tendency to act the moron yet you somehow keep me on a straight course. When you were gone I crashed. Christ, I even hurt Chucky; by accident, but because I lost my temper he ended up in hospital. I was scared, man. I needed you then and you weren't around. What was I supposed to do?"

"Come on, Mo." Clive gave the first indication he had absorbed something his brother had said to him.

"I feel sorry for those Argie families, honestly," said Mo, "But this is about our family and that is always going to be the most important thing in my eyes. I don't suppose your mate Jock or that Welsh guy, what was he called..?"

"Elf."

"Yeah, him. He wouldn't have wanted you to mope about now. What was it his girlfriend said? You were angry at the time but she made a valid point. Life goes on. It has to."

Mo locked his brother in a powerful embrace. All that could be heard were cars splashing through the newly formed puddles on the main road, carrying commuters home from a busy day in the city.

After what seemed like an age, Mo pulled away, a shiny drop of water glistening on his chin. "Pull yourself together," he said. "Let's go back in, eh? A lot of people are here to celebrate with you. The moping and mourning has gone on long enough."

He guided Clive gently back through the double doors.

THERE he was: the big, big man.

Holding court.

Maurice fuckin' Dolan. Head case. Criminal. Woman beater. He didn't deserve to be having such a good time, the master of all he surveys, when his family were at home, no doubt nursing the wounds he had inflicted on them, mentally and physically. It made the watching man sick that others around the table fawned over 'Big Mo', awestruck by his every word. They laughed at his jokes and applauded his cockney wise-guy asides, slapped him on the back and toasted him with their pints. It all just fed his enormous ego.

The watcher recognised most of the characters, a real dodgy lot. Wally, from the boxing gym. Forget knockouts, it was knock-off watches he specialised in. His son Patrick fed a gambling habit by inventing elaborate cons to swindle poor old folks out of their pensions and Handsome Frank was a brutal bare-knuckle boxer whose demeanour was even uglier than his looks. He didn't recognise a couple of the group, but last and not least was the returning hero, Mo's soldier brother Clive. Well, if he really wanted to do the world a favour Clive Dolan could do far worse than rid the neighbourhood of his older brother, a far bigger scourge than any of those Argentines he'd travelled 8,000 miles to fight.

There was an obvious reason why no one wanted to take on the oldest Dolan. It wasn't because he was a nice fella, full of love for his fellow man. It was because they were scared shitless he might fly off the handle at them and they would end up on the receiving end of the legendary Big Mo temper. That 'thing' he carried around with him – carefully wrapped in thick, brown packaging – now rested against his seat, a big deterrent for anyone who fancied their chances. It wouldn't take much for Mo to reach for it either, knowing the gangster's hair-trigger temper. Maurice Dolan had even given the weapon a name: Reg. How juvenile was that?

The watcher despised the man and would do anything to see the smug look removed from his chiselled face, and seeing the package nestled against the chair gave him the spark of an idea. It could be anything wrapped up in there. Anything. A few months back there had been a robbery on a Romford trading estate, a vast quantity of guns and ammunition stolen. The police had issued several appeals, but the goods hadn't turned up. That 'thing' in Mo's possession might look like an ordinary piece of brown packaging but who knows? If someone hinted at an alternative scenario and Mo was challenged about it and acted the wrong way...

The watcher downed the remainder of his pint, slipped from his bar stool and made his way out into the night.

50

DS MAX COOPER blew on his hands, trying to get the circulation moving, as he looked around at the concrete jungle which enclosed him. Max wasn't the jumpy type usually, but a feeling of anxiety coursed like alcohol through his blood, spreading to every extremity on this chilly November night. He clasped the Smith and Wesson Model-10 six-shot revolver firmly, the safety-catch on, its weight clumsy as he manoeuvred his gloves back into position. To think just an hour earlier he had been sitting in the warmth of Barkingside police station tucking into sausage, beans and chips.

Cooper had only been in the area to give evidence at Snaresbrook Crown Court against a bunch of robbers who had ambushed a security van. They had tried to smash their way in with a custom-built battering ram, but the doors buckled before they broke, rendering the job impossible. Forced to abandon their invention, they scarpered, but thanks to Max's Confidential Informant – the career criminal William Dolan – he had tracked the gang to a scrap metal merchants in Lewisham where his team found all the evidence needed to complete the collar.

It had been his first as an official member of the Flying Squad, earning him glowing praise from the bigwigs, but things hadn't been great in court that day. A weasel-like defence barrister had given him a hard-time over his arrest 'procedure' so, anxious to see some friendly faces, he had popped into the local nick for a bite and to catch up on paperwork. It was then that a hand had grabbed his shoulder.

"You Cooper?"

He nodded. "You're needed. Some blokes from the Flying Squad are here. There's a car downstairs, but there's a guy waiting for you in the locker rooms. Got you a snug little bulletproof jacket to wear. Am I right in thinking this is your first active job... y'know, with a firearm?"

"I don't know," he said. "I mean, what's going on?"

"It's all kicked off in Barking, apparently. It's a good thing you're here. The local nick can't handle it. Short staffed. There are a couple of big fireworks displays on. Bloody Bonfire Night was almost a week ago but it seems to cause us grief for a month."

Grabbing his jacket from a seat, Max had followed the local officer out of the door, wondering why he had been asked about his firearms training. It was true that he had been given a four-day crash course in the use of a weapon but he wasn't expecting it to be put to use quite so soon.

According to the briefing he had been given on the drive over, there was a suspected gunman on the loose in Barking. No shots had been fired but an eye witness reported seeing the suspect in possession of a weapon in the Hope and Anchor public house on one of the Barking estates.

Now he stood exposed on a barren piece of wasteland alongside three other officers, his eyes focused on a short alleyway that led from the pub to the giant high-rises that loomed all around him.

"They're coming!" A senior officer joined them, a pair of binoculars dangling around his neck. "I count four or five bunched up and, yeah, it looks like one of them has a weapon. Remember, though, lads, give him fair warning... then shoot the bastard."

CLIVE DOLAN stumbled from the pub, an arm either side of him dragging him into the cold night air. He had done what his brother had asked, immersing himself in the occasion and the alcohol on offer, but though he smiled and exchanged pleasantries with those around him, he regularly lost focus, drifting to that corner of his mind where the darkness lived. At one stage, Archie was sitting right opposite him, plain as day, knocking back a can of Tennants' Extra. When he looked again, though, it was only that lad from the supermarket sipping from a pint of cider.

Everything seemed transient, nothing permanent. Somewhere there was a ball with your name on it, bouncing around in the bingo machine of life, waiting to drop, the caller barking out your fate as quickly as he could say 'clickety click'.

His dad would see these internal reflections as a sign of weakness and tell him to man up, but two months on the other side of the world, where hell really did freeze over, told him his old man's grand declarations were bullshit.

"Bulllshhhiiit!"

To his right, his brother jerked him back up, talking to him as if he was a blind patient, an invalid or a simpleton. "Steady on, son... that's it, one step at a time, watch that old tyre there, come on, you can do this."

It was as if they had been plunged back into the dim and distant past, Maurice teaching his little brother how to walk, pushing him to get it right lest he let down the family name. Dad always told him he had been a slow learner – that he hadn't started walking until well passed his second birthday.

"We thought you was backwards, son," was the unsubtle way his dad put it. "Apparently you was just lazy. Why walk when Maurice could do your fetching and carrying?"

"Bleurgh!"

"Oh, shit," the voice came from his left. "He's had too many of them whisky chasers and done a technicolour yawn. Look at me soddin' trousers!"

Clive tried to focus on the pavement. Had he done that? He could smell it now, his senses awakening. It reminded him of the lethal concoction of stale beer, puke, shit and cordite he'd smelt in the trenches. Hell, the fighting, had he missed it? He span crazily, shaking his bodyguards free, lashing out. The weapon! Where was his weapon? A line of tracer fizzed across the night sky, followed by an explosion that sent him down into the mud and the puke and the shit...

Someone was shouting at him. "Get up! Come on soldier, we've got to get moving." The Major. He was back.

"Put the weapon down, now... step away from the weapon!"

A sharp, angry voice.

Looking up he saw a line of soldiers advancing. Shit! This was real. More firecrackers, the air stinking of gunpowder, his eyes trying to focus on the Argentine advance.

Not right.

Something. Not right.

"Shit, no problem. Look our hands are up." His brother's voice. Clive didn't understand. What was Mo doing here? Had he enlisted? If so, he must have missed the briefing. The instructions had been clear: No prisoners would be taken, on either side. "I've put it down. It's only..."

"Noooooo!" Pushing himself to his feet, Clive barged Mo and the other figure out of the way. "No surrender!" he shouted. "No prisoners!" He lifted the rifle Mo had placed on the ground.

"Frank, grab him!"

A hand pulled at his arm but Clive lashed out, smashing his weapon into the attacker's face. The artillery beat its morbid rhythm above: whizz, bang, karrumph! The voice returned, the one that had to be obeyed, the one that would guide them out of this hell into the light...

"Fix Bayonets!"

"What's he on about?" Mo asking the question. He didn't know about these things. It was Clive's turn to take the lead for once.

"Come on, son. Put the gun down now and step away!" A stranger's voice, ringing in his head. A trick. The Argentines speaking in English. A con, just like those that had waved white flags before shooting the paras as they advanced, one horror story of many in a war without end. He recalled the enemy shouting insults at he and Archie on Mount Tumbledown that time. "Hey Jimmy!" he shouted, remembering the briefing about how Argie soldiers struggled with pronunciation. There was no reply.

Wooziness gone, it was clear what he had to do. The enemy ahead, the covering artillery fire...

"Charge!" He put one foot in front of the other and advanced on enemy lines.

"Get face down on the fuckin' floor and don't fuckin' move!" Max Cooper stood above Mo, weapon trained on him.

"You bastards!" shouted the older Dolan. "You shot my brother!"

"Self defence," said the Flying Squad man. "He was going to do the same to us. He shouldn't have fucking attacked, should he? Our instructions were clear. He had a..."

"...Curtain pole," said another officer, studying the torn packaging. "He had a fuckin' curtain pole."

"It's not a gun?" Max Cooper froze. "Shit! Have a look around, there must be..."

"Sorry, mate, no gun."

Max lowered his weapon, the full scale of his mistake hitting home. "How was I to know?" he protested. "The bloke shouted charge... you heard him. He was going to shoot us. He even said something about bayonets."

A third policeman got up from examining the body. "Dead," he said. "Shot through the head and the heart. Top job."

Smash! From his position prone on the floor, Mo's toe-capped boot jerked out and connected with the back of Max Cooper's knee. As he fell, Mo leapt forward to finish the job. The two other officers were taken by surprise, slow to react as Mo smashed his fists into the face of the copper time and time again. Finally, the other two grabbed their batons, bringing them down once, twice, three times on the crazed attacker. Mo finally succumbed, flopping onto his back as his brother's killer spat blood from a badly battered face. Looking up, Mo saw colourful streaks of light illuminating the night sky, the fireworks reflected in his dark pupils. Calling on his last reserves of energy, he threw a protective arm over his younger brother, who lay at peace now, his war finally over.

51

"YOU want to tell us about it, Maurice?" The Detective Inspector leaned forward, concealing something in his hand.

"Yeah, I want to tell you about everything," snarled Mo, his face inches from his interrogator. "After all, you killed my fackin' brother. Why shouldn't we be mates?"

"Nothing to do with us," said the DI.

"You're coppers," said Mo. "You're all bastards!"

As he said the last word spittle shot from his mouth and landed on the DI's cheek. His interrogator didn't flinch, just opened his hand to show Mo what he had been concealing. The item was wrapped in a small polythene bag to protect it from outside contamination.

"This belong to you, Maurice?" he asked. "We found it in a packing crate in this warehouse down Wapping way, along with all sort of munitions: handguns, rifles, bullets, not to mention bags of jewellery and money... the serial numbers of which match up to a little armed robbery down in Kent. Care to explain?"

"I want a brief."

"Sure. I'll send for one. Still you must be glad to see this, eh? Lovely inscription. I imagine it's got great sentimental value." He turned the object over in his hand. "*To my Fozzy Bear, love you so much, your buzzy Bee, kiss kiss.* How sweet. That you is it? Fozzy Bear? We think it must be because your dabs are all over it."

"Lawyer... now!" demanded Mo, his mind doing somersaults. How had it turned up in a packing crate more than 80 miles away from the cottage in Hastings? The words "Fit up" howled in his ear but how had the police got hold of it in the first place and how had they found the lock-up? Did someone grass him up? That was the obvious conclusion. Either Cozza had found the lighter and planted it so that he could do a deal if the Filth came calling, or Handsome had seen it as his get–out-of-jail-free card. Strange, though, because the ex-boxer would be the one facing a murder rap. Unless both of them were going to point the finger at Mo.

None of it made sense.

BERYL had been up early, organising breakfast for the boys. Even though the nights were drawing in and it was dark in the mornings, Sylvester's in-built alarm system never failed to wake him at 5.30am. She wondered when he would begin sleeping longer. He was four and she tried to recall when Chuck had stopped charging into her room before the first London pigeons had squawked their welcome to a new day.

When she discovered Mo wasn't snoring beside her she thought nothing of it. He had warned her it would be a big night at the Hope. Part of her was pleased he hadn't fallen into bed and slobbered all over her, though she couldn't deny the pangs of unease creeping across her belly, the ones that told her he might have sought sexual gratification elsewhere after taking on a shedful. Though his confession the other day seemed genuine and from the heart, she realised she would struggle to trust a man again after what she had been through.

Turning the radio on in the hope some music might brighten her day, she stood motionless as a news report burst from her transistor. "The man, a Scots Guard who fought in the Falklands, died at the scene and..." At the same time there was a knock at the door. "Hang on!" she shouted, trying to stall the caller while she learned the full impact of what she was hearing. A police inspector was talking now about a tragic accident. "My officers acted in good faith," he said. "This man was instructed to put down his weapon three times but continued to charge. We had been tipped off he was in possession of a firearm and our responsibility is first and foremost..."

Bang! Bang! Bang!

"For Christ's sake!" she wiped her hands on a tea towel, walked into the hallway and threw open the door.

"Fuck off!" she went to slam it in his face but he put his foot there and forced it open.

"Listen, you're upset! I know! I should have told you," said Stan Marshall. "About my wife..."

"You think I'm a mug!" She pulled the door open again, the fury burning on her face, aware she hadn't applied make-up that morning.

"Mum, Sylvester did a poo but came off the toilet half way through!" said Chuck from behind her.

Damn!

A smell of urine and damp invaded the flat, the result of some bastard neighbour being unable to hold his bladder until he got home. "Mum, he's..."

"Beryl, I've got..."

"The shooting happened at..."

Her head span. "You've got to go. Mo will..."

"He's not coming back, Beryl," said Stan. "At least... not today."

The world stopped revolving, went into slow motion. "What?"

"He's OK, but there was an incident," Stan said. "Down the Hope. As I was leaving, there were these police. They had guns. Your Mo, his brother and that scarred boxer..."

"Frank."

"That's the one," said Stan. "The police thought Mo had a weapon in a brown package he was carrying, so ordered him to put it down. He did as he was told, but Clive, well, he grabbed it, hit the boxer with it and then charged the police holding this parcel out in front of him like, well, a gun."

"What?"

"They shot him Beryl. Point blank. He went down and I saw them take the body away in an ambulance, but he was all covered over and I heard on the news this morning... he's dead."

"Uncle Clive..?" The voice of disbelief came from behind her. Beryl turned to see Chuck, his face frozen, complexion white as chalk.

"Go in with your brother now, Chuck," said Beryl. "I'll speak to you later."

"Marched Mo off in handcuffs," said Stan. "He went mad, beat the shit out of this copper. Two of them had to batter him with truncheons to get him to stop."

"I don't understand," said Beryl. "It was a belated homecoming party for Clive. He would have been 23 next week so it was an early birthday celebration, too. Why would they shoot him? In fact, why were the police even there?"

She looked at him suspiciously. "Did you do this?"

"What?" he looked confused. "No!"

"You did, didn't you? You called the fuckin' cops and set my Mo up!" Suddenly her small fists were smashing against his chest, rocking him back with the undiluted strength of her fury. Everything was coming out at once, her hatred, her love, her confusion, her despair. She pushed him up against the wall of the balcony as neighbours poked their heads out of doors to see what the fuss was about.

Her strength sapped, she fell against his body, the tears dropping onto his leather jacket. Gently he guided her back into the flat. In the hallway Sylvester stood, pants around his knees, pointing his finger in the direction of the doorway they had just stepped through. "Chucky gone, mum, Chucky gone," he said.

52

CHUCK had no plan in mind other than to run. His feet pounded down the concrete steps, his intention to get as far away from the flat as possible. His Uncle Clive dead, Dad locked up... the world was collapsing around him.

The man from the market had turned up at their door to impart the news and for some reason Mum had been angry with him. He had never seen her hit anyone before and her sudden display of passion didn't fit with the calm, stoical woman who had brought him up. She must really hate the man for some reason.

The tinny echo of his pounding feet bounced off the claustrophobic walls as Chuck negotiated the stairwell, his mind displaying images of his dad behind bars. It was hard to imagine that giant frame being shut away in a tiny cell. Chuck felt personally responsible and wished he could turn back time and make things better. His dad had told him not to trust the police and now he understood why.

Behind him, he could hear shouting, the stranger giving pursuit. His name was being repeated over and over with a familiarity that jarred with the youngster. "Chuck! Chucky! Come on, son, don't scare your mother like this... she doesn't deserve it. Please, Chuck! I know you're a good boy, don't be like this."

He was right, of course. His mother didn't deserve it but, then again, what did this man know about Beryl Dolan? As far as Chuck knew, they had only met once, at the market. He bet the man would think differently about his "good boy" status once he found out Chuck had been suspended from school for beating up a fellow pupil and had rebelled against his father, talking back to him over the boxing issue. He was hardly candidate for child-of-the-year. Chuck needed to gather his thoughts and talk to someone who could make sense of it all. He needed to see Cliffy.

As he burst through double doors at the bottom of the stairs, the spider-webs in the window glass reflected his image back at him, mirroring how he felt: Cracked, broken, shattered. He sprinted out across the car park, the door banging behind him. Glancing over his shoulder, he could see the man descending the last few steps in the stairwell. He wore a denim jacket, jeans and a T-shirt printed with the picture of a scary witch. The writing beneath said something about a Maiden.

The bloke was scruffy, long unkempt locks flowing out behind him, and Chuck could imagine what his dad would make of him. Plenty of times on the school run in the Daimler Chuck could recall Maurice Dolan pointing out someone similarly dressed on the pavement. "Look at that scruff bum," he would say with a sneer. "Could do with a bloody good wash, eh, boy? Give me five minutes with him, some carbolic soap and a fire hose..."

He felt tears pricking at the back of his eyes as he imagined his dad incarcerated. What would he be wearing? Would they let him shower? Had he eaten? Things hadn't been good between father and eldest boy lately, but Dad had always stuck up for him and the family. Where would they be without him? Uncle Clive, too? Until recently the friendly, smiling man had been a constant presence in Chuck's young life, teaching him lessons which sharply contrasted with Big Mo's black and white view of the world. Listening to his uncle had been a valuable part of Chuck's education, whether they were discussing history, geography, the Army, school or football. Who would he turn to now when he had questions about such things?

How could Uncle Clive survive a war, only to be shot down on the same streets where he had grown up? It was ridiculous. Cliffy had told him coppers were there to protect good people, not kill them.

"Chuck, please!" The stranger was half way across the car park now, his progress reduced to a crawl. Chuck saw him stumble and nearly fall, then bend over to rest his hands on his knees and force much needed oxygen back into his lungs.

Seeing his chance, Chuck drove forward on a wave of adrenaline. Darting behind the giant estate refuse bins, his heart leapt into his mouth as a rat scampered across his path. The smell of rotting food made him hold his breath, while powerful chemicals stung his eyes. Pausing to compose himself, Chuck looked around in order to plan his escape. Then he was off again, squeezing through a gap in the dilapidated playground fence that led on to the recreation field. Ploughing across the cloying mud and clumpy grass, he realised adrenaline could push him no further. His whole body ached: his feet, his legs, his chest, his arms, even his brain. When he reached the bushes on the far side of the football pitch he realised he was home and dry. Bursting through, he came out the other side onto the street and sat on a bench to rest his aching legs.

Pulling a handful of coins from his jeans pocket, he thought he might have enough for the bus fare to the gym. He had found them on the kitchen counter and, despite feeling guilty, had pocketed them before making his break for freedom. Then he had another thought; a lone youngster like him on a bus might arouse suspicion. Probably better to make a phone call. He took the number from his pocket, got up from the bench and went in search of a phone box.

THE battered blue Ford Escort turned the corner and pulled up at the kerb by the rank of shops. The door swung open and Chuck climbed into the passenger seat. "Buckle up," said Cliffy. "Let's go for a ride. Wow, you're in a bit of a sweat... your face is all red. Have you been running?"

"You lot shot my uncle," said Chuck, turning to the policeman. "He's dead!"

"Oh." Cliffy Simpson turned the key in the ignition and indicated to pull out into the steady stream of Saturday morning traffic. "Let's go somewhere we can talk in private. I've heard there was an incident outside the Hope and Anchor last night. I was there earlier in the evening but had gone when it happened. How did you hear..?"

"Someone told my mum... and you've locked up Dad, too!"

"I don't suppose they told your mum the whole story," said Cliffy. "The way they tell it down the station, it was all a terrible mistake. This man – and I swear I didn't know it was your uncle – ran at our officers with what they believed to be a gun in his hand. He was carrying this parcel and they warned him to put it down over and over again. He wouldn't, though. He charged at them, head down, muttering that he would take as many of them as he could. They feared for their lives and one of the officers pulled the trigger. It was only when your uncle was down they discovered the item wrapped up in brown paper was a curtain pole."

"Reg," said Chuck.

"I thought you said your uncle was called Clive."

"The pole," said Chuck. "It's called Reg. My dad carries it for protection."

"A weapon, then?"

Chuck shrugged. "I suppose, yeah. He couldn't shoot anyone with it, though."

"The officers didn't know," said Cliffy. "They couldn't take the risk. Your uncle seemed to know exactly what he was doing."

"He should have done," said Chuck. "He was in the Army; he was a hero."

"He went to The Falklands?" Cliffy slammed on the brakes as a double decker bus pulled out in front of them. "Look, we can't talk here, let's go somewhere quieter."

Expertly negotiating the car through the winding streets, they ended up in a place familiar to the young boy. "I used to play football here," said Chuck.

"I know," said Cliffy. "Hackney Marshes. Do you remember it was that incident with your dad that led to our first meeting? I thought we could wander across the fields, maybe watch a game. Does your mum know where you are?"

"I don't want her to know," said Chuck. "She will only drag me back there."

"We should ring her anyway," said Cliffy. "She has enough worries on her plate as it is. We don't want her launching a police manhunt, do we?"

"No," Chuck said. "They would probably shoot me."

Neither of them laughed, lapsing into silence as Cliffy freed himself from the claustrophobic confines of the car. Chuck got out the other side and they set off across the fields.

Cliffy made the call from a payphone in the changing rooms. Beryl was delighted to know Chuck was with a responsible adult but when she asked him where they were he told her he had promised Chuck not to reveal their whereabouts. "I'll make sure he gets home safely," he said.

"HE was right," said Chuck, his attention focused on his hands as he rubbed them together. He couldn't look at Cliffy. How could he have been so wrong?

"Who was right?" asked Cliffy.

"Dad. He said you were all bastards."

"Do you even know what a bastard is, son?"

"Shut up!" Chuck allowed the policeman a glimpse of the full, undiluted anger he was feeling. On first seeing Cliffy he had been unable to communicate his feelings strongly enough, but now it was just the two of them sitting on a bench he could give full vent to his emotions.

The sound of shouting drifted across from one of the football pitches, two teams of teenagers going at it hammer and tongs. "Man on, Macca, man on!" "Don't let him reach the byline. Jase, that's your job." "Oh come on, Ref! How can that be a foul? Shirt pulling? You're joking!"

"I told you that information so that, you know, you could do something to help us," said Chuck. "Help our mum... but you took it too far."

"You've got it wrong," said Cliffy. "That incident last night, it had nothing to do with me."

Chuck ignored the protest. "It wasn't supposed to happen like that," he said. "You were supposed to arrest him, lock him up for a few days to give Mum a break, but you couldn't stop at that."

Clamming up abruptly, Chuck's mind retreated to a warm day in late June, an incident at the end of the school day when he had punched a boy and ended up having a confrontation with the deputy headmaster. He was still being held in the office when his dad arrived to pick him up. When the headmaster spoke to his dad about the suspension, Big Mo hadn't shown a flicker of concern, just hoisted up Chuck's satchel and stormed for the door. Following his dad to the car, Chuck was bundled inside and driven to the docklands.

He was scared, remembering times in the past when people had been driven there when they had upset the old man. Pulling up, his father had told him: "I'll deal with you later. Sit there and mind your own business and you won't get into any more trouble."

It seemed he was gone forever and Chuck had become bored. He'd started putting his hands down the back of the seats, thinking he might discover some discarded cash he could use for toys or sweets. Instead, he came across something hard and square, warm to the touch. Pulling it out he realised with delight it was his dad's lighter, the one he had been looking for ever since Hastings.

Climbing out into the street with the intention of telling his dad about his discovery, another thought encroached. What if he didn't hand it over straight away? What if he hid it as "insurance" to guard against the worst excesses of his father's temper? He hated being powerless to help when his mum had been dragged around by her hair that day in Hastings. When he had tried to intervene and protect her, he had received a broken nose and a collection of cuts and bruises as a reward.

With a flash of inspiration, he devised a plan. He would hide the lighter in the warehouse in case he ever needed to curtail his father's excesses. It would just take some cunning.

Letting himself into the building, his father and Frank had looked shocked to see him. When he explained he needed the toilet, Big Mo had told him to relieve himself behind some packing crates. Perfect! It had been a simple task to drop the lighter into a crate then return to the car. Chuck didn't even know what was inside them, but guessed they might contain dodgy goods the police would be interested in. He planned only to use the lighter ploy in a worst-case scenario.

"You must believe me when I say it was a coincidence," Cliffy said, jerking his attention back to the present. "Some anonymous geezer rang 999 and was adamant your dad had a firearm. It was our duty to check it out."

Chuck could hear the cadence of the man's voice, but his words were just background noise, mingling with that from the surrounding football fields. Chuck's thoughts were on the day his treachery had got his uncle killed and his father jailed. His motivation had been selfish. He loved his boxing and his dad was going to take it away from him. Chuck knew that once the decision had been made it was final and saw another door slamming shut just when he had found something at which he could excel. After his dad stormed from the gym that time, Chuck had mentioned the warehouse full of dodgy gear to Cliffy, at no stage appreciating the serious damage he had done.

"... What we found in that warehouse won't make it any easier for your father," Cliffy was saying when Chuck zoned back in. "Your dad was storing stolen guns and we suspect one of them was used in a murder down in Kent. There were also the proceeds from an armed robbery in Tunbridge Wells..."

"What?"

"A post office," said Cliffy. "We think your dad and some of his friends were involved."

Chuck recalled a sunny, summer afternoon visit to a small town with his dad after waving goodbye to Uncle Clive on the QE2. His dad had talked to a friendly man in a post office, telling him he was bringing his family down to live in the area. At the time, the news had come as a complete shock to Chuck. It was the first time he had heard they might be moving. He couldn't imagine his dad living anywhere else but London. He would be like a fish out of water. He had meant to ask his mum about the situation but the incident had slipped his mind. Now the pieces fitted together...

"I'm sorry, Cliffy, but I can't come to boxing anymore," he said, having wrestled with his conscience. "I can't be friends with you after what has happened."

"Don't do anything hasty," said Cliffy. "You're upset."

Chuck had made up his mind though, and, like his dad, once he had come to a decision it was impossible to shake him from it.

AFTER Cliffy dropped him off, Chuck sat in the estate playground wrestling with his thoughts. A group of boys were playing on the climbing frame and he failed to notice them interrupt their game and head in his direction. "Hey, whitey, what you think you're doing here? This is our patch." Looking up he saw a tall, black boy blotting out the pale winter sun. He had to be 10 or 11.

Behind the boy came another voice, one he hadn't heard for months. "He's OK, Gabe, I know him."

It was his old school friend Garry. Chuck hadn't seen him since the boy's parents had moved him to another school months earlier. At the time, Chuck had felt betrayed, having been left to stand up to the bullies on his own.

"Yeah?" said Gabe. "Only white boys you tol' me about were the ones that picked on you cos you were black? Called you names and stole your lunch money and t'ing."

"Well... yeah," said Garry. "Chuck's my friend, though. He helped me."

"If he's such a nice boy, why he bunching his fists like that?"

"I'm only doing it cos you are," said Chuck defiantly. If this boy wanted trouble he could have it. Chuck couldn't rely on Garry to protect him. The kid was weak. When he had been challenged he'd run away and grassed to the teachers. Anyway, Chuck was spoiling for a good fight. He didn't care if he ended up taking a beating. He probably deserved it.

"That right, is it?" The boy gave him his meanest look. Chuck stood, knowing that staying seated would put him at a disadvantage. "About time you learned who was in charge around here, whitey."

He lunged, but Chuck caught him off balance, tripping him so that he collided with the bench and bumped his head. Twisting, he shouted to the other boys: "What you waitin' for? Get him!" Chuck was prepared to take them all on but needed to even up the odds. Breaking into a sprint, he pushed past the two boys who were preparing to do their master's bidding.

"Let him go... please!" Garry was pleading, but as Chuck looked back, he saw the other two heavyweight thugs advance towards him. At that speed, he knew they had no chance of catching him. He headed around the corner to the communal dumpsters in the hope of finding some discarded item to use as a weapon.

He saw it immediately – a three-legged wooden table. Looking around, he found the thick, discarded limb and grabbed it just as the boys arrived to close off the exit.

Chuck walked slowly towards them, thumping the piece of wood against his hand just like his dad did with Reg, no longer conscious of the size difference between them. He thought about how his father might handle the problem.

"Never let them see you're weak, boy," the old man would say. "Always go for the biggest, and the others will show you respect, however the fight ends up."

The boys had formed a semi-circle, though their advance had slowed at the sight of the weapon. Chuck felt adrenaline spread equal amounts of fear and anticipation throughout his body. He had to let his instincts and boxing training take over.

Feigning to move one way, he took off in the other, smashing the club against the knee of the biggest boy, who crumpled to the floor, screaming about something being busted. Turning, Chuck advanced towards the others. "Come on then!" he spat menacingly, the club dangling at his side, ready to cause more damage.

The other two boys no longer looked sure of themselves. They could see the fire in Chuck's eyes, the fear having disappeared with the first swing of the club. It was a question now of who blinked first and it was the gang leader Gabe who finally succumbed. "Leave him, boys, he ain't worth it. Just another white, racist scumbag. Watch your back in future, man, cos we'll be coming for you."

"Bring it on!" shouted Chuck, looking him straight in the eye. "You like picking on boys all alone don't you, you bloody coward? Well, why not come back when my gang are with me and we'll have a proper ruck? I'm sure my good old mate Garry there can arrange it. Let's see who's the best gang around here."

Gabe tossed his head, while Garry and the other gang member moved forward tentatively to pick up their injured mate. "We'll be ready," said Gabe. "Come on boys, bring dat idiot." Moments later, they were heading away, Garry and the other boy holding their limping mate between them, Gabe striding out in front.

Chuck turned for home. He was about to put the table leg down when it dawned on him. He never knew when he might need some protection. "Yeah, you'll do," he said. "You're a bit like Reg... I think I'll call you Ronnie."

53

MAX COOPER was totally wasted as he slid from the bar stool and meandered out through the open door, unaware of the two heavy-set men following him. Out on the street, he took a deep breath of polluted Hackney air and tried to remember where he had left his car. In front of him he vaguely made out the sleek, dark shape of a vehicle pulling to the pavement, stumbling as a door flew open in front of him. From the front seat a driver emerged and came around to steady him. "All right, mate?" he inquired. "You look a bit worse for wear. Need a lift?"

Before the Flying Squad officer realised what was happening one of the two men from the pub caught up and bundled him into the back of the car, following him in. He felt something sharp digging into this side. The other man climbed into the passenger seat and turned, training a gun on him, while the driver slammed the back door shut and jumped behind the wheel, turning the ignition. With a screech of tyres they were off and running.

From the other side of him he heard a familiar voice which made his blood run cold. "You shot my fuckin' son: Dead!" said Billy The Kid Dolan, his voice filled with rage.

"Look, I... I'm sorry Bill," said the Flying Squad officer, realising the full extent of his predicament as the lights of Mare Street flashed past.

"I couldn't do anything about it, honestly," he insisted. "I didn't realise it was your boy, did I? Certainly not Clive. I had an inkling Maurice might be involved – it's his local after all. But Clive... He was off his head, Bill. You should have seen him. He bloody charged us!"

"I've only ever done you favours," said Billy The Kid Dolan, sounding far older now than his nickname suggested. "I told you about them guns and I tipped you off about that security van robbery, too. What have you done for me in return, eh? Locked up my eldest boy, and put my youngest in an early grave."

Words stuck in Cooper's throat. "I'm sorry I couldn't save your boy," he spluttered. "Honestly. I tried but, well, he was too far gone. The war must have scrambled his brain. We saw this raving banshee coming towards us screaming that he wouldn't be taking prisoners. What was I supposed to do?"

"Jump on him? Clobber him with your fuckin' baton? There had to have been another way. Why did you think he had a gun?"

"We had an anonymous tip-off."

"And it didn't occur to any of you 'geniuses' that we Dolans might have enemies out there? Don't answer that. I can guess exactly how the local constabulary reacted... 'Oh the Dolan boys are at it again. Someone says they have a gun. Let's go and shut 'em up, shoot first and ask questions later'. Am I close?"

"Look, I... I..."

"Stop fuckin' blubbing, you cunt," said the old man. "You sound like a fuckin' child, you know that? You can't expect me to just let you get away with it, can you? How would that look? I'm Old Testament, me. An eye for an eye; or family for family in this case. Couple of my associates are sitting outside a little house over Harold Hill way at this moment, ready to 'entertain' a young lad and his mummy. We're heading there right now as it happens..."

"You can't!"

"I can do whatever I like. Better believe it. I warned you what I am capable of but you wouldn't fuckin' listen. You need to see this, just to know how serious I am when I make a promise... unlike you, who said you would protect my boys..." His voice tailed off.

"Please..."

“You know, I never wanted Arnold to join the Army but he was dead set on it,” said the old man as if a switch had been flicked, the power suddenly restored to his brain. “Something to do with his grandad – my father. He was a big Army nut and the boy doted on his every word. That’s why he signed up. I tried to talk him out of it, but he was determined. Anyhow... what I find a bit ridiculous about all this is that he goes to The Falklands, survives everything them bloody Argies can throw at him, then comes home and is shot down in the street like a rabid dog by our very own boys in blue. How fuckin’ mad is that?”

Cooper said nothing.

“What about Maurice?” asked Billy The Kid.

“Look, you have to believe it was absolutely nothing to do with me, right? I didn’t even know it was happening,” stuttered Cooper, aware he was digging a bigger hole for himself. “They raided this lock up down at Wapping on the same night and apparently found loads of incriminating things in there: Guns, cash, jewellery... the whisper is they’ve linked it to that post office raid in Kent back in June and the murder of a truck driver. Your boy Maurice is in the frame.”

“Great!” said Billy. “So I am about to lose both sons in one day. Well, you’ve been a great help! I could fuckin’ take that gun there and blast you away now. Better still, maybe shoot you in the ball sack first, just to make you squeal a bit.”

Cooper knew he had to think fast, the alcoholic fog around his brain clearing as adrenaline kicked in. “I owe you,” he said. “I know that and I appreciate it. I can’t get Mo out of the shit, but I can give you something. A nice earner.”

“Our Mo never was the brightest spark,” said Billy, again veering off at a tangent. “He wanted to be big time, but I never thought he had it up here.” He pointed to his head. “Still, this better be good or we’ll be knocking on that door in Essex and introducing ourselves to your family pretty soon. I need you to be there, just so I can see your pain.”

"Heathrow," said Cooper. "I've got a cousin, owes me a big favour. I bailed him out on a number of occasions. He's got a gambling habit."

"What do I want with an airport?"

"It ain't the airport, not exactly. My mate is a security guard at this warehouse. It's owned by a bank. He reckons on the right day you could get away with more than £3m, easy. On occasion they have even been known to store gold and diamonds there."

Silence. A good sign? "Look, I can make sure police attention is ... diverted in another direction. Give you and your mob a free run at it. What do you think? Got to be worth it. You shoot me, hurt my family, it will be bad for business... you'll miss out."

They drove on in silence, Cooper watching Billy the Kid's face for an indication he had bought into the deal. Suddenly he blurted: "Stop the car." They pulled into the kerb.

"Right, Max, I must be going fuckin' soft in my old age but I'll give you one last chance to redeem yourself. What did you say the name of this place was?"

"I didn't," said Cooper, the relief surging through him. "It's a warehouse on the Heathrow International Trading Estate – the company is called Brink's-Mat."

"Let him out of the car," ordered Billy The Kid. The driver came around and opened the door and Max Cooper stumbled out into the night. Watching him go, Billy turned to the henchman in the front passenger seat. "Call the dogs off," he said, before quickly correcting himself. "No... wait. It shouldn't be that easy. Leave the wife and the kid alone. We still got eyes on the girlfriend?"

The man with the gun nodded. "Maybe break a leg or something, just to show him we're serious," said Billy.

EPILOGUE

"DIDN'T bring the boys?" Mo looked somehow smaller, harmless.

Beryl felt his pain. "I couldn't love, I'm sorry. I didn't want them to see you in here, you know?"

"Yeah," said Big Mo. "Can't blame you." He looked around. "Wonder what's happened to Frank... and Cozza. Haven't seen them in here. Maybe they did stitch me up and the Filth have done a deal to protect them."

"No, Mo, they're your mates," said Beryl. "I suspect they've split you up so you can't 'compare notes' like the cops do... you always were the troublesome threesome."

"The old man ain't been in either," said Mo. "Is he intending to visit at any stage?"

"He doesn't like prisons, angel, you know that. I think he feels if he visits they might just keep him here. He said he'll catch up with you at the funeral. It's great they're letting you out."

"With a fackin' guard attached to each bloody arm," said Mo. "It's not the ideal way to mourn your younger brother's death. Bastards." He stared at one of the prison officers standing against the wall as if it had been his idea.

Beryl broke the silence. "Chuck's packed in the boxing."

"Really?" Mo raised his eyebrows. "I feel bad now. He was pretty good. Could have made a go of it professionally – so Wally said. I would have got him another coach if he'd wanted to carry on."

"He seems to blame himself for the things that have happened," she said. "It's nonsense, I know. How can a nine-year-old think such things?"

"He can be a bit intense," said Mo.

"Like his dad," she said. "You in prison, Clive dead... it's affected him badly. They say what happens to you before you're his age can colour the way you are in later life."

"You've been reading them magazines again," Mo said. "Load of old bollocks."

"Yeah," she said. "Well, all I know is he takes after you. Do you know what he dragged home with him the other day? A soddin' great lump of wood. What's more, he called it Ronnie; said it was for his own protection. I put my foot down... told him I didn't want it in the flat. He claims he's thrown it away but..."

"...You think he's hiding it." Mo chuckled. "Sly bugger. Talking of Sly, how is my youngest?"

"Eating me out of house and home as always. Into everything, like most toddlers. You can see his little personality coming out a bit more each day. School next year!"

They sat for a moment in comfortable silence, Beryl twisting the wedding ring on her finger. "How would you feel about another one?"

"No thanks," he said. "Last one was lukewarm."

"Not a tea, you divvy. A child!"

"Oh," he thought about it. "Well, if one of my little swimmers escapes from here we'll call him Ronnie Biggs after that train robber who had it on his toes." The idea made him laugh out loud.

"I wouldn't worry about that," she said, gripping his digits tightly.

He looked into her eyes, trying to form meaning from her words. "Eh?"

"Three months," she said. "Amazing, isn't it?"

Tears sprang to his eyes. Mo held his nose, trying to fight them back. He was crying and smiling at the same time. "For God's sake," he said. "This will do nothing for my rep."

"No." She laughed, grasping his hands even tighter.

"How do you know?" he blubbed.

"Oh, the stork dropped me a note," she said. "Silly plonker! How do you think I know? The doctor confirmed it this morning. I reckon it's another boy."

"Really? We're due a girl you know."

"Next time."

"Got a crystal ball have you?" he wiped away another tear; smiled.

"Maybe." They fell silent, looking into each other's eyes.

"I love you, Bee."

"I know," she said. "So what should we call him?"

He sensed that she had changed the subject. It was too early for her after the affair. He knew his disloyalty had hit her hard.

"You're pretty sure about this, aren't you?" he said.

"I tell you... it's a boy. I can feel it... let's call him Clive."

Mo thought about it. It was a great idea to honour his brother, but didn't fit in with his plan.

"Ever heard of a tough guy called Clive?" he asked. Then he had a brainwave. "No. Remember Dad always called him by his middle name, same as my grandfather. We should call him Arnold! We've honoured Norris and Stallone, we can't ignore Schwarzenegger now, can we?" He grinned.

"Arnold it is then. We'll call him Arnie for short. I like it."

The truth hit him like a punch to the gut. "I may not be around for him... or her," he said. "I don't fancy my chances of walking away from this one."

"You can't give up now!"

"I might as well," he said. "You don't know the judge."

"You do? How?"

"I didn't recognise the name but my solicitor showed me a picture of him. We have a past."

"Then get him removed from the bench for God's sake," said Beryl. "Or leave him there and claim a mistrial. Anything!"

"I can't admit I know him, though... and if I did he would probably deny it. What's worse: He's going to love sending me down."

"You're talking in riddles, angel."

"Sorry," said Mo, he squeezed her hand. "Let me start from the beginning. Just about a year ago I was parking up to see the guru and this skinny little oik told me to move my car..."

ENDS

About the Author

Reviews and ratings are the lifeblood for Indie Authors and can make the difference between climbing to the top of the charts or floundering in the bargain bin, so if you like Nick's work please leave a review on Amazon or Goodreads. Also check out his website www.theripperfile.com

Nick started writing the Boxer Boys series when his dream job as Welsh Sports Editor of the News of the World was torn away when the paper closed with 48-hours notice. He released Crossing The Whitewash in August 2015 and this is his second novel. He is married to Liz with two children, Jemma, 34, and Olivia, 7.

Printed in Great Britain
by Amazon